PENGUIN BOOKS
SONG WITHOUT END AND OTHER STORIES

Neelum Saran Gour is the author of four novels and two collections of short stories. Her work is included in several anthologies. She has also edited a volume on the history and culture of Allahabad and translated her work into Hindustani. She is currently professor of English at the University of Allahabad.

SONG
without End
and Other
STORIES

Neelum Saran Gour

PENGUIN BOOKS

An imprint of Penguin Random House

PENGUIN BOOKS

USA | Canada | UK | Ireland | Australia
New Zealand | India | South Africa | China | Singapore

Penguin Books is part of the Penguin Random House group of companies
whose addresses can be found at global.penguinrandomhouse.com

Published by Penguin Random House India Pvt. Ltd
4th Floor, Capital Tower 1, MG Road,
Gurugram 122 002, Haryana, India

Penguin
Random House
India

First published by Penguin Books India 2011

Copyright © Neelum Saran Gour 2011

All rights reserved

10 9 8 7 6 5 4 3 2

ISBN 9780143414544

This is a work of fiction. Names, characters, places and incidents are
either the product of the author's imagination or are used fictitiously and
any resemblance to any actual person, living or dead, events or locales
is entirely coincidental.

Typeset in Adobe Garamond Pro by Eleven Arts, New Delhi

Printed at Repro India Limited

This book is sold subject to the condition that it shall not, by way of trade
or otherwise, be lent, resold, hired out, or otherwise circulated without the
publisher's prior consent in any form of binding or cover other than that in
which it is published and without a similar condition including this condition
being imposed on the subsequent purchaser.

www.penguin.co.in

MIX
Paper from
responsible sources
FSC® C047271

This is a legitimate digitally printed version of the book and therefore might not
have certain extra finishing on the cover.

To the memory of Meenakshi Mukherjee who commanded:
Never mind the market, write for me.

One of the stories in this random collection was written in 1981, and one as recently as 2011. The other stories found themselves, with a little help from me, in the intervening space of thirty years. The utterance changed and the pace and the voice. The concerns did not. Together, these fifteen pieces add up to a larger story of inadvertent contrasts, of a changing landscape and language and the shifts and reinventions of a writing life. The essential story lives in the interstices and if you look for it you might find it.

Neelum Saran Gour
Allahabad

CONTENTS

CONTENTS

Play

I went to Jatin and said, Boss, I'm kind of tired of this role. I want a change.

I had been careful to time this interview at two in the afternoon, the safest time with Jatin, I'd calculated. After seven in the evening he was drunk and apt to turn cutting. Before noon he was bleary and befogged, nursing his hangover. Between 12.30 and 2 p.m. was his mellow hour, his vile temper softened by the dosa-idli brunch he had at the Coffee House and the slavering attention of the fawning waiters there in their limp turbans and cummerbunds.

He jiggled the mouse round, clicked the save button and closed the page he was working on. Then he directed his deadly stare at me. What's with you, man? A change? Consider yourself absolutely free to join another group if you wish. Please yourself.

I bit my lip. Had I overstepped? No, no, I bleated. Don't get me wrong, Boss. I didn't mean a change of group, please. That's not what I'm getting at.

Then what the fuck are you getting at, please? He switched the PC off and swivelled his chair around in a mighty swirl to face me squarely. I quailed.

Boss, I only meant that I'm tired of playing . . . the postman each time. I mean . . . it's way too dull. I mean it's not exciting enough, no zing, and I could do other roles . . . anything else that you might think okay . . . My voice trailed off in nervous confusion.

1

He demolished me with a withering frown. Began speaking in his high empire Brit tones.

It may have escaped your attention, Mister Banerjee—(my name is Partho, but when Jatin's steamed up he addresses the cast with scathing formality)—that you have put in less than a year with us. And one of the things I've learnt, after twenty-five years of hands-on experience, is that you can't make a pup perform a grown dog's tricks.

That settled me. I smarted, incensed, and found myself bound hand and foot to the postman's role. One hell of a useless role it was. I had to utter only two lines: Is that so, moshai? And: The address on the envelope is 36-B, Gobindopur Lane—that's the flat you live in, na? Just two pathetic lines and not much chance of rising to great heights of thespian splendour with those. I had to come in on a bicycle and stop mid-stage on being hailed by Mayank who played the lead role of Pranesh Mitter. I had to get off the bike, prop it against me and peer at the letter that Mayank held under my nose. It was an old-world bicycle with a wicker basket and a lamp. I wore an old-world postman's khaki uniform, cap and all. I had to prop the bike aslant against my hip, frown at the address, read it, look baffled and utter the second line. I'd tried a shrug but the Boss shot it down. Too Western, he said. I didn't know what to do with my hands and the Boss said I could hold on to the handlebars and sort of crane my neck to the side and look over Mayank's shoulder so I did that.

The trouble was that on the opening night when we performed the play *Five Letters* at the Natya Bhawan there was my entire lane in full strength sitting in the audience! The entire extended family, all our aunts and uncles, all the neighbourhood aunties and didis and dadas, everyone, just everyone who knew me turned up to applaud the rising star, some family jokers even, fuck all, taking videos of my big scene! My bike, my khaki costume and my two lousy lines came in for much banter afterwards and I was at the end of my tether with all the teasing and scoffing, although I did better as a real-time family courtyard actor affecting a good-humoured charade of mild forbearance than as an on-stage postman!

Now for eight rotten months I'd done the postman—in Kolkata, in Benares and Bolpur and Allahabad, in various provincial, suburban and metropolitan theatres, in upscale gatherings and cosy colleges and conferences—till I was fed up to the teeth and I made that timid attempt to sound the Boss for a change and he stamped me underfoot and danced over my corpse!

He wasn't a bad sort, our Jatin Boss. There could be no doubt about his genius as a director, although he was apt to go all intellectual in our after-rehearsal addas and bore us with discourses on the interplay between the lived life and the enacted life, on the many psychosensors and existential filters through which life is made to pass in being processed into art, on the self-destroying choices that make an artist's reputation and break his genius, on the hyper-vision of the director, on the multiple, alternate, inverse or counter possibilities that branch out of the essential stage situation. We didn't follow the thread, didn't even try to. We were used to his exalted ramblings and so we sat with our tumblers of masala chai, busy with our own thoughts. I often wondered why this great, gifted director, this weighty intellectual, never saw that we were only acting interested, looking awed and edified in a masquerade of dutiful discipleship, when no one, I swear no one, knew what the hell he was going on and on about.

Only Mayank sometimes risked pulling Jatin's leg, going all cross-eyed when that talk of 'hyper-vision' was on, but then Mayank Mukhopadhyay was our seniormost actor and so he was the natural choice to take the lead role, that of Pranesh Mitter. Now that was one role that'd struck fire in my heart, Pranesh Mitter's. I knew all Mayank's lines, every full stop and comma and pause and hesitation. I wondered if I would ever get to play that role—Pranesh Mitter in the old classic *Five Letters* by Neelbandhu Ghoshal who died in the mid-seventies. Mayank carried off the role pretty well but somewhere deep down I believed I had it in me to do a better Pranesh

Mitter than Mayank could. Mayank was a method actor whereas I was—how to put it—more on the inspirational side. I believed in the suspension of self. I believed in going beneath the skin of the character and all that stuff. The postman just didn't allow me a free exercise of inspiration.

Now consider the great potential of Pranesh's lines—the way he looked straight at one of our crew sitting in the fourth row and said: You, moshai, in this world where worth means net worth alone, let me see what you're made of. You have an eight-digit salary or maybe you're a corporate czar and own your own company. You work hard and party hard. You inhabit what's called the luxury lifestyle space. You own a BMW, a Volkswagen Beetle, a Mercedes Benz, a Chevrolet Aveo, a Mitsubishi Lancer. Am I right?

And the actor would answer, Absolutely right. But how did you know? He'd do it sitting down so most of the audience only heard a voice responding from the pit of the dark hall. Gave it a nice resounding anonymity. Then Pranesh went on: Ah, one look at you and I knew you. You have twenty different credit cards and membership to all the upscale clubs, the Tolly, the Calcutta, the Bengal Club, the Saturday. Even by tie-ups the Bombay and Madras Gymkhanas, the Willingdon, the Raisina. Maybe you go to the World Economic Forum at Davos each year. You know the managers of the best hotels and their best suites and spas. Maybe you dream of your own helipad and yacht, now that you've got everything from the good, glamorous wife to the good glamorous girlfriend. To one you gift diamonds and the latest Hermès perfume on Valentine's Day. To the other you give gourmet cakes and aromatherapy for her dog. You have children studying at Harvard Business School and MIT. You can look forward to a mellow retirement spent between the golf course and the home theatre system, reclining on the board of half a dozen companies, travelling to corporate conclaves and being an active and important personage in the think tanks of the government, with all your medical expenses borne by the directors' scheme of your ex-company. And when you die it shall be in seven-star comfort, cosseted by the best super-specialists that money can lure.

Mayank delivered that bit in a charged and simmering undertone. More like a compelling harangue than an introspective aside. Much of Pranesh's speeches had this tone of pressured interiority. Even a tortured, stylized rhetorical pitch, so low and tense that you could feel the emotional stretch, like a palpable weight, all the way down the hall. That was Mayank's strong point as an actor. His personality could overwhelm the entire space, even when we performed the play in translation, that stiff, textbook-like translation that completely killed the living language of the original. Even when Jatin tampered with the original. For example the lines I just transcribed. They weren't part of the original. They were 'topical updates', as Jatin called them, and not very smart ones at that. In the updated version Jatin made Pranesh pick up a magazine and flick idly through its pages. There were lines scattered with references to design houses, Gimonnet champagne and Armani suits, Dupont and Montblanc pens. Watches from Tissot, Longines, Chopard and Jaeger-Le-Coultre. Fragrances from Calvin Klein and Escada, variously described as fruity, flirty and floral. Bags from Prada and Louis Vuitton and Judith Leiber. Shoes from Lanvin, Gucci, Valentino and Jimmy Choo. Jewellery from Gaultier, Piaget and Dior. And collectables, covetables and clothes for the fashionista wives and girlfriends created by every headline haunting designer that ever strutted his stuff on the ramps at fashion weeks.

The original lines were something else now. Actually there were problems in this play. Everything in it hinged on the five letters that the postman brings. But Mayank argued with Jatin, who wrote letters nowadays? Could the homely handwritten letter exist in the same conceptual universe as the upmarket ambience of the helipad and the jacuzzi? Wouldn't the letter writer have much rather used a cell phone or sent an email? No one writes letters now, Boss, we agreed, so cut out the contemporary stuff. So Jatin went back to the earlier version although he did it complaining that such a period-specific play like

Five Letters and a young audience were a mismatch and it would only be an older audience that would be in sync. So what, Mayank took Jatin on. Why must everything be targeted at the young? Let's keep it consistent, he said. The issues are always the same, believe you me. I'm not very sure about that but Mayank said it with such conviction that Jatin had no choice but to go along with him. We went back to lines about the chairman of Macneill and Maguire, the luxury apartment in Belvedere, the navy blue Buick, the olive green Austin. We reverted to Dubonnet and Campari, Pina Colada, Gin Fizz and Planter's Punch. Kent King Size filter cigarettes or Rothmans. Our flights changed back to TWA, Alitalia and BOAC and our hotels were scaled down to Taj, Park and Sheraton. There was the lovely musical wife who played the piano and sang, and the Anglo-Indian mistress who danced at Firpo's, the baganbari in Narendrapur and the prodigy sons at Oxbridge. And the salary package fell to five digits but that was what the author had scripted, not our director.

Perhaps the issues really did remain the same and to hear the rest of Pranesh Mitter's monologue, delivered in Mayank's charred, self-parodying tones one realized that nothing much needed to be 'topically updated'. This play by Neelbandhu Ghoshal had been a hit in the seventies when Left-wingers were a brand much in fashion. Neelbandhu himself wasn't ever a champagne socialist but a reclusive grassroots writer, but the theatre circuit made big capital out of his work. It struck a chord even now in our glitzy, globalized, gift-wrapped time. When Pranesh swung around, arms folded on his chest, one shoulder hitched a bit higher than the other in a challenging, in your face, assault-mode posture, smouldering with rancour, and said to the audience: 'No, moshai, not a chance, whatsoever!' you knew he spoke for millions. When he said: I once tried to draw up my own list, the things that were mine, and I found ten things, and that made me feel really rich because honestly I hadn't expected so many. Let me go over my list. There's my job at the census survey office. There are my old parents back in the village and their palm-leaf shack. That makes four things. There is this rented room but it's only half mine, so that's four and a half. And then this string cot, that stove there, that chair . . .

Here the stage lights began coming on, long cones of white light, their beams groping the empty space before alighting on the spare contents of Pranesh's ragged room. A wooden chair with a straight back, a wobbly table of rough, unpainted wood, a black tin trunk, a clothesline strung across with a heap of soiled clothes piled on it. A stool with an earthen water pot. A bucket and a mug. A kerosene stove and some aluminium vessels on the ground. As the arm of light fell upon each object, the audio system produced a sort of subliminal beep. That was Jatin's idea and it served to underscore the substantial countability of each item in Pranesh's inventory. A positive tick mark for personal valuation. I sometimes felt that it produced an unnecessary documentary impact on an existentially intense scene but I could understand why Jatin chose this sequential itemization. It sat well with Pranesh's next passage and by the time he had pointed out each humble object in a brutal, inversely swaggering way, all the lights had come on softly and the bareness of the room in all its shabbiness stood exposed in a sort of naked self-flaunting.

I was wrong, said Pranesh. It adds up to fourteen and a half things. Not ten but fourteen and a half! But I can do still better, you know, and it's a game I play with myself. I can come up with another catalogue—all the things I do not have and will never have. And this list is so impressively long that I end up feeling rather vain at the end of the show. I say, moshai, here's what I don't have. Does anyone have a longer list? But that's all idle heroics. Of course, for everything that you don't have there's someone who has less. Just as for everything you do have there's someone who has more. Note that down, mister, you of the Belvedere and the Buick and the baganbari! At some time that thought might come in useful.

This last thrown at the audience before the big mock-Shakespearean soliloquy took off.

Sometimes the queue at the station counter is twenty yards long and the buses that cruise out of the bus adda tilt to the side with the weight of men. I fight my way in, then push my way out, get off at the last crossing and walk the remaining three kilometres because the rickshaws have hiked up their fares. Can my wife advance beyond her beautician's assistant job? Can my children win scholarships? Can I take out a housing loan?

Here Mayank gave vent to one of his raucous demon laughs, designed to make the audience jump. Not even this, not even this! You want to know why? Because, dadas, didis, dadus, didas and chhoto-shona-monis, I don't have a wife, not being married, you see, and I don't have any kids, not having a wife, ha, ha, reminds me of a joke—Pardon me, madamji, are you married? No? Then, pardon me, madamji, how many kids? You know the rest. Or the other way round—Pardon me, madamji. How many kids? Two? Then, madamji, one last question—are you married? What a sick joke that was in the old tea shop addas but okay, you've got the gist. I'm not a married man, can't afford to be. I don't own a house or furniture. All this is rented. I don't wear branded underwear but I say I'm doing fine, thank you. But you don't believe me, I know you don't. You think it's all a cover-up. You think I'm jealous and although I shout at you that I'm not, I'm not jealous at all, I ask myself, here in my empty room, am I? Am I jealous? Would I rather be you? Am I jealous? Of course I am.

Here the lights faded, leaving Pranesh's blurred form pacing the stage, barely visible. It's one of the passages Mayank did brilliantly but one I felt I could do still better.

Of course I envy you. I remember walking down a street envying this man's car and that man's wife, this man's dog and that man's kids. This man's skills and the other man's luck. This man's muscles and that man's brains. It was that way with me. I was marked out to be denied, I'd convinced myself. Ineligible, past the age, gone to seed, not up to the mark. I was an insect under a paving stone, though even an insect generates offspring. I was just a bilious heart. A sawdusty taste of the mouth, a nauseous, insolvent life grinding away. Eating in the corner dhaba or boiling two potatoes with my rice in that aluminium pot there on my kerosene stove and swallowing it down with a dash of salt and a teaspoon of mustard oil. Then something strange happened to me. Something very commonplace. But it turned my life around, it did. Very commonplace.

And that's when the speakers produced the sound of a jangling door chain and I tossed in the first of the five letters. I didn't come in yet, mind you, wobbling in on my bike in my khaki cap and uniform and my sack of mail. I made no appearance at this point. But Pranesh sped towards the place where the blue inland letter had fallen, taking his time stooping and picking it up, frowning over the address, before his next big scene began. He read the name on the inland—Deb Barat. The address—36-B, Gobindopur Lane, Off Binoy Mullick Road. He mused, I don't know any Deb Barat. But this is 36-B, Gobindopur Lane and it lies off Binoy Mullick Road. Someone else's letter. Must be the new postman. I must look out for him and give this back to him. But how? Tomorrow is Friday and I'll be away at the office and this fellow comes in the afternoon, so? Maybe the neighbours might know where Deb Barat lives, or the woman at the paan shop . . . While uttering these lines in an audible, preoccupied mumble, his hands have, seemingly working on their independent volition, gone ahead and torn open the inland. Pranesh regards the unfolded letter with amazement.

What's this? he exclaims. Well, it's done now. Let's see what this is. It's a nice, refreshing sort of feeling, that this might have come for me. Me. A man with no fixed address. A man of temporary habitations. Why is it exciting to read someone else's mail, to filch something in stealth, even a rag will do because . . .

He did not complete his sentence. Absently removed a towel from the armrest of the old chair, flung it vaguely at the cot, seated himself, swinging one leg over the other, slipped off a sandal and began to read:

My dearest Debu,

Why haven't you written after your tiny note that said you've reached and found a place to stay? Didn't my letter reach you? I gave it to Dhrubo to post but he's so careless. I'm not sure if he posted it at all. And I dare not ask him, he's that moody.

The lights dimmed. A single yellow beam traversed the murky space and fell on Pranesh's lowered head as he read aloud in an intent monotone. The voice slowly changed to a woman's, acquired an undulant rhythm, then a spark of living self, a leap into personality. It was a mellow, private voiceover now. Pranesh read on, moving his lips.

Dhrubo's become strange. Ever since the results were declared he's been low. Two whole days he just lay in bed. Wouldn't speak. Wouldn't eat. At night I awoke to find him out in the yard, smoking bidis with two other boys. They saw the door open and slipped away. I asked him who they were and he said Shyamol and Baptu-da. I asked what they were doing at this hour and I got no answer. I am so worried. A growing boy needs a father around. A mother is no good. Without old-fashioned fear all the love in the world can fatten in its own syrup and rot, as my grandmother used to say.

Jatin had made creative additions to this voiceover. Made a strong gust of wind blow the words about. Introduced street sounds—the hoot of a cycle rickshaw and the rattle of wheels bearing down on gravelly ground. A dull hammer beating on an iron girder far away. The cry of a vendor selling green coconut milk. The drums and bells of a wandering singer and the tinny clang of trams passing. Above it all the chime of a clock followed by its steady ticking in the pauses. It worked beautifully in a dark hall. Kalyani, our diva, who played the role of Jyotsna, had a voice to die for and in the breathless darkness her voiceover created the illusion of a lone plaint rising out of the hum and buzz of an immense city. This play, like many others of its time, was made up of lengthy intersecting introspections and in the hands of an unimaginative director it might have sent a modern audience to sleep. Jatin managed to break up the length of the uttered lines by subtle interventions that got a calibrated array of signals working on the audience's peripheral reception. There used to be pin-drop silence as Kalyani's voiceover filled the hall.

I said to Dhrubo, Never mind the results. Go, get the mark sheet. By the grace of God you'll never want for anything, son, neither a roof over your head nor two handfuls of rice. But there's no sign of the mark sheet yet. I brought him an admission form from the Pitmans Institute branch at Aamtola. It's an eight-month course in typing and shorthand. But he tore it up and flung the pieces in the garbage pail. You'll want me to take up plumbing and radio repairing next! he shouted at me. Is that what I'm good for now?

A rear curtain has risen. A number of screens have come alight at unequal heights. Some critics had called it a mongrelization but they couldn't have been more wrong. It worked. It spun a web of sensory detail around the audience's consciousness. There was never a dull moment in this mixology—photography, cinema, music, theatre and dance. Genre-busting convergence they call it now. The voiceover found visible action above and all around Pranesh. The letter came alive as silent film, as shadow play, as a slow dance drama, as a puppet show, some of the action on the screens and some on the stage. The great thing was that it happened seamlessly, each dimension of dramatization taking the audience by surprise but pitched with perfect contiguity alongside the others. The audience's attention was so cleverly diverted to the screen on the left that they never noticed when Jyotsna and Dhrubo entered in the flesh to carry on the enactment of the contents of the letter. At some point the circle of lights converged on the two, leaving Pranesh out, and the mime flowed naturally into dialogue. You had to see it to be part of the throbbing pulse of the performance.

What's to happen to a boy who fails in every subject and whose parents can't afford tuitions. There should be some way of handling this rage. I live in constant terror. I said to him, on the third day after the results. I said to him, Why don't you appear in the exam again as a private candidate? I'll speak to Bose sir. You can study

something . . . something like history or civics. Then you can go on
to do a BA. Privately by correspondence. Maybe you can take up
tutoring schoolkids. What for? he shouted. You want me to starve
on the streets of Kolkata? Our Bose sir didn't starve, I tried to argue
with Dhrubo. He wore a fine lawn dhoti and a silk Panjabi and he
carried a pocket watch the kind Gandhiji had. He ate fish seven days
a week and got his daughters married in style. All by teaching the
children of rich folk. I said that to Dhrubo but in my heart I thought,
Who will accept a failed student to tutor his kids? But all this was
just to deal with the rage of the moment and I've learnt to act. Ah,
the strain of this acting, this show of sweet patience. Join Pitmans
and learn to type, I tried to tell him. I'll get you another form. And
what will I do then? he wanted to know. I said, Son, you go round
to the court-kacheris and see for yourself. See how busy the court
typists are. You go to College Street and walk down the lanes and see
them busy typing things for scholars—book writers, doctorate writers
and suchlike. Fifty paise a page. Imagine! He said, How will I go to
Pitmans? It's far and it's not on the bus route. I said, What's wrong
with your bicycle? It's the most intelligent way to get around. Even a
horse needs fodder but a cycle needs nothing. But Dhrubo said no.
His friend Mithu has just bought a scooter—a Bajaj Lambretta, he
said. He won't cycle to work when his friends are buying scooters. I
can't buy you a scooter, I said flatly. Why not? he wanted to know.
You won't buy me one, Ma, because you think me a no-good fellow.
It broke my heart to hear him say that. I think you are as good and
better than anyone who passed the toughest exam anywhere! I cried
out. But he pushed me away and said, You don't. You're pretending
all the time. You're such an actress, Ma. You think me useless and you
wish me dead. That chilled me to the soul. Just the other day I read
in the *Amrita Bazar Patrika* how a student hanged himself because
he failed in the madhyamik exam. These wrong-headed boys can be
so wilful. I will do anything for you, my child, if you would only do
this Pitmans course, I pleaded. He looked at me very straight and
said, Baptu-da has found out about a second-hand scooter. Will you

buy it? How much is he asking? The owner, I mean. Two thousand rupees, he tells me without shame. I don't have two thousand rupees, I told him. I was so angry. Then he says, the brazen lout, I won't go to Pitmans. Why have you gone away, Debu, leaving me to handle such bad children? Because Mona is no better than Dhrubo though she's been a bit quieter of late. I said to Dhrubo, Let me write to your Baba and ask him to arrange the money. Oh, he won't do a thing! he snarled at me. He never has any money for us. Only for himself. I don't want to complain, Debu, but that does seem so, though you'll be angry hearing me say this, as you always are. I see that I have to surrender on this point. I may have to sell my mango pendant gold chain but there's no way out. After all, everything is for the children, isn't it? The roof is leaking. In places the thatch on the kitchen is like a sieve and you can see the moon shine through it. When it rained last week that rack on which we keep our shoes got soaked. And the old wooden crib in which we keep our rolled-up mats. But I can't handle the workers alone so I'll have to wait a bit to get the thatch repaired. And anyway we need the money for this wretched scooter and then the Pitmans Institute's fees and there's Keya Kaki's daughter's wedding round the corner. They gave us a tea set for Shubhra's wedding, remember? So I must give her something—I've thought of a set of payesh bowls. I don't feel like going out these days but I have to go. It will be strange, dressing up and going to a wedding house alone. I've lost so much weight and am as thin as can be. So thin, I'm ashamed. Were you ever ashamed of me? Or have I been imagining it? I could never pluck up the courage to ask you. I was so scared you might say yes.

Jatin, when he was in that 'topical updating' fit had tried changing the scooter to a bike, Pitmans to a computer skills institute, the tea adda to a cyber café. But, as I said, we convinced him to stick to the original seventies' script. Suddenly one afternoon he calls me and says, Rehmat is leaving us. I want you to take on Dhrubo's role. Rehmat leaving? Why? He doesn't like playing Dhrubo, and this, as you know, is something I don't encourage in our group. It's not for an actor to pick and choose what he likes doing or what he dislikes doing. You've got to do what's assigned to you and if you're dissatisfied you can bloody well walk out. So, Mr Banerjee, you're doing Dhrubo's role henceforth. Notice the Mr Banerjee!

I wasn't pleased. Dhrubo's a sixteen-year-old, Boss, I protested. And look at me. Can you pass me off as a sixteen-year-old, even with make-up? He smiled his nasty smile. We'll put you in a corset, Mr Banerjee, if we have to. Meanwhile there are sit-ups and crunches and places like gyms, so go, will you. There was nothing for it. I half admired Rehmat who'd had the spunk to walk out but I know myself. I don't have it. And my mother was so pleased with my so-called acting and so patiently awaiting great performances from her son that I thought, hell, here's where I set about doing in life that that oaf Dhrubo can't do in the play—live up to my Ma's hopes. So Dhrubo I became, that sullen, slow, loutish bloke, that pain in his parents' neck, just to cover myself with glory in my real-life Ma's eyes. She was so different from my stage mother and so much the same. In the silent films that came alive in the multiple screens a slender, small, middle-aged woman moved about an old thatched homestead. That was Kalyani-di who played Jyotsna. In daylight you'd say she was a bit old for the role like I was for Dhrubo's. Her face had acquired a cadaverous look and the skin on her forehead was flaky and lined. But under the footlights she looked a well-preserved, even fetching forty and her gentle, pain-cleft young girl's voice spun a web of innocent and questioning despair. In the silent film that preceded her physical appearance on-stage she flopped down on a step, undid a knot in her anchal and set about counting the coins. Behind her was a veranda with a crumbling old rack, an old wooden cradle stuffed with rolled-up mats and folded kanthas, and some bits of beat-up furniture. At the back of the house was a thicket of coconut palms and a clump of banana trees waving their fanlike arms along the thatch, and a musty pond filled with water weeds a little way behind. She called me by name. Dhrubo!

Ai, Dhrubo! Show yourself, child! And I entered the stage from the right in answer to her call.

But before I did so, Pranesh was bending beside his cot, pulling out his black tin trunk and unlocking it. He rose to his feet, closely studying what appeared to be a bank pass book. His whisper was pre-recorded in our audio, so even the last row was privy to his moment of truth as he mused: My son Dhrubo wants a second-hand scooter now and I must caution him to check out its engine, its papers, whether it's ever been in an accident. If that's what's needed to make him feel positive we've got to scrape together the money somehow. Maybe he'll stop feeling like a failure then . . .

Pranesh consults the pass book, then the audience. Shall I pull off an absurd stroke? Shall I send her a cheque or a money order? Ah, no, no, she'll see my signature and wonder who it is.

He flicks the inland over, checks.

And anyway, there's no return address. And who the hell am I to play God though it's good to feel we're sometimes allowed to do so, like a child wearing his father's shoes. But for all I know it's all vanity, not kindness, and we must be very sure exactly what it is. And also, who am I, tell me, to take these grand postures? No shit in the arse and a banquet call for the pigs, as they say, excuse me, it's so to the point. And another thing—why am I forgetting that I am not this Deb Barat, whoever he is. Though I keep lapsing. I keep feeling like I've become him, even if it's for a brief while, and this woman here is my woman and this unruly boy my son. If I had married, who knows, I'd have had a wife like this, a son just so . . .

And that's when I came and stood before him and said, Baba, Ma said . . . she said you wanted to see me . . .

Then Pranesh frowned and said in a crusty voice to me, What's the problem now?

I hung my head and fidgeted in silence and Pranesh proceeded, She tells me you want a second-hand scooter.

I looked up, said, Yes, Baba.

He looked me up and down. Have you examined this scooter?
I shook my head, said, No, Baba.

Then go and examine it, said Pranesh sternly. Be sure to check
with the mechanic and see to the transfer of the name.

I flushed, broke into a shiver, darted a look from him to Kalyani-
di, my stage mother, who'd come up behind us.

Why didn't you speak to me instead of worrying your mother?
demanded Pranesh wrathfully.

That's just what I told him, Kalyani fluttered. I said, Let your
father come home. He'll see what can be done. It's all right by us
that you haven't done well in the exams but there's always next year,
and meanwhile there's Pitmans . . .

Let me handle this, Jyotsna, interrupted Pranesh. He turned to
me. Before we give you that scooter I must tell you that I myself
never had one. I walked six miles to the village school. Then the two
of us, Milon and I, shared a broken bicycle. It was stolen and we had
to walk again. But we were never ashamed, never. So I say, learn to
be yourself instead of trying to do what you see others doing. And
do it confidently, as I did. Above all, don't worry, Dhrubo, my boy.
I have fifteen years of service left. Enough time for you to get well
settled and your sister as well. But there's one thing I insist on—let
me not hear that you've been misbehaving with your mother again,
is that understood? And let me not hear you've been wasting time
at the adda instead of . . .

But Dhrubo has slipped away in the middle of his father's lecture
because all the while Pranesh has had his eyes fixed not on him but
on Jyotsna. And as the light ripens on Jyotsna's form—I should say
Kalyani-di's form—soft music begins playing, a Bengali love song
in Hemant Kumar's voice:

Koto deen poray aylay, ektoo bosho.
Tomai onek kotha bolar chhilo, jodi shono.

I'll translate that one for you:

So many, many days have you taken to come, do be seated.
There's much to tell you, if you will only hear me speak.

This too was an interpolation by Jatin but a good one. The song didn't play to its end but was abruptly interrupted by the cry of a hawker and the revving of a van's engine. Jatin had carefully built up the illusion of a by-lane going about its business, filling the empty pauses of Pranesh's monologues with crowded details. An earlier director had used a split-level stage and a still earlier one had given this play a solidly realistic interpretation. But Jatin had used off-stage audio to marvellous effect so that the drama of a real world flowed alongside Pranesh's on-stage progress. Quite as the play was intended to do—but more on that later. Let me get back to Mayank playing Pranesh through some of the most difficult and engrossing sequences. Kalyani's voice is heard faintly as he turns from a rear screen window to the letter he holds in his hand.

Were you ever ashamed of me? I could never pluck up the courage to ask you. I was so scared you might say yes.

Only the first lines are in Kalyani's voice, the rest in Mayank's.

Pranesh consults the audience. She asks me, am I ashamed of her? Shall I tease her a bit and say, You're right, I'm so ashamed. I don't know where to look when we're out together. She so desperately wants my approval. What power my words have over her. The hurt will come into her eyes. Which will taste better—the flavour of my power over her heart or the pang of her pain rebounding on mine? She's no beauty, granted. Look at her. She's thin as a scarecrow in a brinjal patch. Dark as a brinjal too, poor girl. And all this hard work has taken its toll. Dhrubo and Mona are no help at all. If anything, their antics have aged her a good ten years. It's such a pity I'm not at home to help her a bit but a job is a job. And when my superiors in the selection board asked me if I was willing to go on transfer anywhere in India, I said yes, isn't that part of my service agreement? Anything you say, sir. So this rented room and this rented string cot and chair and table and all I can call my own are the clothes on that line and that tin trunk beneath the bed. She's alone handling her life, I'm alone handling mine—that's life.

It may not come as a surprise to you but I have frequently been with women. It's less often now. Somehow I've lost the taste for that sort of thing. In the gardens of Outram Ghat or Victoria Memorial. You picked a woman. She took out a plastic sheet from her bag and unfolded it on the ground. Or relieved your itch with her mouth on a shadowy bench or stone step. Yes, and some years ago I had a thing going with a woman in my office. A sub-staff, as they call them, quite a good-looking piece. She had a good man for a husband but she liked having me around too. My wife doesn't know. I also slept once with my landlord's daughter when I was living in Ranaghat. She was only eighteen years old and fair as a rajnigandha flower. Fairer, much fairer than my poor brinjal-purple wife. But, to come back to what I was saying, what answer can there possibly be to this question? Ashamed of you? Nonsense, what an idea! How can I be ashamed of you? Have you taken leave of your senses? I'm proud, proud. You've done me proud, Jyotsna. And you're perfect, just perfect for me. I have eyes for no woman but you. I must remember to say that to her when her next letter comes. It will make the poor girl happy. God knows she deserves it.

The screens come on softly, one by one, randomly here and there, scattered all over the stage at various heights, of various shapes and sizes, littering the space like a cinematic collage. Kalyani's various moods and moments. Bending over a courtyard pump, filling a metal bucket with water, working the handle of the pump up and down. Wringing a saree and spreading it on a clothesline to dry. Chopping fish with a curved cleaver. Staring at an overflowing windowful of rain. Swiping at her beaded forehead with the trailing end of her saree. And, dominating the smaller screens, a large close-up of her face. Parrot nose, anxious eyes, hair pulled back and knotted in a coil, a big red smudge of vermilion between her brows.

Did you see him then? asks Pranesh.

Who? asks the woman on the screen.

The doctor.

No.

Did you get your tests done at least? What's your fasting sugar like now?

I've forgotten, I tell you. I'll have to check the old report.

Pranesh is furious at the apparition. What do you mean forgotten? You haven't had the test, you mean?

Okay, so?

Your last report was something like Fasting-190 and PP-215. And your blood pressure was well over a hundred. And you still go on taking that lump of jaggery after every meal.

She giggles. Ah, you make it sound like a cricket score. It's only jaggery, not sugar. And date palm jaggery at that.

How stupid you are.

Yes, it's what I tell myself a dozen times a day. How stupid I am. See the way I slog and work myself to the bone and nothing ever goes right for me.

There are tears of sudden exasperation in the oversized eyes of the woman's close-up. If I drop dead slogging one of these days that jaggery would have been well worth it.

Now, now, says Pranesh testily. I didn't mean it. About you being stupid. Just forget it. Let it go, Jyotsna.

That's just my problem, says the figure, bending over the bucket at the pump. I can't forget things and I wish I could, says the figure hanging up the saree on the clothesline. I remember too much, far more things than other people do, the face at the window says. My memory is my problem, what a tyrant it can be. It hangs on to things and won't let me rest, says the woman with the cleaver. Sounds, colours, tones of voice, expressions . . . God, I often pray, let me remember less! sighs the close-up of Kalyani. What's the use of hoarding so much in one's mind? It's not good for me. But then I sometimes feel that to remember is to possess forever. Never to lose anything. The thought is always more real than the thing.

Here the figure at the clothes line smiles suddenly, tenderly. The voiceover modulates, changes in timbre, gathering distance and a shadowy resonance.

For example, it says, that elephant ride in the college fair. I didn't know you and I was so shy. I found myself sitting in the elephant's howdah and I was unsteady and nervous. Sorry I'd been talked into this. I clutched at one of the ropes but it chafed the elephant's bottom and he began wiggling to and fro and the mahout shouted at me and then I lost my balance and felt myself pitching over the side. Then you turned and reached out and grabbed me about the waist. Do you remember? the image asks.

Yes, answers Pranesh.

And that time when we took the steamer at Babughat. You bought me a newspaper cone of puffed rice and gram. Plenty of chillies it had and a squeeze of lime and a dash of oil. I remember the taste exactly. You said then, What can a poor office clerk offer his wife on an outing, say? This and maybe some ice cream. But, believe me, little girl, you told me, one day you'll see me the Governor of West Bengal and we'll live in that huge villa with the lions on the gatepost. And I laughed and laughed. Do you remember?

Yes, I remember it all, answers Pranesh.

Then it rained heavily and the streets were waterlogged and public transport came to a halt. The gutters filled and overflowed and the future Governor of West Bengal had to carry his bride across a drain and deposit her in a tana-rickshaw. Do you remember?

Do I? Of course.

Do you remember how we used to walk through New Market and we couldn't buy a thing, no, not a thing. All you bought me were little jasmine ropes for my hair and hustled me out of the shops because I grew sadder and sadder, seeing all those marvellous shop windows and I grew bitter and spiteful with you. Now when I walk past the same row of shops, it's funny but nothing attracts me. Desire is such a short-lived thing, I've learnt. Is it that I've tamed my heart forever and locked it up?

I'm the same as you, Jyotsna, Pranesh agrees. He turns to the audience. There are times when I desire nothing at all, he says, just good news of Mona and Dhrubo, and Jyotsna is in good humour.

When Kalyani had an accident and broke her leg two days before our Samvada Theatre show in Delhi, Jatin came up with the daftest of ideas for me. I was indignant. No way, Boss. What d'you take me for? I shouted, for once forgetting myself. A cross-dresser, huh? Oh, shut up and listen to me, snapped Jatin. You know the script well. We don't have an understudy and anyway it's too late to call in an outside actor, and if you act cussed now we'll have to call off the show. Why don't you take it as a challenge? And you don't have to speak at all. Most of it's voiceover and we can record Kalyani's voice and make changes in the bits in which she does have to speak. No problem at all. You're asking me to do a woman's role? I shrieked, near hysterical. Do I get you? Absolutely, he said. I'm not asking, I'm insisting. All you have to do is mime and use a bit of effective body language to go along with the voiceover. Do it, man. Put in some practice. Prove yourself. I'm sure to fudge it up, I grumbled. And it isn't me that'll be proving anything, Boss, it's you. I took one last ineffectual sock at him. You want to gloat—Look, I've even made a male actor do a female role once. Good for me, na? he rejoined nastily. There was nothing for it. I had to fall in with his wishes. But thank heavens our signboards and fliers and handbills still carried Kalyani's name.

It was a weird and mind-boggling experience, playing Jyotsna. Mercifully I didn't have to spout dialogue and I knew how to step and how to use my body. All that arati dancing and drumming practice in the Durga puja pandals came in handy. Gave a certain fluidity to my movements, moderated their angularities. But I'd never been so nervous. I remember parts of that performance vividly.

Kalyani's voiceover lowered in a confidential tone, with an intimate, chancy hopefulness sparking it: I don't know if I should be asking this, but do you still find me desirable?

Pranesh broke into a laugh. What do you think? he asked.

That's no answer. I want a yes or a no.

Why do you hold a gun to my head?

Because your answer can make or unmake my day.

Pranesh discovered the zest in small cruelties and the power. And the knowledge that injury can be inflicted and recalled at will.

Then the answer is no, he teased.

All the screens faded to a faint blur. The stage was in darkness for a long moment. Then it lit up to a dim bare visibility. There were two figures, one stretched out, one half sitting on the cot. They had crept in unnoticed under cover of the momentary darkness—Mayank playing Pranesh and me playing Jyotsna. In the voiceover a woman's voice resumed its forlorn rhythms of provocation, seeking, complaint.

Now I know why you never bother these days. You don't linger over my body as you used to. You don't whisper to me in the dark. You don't nibble at my ear lobes or kiss the arch of my instep. You are in such a tearing hurry. I haven't felt loved in years. I sometimes think that all you want is to prove to yourself that you can still manage to do it. I'm just a dummy in a trial. I might as well be a beaker or a test tube or a bell jar in a lab. You've forgotten who I am completely. You're only trying to prove yourself. To tell you the truth I haven't got your kind of conscience. And to tell you the truth no man attracts me now. Not even you. But I've got to prove something too. I have to prove myself worthy of being loved. Of holding on to love. Unless I do so I'll fail myself. Once I asked you, Tell me what you think of me. Tell me truly. You said, Truly, I say that I think you a fool. I know, I know what you mean, ah, too well. A fool because I've loved you. A fool because I've never known your other truths. A fool because my heart rejoices in your lies. What an actor you are, oh, I hate you so much. I want to howl my heart out. Enough! Go, go now. Get out of my sight! Let me not set eyes on your false face again. Instead see what a fine show of love I put up . . .

Aah, isn't she tiresome, this spitfire? exclaimed Pranesh to the audience. There's nothing worse than a nattering shrew. Jyotsna's harangue was delivered in the voiceover while I sprang up and circled Pranesh in charged balletic challenge before Jyotsna's anger cracked and she hurled herself on to the cot again in a convulsion of weeping.

Pranesh tore his hair in exasperation. What have I done? Jyotsna, stop! What's wrong?

Have I said anything I shouldn't have? Look. Try to understand. I've lived alone for years. I've lost the graces of company. I say things I don't mean. Sometimes I say one thing and you understand another. Sometimes I say things out of sheer perversity.

Jyotsna: What am I to think when you always avoid giving me straight answers. Just now, when I asked you something for my own self-respect, would it have cost you a fortune to say yes? I wonder, Debu. There's much that I wonder, reading the afternoon Bangla papers. Have you ever been with women, Debu? Tell me. Tell me honestly.

Pranesh (bursting into a fit of rage): You insult me, woman! What do you take me for? What do you think me? After all these years together you still don't know me. Have I no honour in your eyes?

Jyotsna (sitting up, stunned): No, I didn't mean . . . I was just . . . (The voiceover stammers.)

Pranesh (thundering): What else could you have meant? That I'm a dishonourable, immoral man!

Jyotsna: Oh, I'm sorry, sorry.

She has propped herself up, encircled him with her arms from behind. He shakes her off.

Go away, he says, grim. You just won't let me live in peace.

Jyotsna: I said I was sorry. Forgive me. I won't ever say such a thing.

Pranesh: You keep saying sorry and you go on doing and saying the same things.

Jyotsna: It's because I'm afraid.

Pranesh (gruff): What're you afraid of?

Jyotsna: I'm afraid I'm not good enough. That things aren't as they seem. But please, it won't happen again.

Pranesh: Then understand once for all—the next time you utter such shameful suspicions I shall walk out, just go off, and you'll never see me again.

Jyotsna: Oh, don't. Whatever can I do without you? Scold me. Punish me any way you want, but don't leave me. I can't carry on without you and you know it. Come to me. Please, Debu. Come. Let me soothe away the hurt I've given. I'm a monster. I promise it'll never happen again. Come.

I suppose it was the light guy's forte, getting the violet shades to thicken to an impenetrable concentration while faint music rose, the pace of the darkening and the quickening of the music exactly in sync. Urgent whispers filter through the speakers of the audio system.

Pranesh: What shall I do to make you feel good again, my love? Tell me. Teach me again. I am a lump of selfish flesh. An unrefined oaf. A creature of limited imagination. And a woman's body is such a judging, finicky thing. Shall I do it this way? Or this? Am I doing it right? Tell me what to do.

Give me poetry, she demands. Give me words. Rabindranath.

Here Pranesh's level, detached voice confides in the audience: What to do? I cannot remember a single complete Rabindranath poem. Yes, those mornings in the suburbs, when the day began with a singing voice practising in the next house . . . I never saw the singer but the words . . . the words . . . ah, yes.

'When my rooms have been decked out and the flutes sound, and the laughter there is loud, let me ever feel that I have not invited thee to my house . . .'

Jyotsna's voice: Yes! Go on doing that. Yes. Go on. Don't stop.

'Let me not forget for a moment. Let me carry the pangs of this sorrow in my dreams and in my wakeful hours.'

Oh, please. Don't stop. Yes.

'I am eager to die into the deathless . . .'

Oh that one! I know that one! Please. Yes. Don't stop. A bit faster.

Pranesh's voice, a toneless aside: What a tough exercise. Did I ask for a Tagore-loving wife? Then he goes back to recovering the lines.

'I shall tune it to the notes of forever and when it has sobbed out its last utterance . . .'

Here his memory fails him in the exertion, the sheer explosive distraction of what he's at. But gasping, Jyotsna's voice brings out the words, garbled, aching, in an airborne symphonic climax:

'. . . Lay down my silent harp at the feet of the silent.' She utters a deep sigh and falls still. A sarod begins its trickle, droplets of notes gathering into a steady downpour. The tabla erupts in a crackle of stuttering lightning.

Tell me, she implores, tell me what I mean to you.

And though he has never been seven times round the fire with her in living memory, it is as though the chants of the marriage mantras have lain in his soul and he whispers: You are the mother of my children. The preserver of my coffers. The keeper of my home. My other self. Fellow kindler of the sacrificial hearth. Companion nurturer of my ancestors' manes. Protector of my wandering heart. Wayfarer to the future. Path lighter to my moksha. Soul friend.

Curtain.

When the curtain rises again Pranesh is sitting at his table alone, still clutching the letter. One hand clasped to his forehead. All the screens have melted away. He wakes from his trance, looks around, looks to the audience and slowly rises from his chair in disbelief. Gone? Where did she come from and where did she go to? he asks. The mind will never get to the bottom of this. All we have are theories but no one knows. So much of her. Gone in a trice.

He regards the letter, holds it away at a distance from his eyes in order to focus better. Did she step out of this? Did all the things I've managed to possess come out of this? Let me count and see. I've acquired a son who's training to be a typist, who's lazy and refuses to cycle to work. The son has just bought a second-hand Lambretta scooter. I have a wife who is thin, diabetic, harried with housework and troublesome kids, a wife who's felt unloved for years. Who loves to hear poetry while making love. I now have a house with a leaking thatch, a rack of old shoes, a crib full of palm mats. Yes, and I have a daughter too who's a handful but a bit quiet lately. And there's someone my wife calls Keya Kaki who has a daughter who has a wedding coming up. More, I've suddenly acquired a head full of memories. I once sat with a young girl on an elephant at a college fair. I grabbed her about the waist as she almost fell off. There was also a mahout who shouted at her. There was an elephant that jiggled its bottom. I bought a paper cone full of puffed rice and gram and an ice cream for a young wife on an outing and I carried her across a gushing gutter in a waterlogged Kolkata street. I walked with her through the maze of New Market and we were so poor we couldn't afford to buy a thing. And she was angry with me and showed it. I have once bitten a woman's ear lobes and kissed the instep of her foot. I have sat through her storm of accusations and tears and all her protestations of hate and of love. And I have recited broken lines of Rabindranath while making love. I'm getting to be a fellow with a crowded life! A full, eventful, connected existence. But what I want to know is, where the hell is it all coming from? From this paper in my hand or my own head. What's that she said? The thought is always more real than the thing.

Awesome! boomed Jatin's baritone. You're going great guns, man! I always knew you'd pull it off. Don't give me any of that! I snapped. I was, like, fuck the stage and all these smart-ass guys. Can't you see how rattled my nerves are, playing a woman? Frayed, that's me. God, don't you even begin to realize the state I'm in by now, Boss?

He looked at me with interest. Aw, give us a break, what's with you? Don't tell me your sleeping Yin's been activated. Think. Are you still hetero? I mean, how d'you feel about yourself?

They made fun of my sleeping Yin, of my progress into pink. They made drunken verses ending in 'pink' and 'think' and 'shrink'.

I laughed wanly, wimp that I am. I laughed my ass off and kept my troubles to myself. I couldn't get Jyotsna's lines out of my head. I heard them playing in my mind even while I slept.

It was not as if Jatin was unaware of my strange distress. Because one day, quite out of the blue, he called me and said: For how long are you going to fool around, Partho? Don't you think it's time you took the male lead? Pretty stupefied, I was. You mean Pranesh's role? Yes, you damn fool. What's up with Mayank? Mayank has to go to Mumbai for a contract. In case you don't want to take it on, tell me by tomorrow. He hung up.

In case I didn't want to take it on? I was speechless with the thrill of it. After a year and a half of waiting, doing roles I didn't want to do, here was the Boss offering me the role of my life, asking me whether I wanted it or not!

So Pranesh I became, Pranesh in all the epic majesty of his angst and the troubled exhilaration of his quickening inner life. Pranesh tearing open Jyotsna's next letter which the postman has thrown in and pacing the dark stage reading it aloud:

It's Mona now, Debu. She doesn't know I go through her cupboard every day—it gives me clues as to what she's up to. And two days ago I found something that terrified me. I haven't slept all night with worry and I can't confront her with it. She scares me, this difficult, quarrelsome girl. There was a carton of condoms, Debu, hidden beneath a pile of clothes. A full carton. And in the locker—which she always leaves unlocked—two gold bangles that I've never seen before. Real gold. Have you any idea what all this might mean? What's she doing? Who's giving her these things? She tells me she has to work in the college library till late and I know well enough that studying is the last thing she's doing. Then Keya Kaki's friend, Sarvani, spotted Mona getting off a bus at the racecourse stop and with her was a man. They were heading for Victoria Memorial where, as far as I know, only lovers go, apart from regular tourists.

Here Pranesh begins quivering with tension. Now that Kalyani was back we reverted to the earlier draft of the play in which the scene was enacted onstage with a voiceover occasionally providing a commentary or an observation. The rest of the scene was a pretty conventional rendering.

Enter Kalyani: I asked Dhrubo to keep tabs on Mona. I couldn't tell him what I found in Mona's cupboard but I told him that I suspected Mona was seeing someone and so it's best for us to find out who it is, whether he's okay or not, before we talk to her. But Dhrubo, you know how he is.

Enter Dhrubo: You're asking me to spy on Didi—did I get you right?

Kalyani: I'm asking you to keep a watch on her.

Dhrubo: Comes to the same thing.

Kalyani: You can call it whatever you like, I don't care.

Dhrubo: Well, it can't be done.

Kalyani: Why?

Dhrubo: D'you think I can escape her seeing me? Is this some kind of cloak-and-dagger spy story where I go around shadowing my sister wearing a mask?

Kalyani: Can't you . . . can't you ask one of your friends to do it for you? Someone Mona doesn't know.

Dhrubo: Hmm. Okay, let me think.

Kalyani: Why not that Ranjit? The one who came to see you yesterday?

Dhrubo: What should I tell him?

Kalyani: You'll have to tell him that we're worried your sister is having an affair with the wrong kind of man.

Dhrubo: I could. But there's another little thing. What'll you give me?

Kalyani: Give you?

Dhrubo: To do this and not tell Didi.

Kalyani: Why, you . . . you unspeakable boy!

Dhrubo: No, seriously, there's a two-in-one cassette player I could do with.

Kalyani (sighing): What would it cost?

Dhrubo: I'll find out and let you know. And there'll have to be something for Ranjit as well?

Kalyani: Him too?

Dhrubo: Naturally. Why ever should he agree to do this for me?

Kalyani (hopeless): Would fifty rupees do?

Dhrubo: Make it a hundred.

Here Pranesh breaks in, walking right across their field of movement, unseeing, lost in his musings: Ah, poor, poor woman. Such a vicious fellow this boy! What have we ever done to deserve such grasping offspring, God knows there's nothing in my karma or in hers . . . Shall I send her the money? But again, the old problem. And seriously, what *is* this daughter of mine up to? My heart sinks at the thought of it. The Victoria Memorial gardens at dusk! Oh, hell, hell, hell! And here comes the girl herself, stomping in, all in a froth.

Enter Mona. Her face is flushed, her eyes snap with rage.

Kalyani: Where have you been?

Mona: In the college library, where else?

Kalyani: That's not true.

Mona (eyeing her mother): I've been out on work. I'm working on a college project. But that's not what I want to discuss now. What I want to know is how dare you set up that rotter Ranjeet to shadow me? What d'you think you're doing?

Kalyani: I don't know what you're talking about.

Mona: You know very well. What an actress you are, Ma! What a liar! You set up this rascal to spy on me and pretend you know nothing about it.

Kalyani: Mind your tongue.

Mona: You mind your tongue yourself!

Kalyani: How d'you know I set him up?

Mona: He came up to me. He had the audacity to say, 'Your Ma has paid me a hundred rupees in advance to keep tabs on you. Now what're you going to pay me to keep my mouth shut?' I . . . I hit him with my bag and . . .

Kalyani: Yes, go on. What are you going to pay him to keep his mouth shut? And may I now ask, shut about what?

Mona: Oh, I hate you, I hate you, Ma!

Kalyani: Who is this man you're going around with?

Mona: Mind your own business. Get out of my life!

Kalyani: It *is* my business. I found a whole carton of . . . of condoms in your cupboard. Under your pile of kurtas. And a pair of gold bangles.

Mona: Ah, you've been going through my cupboard! How dare you? How dare you?

Kalyani: Who is that man? Answer me.

Mona: If you must know, he is my project supervisor.

Kalyani: What is his name?

Mona: His name is Dr Mohit Lahiri.

Kalyani (grimly): I'll have to visit your college one of these days.

Mona (shouting): Oh you will, will you, will you?

Kalyani: I want to ask Dr Mohit Lahiri why he's made my daughter keep condoms in her cupboard. And I want to say thank you for those gold bangles but we don't accept such . . . such payment in our family.

Mona flies at Kalyani and tries to claw at her face.

Mona: You are such a bitch, Ma! I wish you'd die!

Kalyani: Nothing you say has any effect on me, girl. I insist on knowing the truth.

Mona: Okay, you want the truth and you shall have it. Lahiri sir is supervising my project on prostitution in public spaces in Kolkata and we are doing it for an NGO called Mritunjaya. We interview the women in their usual haunts and give them condoms and literature and coupons for free medical examinations. You want to know about the bangles? I'll tell you, I'll tell you, Ma! Many of the women have become my friends. Yes, you can turn your nose up but they're fond of me. One of them's called Bijoya and these are the bangles she bought with her savings for her daughter

for when she's older. She didn't know where to keep them safely
so she asked me. And now, Ma, I'm not going to stay another
moment in your house after what you've just accused me of. Just
give me ten minutes and I'll be packed and gone.

Kalyani: Stop! You can't do this. Where'll you go?

Mona: I'll go to Lotika's.

Kalyani: No, Mona, stop. I'm sorry I was hasty.

Mona: Hasty? I like that word—hasty! Slinging mud on me, spying
on me, getting outsiders to spy on me—hasty!

Kalyani: No. I'm sorry. I was worried. Times are bad. People aren't to
be trusted. You're so young. I'm all alone looking after you . . .

Mona: You won't be looking after me any more!

Exit Mona and Kalyani.

Kalyani's voiceover: And as if that wasn't bad enough, here's a fresh
bit of disaster—from Dhrubo's end. I thought to myself, let her
go and cool off a bit. Tomorrow I'll go to Lotika's and bring her
around. Then Dhrubo didn't return. And this morning there
was a knock on the door and Sub-Inspector Mullick from the
police station was standing there. He asked me where Dhrubo
was. I said I had no idea, that Dhrubo hadn't been in all night.
He said, Shrimoti Barat, I've come to warn him. I could arrest
him if I wanted but your husband is known to me so a warning
is fair enough. I asked him what the matter was. He said Dhrubo
and his friends had been collecting donations for puja pandals,
pretending to be members of the Jagrihi Club. He said an
elderly couple who were acquainted with the club's office bearers
informed them and the club had lodged a complaint with the
police. He said Dhrubo and his rascal friends then threatened
the old couple. And now Dhrubo is in hiding. Oh, Debu, was
there ever a woman as hard pressed as me! I think I'm going mad.
I wish you were here with me to handle all this but you don't
write a line and don't take any interest in us. Maybe you're tired
or busy or on tour but I can't wrestle with these troublesome

things alone, I swear by Ma Kali. I think I'm going to have some kind of a breakdown . . .

Here Pranesh slowly rises to his feet and puts the letter aside, saying, Over my dead body! Ah, this poor, poor wife of mine. There's a limit to what one poor soul can endure. Shame on me that I can't lift a finger to help. But clearly, enough is enough. I see I'll have to take things in hand. Mona first. I wonder if my daughter spoke the truth or if she's just another slick actress and an arrant liar? Is she really working on a project or is she fucking around with this Lahiri cad? Why would a woman pass on her gold? That does seem a bit incredible to me. A whole carton of condoms—sarvanash! They must be—oh hell, what a loathsome thought! My daughter. Oh, I could wring her neck! It's only too probable that she's pulling a fast one on her poor helpless mother. It's only too probable she's running wild with this scoundrel. Lying in the grass, smooching in taxis or groping in dark movie halls—ah, I know the scene. Wait till I catch her! I'll break every bone in this Lahiri's body. Ah, there they are! That's them. I'm absolutely sure.

All of a sudden Pranesh points to a couple sitting in the third row. He comes leaping down from the stage, pounces on the man, collars him, hauls him to his feet and drags him towards the stage, shouting, You haramzada! I know you! What are you doing in this dark cinema hall with my daughter?

The girl begins to scream. Let him go! Let him go, you beast! Have you gone mad? What are you doing? How dare you?

There is a scuffle in the aisle. The man shouts: Leggo! What the bloody hell d'you think you're doing, man? I'll settle your hash for you.

Clearly an Anglicized upper-crust voice. Pranesh drags the man on to the stage, the girl running frantically along. You'll be sorry! she shouts. I'm going to complain to the actors' union. You can't assault innocent members of the audience like this.

Pranesh will not let go of the man. Kindly explain, you bastard, what you're doing with my daughter.

I am not your daughter! shrieks the girl. Are you crazy? You'll pay for this!

Not my daughter? asks Pranesh, releasing the man. He appears to be in a daze.

And this isn't a movie hall, shouts the girl. It's the ICA theatre and this is a play by Neelbandhu Ghoshal and we're plain ordinary people who've bought tickets to see you perform! The man dusts himself, straightens his collar, pats down his hair.

If you're part of the audience, says Pranesh, disbelieving, then who am I?

Let's calm down, says the man. You're probably stressed out and under some sort of a delusion. You're Pranesh Mitter imagining that you're Deb Barat, the man for whom the letters come.

Am I Pranesh? asks Pranesh, confused.

Actually you're not. You're only acting as Pranesh. But—the man produces a play bill and consults it—in real life you're Partho Banerjee.

It's complicated, says Pranesh ruefully. Let me figure this out. You're quite sure you're not my daughter Mona?

No way, says the girl.

Have it your own way then, says Pranesh in a defeated voice. I am very sorry for my misbehaviour. Go back to your seat, madam. Accept my apologies, moshai. No hard feelings. I seem to have forgotten my lines.

The man slaps Pranesh's back. No hard feelings, old chap, he assures. We all forget our lines sometimes. Then someone comes along and prompts us.

The couple return to their seats.

Hah, cries Pranesh, where's the sala prompter? You in there? he calls into the wings.

Here! answers a voice.

What're you doing, sleeping on the job? I've forgotten my lines. What's my name?

Pranesh Mitter, answers the voice.

Is that my real name? asks Pranesh.

No, only in this play.

I'm all mixed up. Am I someone else outside this play, then?

Don't be ridiculous, scolds the prompter. You're our Partho. Actor, thirty-two, male, resident of Kolkata, West Bengal, India. Come to your senses now.

Ah, I remember it all, gasps Pranesh, addressing the air. What an embarrassing mistake that was, Jyotsna. I was quite sure it was our Mona but it turned out to be a complete stranger. Why do my eyes fall on complete strangers and I think I know them through and through? But again, why do the ones I think I know through and through become strangers to me? But leave it all to me, Jyotsna, my dear. It was a genuine mistake this time. I, as they say, forgot myself, I really did and had to be—how to put it?—recalled to myself. But I'll get to the bottom of this. It's all because of that rascal prompter. Here, man, come and show yourself. I see I've got to keep you somewhere where I can see you all the time. Come on out!

By now the play had broken out of its mould and spilt its contents all over and the line between make-believe and reality had blurred.

The prompter comes in, script in hand, looking shifty.

Pranesh: Ah, there you are, mister. Look up that rag in your hands and tell me what I'm to do now. I seem to have lost the plot.

Prompter: You get down to cooking your dinner.

He considers the script. It says here, Pranesh Mitter crosses over to the right, squats on his wooden plank in front of his kerosene stove. He takes out three potatoes, a kitchen knife and an aluminium pan. Then he rises and comes to sit on his cot, placing the pan on his knees and the rest beside him on his bed.

Pranesh obeys, parodying every action.

Prompter: Pranesh begins to peel the potatoes.

Pranesh: Right-o! Pranesh does just that. What do I do with these bloody potatoes?

Prompter: You light the stove and put them on to boil with the rice and then mash it all up with salt and a bit of oil.

Pranesh (gravely): Okay, okay. I do just that, but, hey, I've run out
    of salt. You'll have to run along to the corner store and get me
    a packet.

Prompter: You sure you're going to be all right without me.
    Suppose you forget your lines again? This audience might
    turn restive.

Pranesh: Okay, leave the wretched script here. Here on the other side.
    Not in the potato pan, fool! The other side, I said. That's right.
    I'll look it up if I forget my lines. Now go, will you. Be off with
    you and be back in a jiffy.

The prompter leaves. Pranesh looks sideways at the sheaf of loose
sheets while continuing to peel the potatoes, muttering: Here's the
bloody script of my life—everything I have to do. Complete stage
instructions. But . . .

The lights go out. And Pranesh swears, Oh sarvanash! Now
there's load shedding and what's the use of having the script of my
life beside me if I can't read a word of it? Hey, light dada! Get the
generator going. I need just a bit of light on this script, please.

The light technician appears, carrying a lantern.

Light technician: Here, brother. Make do with this while we get the
    generator started.

Pranesh pulls the table alongside the bed, places the lantern on
it and holds up the script to the light, screwing up his eyes in an
effort to read.

Pranesh: It says here, Pranesh takes a handful of rice in a platter and
    starts cleaning it. Right-o . . . handful of rice. Ah, I clean it. So.
    (Street sounds)

Pranesh: But where's the rest of the script? It seems this fool of a
    prompter has gone off with the next sheet. And this lantern's
    no help. Whatever will this audience make of me now? I see
    I must do something at this point, say something, but what?
    Director babu!

Pranesh calls out loudly: Director babu! Tell me what it is I have to
    do. I've forgotten my lines—just blanked out. And the prompter's

gone out for a bit and maybe carried away the next page by mistake.

Then Jatin's beery, baritone reprimand booms on the audio system: You've sent him away at your own risk, don't ask me anything now.

Pranesh: But what do I do now? I've forgotten my lines, director babu, sir. It's your play as much as it's mine.

Jatin's stern voice: Do whatever you can take responsibility for. If nothing occurs to you, just wait. Go on peeling the potatoes, cleaning the rice, whatever's on hand.

Here Jyotsna's voice undercuts the director's voice. It seems to blow in, a sighing whiff of a breeze. Oh, Debu, I've overloaded you with my troubles. This is interrupted by a whirring squeal of the sound system—an effect ingeniously produced by our sound guys. Above this whirr there is a loud hammering on the door. It is repeated, louder. Still louder. And Pranesh curses: That must be the sala prompter back from the bazaar. Come in!

No one does.

Pranesh: What's going on here? Is it load shedding or has my mind blown a fuse? Was the voltage too high, for God's sake?

There is complete silence. Then the jangle of a door chain against old wood.

Pranesh swears irritably: I can't see in the dark. Where are the damn matches? Just a moment. Who is it? The door's open. Push it, will you.

Deb Barat, comes the answer. Deb Barat is my name. The lights come on all of a sudden, every bulb blinding, stupefying the eye.

A man enters the room, stepping in tentatively. He looks around unsure of himself. He looks at Pranesh's table and chair, the aluminium pan with the half-peeled potatoes, the dish of cleaned rice, the string cot with its rolled-up bedding, the kerosene stove at the rear, the clothesline with the piled-up clothes. He obviously does not know how to begin and while he pauses in a frozen instant,

Pranesh rises to his feet, lip-syncing to his own voiceover coming through the speakers: I knew this was going to happen some time. He has turned up at my doorstep to recover his letters.

Pranesh wastes no time. He pulls out his old tin trunk from beneath his cot and takes out the five letters. He holds them out to the stranger, saying: Here they are, moshai. His words are brisk, simulating a confidence he is far from feeling. He turns to the audience and speaks, his voice snagging around the words: There it all goes, the life I received as a gift of grace. There goes my house with the leaking roof. There goes the poem I recited while making love to my wife. There goes my wife as well. My quarrelsome daughter and her mysterious lover. My black sheep son and his Lambretta scooter. He's here to take it all back and why shouldn't he? It wasn't mine. It was something I stole. No, stole isn't right. It was something I received and kept and now that he's here I feel so shamed, so bereft. Such a loser. But no doubt, he's cut up and expects an explanation. Won't you sit down, Barat moshai, and let me explain?

I'm usually called Debu, said the stranger, sinking into Pranesh's chair. He holds the bunch of letters awkwardly like an ungainly gift. A great annoyance shows on his face.

Ah, I know how you must be feeling, sir, murmurs Pranesh, shamefaced. You notice that there are five letters. The envelopes are torn open and the pages rifled through. They have been unfolded and read and put back dozens of times. I plead guilty, moshai. Believe me, I have no excuse except idle curiosity. This is a dull sort of place—nothing much to do, no circle, no adda. Absolutely nothing to do except cook one's meal, eat and sleep and go to work at 8.30 the next morning. At my office there's a staff of four and they're all men with families except me. I opened the first letter and it seemed interesting. Then I opened the second one and then came a third and a fourth and a fifth. Believe me, Debu-da, I meant no harm.

Please don't apologize, sir, protests the stranger. Don't think about it.

But you must have missed them surely, says Pranesh, contrite. You must have waited and wondered why your wife had not written. You must have worried about Jyotsna and Mona and Dhrubo . . .

He stops short, confused. He feels such discomfort merely using those names with such unwarranted intimacy. No matter that he'd built a complete life with them. Fought with, slept with, scolded, threatened, forged such a connection with them that it could only be karmic. Something left over from a past self or even a backwash of an uncharted future, a seepage through the membrane of time from an alternative life in a parallel universe. Why else was it so hard to uproot their names from his heart? But it had to be done, this thing, no matter how deep the roots had gone, into what impenetrable subsoil of his dense unremembering.

He has been murmuring these thoughts aloud. This was a life that wasn't mine to claim, so let my besotted heart loosen its hold and let me give it all back without flinching to this lucky man to whom it belongs. I'm sorry you haven't been able to answer your wife's letters, sir. You can do it now. I know how it feels to be alone, without family, home, furniture, trees and books and knick-knacks and all the rest. Not that I've ever had the good fortune to own any of those but I know how it must feel to you . . .

Stop. Please don't carry on like this. Deb Barat has stood up wearily to stretch his legs. To tell you the truth, I wouldn't have answered any of these letters.

Pranesh has come up behind him, baffled. Why ever not? She is alone. Has problems. Your son's wanted by the police. Your daughter's going out with a strange man. But I beg forgiveness, I'm intruding again into your private matters.

Not at all, says Deb Barat. Since you know so much about my what you call 'private matters', moshai, let me tell you something still more private. I applied for this voluntary transfer. Yes, actively pursued it and all. To get out. It was too much to endure, believe me. Day in and day out, the claims, the charges, the demands, the exhausting, unrelieved accountability. The same cloying, sickening, soul-breaking caringness of it all! One is born for better things. I got away, sir, and I can't tell you what a relief it is to be on my own. How sane it feels to me. I seem to be breathing fresh air, I who have only inhaled noxious fumes all these years till I was choking for breath. Do you wonder at me?

Pranesh stands staring, shaking his head. His voiceover murmurs his thought: He asks me do I wonder at him. I wonder at him and at myself too. To think I hanker after all that this man has run away from. All that heart-warming, the elation that he calls toxic excess. All the ravenous aches and the dark unforgiving, the wounding and the grieving that burn away at us like an illness, and all the holy rapture, the mercy! But I crave that blessedness and he flees from it. He has it. I don't have it. Neither of us is happy.

Deb Barat has walked up to the barred window at the rear of the stage. He gazes out. What a great view you have here, he says softly. I like the way the lane slopes down to the pool there. And those lights in the water. If it looks this nice on a moonless night, how much nicer it must be on a clear day. I envy you, moshai, you are a lucky man.

He turns round to survey Pranesh's room. You have all this empty space to yourself. Nothing to break this sacred stillness. No earthly worry to vex you. No one to be responsible for. How free you must be, sir.

Pranesh joins him at the window and looks out. I see nothing, he says. Just the lane and the bazaar and the community pond. But what are you doing, moshai?

Tearing up these letters, answers Deb Barat. He tears the letters up into small shreds and tosses them out of the window.

But you didn't even read them! exclaims Pranesh.

I didn't come here for them, says Deb Barat. I came to borrow a torch if you've got one. I can't find mine. I've moved in three houses down the lane and I thought somebody might have what I couldn't find.

Ah, Jyotsna, murmurs Pranesh's voiceover. Did Dhrubo come back? Was Mona speaking the truth? Somebody has what I couldn't find and thanks to him I won't find my answers either.

Deb Barat heads for the door, saying: I shall tell the postman not to throw unwanted letters in the wrong house again. Nomoshkar, dada. Good to have met you. I'll look in again.

The play ends there. Having soared into its own meta-reality its quiet touchdown is smooth, leaving the hall in absolute silence.

Not my touchdown though. Apart from the first handful of performances I found that the role of Pranesh Mitter zapped me no end. I can't define it as disappointment exactly. More like a misplacement of expectation. I guess I was tired of living with the soul's awful complexities. It had all seemed awesome so long as I saw others performing the role but once I was the one acting, I wasn't sure. This wasn't the great role of my life, I was sure of that. What that great role that I was waiting to play was I didn't know but it most definitely wasn't this one.

I chose to approach Jatin at two in the afternoon. He jiggled the mouse round, clicked the 'save' button and swivelled his chair around to face me.

Boss, I said, I'm looking for something pared down. Something solid and commonplace, not yawping around in an internal audio mist or someone else's trapped thoughts. I want to play the real, the here. Boss, let me be the postman again. Just for a bit. Now that Mayank's back . . .

Why the postman? He transfixed me with a stare that went through me like an electric drill.

Because he's the coolest guy of the bunch. Because all he has are a bicycle and a bag and two lines to speak. He's not out to grab eyeballs, if you know what I mean. He's not an attitude junkie.

But suppose Rehmat or Mayank go off again?

I'm okay with playing their roles again. Only, just for a bit, once in a while, between playing different roles, Boss, let me be the postman again.

Suddenly Jatin smiled, so benign that the thought went through me in a flash—hell, this guy's been acting a part all this bloody time!

Oh okay, he said. Just for a bit, once in a while.

I reckoned that was enough for me. Just for a bit, once in a while, in between playing different roles, to know what being happy really was.

Song without End

Finally, room number 12, the last in the row of private wards, and Dr Mehta's favourite.

The patient sat up in bed.

'May I borrow your spirit, doctor?'

'I beg your pardon?'

'What I mean is, may I borrow some doctor's spirit from you?'

Dr Mehta couldn't help laughing. 'What d'you need it for?'

'Oh, just as a cleaning fluid. See this record of mine?' He reached out and lifted a worn-out LP from the bedside table. 'It's got a lot of dust in its grooves. I'm trying to clean it up.'

'Song without End' read the doctor on the sleeve of the record.

'In fact,' confessed the patient gleefully, 'I even went down to Civil Lines, looking for some record cleaning fluid and a new needle for my old stereo. Couldn't find either. Obsolete gadgetry, I was told.'

Dr Mehta's face grew stern. 'You left the hospital?'

'Yes. In defiance of all your commands.' The patient grinned.

'Damn you, Narendra! Who gave you permission to leave this ward and go hobnobbing about town?' demanded Dr Mehta, wrathful.

The patient knew just how far he could stretch the bonds of an old small-town friendship. 'I don't need anyone's permission once I've set my heart on something.'

All the interns were having trouble keeping a straight face. These little exchanges every morning and evening enlivened the rounds. But Dr Mehta was not amused.

'I see,' he said drily. 'And how exactly did you go on this . . . excursion?'

'I walked.'

'Walked! And however did you negotiate the traffic? You aren't even steady on your feet yet.'

'Easy. I had my stick. I even thought of fixing a large L on my back.'

Here everyone burst out laughing, Dr Mehta too. And when the merriment subsided, Dr Mehta marshalled all the severity at his command. 'You're not to repeat this sort of thing!'

'Why not?'

The doctor answered with his patent cardiologist's quip: 'The heart has its reasons that even cardiologists can't guess, Narendra.' He fixed on his patient a piercing stare. 'It might interest you to know the medical history of your next-door neighbour in this wing. The number 11 guy. Almost ready for discharge now. But like you a case of singular cussedness. Very fussy patient. Fussy and interfering. Even when he was suffering from severe bleeding in the lungs, when the air pockets in his lungs were filling up with blood, he wouldn't let us put in the breathing tube. He knew he would die but he just wouldn't have it. We had to browbeat him—literally. We'd done all we could. Cardiac catheterization. Putting in a drug coated stent to clear the blocked-up artery. Giving him intravenous blood thinners to stop the stent clotting. Then the bloke's absolute stupidity about the tube! I told him that I had handled similar cases of blood thinning but a few days of ventilator support and intubation could take care of that. But he refused. Nothing we could do about it. It was the fellow's wilfulness against the simple mechanical predictability of what we were suggesting. Exasperating. Especially after we'd tried all the other things—supplemental oxygen, diuretics, pressurized face mask. Then of course the crisis. He was breathing forty times a minute. His oxygen saturation was falling fast. I had to hector at him—got the anaesthetist to get ready to intubate him whether he liked it or not. And when we managed to, my God! The blood in the tube rushed up like a jet of high-pressure water up a pipe. Even our masks and gowns were sprayed and by the time the central intravenous line was located, he'd begun swinging from side to side like a body out of control. It was touch and go. But then we managed to kind of grab the controls.'

Number 12 was appropriately awed. 'So did he make it?'

'I told you he's almost ready for discharge. A smallish tube made all the difference. The lung bleed went on for some days and we had to give him heavy blood transfusions. Then his BP kept falling and rising and his temperature too. But we made it.'

Dr Mehta crossed over and stood at the foot of the hospital bed. Then he said very earnestly, 'Look, I really needed to scare you, Narendra. You're on the wrong side of sixty. The finest case of mitral stenosis in recent months. I'm not too happy with that valvotomy we did on you. I've been reading up on your case . . . Anyway, I'll let you know what we've decided in a day or two. Meanwhile, do curb your excesses. Listen to your music, read your books, but just take it easy . . .'

'Hish! You're like a nagging wife, Mehta,' protested the patient. And as the doctor turned to go the patient called after him, 'Don't forget the spirit, Mehta!'

'I shan't,' called back the doctor. The juniors knew that their chief always left this particular ward cheered.

The next morning Dr Mehta found the patient tinkering with an ancient contraption on the table.

'What's this?' he asked. 'Why, an old turntable record player! Battery operated?'

'That's right,' said the patient. 'I sent for it—and a batch of my old records.'

'Ah,' remembered the doctor, rummaging in his pocket. 'That's the spirit, man.' He handed over the bottle of spirit.

'Thanks,' said the patient. 'Now I can get the old things turning smoothly again.'

'But what an old ruin!' exclaimed Dr Mehta, examining the record player. 'I had one of these about thirty years ago. D'you mean to say it actually works?'

'Occasionally. Let me get my records polished and I'll play them for you. Do you have any spare time today?'

The doctor reflected. 'I can manage a quarter of an hour maybe. Just after I go off duty.'

'Good, I'll have my Mozarts all cleaned up in an hour. I read in the paper that some of his lost compositions have been unearthed and I simply must get hold of them, but meanwhile I have to satisfy myself with these.'

'See you at one-thirty then,' said Dr Mehta. There was something disturbing that he had to break to this patient. Tactfully.

'How about a glass of juice out of the old flask, Mehta?' offered the patient when the doctor appeared at 1.30. 'It isn't infected, you know. No bird, swine or any other species of the sneezy-wheezies in the news.'

'I hope it is infected,' smiled Dr Mehta.

'Eh?' The patient looked puzzled.

'With your special swaggering bravado. I could do with a bit of that myself,' complimented the doctor, settling down. 'What's this now?'

The patient selected a record out of the dozen strewn on his bed. 'This, my dear Mehta, is the Turkish Concerto.'

'Oh, oh!' mocked the doctor affectionately.

The old turntable creaked into motion. It swung its shining black weight in unsteady, wobbling circuits and a breath of music fluttered into the room. Little trinkets of melody went reeling on the floor. Whimsical phrases of tune somersaulted up to the windows.

The patient closed his eyes, enthralled. And when the disc swirled to a final stop, he opened his eyes and said slowly, 'D'you know, Mehta, I once went all the way to Vienna to stand by this man's grave for a moment. Yes. In return for that hair-raising harangue you flung at me this morning, I must repay you in kind, whether you like it or not. It was in a remote cemetery called the Beidermeyer Cemetery of St Marx.'

It all came back to him and he spun out the visions as best he could. A slow-flaming Austrian autumn, all the leaves glinting in a slanting gold drizzle, a lotion of sun tippled over the boughs. The air like a fine membrane, crackling like unfolding cellophane as one walked through it, looking for that grave. A large, lonely cemetery, entirely baroque, with cherubs and angels leaning over mildewed crosses—cast-iron benches—shaded avenues smoking in a sifted dust of light. And that particular grave—a pillar with his name on it, Wolfgang Amadeus Mozart, in a small bed of flowers. And all round it, under the branches, such an inlay of faint sparkles on the ground.

'I thought I had to say something to him but I felt such a fool. So all I said was: "I've known your music for years. I've loved it. Thank you." I even visited his home. The address was 5, Domgasse. And the name of the house, Figarohaus. A house with an ordinary enough approach . . .'

Two arching doors, up a narrow stone staircase and then a polished door with that name again. Into a beautiful inner lobby with pink frescoed walls. And in large glass cases his work, scribbled on yellowed sheets in his own hand. A small, slanting, elemental code.

'It was funny, coming straight from the grave of an absent man to the physical presence of his work. I thought: Here's the music he composed, and there lies the hand that wrote it all—decomposed . . .'

It was at this instant that Mehta thought fit to pull his patient's leg with a teasing interruption. 'Good God!' he breathed in gentle malice. 'But what a wretched philosopher you are!'

The patient looked immediately abashed. 'Sorry,' he said. 'But I do get carried away at times. Did you like this piece? It's my favourite.'

'Very much indeed,' said the doctor. 'But I do wish you'd change this old record player of yours. Get a better music system, a CD player maybe.'

His companion was incensed. 'Whatever for?' he demanded. 'I've been getting this one repaired for *years* whenever it breaks down. It isn't going to change the notation, is it?'

'No, but a superior music system shall make the same notation shine through better.'

'Rubbish!' dismissed the patient. 'But something in that. The other day I tried cleaning the soundtrack of *Song without End*—a film about Liszt—with a nasty acid powder recommended to me by a friend. It ruined it, erased the music entirely. Makes *you* humble, doctor, to remember how all that magic is contained by a physical object after all. And when it's damaged . . .'

'You can always go buy another one. Other cassettes and CDs continue playing the same music, you know. You won't find a record like this but one's got to move with time and technology.'

'That's some comfort. And the notation's all written down somewhere. Maybe I can train myself to hear it in my head, without disc or tape.'

'The day you do that I'll refer you to our neurosciences research wing.'

The patient took a long quaff of juice and pulled the doctor's leg. 'You and your wretched medical textbook mind, Mehta!'

And the doctor laughed, enjoying himself, and retorted, 'You and your wretched decadent European mind, Narendra. What're you doing here, anyway? In India's sprawling cow belt?'

'Nonsense, it was a cow belt when the Aryans came. It remains a cow belt still. Rather more reliably bovine. Though personally I choose to call it pastoral!'

The doctor held his sides and roared with laughter.

'No, honestly.' The patient wiped away the tears of merriment from his glasses. 'I feel quite at home here. Quite an Orpheus, in fact.'

'Good for you. Strum your lyre while Rome burns, man. What was that fellow's name now? Orpheus, wasn't it?'

'Your ignorance, Mehta, is quite shockingly abysmal! That was Nero. Medical practice has undermined your cultural quality. Well, well. Look at me—a retired teacher. Financially low-class, culturally high-class. On the whole I flatter myself. I insist it's better than being financially high-class and culturally low-class.'

Never in this hospital had Dr Mehta laughed with a patient more. 'What a bloody snob you are, Narendra!' he exclaimed.

'Oh, absolutely. Not that I'm above middle-class or middle-brow activity, Mehta. Drink up now. Did I tell you I'm quite a political animal now? I'm heavily into caste politics.'

'You?'

'I am now a micro caste unto myself. And anyone who shares my tastes and values belongs to my caste. I call us the sabhya-jan caste—men of culture.'

'Sounds like a marginal political party. That'll never ever win an election.'

'Oh, I won't even try. I'm content writing outraged letters to the editor in the Queen's English and the purest Hindustani. Or filing public interest litigation suits or right to information applications. I have my hands full.'

'You've come a long way. Citizen activist, eh? Marx to Mozart to this . . .' teased the doctor.

'Mind you, I'm not saying that I'm not an okay-enough candidate to contest an election. Not distinguished for any excellence but not remarkable for any lapse, which makes me a being of rare ethical clarity, you'll agree.'

Dr Mehta suddenly looked at his watch. 'Oh my God! It's past two-thirty! I must be off. Thanks for the juice. Oh yes, before I go—we've decided to operate on Friday—eight in the morning . . . Let's try giving you a synthetic valve this time. It's your third operation, you know, so . . .'

The patient had tensed. Dr Mehta rose to his feet and said softly in an altered tone, 'Not to worry, Narendra. Leave this third operation to me. I'll see you through. We'll have you—how d'you say?—fit as a fiddle.'

He gave the patient's shoulder a gentle squeeze. For a long moment neither spoke. Then, the old roguish grin returned and the patient asked playfully, 'Are fiddles fit, Mehta?' And Dr Mehta grinned back, relieved, and asked, 'Medically or musically?'

They laughed. The patient shrugged. 'Mozart might know. Who cares,' he whispered. 'Not I. Operations are your line. Opera's mine.'

'Both, my dear man, need a theatre!' remarked Dr Mehta. At the door he paused, embarrassed by his own stirrings of sentimentality. 'Remember what I said, Narendra. Friday morning at eight. I'll see you through with this.'

They tried hard at the hospital to keep the news from him but such things cannot be hidden. The hospital went into deep mourning for a day. It was in silence that he learnt that Dr Mehta had died of a sudden heart failure.

It was in silence too that he received the news that he was now to be operated on by the young Dr Venkat Rao, Dr Mehta's prize student and just as well known a surgeon.

And it was in silence that he was wheeled on his gurney to the pre-operating room, seven o'clock on Friday morning. All he heard, lying on his back, was the trundle of the wheels on the uneven floor. 'Tumbrils!' he thought absurdly, and stopped in amazement as a little click sounded in the interiors of his brain and a familiar voice scoffed, 'Tumbrils! For God's sake! This wretched, decadent European mind of yours!' It was of course his own mind, he told himself, playing out its accustomed circuits of preserved tones.

The solemn light came on. The masked faces gathered round him in a gentle, radiant hush. The anaesthesia lulled him slowly into sleep and his far-flung mind resumed its several secret lives.

That was when they heard him quarrelling in a broken mutter. 'What an astonishing old joker, really. Well, thanks very much for the pleasure . . . of your company, Mehta.'

They did their best but he hadn't a chance. The scribble of the electrocardiographic tracing on the cardiac monitor scripted the draft of his physical continuity like the score of a wayward composer. He slipped away, still under anaesthesia, out of the dark, damaged grooves of his own recorded being and beyond their repair or recall. Dr Venkat Rao never knew who it was who performed that operation.

Connectivity

To be old was to never be surprised at anything. To have seen dreadful things happen to decent people and decent people driven to do dreadful things. Amitesh Shankar used to feel, Hey, I'm just the same as before. It's the world around me that's changed. The mind's entrapment in time seemed to be the central mystery of living, to which somewhere in the recesses of the brain there lay a mislaid master key. But lately he'd begun doubting even this. It's not just the world that's grown different, it's me as well who's aged and lost interest. But a man couldn't just dig in his heels and go into cussed denial. Even if it was a bit late in the day, one had to roll up one's sleeves, pull up one's socks and get moving rather than mulishly defy change. Which was why he was here in the autumn of his life, engaged in this gory war.

He could hear the mutter of machine-gun fire. Then a deafening boom. On the sooty horizon a ghostly light throbbed. The sky was wiped out for a moment before an ashen glow erupted and sank, pulsing like the light of a low voltage moon. His heart was pounding. His mouth felt like sandpaper. He'd give anything for a drink of water. He groped for his flask but he seemed to have lost it in the confusion. He swallowed spittle, gasped, and the smoky air seared his straining lungs till he thought he'd choke on its fumes.

He saw a man sink to his feet, holding his head, weeping: 'Man, this is hell, this is hell. I want to go back.' It was a foggy voice cleft with pain. Squatting in the mud, he moaned: 'Man, I can't go on.'

There was continuous machine-gun fire onshore. Thunderous blasts. Far away he could see two rows of boats. Suddenly a boat exploded and he saw bodies tossed up in the air.

You had to somehow get to the shore. You had to reach the row of barriers, ducking the bullets. Men kept dropping dead around you, fellows you'd known. A verse came into his head: 'Watching, we hear the mad gusts tugging on the wire, like twitching agonies of men among its brambles . . .' But this was no time for poetry, and anyway this boy wouldn't understand a word. Right now there was the steamy desperation of panting from barrier to barrier. You couldn't shoot back because the enemy was on an elevation.

'Heads down!' Then five or six orders about reaching the line. His arm ached with the weight of the Thompson gun. The captain shouted: 'Sergeant, go down to the beach and get those Bangalores!'

Staggering furiously to the wall, barely scrambling into its shade, finding temporary cover. But that wasn't reprieve enough. There was more to get across. A line of wooden posts strung with spiky, fanged wire that grazed your hands and tore rents in your uniform. A Red Cross man came, bent double.

He looked enquiringly into the tense face of his companion. The boy was squinting hard with concentration, trying to pick out something beyond the visible horizon. His face was tight with the strain of it.

'What now?' Amitesh signalled his helplessness.

'Go on,' whispered the hardened voice. 'Press W.'

Amitesh felt like a beaten man, the one who'd cried 'Man, this is hell. I can't go on.'

'By the way, what's a Bangalore?' he asked, offhand, trying to relieve the stress.

'It's a long bomb. You carry it like this. You fit it in, then it goes bang.'

Where the hell am I? asked Amitesh. And what am I doing here? Stupid question, he chided himself. Right now I'm not

Amitesh Shankar, seventy-year-old retired bureaucrat, fond grandpa, holidaying senior citizen and all the rest of my several selves. At the moment I'm Sergeant Powell and this is Omaha Beach. It's 6 June 1944, not 31 December 2006, and we're in the middle of Operation D-Day.

'D'you know,' he told the kid, 'this may be a game for you but we read loads of books about it. The father of one of my pals was killed in one of those operations.'

Coincidentally, on this of all days, he thought of Godfrey Jennings. Godfrey Jennings who'd stayed back when his mother left for Australia in 1951. Godfrey Jennings stepping on to the Tolly Club dance floor, wearing his silver cloth waistcoat, with Veronica on his arm. He used to joke with Godfrey, 'Are you paid by the Tolly to get the dancing started?' Because even at sixty Godfrey and Veronica were fabulous dancers. Old-world tangoists, waltzers and foxtrotters for whom the admiring teeny-boppers gradually cleared the floor to stand and watch.

This New Year's Eve he didn't go to the Club as in earlier years. He had other plans for himself. When his daughter and son-in-law offered to take him along he'd refused. He'd stay back with the kid.

'Oh no, you mustn't, not tonight for God's sake, Papa. You must have fun!'

'I'll have fun, don't worry about me,' he reassured them. No more of the Tolly, not after that disastrous piece he'd done for the *Clarion*.

'But what'll you *do*?' The guilt was eating into them.

'I have exciting plans,' he said.

'Like what?'

'I'm going to make myself a drink or two. Let my hair down. Put my feet up. Hobnob with the future. Tell grandpa's tales, like Namita tells her grandma's tales to Milind's kids. Watch TV, check my mail, you get the idea?'

His daughter looked from him to her solemn nine-year-old. It was obvious that Dinks didn't exactly share his grandpa's enthusiasm.

'Okay. Suit yourself. Dinner's in the kitchen. Microwave it. And Dinks, no tricks. Look after Papa. I'll keep tabs on him,' she assured Amitesh.

His daughter wore a sleek black lycra midi-dress, off one shoulder and cross-hatched across her back. The kind that Deborah Kerr or Rita Hayworth wore in old copies of the *Illustrated Weekly of India*. Neha had copper highlights in her burgundy hair tonight. But there was nothing even remotely Errol Flynn- or Gregory Peck-like about his son-in-law Rohit. The fellow had messed up his hair with some sort of awful gummy mousse or gel and drawn it in unkempt bristles across his pale forehead, as though he'd towelled his hair and left it uncombed. He had a tiny Saracen beardlet on his chin too. What the hell have you done to yourself, man? Amitesh had almost demanded, then recalled the golden rule for senior citizens: Don't ever fault the young. Rohit was thirty-five and looked it, despite the divergent-thinking hairstyle. Amitesh's daughter Neha was well kept but lined and edgy. Both of them corporate execs who worked hard to look young. For his part he was happy being seventy years old tonight. To be left with fewer stakes was to be left a freer man.

'C'mon,' he said to the kid as soon as the door clicked shut and he heard the car rev up outside. 'Let's see you teach me to play a computer game tonight.'

Hobnobbing with the future seemed full of promising possibilities.

The kid was mindful of his obligations as host. Not for nothing had his mother looked daggers at him. But the game had made Amitesh all jittery. Hobnobbing with the future had only meant being sentenced to rigorous imprisonment in somebody else's past.

'Deepak,' he said after an hour of it, 'it may be great fun for you but I think I'll stop here.'

At Sherwood College that day in 1944 the headmaster had called Godfrey to give him the news and a prefect had escorted him to the head's chamber and escorted him back and watched over him in the playground at recess time and at evening prep so that no one bullied him or pulled his leg. And that made Godfrey feel stranger still. Like the privileged owner of a solemn fate. Amitesh wondered whether Godfrey was at the Tolly this evening or away in Australia, whether he had a grandchild who played computer games like this one.

'Let's go watch TV for a bit,' he suggested with tentative hope. The kid, still on his best behaviour, agreed.

Amitesh sank into the sofa and surrendered himself to the seduction of the TV. The kid lounged in the armchair alongside, holding the remote control like a sceptre. Models sashayed down the ramp on Fashion TV. VJs mouthed saccharine phrases. Rockstars husked and hammered the air. Newsreaders snapped crisp headlines above the running screen type. The visuals had no sooner settled than they were whisked aside by others. The air was frayed with incomplete soundbytes. Littered with snipped-up images. Amitesh had trouble focusing and unfocusing. Scenes from Bollywood films flicked on and flittered off. Half lines of songs. Bitten off sentences, aborted in mid-grasp. It was disorienting and it made him restless. Little beast, he thought. The attention span of a quarter of a minute, was it? Enough to unhinge the calmest viewer. He checked himself halfway through thinking, This generation! and instead began planning occupation with craft and strategy. If I can just manage to get hold of the remote . . . by distracting him maybe. Suppose I told him grandpa's stories . . . That was a doomed formula, he knew, but no harm trying.

'Would you like me to tell you a funny story?' His voice sounded bogus, even to himself.

'Uh-huh,' said the kid.

Amitesh didn't know if 'uh-huh' meant yes or no. But the way it was said was forbidding enough. Against its grim mistrust he just couldn't do the once-upon-a-time spoof. He couldn't but help tripping and falling headlong into another cliché.

'When I was your age . . .' he thought fast, keeping the remote in view, seeing it out of the corner of his eye.

'Um.' There was the smallest inflection of encouragement which Amitesh seized upon. 'When I was your age I used to collect stamps. Do you collect stamps?'

'Yup.'

For the crack of a second a passing thought perplexed him. How *do* you collect postage stamps when most letters aren't posted any more?

'Do you have an album?' he risked.

He remembered trading stamps with friends. The stamps he acquired, wrapped in the silver foil of Fruity candies. The paper hinges he made and pasted laboriously into the boxed spaces of his album. The long negotiations with rival collectors over the exchange of duplicates. He had the precious Mahatma Gandhi commemorative stamp of 1948. He had the Air India International first flight commemorative stamp, also of 1948. And best of all, the Indian independence commemorative stamp of 1947! He had about thirty stamps of Lenin alone.

'Why don't you show me your stamp collection? Maybe you'd like some real, old stamps that I've got back home in Lucknow.'

There was no answer. Amitesh repeated his offer.

'Let's see your album now.' He kept an eye on the remote, hoping the kid would go off to fetch his album. But the kid didn't budge. Instead he picked up the remote and held it fast as though reading his thoughts. He jerked his head in the direction of the dining room where the family PC was.

'There?' asked Amitesh, disbelieving. 'On the computer?'

'Yup.'

A virtual album! In a file!

'D'you exchange stamps?'

'Yup.'

Amitesh gave up on this one. Still, the remote.

'Come on. I feel like a different sort of game. Like snakes and ladders. Or carom. Or . . . or Ludo. Have you ever played Ludo, Deepak?'

The kid looked puzzled. 'Lido?'

Amitesh sighed. 'Okay, why not cards?' he suggested, spotting a deck of cards on the DVD stand. 'Rummy, teen patti, khichri, anything?'

The kid had suddenly brightened up. He sprang out of his chair and fetched the deck of cards, still holding on to the remote.

'Uh-huh!' signalled the kid and this time his enthusiastic tone seemed to be 'great!'

Amitesh picked up the cards, fuming inwardly. Who does he think he is, this gen-next technobrat? Ordinary conversation's beneath him? Does he usually converse in shrugs and grunts with people outside his own peer group? If I distract him, maybe I can sneak away the remote.

'Now what shall it be?' he asked heartily.

'Khichri,' voted the kid, volunteering a word at last.

'Right-ho! Khichri it is!' Amitesh dealt the cards.

They gathered up the loose cards in two neat piles. Then, like two elegant Lucknow nawabs competing in sportsman-like chivalry, each signalled the other to start. The kid waited. Amitesh waved the offer gallantly away with a courtly 'After you'.

The kid, his face impassive, threw the gambit. 'Two of spades.'

Amitesh picked up the topmost card in his pile. 'Three of clubs.'

The kid sniffed fastidiously, fidgeted and produced his card.

Queen of diamonds.

Ten of hearts.

Amitesh clowned, danced his fingers round his pile of cards, wondered if he should say 'Eenie meenie mo' or some such silly thing, then wisely decided against it.

Six of clubs.

The kid watched, frowning intently. Funny that one strained so hard even when one knew it was all a game of chance.

'Four of clubs!' cried the kid gleefully, scooping up the lot.

'Oh hell!' Amitesh groaned in mock despair. 'Okay, you start now.'

Five of hearts.

Ace of clubs.

Four of spades.

Amitesh hid his own three of spades artfully, a trick learnt long ago, and brought up a two of diamonds.

'Jack of diamonds!' The kid mysteriously produced his winning card with a quick movement of the hand that Amitesh instantly recognized. He hid his amusement in an expression of carefully studied consternation.

'Winner twice over!' he sighed, chuckling inwardly. He knows how to cheat at cards but he doesn't know that I do too!

The kid pawed up the cards, producing a fresh gambit.

Queen of hearts.

Amitesh's hand moved closer to the remote.

Five of clubs.

Six of hearts.

Amitesh pulled at the remote in deep abstraction, picked it up.

Ten of clubs.

The remote was now firmly in his hand, his fingers playing on the buttons.

'Joker!' cried the kid.

Amitesh started, looked around and glared at the kid. Are you addressing me, sir? his old headmaster at Sherwood might have demanded. Then he saw the kid joyously flourishing the fool in motley, dressed in pied breeches, doublet and hose, with a bell at the tip of his cap.

'Ah,' he breathed. 'You win.'

The kid uttered a whoop, scooped up all the cards. Amitesh arranged his face in an expression of geniality. I believe they're called 'smileys' now, he thought wryly. He put on his reading glasses to study the buttons on the remote better.

'Here it is. Twenty-six, eh? Let's see what my friend Bean is up to now.'

'That's two hundred chips for me.'

Amitesh looked up, startled. Did they measure cards in microchips too, dash it, real cards made of paper and print?

'What's this now?'

'That's two hundred bucks—two hundred rupees—for me, Nana,' announced the kid as though explaining to an imbecile.

Amitesh was outraged. The kid clarified the calculation, suddenly fluent. 'Three rounds are three hundred bucks. It's the Saturday rate in our colony. But you can give me two hundred only.'

The idea dawned on him slowly. No game without cash, eh? Giving me a concession too. Most kind of him. A New Year's Eve baksheesh to his poor old grandpa.

'Two hundred chips, Nana,' the kid persisted.

Amitesh reached for his wallet. 'Okay,' he said. 'You win as usual.'

That's it, he thought. Heads you win, tails you win too. He handed over four fifties, sank back against the cushions of the sofa, toying with that useless trophy he'd strategized so craftily for, the remote.

He saw Mr Bean painting his living room wall. He saw him sawing through a picture. He saw Mr Bean brush his teeth, shave, wash and dress while driving a car. He saw Mr Bean accidentally kidnap a baby. He saw him trying to make a sulky child laugh. He felt as sulky as that little fellow on the screen and he turned to his particular little fellow, the monster brat beside him.

'By the way, Deepak,' he asked, 'what'll you do with this cash?'

'I'll go buy a Valentine's gift for my girl,' said the nine-year-old seriously. 'And I'll take her out on a date tomorrow.'

Amitesh swallowed hard. 'A date, eh? What's she called?'

'Googlie,' said the kid.

'Is that her real name?'

'Nope. It's Gunjan. But I call her Googlie.'

'Okay. And what does she call you?'

'Yahoo,' answered the kid with a grin.

Amitesh turned to Pogo again, a little out of his depth. After a while he put the remote back on the table and rose. Might as well try something else. Better than this, being indulged by this technobrat who sat patiently suffering his dotage. For a moment he wished he'd gone along to the Tolly Club.

That was when Kolkata was still called Calcutta. Amitesh remembered those New Year's Eve bashes long ago when he'd gone club crawling all over the city. From Bengal Club to the Saturday Club, from the Saturday Club to Calcutta Rowing and finally to the Tollygunge Club. He remembered the floodlit lawns, bejewelled trees, afloat with a witch-cauldron mist of mauve and green light blowing about the air. Bonfires and milling crowds. Strobe-lit dance floors steaming with light. Everything from Nat King Cole, Frank Sinatra, Engelbert Humperdinck and Tom Jones to the Beatles, Abba, Boney M and Diana Ross. Sometimes Usha Uthup—she was called Usha Iyer in those days—put in an appearance and he stood up in the audience and gave her a standing ovation. Desmond and Satish and Niranjan and himself. Namita hadn't liked dancing because of the pain in her foot.

Those were his senior bureaucrat days when his vast apartment in Alipore Estates looked down on the city from the ninth floor. Ninth Heaven, he used to quip, and sometimes Cloud Nine. His balcony overlooked Alipore's lawns on which the jacarandas cast frail, creped petals. A flaming gulmohur tree held up its buoyant parasol just beneath his balcony, its outspread branches lifted in a sort of aerial ballet. He remembered the curlicued cast-iron garden lamps with their frosted bulbs brimming over with waxen light. When they all came on every evening exactly at six-thirty it was, as Neha used to say on her evening walks, like nine moons lighting up in the sky. Landscaped hillocks with crafted palms. From the windows of his dining room he could see the high-rises piled up like fitted and towering Lego blocks sprouting in the chalky morning light. And the blurred dome of Victoria Memorial behind the creeper-hung decks of the Taj Bengal Hotel. From his study he could see the terrace nurseries of Woodlands Hospital. A walnut-brown stone church. Beacon lights glowing up the horizon above the faraway Kidderpore

Docks. And from the opposite window the shady Mayurbhanj Avenue joining up Diamond Harbour Road. He could see the trams snail along and imagined their fusty trundle. On clear days the lines of the far distant Howrah Bridge were pencilled harp strings. What else could he remember? Cheesy lampshades and an ivory-coloured mock fireplace. A matt-finished wall with a curdled plaster finish. There were venetian blinds on the bedroom windows through the slats of which long peels of dusty noon light fell slanting on the floor. Sounds. He could still hear them, recorded somewhere in his brain. A doorbell that sprayed a fine tinkle into the air of the lobby. A grainy surf of traffic noises ebbing about the tepid Calcutta sky. And a lift that sounded like the groan and haul of waves breaking and receding on a beach. On New Year's Eve the estate buildings were illuminated with scallops of dangling bulbs.

And golf, of course. Every blessed Sunday. By sunshine or rain at the Tolly links. He once wrote an article about a caddie who claimed to be descended from a branch of Tipu Sultan's family. He liked doing that kind of thing—articles about caddies and drivers and people like that. Recently, much after retirement, he thought of doing some freelance writing again. He did a piece on the golf hamlet of Martinpura near Lucknow but the Sunday supplement of the *Times of India* sent it back with a polite rejection. He'd looked at his typewritten manuscript in disbelief. In the old days being rejected by the *Times of India* was out of the question. Now there were strange markings on the page. He promptly wrote another piece on the twin festivals of Dusshera and Diwali and sent it to *Indian Voices*. He was rather proud of the way it'd turned out and he titled it 'Season's Meetings'. He vetted it carefully one last time before sending it off.

Season's Meetings

Often the spectacle and ceremony of a popular festival takes on added significance, highlighted by some touching human detail. Dusshera and Diwali shall always be associated in my mind with two pious and unassuming men.

Shubh Karan worked as a driver in an insurance company and he had a passion that fuelled his personal life, a deep devotion to Goddess Durga. Every Dusshera he organized a puja in his house. He had learnt clay modelling as a child and the larger-than-life image of the goddess was his own handiwork. The lion, the demon, the weapons in the goddess's ten hands, everything was fashioned with meticulous artistry after office hours. After the evening worship slum kids enacted plays written and directed by Shubh Karan himself before an audience made up of slum families. All this was done in the space enclosed by a small circle of ramshackle houses. Shubh Karan came to Lucknow as a child of fourteen after failing in the Class 8 examinations. For nine years he worked as a daily wager, earning seven rupees a day, before he acquired his job. Since then he had graduated and done his MA in Hindi literature, built his tiny house, married and raised a family. He continued to support his old parents and later began organizing educational programmes for the children of ragpickers. 'Everyone manages to live for himself, sahib,' he said to me once. 'It's when you can do something for others that . . .' He fell silent, overcome by awkwardness. He narrated a touching incident to me on another occasion.

Once when he was twelve and living in his native place in the hinterland of Gorakhpur, he had made an image of the goddess. By accident or ill luck the image broke a day before the consecration. He wept bitterly but set to work. Helped by his old peasant parents, he worked feverishly all night and by morning the new image was ready!

Diwali for me cannot be detached from the memory of old Mohammed Shafi. One Diwali morning I drove thirty kilometres out of Lucknow, headed for the village of Sisendi in the interior of Mohunlalgunj. There was a smoky October chill in the air. Mohammed Shafi was not well. He sat on his charpai, huddled in an old filthy quilt, although winter was still a couple of months away. I showed him the article I had read in a magazine and had carried along. He made me read it out and translate it for him. He took it and studied his photograph with a disapproving pout. Then it was circulated among the assembled audience, three generations of progeny. 'It's true,' he told me. 'For thirty-five years I have been making fireworks. Making fireworks for Diwali and Shabbebarat and also for wedding processions is my family profession. We used to make crackers for the nawabs of Avadh. Making crackers is an art. People drive down from the city. Orders come well before the festival season.' He told me how he varied the chemicals to make anars, chakris, chhatris, mahtabs and rockets. Over cups of milky tea he spoke about the sound capacity of various kinds of bombs. When I rose to leave he made his grandsons load a big basketful of assorted fireworks into my car. He was stung when I offered to pay and grew expansive when I accepted defeat. 'This is how I celebrate Diwali. I distribute crackers for free to whoever happens to come by. Naseeb has brought you to my door this Diwali.'

Mohammed Shafi is long dead. His family has disbanded. Muslim families who traditionally made crackers and fireworks have had to pick up other jobs—for very obvious reasons. A world has ended.

It had come back. Some young spark at the editorial desk had tried to readjust his sentences, make his syntax informal, put 'landed' instead of 'acquired' and a question mark against 'progeny' and 'expansive', before finally giving up. Amitesh could well imagine the hair-shrugging young editor saying: 'Basically, what I mean is, like, your vocab is way out of sync with now. There's no way I can make it work. And basically what folks like to read about are celebs and things, not drivers and old villagers.'

Oh yeah? he mentally mimicked the jokers he routinely met in the malls. Oh yeah, I know. People like to read about film stars and CEOs and India's big billionaires. And hoteliers and wine tasters and hi-fi chefs and fashion designers and software wizards, eh? Lifestyle guys. Not drivers and villagers, unless it's in a fashionably—what's the word? Ah—'subaltern' paper. I'm so hopelessly out of sync. He recalled the snippet he'd kept, a cutting from a popular rag. It was titled 'Guru Gyan' and it was supposed to acquaint twenty-first century young readers with Immanuel Kant. There were hilarious subtitles like 'Who Is This Dude?' 'What Makes Him Cool?' and 'Cool Quotes'. And under the 'Cool Quotes' head the sober voice of Kant pronouncing: 'Science is organized knowledge. Wisdom is organized life.' And again: 'We are not rich because of the things we possess, but for what we can do without possessing them.' It tickled Amitesh so much that he cut it out and kept it in his old copy of *The Critique of Pure Reason*.

Basically, what I understand, like, is that I've got to catch up with the times, he told himself. There's no way I can survive this age unless I resign myself to turning into a mentally lapsed, muffled, carpet-slippered, baggy-trousered, spit-dribbling, doddering old fogey. I must update. Get in sync. Or else sink! It was this which underlay his secret New Year resolve. To catch up with the present, all in one month. To learn how to use bizarre gadgetry, get tech-savvy, right? This was going to be the first night of his personal—what was the word?—ah, 'makeover'!

To the computer then after pouring himself a quick whisky and soda. He'd learnt to receive emails and was pleased to find a New Year greeting from Chris Morton in his inbox.

The magic of it was just beginning to dazzle him. You clicked, you waited a micro-moment and there you were, connected. Was this the interconnectedness that philosophers spoke of, every particle to every other particle in a comprehensive sentience? Much before he began enjoying the technology, he'd begun enjoying the idea, romanticizing it, relishing its promise of potential bondings, unconfined by the constraints of space or age or even identity. No matter that people faked personalities and no matter that name, age and circumstance could be invented. One connected with a hypothetical self and who knew what reverse realities lay even in the falsehoods.

Password. That magic word unlocked the gates to the mystery and there, on top of his list of incoming mails, was Chris Morton's name. This was a new pleasure, this instant contact. He'd caught up with old friends in American and British university campuses or living in retirement in quiet suburbs. Earlier, the postman dropped annual greeting cards into his mailbox and his eyes had registered the pace and pulse of handwritings long known. He'd seen Merry Christmas change to the politically correct Season's Greetings. And he'd learnt the barest of bare essentials about those lives on the other side of the globe which, come to think of it, shrank to just what the children were now doing, their location shifts, their personal copings with illness or bereavement and a dogged joke or two to indicate obdurate defiance to it all so long as one could go on managing that.

He'd sent all his old friends his newly acquired email address. Beneath Chris Morton's name were a bunch of others, some nonsense ads and some spam.

'Keep away from attachments,' his daughter Neha had warned.

And he'd quipped back: 'Yup,' mimicking his grandson, 'that's what we've always been taught by our gurus: Keep away from attachments. And I don't mean your management gurus.'

She'd clucked: 'Stop being funny, Papa. You'll introduce a virus if you go opening these strange mails.' Quite like the way his wife Namita used to cluck: 'Be serious, Amiteshji, and put on your muffler. You'll catch an infection.' Well, interconnectedness did involve the free passage of destructive microbes. So what you did was work on your immune system and run your personal custom-made antivirus meditation programme in your head. I'm learning, he thought, and repeated: Keep away from attachments.

'And, by the way,' Neha had considered him with ironical amusement, 'there happens to be a site called www.guruji.com that trawls the cyberspace, hunting for material interesting to Indian users.'

But Chris Morton wasn't a stranger, so he clicked. And while he waited he thought back to that lovely winter in Boston, two decades ago, and that evening back in from the snowy pavement walk and that sharing of parent-lore between the two of them. Bipolar mother and anguished father. Scraping, scrounging mother and alcoholic father. Upstaging sisters and devoted dope-done-in kid brother. And pets who died.

Open sesame. The page opened. The thing to do now was to click on Attachments, then sit back and watch the virtual sheets flutter across the screen, to land in the virtual bin.

Chris's mail said: Hi! Happy Nu Yr. My Nu Yr letter is in PDF.

What's that now? wondered Amitesh. He clicked on Attachments repeatedly, to no effect. He kept pondering the message in growing bafflement: To find relevant application go to web to open file. By the end of the sixth try he was forced to swallow his pride and humbly appeal to the gen-next specimen next door.

'Deepak,' his voice to his own ears was disgustingly craven. 'What is PDF?'

It took the little beast fifteen minutes of brisk keyboard jiggling, with occasional spells of waiting with an expression of maddening forbearance on his face.

'What're you doing?' asked Amitesh meekly. 'Downloading Adobe Acrobat Reader,' was the curt reply. Amitesh asked no more, reluctant to risk parading more of his personal ignorance than was strictly necessary.

'Here.' The kid pushed back his chair and rose, crisply competent. 'There's your letter.'

'Thanks,' said Amitesh and turned to Chris Morton's long page.

Hi,

In the last few months I've been in Japan, studying corporate adaptations of New Age Buddhism in contemporary neoliberal societies. While there I grew interested and got hold of some fascinating Japanese screens. It's there that I met Hazel who's doing Shinto studies in Nagasaki. One of the high moments of my stay was when I found myself in this little shrine which had a wishing tree. I suspended my scepticism and tied a white ribbon and actually said an old-fashioned prayer for Delia and Jake who're high-school sweethearts seriously planning their marriage. On my way back to the US I visited Hawaii where I ran into Toby Madison who'd been part of a proactive war resistance group called Sanctuary during the Vietnam years. Back in Boston from Norway earlier this year I set myself to work on my study of the ethnos of cultural assimilation in corporate patterns and hammered away at it, thumping out 4000 words a day, seven days a week. The piece appeared in *Postmodern Culture Studies* in their forty-ninth volume, the July–Sept issue. This regimen did me a world of good and took my mind off the messy split that Helen and I had in February. We'd been working hard at making our marriage work but it took some doing to accept that it wasn't any good. March was harrowing but we've survived it. Helen now lives three blocks away and Delia can scurry to and fro between the two apartments and insists she quite likes it this way, having two homes instead of one. Jake's parents are separated too so between the two of them Delia and Jake have four homes! Delia is up to her teeth playing drums in her band The Minotaurs. Maybe she'll major in music. We spent a quiet Christmas, our first since we split. Helen and I met briefly for supper and Delia kept us company before flying off to Cologne where The Minos were to perform at a rock fest . . .

Amitesh read the letter to the end, feeling obscurely sad, whether for Chris or for himself, he wasn't sure. He remembered Helen well and Delia as an infant. Chris wasn't sorry for himself and was handling his life as best as was possible, given his kind of world and his range of freedoms. Amitesh wondered if Chris had enjoyed a superior quality of choice in his life, a more finely asserted and demanding standard of happiness as against his own quiescent, unbargaining history. Chris seemed never to have settled for anything less while Amitesh had taught himself to settle for whatever came. Even to argue around his disappointments and readjust his demands. At the end of the day, who was to decide which was wiser? To have known the dark mess of troubled living and losing or to have practised all the cautious rules of a hygienic conscience and be left feeling vaguely bereft?

But he was missing something here. An intimacy of voice in this public space. For this letter was like something shouted across a highway at rush hour. Addressed to about thirty people. The names were there, stacked in rows of running type—Barnabus, Julia, Mike, Paddy, Heather, Ludmila, Masako, Simone . . . All with the circled alpha locating them precisely in the cyber-empyrean as surely as ISBNs and bar codes identified books. Amitesh felt uneasy, unalone and shadowed in this haunted room. Chris Morton wasn't talking to him, looking him in the eye, clearing his throat, hesitating before an awkwardness—though he'd heard that that too was now becoming possible. Chris Morton was making a balance sheet of events for a score and a half people and Amitesh felt lost in this spectral crowd of strangers.

But there were new options to loneliness. Amitesh had researched the procedures and inside conventions of Internet chatting, sat with paper and pencil, taking notes, alert to all instructions from a very concerned daughter. By now he had compiled a lexicon of codes and he'd pored over them as a nursery schoolkid might pore over his primer.

Capital letters are rude. Small letters are polite; plz is please; wats is what's; gr8 is great; u is you; y is why; tc is take care; tu is thank you; lol is laughing out loud; pm is private message; tom is tomorrow; btw is by the way; gtg is got to go; brb is be right back.

He practised this new script on a piece of paper: U R dumped. I h8 U. V R thru. Its ovr. Its nt wrking. And lol-ing to himself he added gleefully: its wrking. im loling to mslf.

So here it went. As told, three boxes confronted him: asl was age, sex, location. Should he lie? He filled in the answers, lying twice. But here it wasn't a moral thing. It was imagination-flexing, fact-flexibility, flexi-creativity, call it anything. What curious names the others had. Coolguy, Beyonce-babe, Sweet'n' sour, Etna!

Indian? Wer from?

Kolkata, he typed.

Dats Gujrat?

He lol-ed some more, sitting in his chair.

Ya, he flexi-facted some more. Werfrom?

L.A.

Ach, these Americans! I know all about L.A. and they go put Kolkata in Gujarat.

Name?

He typed carefully—Met-U-Selah, reasonably sure the allusion meant nothing at all to Etna out there. It obviously didn't.

Hi, Met. U no L.A.?

Ya, Amitesh typed. Wat's it like 2day?

Like shit, came the jaundiced answer.

U like rock?

Ya.

U no the band 2-el?

To let? asked Amitesh warily.

No. Tool, came the answer with a lol. Dats a song by MJK. Maynard James Keenan of Tool. Its abt h8ing everything. Called NEma.

Nema?

No. Enema. Lol. Its abt sexual abus of kds.

How ds it go?

Lk this—the only way to fix it is to flush it all away, I wanna watch it all go down. Mom please flush it all away. Lk it?

Amitesh didn't know whether Etna meant 'like' or 'lick'.

Wats this? he sought, earnestly trying to get it right.

Song.

Ok. I C. A scatological song, he remarked primly.

????

Scatological, spelt Amitesh politely, not knowing how to compress it. It means sumthing 2 do wid bodily excrement. He just couldn't bring himself to write things like shit, piss, fart or snot to an absolute stranger.

But this one had a sense of humour and maybe even language. He wrote: Shittological? Incrementally excremental? Then a row of smileys appeared.

Incredibly execrable, spelt out Amitesh and added a smiley too. But how the hell could one shorten this fabulous wealth of words without losing all the wicked wordplay? He wasn't making much progress at this new language.

Ders dis film in vich dis guy stuffs de heroin up his, informed his chat friend.

De heroine? asked Amitesh, appalled.

Another lol. No. Heroin. Drug. Dis guy stufd it up his.

Y? Amitesh queried chastely.

2 smugl it.

Den?

He ws dopd. Den it wor of an he hd 2 go to de 2l.

Tool? asked Amitesh, feeling out of his depth.

Toilet, man. He shat de stuff out. Den he rembrd hed sht it out so he plonked hs hands in de sht watr 2 gt it out.

Amitesh felt his stomach turn. What was going on here? But Etna was in great form.

A scatological film cald Trainspotting. Incredibly excremental, wrote his opposite number. Sht isn't logical. Logic is sht.

Amitesh had had enough but Etna changed tack. So Met wat u doing 2day?

Wat u doing? asked Amitesh courteously.

Gtg 2 a bash.

No bash 4 m, typed Amitesh. Ive jst gtg 2 somplac tom 2 c if I cn gt rum 4 myslf. Big qs in de markt 2nite. Gt 2 q up b4 de counter.

Wt u need a room 4? Cing a gal?

Amitesh was put off. I meant rum, nt room. To drink. U drnkng?

Im a t totallr. Im feelng real cd 2nite. No 1 2 c. No 1 2 d8. U cing any 1, Met?

No 1 2 c, answered 'Met' in companionable solidarity.

8 anythng gud?

On a diet. I hv a heart prblm.

Luv?

No. Cardiac.

Ooops.

Its ok. So no bash 4 me. I 8 a pl8 of gr8ed salad wid 2na fish. I musnt put on w8.

In a fit of newly acquired fluency with this crazy Morse, he confided: Im nt 2 gud wid intrnet chatting. Dis my fst time.

A smiley appeared. And the words: Gud. Gr8. Alwas rembr 2 use a condom.

Amitesh was stung by the liberty. He decided to ignore this coarse dig in the ribs and went on.

Im xperimentng wid a makeovr job. Gt 2 no many new things. Nu yr plan. Ive gt 2 b sum 1 new.

Like Howgal?

Lik wat?

Opal Mehta etc. Any relation? Mehta–met?

No.

Met, wen u gt kissed, gt wild and gt a life, c me 4 a d8.

Did this joker know who he was talking to? Amitesh seethed. Why, I might be old enough to be his grandfather and he dares to joke with me about shit and kissing and condoms and stuffing things up the anus! He began typing very fast, forgetting the newly learnt script.

I hold very strong views on plagiarism. I saw piles of that plagiarized book on the footpaths of Russel Street and Chowringhee but I didn't buy it. No one seems to think that buying a plagiarized book amounts to giving your consent to corruption. All we want is good bargains and in the process we get a whole lot of things we never bargained for. That young lady got caught but there's so much of the same thing going on in this blasted cut–paste age. There's no concept of right and wrong and this is where we've all run amok . . .

Ok by, wrote Etna and exited, dropping a smiley as he did so. Amitesh looked at the pancake disc split by its idiot grin and clearly read its scorn. He logged out slowly, annoyed at all the meaningless misconnections, the meandering forays that led right back to his own isolation.

There was still the mobile phone, Amitesh thought. Maybe he could call up Satish or Niranjan or Desmond. He was in no mood for text messages. For God's sake, he wanted a human voice and nothing less. There was the TV clacking on in the next room, if you called that the sound of a human voice. Like many people, he left the TV on through lonely evenings, chattering for hours, unviewed. But somehow it wasn't quite the thing tonight. He wanted more than a voice. He wanted a person behind that voice, a real human being speaking a real, full-bodied language, not a cryptic abbreviated signalling. No sms-ing. That was too much of a strain on his powers of compression, he who'd lived in the time of sparkling table talk and literary banter that was a subtle, sporting contest in style.

He picked up the cellphone and diddled. And was exasperated to find that its language system had changed somehow to Filipino! He felt sudden fury at it. So what the hell am I doing in this world, a migrant from the past, trying to learn new forms of communication, make new connections? He'd read in an article in *The Hindu* that very soon wristwatches would be obsolete, that newspapers were already on their way out. Everything would be concentrated on your mobile phone. It was called 'convergence'. Your mobile phone would show the time, make your appointment schedules, screen films, bring you games to play, even take snapshots of your clogged pipes that you could mail as jpegs to your plumber. They would open the garage door, start your car, teach you to strum the guitar. Amitesh had jotted down the paragraph in the diary that he kept in his pocket: 'Technology evolves irrespective of our desires. Its onward march leaves us in the lurch, haunted by memories of things we used to do.' Now Chinese PCs could recognize the quintessential you and needed no password. No matter that you'd aged, plastered your face with a mud pack or had cosmetic surgery. The PC knew who the fundamental you was. Which was more than you knew yourself.

He pressed the buttons on his cellphone, cursed and gave up, thinking wryly: Ders no wy I cn gt it rt, gd dm it! That last 'God damn it' struck him in shorthand. He'd invented it himself! Cool, he grimaced. But how to bridge this chasm between Filipino and English without appealing to the monster brat's sufferance? He could barely make and receive calls and the rest was trial and error. Mostly error. No way, he swore, rebellious. No way.

There was still the old-fashioned landline. But Satish's number was impossible to get through to. 'The number you are trying to reach is currently switched off.' Niranjan's line clicked on and his thin, careful voice spoke: 'Hello. I'm out at the moment but if you leave your message I'll get back to you as soon as I return.'

Amitesh hung up without a word. Did I ask for Niranjan's voice? I got that, only it was a recorded tape. Get back to you? Could one ever get back? What was the difference between 'meet' and 'meet up'? Going by the vibration of it, 'meet up' was a purposeful, focused act while 'meet' was, well, just be in chance connection, casual and unmotivated. He was the 'meet' sort, not the 'meet up' sort, he reflected with rising bitterness. The back-slapping, chancy, chatty-barber kind, the 'yaar' and 'saala' kind. No wonder my chosen name on the chat site was 'Met-U-Selah'. Methuselah! But maybe I'm reading all this into ordinary word shifts. Who calls a wife a 'helpmeet' now? He smiled at the thought, relaxed and tried once more. Desmond's number. To be answered by a melodious voice: 'This number does not exist.'

For a sinister instant he wondered if Desmond was dead, then dismissed the pang and tried to call Namita on Milind's cellphone. And was put in his place by the summary revelation: 'The number you are trying to call is currently out of reach.' Out of reach, he brooded. So much within reach and so many people out of reach. Well, Namita had been out of reach for a long time. She seemed to have receded into an antique world of her choosing. He felt let down, thrown on his own scant resources, baffled by her forgetfulness which had swept him away from the focus of her priorities. It had already happened, he knew. Sometimes he felt impelled to call her up just to remind her he existed. 'The number you are trying to reach is busy.' How typical. There she was, simulating renunciation, dramatizing non-attachment, doing the vanaprastha thing, that third stage of life, occurring roughly at fifty, when the sages recommended withdrawal into the deep forest, all one's human responsibilities complete and all one's emotional connections over and done with. She was dramatizing the cherished Indian fantasy of cutting loose, imposturing it for some intensely personal reason. Non-attachment? Like hell you're unattached! You're deeply attached to your own bloody self and making some sort of a point. You cling to your own self like a vine. You don't know who that self is but the Chinese computer knows—ha, ha! So don't give me any of that! Don't give me these spiritual theatrics! Rama sent his wife Sita into exile, look here's Lady Sita going off into exile on her own . . .

He'd taken to talking aloud to her and he was doing it now. Speechifying wrathfully to his absent wife. He shut up suddenly, irritated. This was a damnable evening, no mistake about it. He poured himself another whisky. Came back and sat beside the telephone. Took a sip, swore, picked up the receiver, began dialling digits randomly in a fit of defiance.

In a mist of oncoming tipsiness he heard the phone ring somewhere. He wasn't sure if it wasn't just ringing in his head.

'Hello,' he said.

'Hello,' said a man's voice. There was a pause. 'Who is it?' A limp, dusty voice.

'This is Amit,' said Amitesh, very low. There was a lot of disturbance in the line. A gritty, scouring engine buzz. Was it telephonic static? Traffic? He thought he heard a faded beep. A siren? He took a handkerchief out of his pocket and put it carefully on the mouthpiece, the way the fellas did back in college when they made crank calls to the girls in the women's hostel.

'Oh, Ahmed. The dog didn't die.' A flaked, tired voice it was.

'Didn't he now?' responded Amitesh softly.

'No. I watched from the balcony all day. Twice I went down to check. It was quite okay . . . What's funny is that nothing at all seems wrong with it.' A stringy, shredded voice with thickets of darkness between the words.

'Did you think something would go wrong?' Amitesh could sense his own disguised voice funnel down. He could experience its descent and where it came to rest and find lodgement in the other's reception. He could feel the stir of its riffling, the disquiet in the other's posture.

'No, I mean, that stuff had silver foil on it, Ahmed. And pure ghee and raisins and cashews and things.'

'Dogs have stronger digestive systems than us,' risked Amitesh.

There was a jump in the voice. 'No, what I mean is, he wasn't sick. After I gave it to him I was terrified. I didn't want it to die. I've heard that poisoned stuff sends you into convulsions at the end. So I checked several times. But it's fine. What could it mean? Why did she bring me that halwa?'

'She did?'

The voice was unpractised in lengthy conversations. Gauche. But once the syllables had unlocked, the words tumbled out in a ragged rush.

'Yes. I was stunned to see her standing there on my doorstep. She looked funny. Something scary about her eyes. She was holding this covered bowl. She said, "Beta, it's Nitin's birthday today. I made some moong dal halwa. I've brought you some."'

'Nice of her.'

He could hear a sharp intake of breath. 'Nice! After the fits she's been throwing? On the stairs! In the lift! I wanted to ram the stuff down her throat. But I just nodded and took it. Closed the door quickly. I nipped down to the street. Fed it to the black stray dog near the Parag milk booth. Just to see . . .'

A naked, flinching pause.

'Yes?' said Amitesh, playing it by ear. He could feel the quickening of agitation.

'But the thing is—nothing's happened to him. It's been twenty-four hours. He's fine. Absolutely normal.'

'You thought he would die?'

'I was sure he would die.'

'You thought it was poisoned—the halwa?'

'Yes.' Very low and murky, confidence thinning.

'Now you know it wasn't.'

'Yes.' There was another pause. 'What does it mean?' The question raked the air.

'It means . . . that she wasn't trying to poison you.'

'But she hates me!'

Amitesh was shaken by the violence in the tone. 'How do you know?' he ventured, thrilling to the drama of this unexpected encounter.

There was an impatient click of tongue against palate. 'Don't you remember, Ahmed? Didn't I tell you the other day? You must have forgotten.'

He decided to push this hazard a bit more. 'In the lift, you said?'

'Yes. I was going up to the seventh floor. From the second. She'd come up from the ground floor. She was standing there alone. She saw me get in and she backed away against the wall and pressed the third floor button. I said, "Auntie, why are you getting off on the third floor?" She looked crazy, panicked. She started screaming, "I'll take the stairs, by God I will. I'm not going up in this lift with you! God knows what you're carrying in your bag! God knows what you and that brother of yours have been up to!" She rushed out when the lift reached the third floor and she climbed all the stairs up to the eighth floor.' The voice had grown breathless.

'Strange.'

'No. At Nitin's funeral, when all the building people went to meet her, she wouldn't talk to me. I said to her, "Auntie, I'm shocked."

She looked away from me and hid her face in her odhni and began to weep. And then she said, "Go away. Please go away."'

'Why you?'

'Because ever since Aijaz disappeared they've all started saying he's been picked up. And maybe he hasn't been picked up but has just gone off like he used to . . . She thinks he's got something to do with the train incident . . .'

Amitesh felt a cold breath of horror. Where had he landed, what dreadful area of delirium or threat? 'What did you do?'

'I just left. Everyone was looking at me in a funny way.'

'Yes?'

This pain hadn't settled. It clamoured, tore about, stretched the vocal cords to cracking. 'Yes. They look at me like that. Keep stopping me and asking, "Where's your brother Aijaz?" I say I don't know. Once someone said, "Of course you do." I walked away. They've stopped saying hello to me. They just come right up in a frightening way and they say, "Where's he gone? Where's your brother? Don't you know? You must know." How can I tell them anything when I don't know? When the police kept me in the lockup before Saleem Bhai telephoned, that's what they kept asking me at the thana, "Where's your brother? Where's your brother? Where's your brother?" I kept saying, "I don't know. I just don't know!" For Allah's sake, how can I be responsible for what Aijaz does or doesn't do? My back still hurts and now I have nightmares in which the constables and the neighbours and the whole market keeps shouting, "Where's your brother? Where's your brother? . . . "'

'But where is he?' whispered Amitesh, shivering.

'I tell you, Ahmed, I don't know. He used to keep going off. You know that. Some nights I dream he's in prison and he's being tortured.' There was the faint nick of a catch in the voice, a sob. 'I think I can hear him screaming. I think I'm lying here safe in my bed. I have bathed. I have eaten. But Aijaz is being tortured somewhere . . .'

The voice circled the steep pit of awful knowing. The shudder came through and at his end, Amitesh shook too, receiver in hand, the handkerchief almost slipping away. Fear beat in the air.

'I read about those prisons in all those strange places—where they set dogs on you and give you shocks and put things into your private parts and make you roar and howl and beg. And I think, suppose he did something after all? Suppose they make him howl and beg and suppose he screams, "I did it, yes, yes, yes. I was one of them." I can't sleep, I can't eat, worrying about Aijaz and worrying whether he was part of something.'

Amitesh could hear a heaving, a gasping and snatching at half-choked words. 'Ahmed, this is hell, this is hell. I can't go on.'

Badly shaken, Amitesh held on to the receiver connecting him to the voice. Unable to utter anything, unable to let go. His own voice had an odd hoarseness when he spoke again. Treading thin ice ever so cautiously. 'Didn't Aijaz ever mention anything to you?'

The voice grew exasperated. 'Aijaz? Not he. He always left me out of things. Always. Since we were this high. He was always Abu's boy. Me, I was nothing, no one. Always going off by himself.'

Amitesh's mind was racing. By now he'd worked out some of the scene. But there were large opaque patches. Who was Nitin? The woman's son. She didn't want to be alone in the lift with this man. I don't know what you're carrying. Where is Aijaz, your brother? Police lock-up. Nitin's funeral. Go away, please go away. He dared not risk seeking further details but this question he just had to ask.

'Why did she bring you the halwa?'

The start at the other end was palpable. 'I don't know.'

Another risky question. He could always hang up if things went out of control. He made it sound like a statement, not a question, feeling his way forward from that bit about Nitin's funeral. 'Nitin died so . . .'

He'd manoeuvred his opposite number perfectly. 'They said it was instant. His head was blown off. Still, there was a post-mortem and all that. He couldn't have felt a thing. Even after so many months I can't forget her shrieks when they brought Nitin's body.'

A long, simmering silence. Amitesh inched forward. 'Still, the dog didn't die.'

'No.' Very soft. 'She'd gone and put cashews and things in it. Silver foil on top. What could it mean?'

'It wasn't poisoned.' A micro-move further.

'She called me by my childhood nickname—the one she'd heard Ammi use when she, Ammi and Salma Khala used to knit through the afternoons and we used to play cricket in the yard. Long ago—fifteen years?—I don't remember. No one calls me that any more. Except you sometimes, Ahmed, when you happen to remember. I'm grateful that you do . . .'

Amitesh panicked. The voice went on. 'With Abu-Ammi gone and the rest gone too and Aijaz missing, Allah knows where, no one calls me that and you can imagine what it means to be called by the name your parents used when you were a small kid, and every time you call me that it . . . it makes me feel so . . . supported. Ahmed, are you there?'

Amitesh's hand was shaking. He couldn't trust himself to utter a word.

'Ahmed?'

'Yes.'

'Why did she bring that halwa?'

This stretched voice with the sob clotted in its grain had him ambushed. Back to the wall and nowhere to flee. His temples throbbed. He held his breath and swallowed.

'Ahmed?'

Slowly Amitesh put down the phone. He mopped his forehead. It was 31 December but he was sweating.

In the adjoining room a giddy band was playing on the TV. Amitesh's breath steadied and he went to open the window. He returned to the cabinet to pour himself another small whisky and, as he was pouring the soda, the understanding came alive in his

brain that he had lost that voice forever, that he was in no position
to substantially help or heal anyone beyond the barely minimal and
that was perhaps the real trouble. No, he thought with quickening
urgency—there's still the redial button. I don't know his name and
he doesn't know that I'm not Ahmed, what with all the telephonic
disturbance and the defrauding handkerchief, and quite obviously
he didn't have a caller-ID phone, but the answer to his question had
gathered in words so simple that it took a while for Amitesh to spot
and straighten them out.

I want to tell him, thought Amitesh, I'm not Ahmed and I don't
know your name. But I know that she brought you that halwa because
human beings still have some scraps of chivalry tucked away in their
terrible hearts and that sometimes certain buttons get pressed. We
keep our cellphones locked up in our bags, the way we carefully lock
up our hearts. But sometimes we forget to do so.

The right words had not come when needed but the redial button
offered a second chance. For the first time Amitesh was thankful for
technology. He had to get back to that voice and, balancing his whisky
in his hand, he made for the corner table where the phone was placed
and pulled up his chair again, picking up the receiver.

Only to hear the brat's voice on the extension in the sitting room,
chattering avidly: 'Hello. Googlie, Happy New Year! I love you!'

Amitesh heard the froth of laughter in the little girl's voice as she
said: 'I love you, Yahoo! Happy New Year!'

The kid had pre-empted him. And there was no memory system
in this bloody outdated phone, he cursed involuntarily. Upset, he
put down the receiver and sat staring at the phone in a state of
immense loss.

'Whatyadoing tomorrow, Googlie?' the brat's spooney voice
drifted to his ears from the next room.

Amitesh went and stood at the window to still his head. He saw
Kolkata spread out before him, strewn with lights. Streets, avenues,
lanes met and cross-hatched in long strands of illumination. The
high-rises were festooned with loops of light, thousands, millions of

Chinese bulbs trailing into motifs, arabesques, skywriting, ads—the flamboyant signature of a feisty city. A glow rose from the earth to the sky like sifted fire dust. There were also big shapeless blots of impenetrable blackness which might be the Maidan or the parks around the lakes.

Snatches of his recent conversation floated into his head. I have bathed, I have eaten, I'm lying here safe in bed but my brother is being tortured somewhere. The blinding words—they make you roar and howl and beg. Go away, please go away. He saw the lady covering her face with her odhni. The young man—surely he was a young man if he referred to his childhood being fifteen years ago—tossing in bed, his unblinking eyes hungrily raking the dark night.

Dulled, Amitesh stood at the window, whisky in hand, looking down upon the world, that grid of meshed, interlacing lights, and felt himself belong to its large life, this perverse, bruised, besotted convergence of contingent intersections. I am well slept, bathed and fed but my brother is being tortured somewhere.

Behind him he heard the brat laugh and say: 'Ya, I know. I'm sorry, so, so, soooo sorry, IloveyouIloveyouIloveyou, there's no way I can tell you Iloveyou . . .'

At the window, Amitesh, sober despite three whiskies, thought of praying.

A New Year's Party

They called him Uncle Scrooge. Not that he was a miser or had ever displayed any special proofs of callousness but his widower status, his solitary spartan ways and his accounting job somehow tempted the literati of the neighbourhood to draw some rash parallels. Especially in the Christmas season.

True, he worked on Sundays and all holidays including Christmas but that was because there was little else to occupy himself with. This Christmas Eve was no different.

Geoffrey Fernandes, old Geoff, worked until dusk fell and when the lights began to shine outside his fourth floor windows, he decided to call it a day. On this day the stenographer, the two clerks and his partner had taken the second half off and the responsibility of closing the windows, switching off the lights and locking up was his. Pocketing the keys, he creaked down the old wooden staircase, sixty-four moaning steps, and emerged upon Metcalfe Street.

A Calcuttan Christmas was a sight in itself, reflected he, walking down Chowringhee. An English dish with Portuguese sauce upon a Bengali bill of fare! The shades of night cast a generous covering over the city's many destitutes and if a street light fell upon a haggard, hair-naked woman or if a thin claw was thrust beggar-wise under one's nose, it only lent a certain Dickensian aura to the place. This was the city of the Fagins and the Dawkins and the Nancys of God's unchanging world, thought old Geoff. And he, poor old Scrooge, nasty old Scrooge, locked up in himself.

It was also the city of the Doras and the Rosas! The air was aswirl with the gold dust of galaxies of little giggling electric bulbs, opening and closing, winking, racing to left, racing to right, falling flat, a little wink here, a little blur, dip, blush and twinkle there, all a vast chorus in a hilarious musical comedy of light. Now a slow minuet and now a roaring rumba. Gold dust, river mist, tinsel and gloss, the very streets gift-wrapped in crackling tissue, tied up in little leaping festoons and scallops of streamers, looped and twisted and knotted and dangling with rainbow baubles, and a syrupy, confectionery smell everywhere! Gracious, thought old Geoff, what a long line at Flury's! The Bengali does not bother much about his bread but he loves cake. Witness the rows of piled-up plum cakes, five rupees a piece, sixteen rupees a piece and twenty rupees a piece, all spread out or towering in little cocoa hillocks upon cloth spread upon the pavement. The giddy doors of restaurants swing open, swing shut. Their ceilings are hung with tinsel stars, gauze demons, cardboard moons, crazy puppets. And a laughing, lewd, husky music, all asleep and a-staggering, floats out and teeters down the street. Old fat men wearing paper caps, claiming to be Mickey Mouse or Superman, blowing straw whistles, foxtrotting without partners, or taking swigs out of bottles. And, tonight's carol singers already upon street corners, sitting upon rickshaws, tuning up with a few delightful, unholy lyrics, the ethnic dholaks a-thump, the fiddles shrilling higher and higher, the harmoniums trickling and snorting in unheeding mutiny down the scale, and naughty voices croaking naughty, crazy words with expressions of soulful piety! Crowds of applauding jokers, drunks, dancers, teeny-boppers.

Geoff turns into New Market to buy a few flowers. A couple of long-stalked tuberoses, smelling of paradise and a romp in a monsoon garden and a sleep in a wreath-strewn grave. A scent which brought in memories of the future and hopes of the past. A tuberose for the vase, a bottle of Army rum and a token plum cake—that's Christmas for me. Finally a long trudge up the stairs to his apartment on Kyd Street, the unfailing crash against the bicycles in the dark corridor, the unlocking of a door and the click of an electric switch. A buoyant, bouncy voice is heartying up the room. A lady smiles winningly and music strikes up. Calcutta television gives Geoff Fernandes dozens of joyous companions upon this evening of evenings. He drinks his way slowly and purposefully down the bottle. Ants hear of cake crumbs and descend in their hundreds to carry away the loot.

There is still the most important ceremony to perform, the two letters to write to the only two persons in the world he cared to invite upon New Year's Eve. My dear Alphonse, he scribbled. My dear Sheena . . .

They never, never dropped in together. How could they? Their trains arrived at different hours of the evening. Hers came in at 8.45 and she being a flighty, bubbling creature who loved to dawdle before shop windows, daydreaming, was ever late. His came in at 3.00 so he was usually already in before Geoff returned from office, laden with his parcels.

The key was in a crack above the mailbox. Old Alphonse knew exactly where it was and he knew how to make himself comfortable in the old apartment. After all, hadn't he lived in it for years and years before Geoff took over?

What point was there in coming home early?—was Geoff's argument. After all, the old guy would be fast asleep after his journey and absolutely at home.

Planning the eats was the tricky thing. No sweets. The old one was diabetic, the young one probably on her perennial diet. Nuts? But what about his teeth? Slices of off-season pineapples, cookies, wafers, cheeselings, mince-pies and grilled chicken off a cart. Fine, fresh rolls and tins of cheese, tins of soup, slices of salami and ham. He had that bottle of Johnny Walker tucked away for some such glorious day. But what a lot of packets and only two arms to load them on. Well, he'd done his best for them—they were hard to please, those two, but surely they'd see at a glance how much thought and money and affection had gone into the feast. So he reflected, struggling up the dark, old stairs, carefully balancing his way lest a single item fall.

The lights were on in the apartment and what a comforting feeling that was—to feel that somebody was already there in that chilly, empty home before him. He pushed open the door.

There was his battered old overnighter on the floor but where on earth was he?

'Alphonse!' cried Geoff. 'Where are you, Alphonse?'

A low grunt from the loo set his mind at rest. The old fellow's bowels were a problem—always had been. They roared, rumbled and revolted at all hours.

He dumped the parcels upon the table. The checked table-cloth was already laid, the TV going full blast. A rumpled cushion upon the rocking chair, ash upon the threadbare rug—Alphonse had smoked and slept, leaving these marks of his presence. Geoff sank slowly down into the armchair, savouring the soft assurance of another unseen human presence here with him and here before him. It was comforting not to stride into a void. 'Oh, there you are, Alphonse!' cried he rising to his feet as the old figure came shuffling out, holding himself aslant, taking the short, sudden steps of a very old man.

'Happy New Year, Alphonse!' he cried warmly. 'Er—ring out the old, ring in the new, you know, Alphonse, old chap!'

The old man grunted and shot him a sharp, accusing look. His faded grey eyes could pierce holes through one's skin, thought Geoff.

'Not so soon, dash it, Geoff!' came the baritone protest. 'It's four hours to go.' He lowered himself slowly down into the rocking chair.

'Always in a hurry to ring out the old—eh?' He shrugged cynically.

Geoff laughed uproariously. 'Ha-ha-ha indeed! Touchy, Alphonse?'

The old man waved an invisible fly aside. His eyes went round the room, warming upon old bric-a-brac, puzzling over new books, peering at pictures.

'There, Alphonse, that's you.' Geoff pointed at the yellow monochrome upon the wall above the mock mantelpiece. 'Remember yourself?'

'Hmm,' responded his guest. 'You still have it here?'

'You're decorative, you know. Add quality and atmosphere. I'd cherish that portrait even if I didn't know you from Adam. As it is, I'm fond of that fluffed cravat and those collar studs and that air of supercilious gravity, Alphonse. There's aristocracy in 'em all.'

'They weren't bad,' conceded Alphonse. 'What's that you got on the wall?'

Geoff scanned the far end of the room. 'That? Don't you remember? It's an old print of yours—a Rembrandt called "The Philosopher". Used to lie about in your files. So I decided to salvage it and put it in a respectable frame. The fellow did a good job. Like it?'

'Um,' assented Alphonse. 'You've had them chairs polished.'

'Same old things,' informed Geoff. 'The upholstery was all gone. I had them done up. How d'you find 'em?'

'Terrible,' snorted Alphonse, closing his eyes upon a satisfying inhalation of pipe.

'And that . . . that object?' He opened his eyes and pointed at a yellow fibreglass garden chair Geoffrey had picked up at an auction.

'That's a washable chair, Alphonse,' explained Geoff.

'A washable . . . chair!' The old man's eyes shone with merriment. 'How every extraordinary! A washable chair!' His shoulders shook with convulsive laughter. 'How very strange! A washable chair, to be sure!'

Geoffrey was beginning to find this senile humour trying.

'What's strange?' asked he testily.

'Why should one wash . . . a chair? Ho, ho, ho!' went the

old guy and collapsed in spasms of wheezing laughter. Geoffrey shrugged, rose and strode to the sideboard and stopped short all of a sudden.

'What's that now?' asked he in wonder.

'For you, lad,' answered the merry old man. 'And a Happy New Year to be sure.'

'A Dom Perignon! 1952! It's terribly good of you, Alphonse.'

'Don't mention it,' wheezed the guest. 'Ring in the new, my lad.' He pointed a threatening finger in Geoffrey's face—'but never, never ring out the old.'

Geoffrey laughed. 'I never do, I never do, Alphonse. It can't be done.'

'I'm afraid,' he went on, unlocking a cabinet, 'that I haven't anything equally splendid for you.' He extracted a small packet from the recesses of the cabinet and slapped it heartily upon the peg table beside the rocking chair.

'What is it then?' queried the guest.

'Something you like,' said Geoff affectionately. 'A whole book of crossword puzzles. Keep you busy all evening. And a detective novel to set your wits racing. Keep you busy all night. Remember last year?'

A gleeful grin cracked across the guest's face.

'Just so,' said he. 'Quite so.'

Those crossword puzzles would almost all be worked out in a couple of hours, Geoff knew. Some of the tougher ones would be left for Geoff to work out. That detective story would tease the old man out of all thought and speech and he would pester Geoff for his opinion and his own detective devices until next morning. The old man slept badly—his sleeping was done in the afternoons.

'Oh, by the way, I have last year's crosswords all worked out for you. Took me some time, you can bet. Some still remain to be solved. But Sheena is clever . . .'

'Sheena?' The old man sniffed. 'That young lady is to be here again?'

Geoffrey nodded. 'Charming, isn't she?' he asked. 'She'll help us work out what remains of that puzzle book. Maybe she'll tell you who murdered Alfred Fletcher on the night of 21 November.'

'That,' said the old man, 'is a silly young piece.'

'But you can't deny she's enchanting and full of fun and ideas and she has answers for everything.'

He looked at his watch. 'She should be here now. I don't know where she's got to.'

He went and stood by the window. Down below the number 59 tram shuttled past, clanging all its bells, rattling upon its guttural track. A nippy south wind stole in, wet from the Bay of Bengal. Taxies scurried about in 31 December frenzy. Rickshaw pullers still raced, hot-footed, bearing little old Chinese ladies in pyjamas and jackets and puckered parchment faces. The shops began pulling down their shutters.

'Relax, Alphonse,' Geoff called over his shoulder. 'How 'bout those crosswords now? Or wait. Let's open up that Johnny Walker. The night is young, as they say. She'll be here soon. Bound to be.'

Nine-thirty and still no sign of her. The party couldn't begin without her and here was this old fellow getting restive. Geoffrey clicked impatiently, glass in hand, at the window. She was the limit. She loved making them wait. It was one of her little ways.

'Sorry, Alphonse,' he muttered, apologetic. 'I guess we'll just have to do without her. You carry on with those puzzles—I'll go warm up the soup. Let me fix you another drink.'

'A silly young piece,' he heard Alphonse grumble into his beard. All the same it was all too obvious that Alphonse, like him, Geoffrey, was impatiently waiting for the giddy girl to arrive. The anxious look he threw at the door, the start when footsteps sounded on the stairs, all bespoke suppressed anticipation and restless suspense.

He carried in the soup tureen from the kitchenette and set it centrally down upon the chequered tablecloth. He undid the packets of wafers, spread butter and cheese on rolls, arranged pineapple slices upon a plate and the festive chicken upon another, brought in more

dishes, bowls, spoons . . . That was when a door banged shut, down
below, a cab started, a bell shrilled and presently a flurry of high-
heeled shoes clattered up the stairs and a strong whiff of cologne
swept in with the breeze.

Alphonse dropped his book upon his lap. Geoffrey dropped the
spoons upon the table.

'She's here!' he cried, excitedly. The old man nodded joyfully and
the door burst open.

'Oh, Geoff, old boy!' cried her high, childlike voice. 'How
unforgivable of me, I do declare! I've kept you guys waiting.' She
flung her bag upon the settee, pirouetted round and hugged Geoff,
stared in mock astonishment at Alphonse, reflected and pecked him
on the cheek.

'Sorry, old bear,' she cooed. 'I didn't mean to be so late but . . .
anyway, its fun to have folks waiting for you, isn't it? I love doing
it. Fancy having a life in which nobody's waiting for you. And this
. . . this Neanderthal man? Whoever's he? Oh, oh, it's Alphonse. My,
isn't he old! I took him for your prehistoric orang-utan.' She tinkled
out her kiddish, outrageous giggle. And Alphonse always so sensitive
to her words, or didn't she know that? 'Peanuts, baboon?'

Alphonse was white with sudden rage. 'I imperfectly comprehend
your import, young lady,' said he stiffly in his best Oxonian accent.

'Oh come, Alphonse, drop that courtly air. Anyone would
imagine you're a stuffy old earl that the taxidermist has filled up
with rotten straw!'

'I insist,' said Alphonse gruffly, 'on a proper observance of form.
I am considerably older than you, lady, and I take strong exception
to your language.'

'Why, what's wrong with him?' cried she, stung. 'I haven't been
here five minutes and there he goes again. What you need, sir, is a
string of good, contemporary, soul-stirring profanities and I've a
mind to let you have 'em, and gratis.'

'Sheena, please,' begged Geoff.

'Is this propah? Is this right?' she mocked.

'I do believe you're mad, both of you. You're like oil and water. Can't mix. I call you here and the moment you set eyes upon one another you fly at one another's throats!'

'But this . . .' he flung his arms out despairingly, 'is my party. I'm going into the kitchen. Kindly let peace be restored by the time I return.'

They sat opposite one another in perfect harmony, smiling amiably when Geoff returned, carrying the glasses. Suddenly the comedy of it struck him.

'Sorry, old girl,' he smiled. 'I guess you just got us both het up with waiting. We're old chaps, you know, and prolonged tension, stress . . .'

'And I . . .' she put an arm round Alphonse's shoulders, 'got het up with guilt. Stress . . .' she smiled winningly into Alphonse's disgruntled face, 'is right.'

'Anyway,' said he, popping the Perignon, 'whatever have the two of you been saying to one another to re-establish such peace?'

'Nothing,' barked Alphonse.

'Nothing,' giggled Sheena. 'We're at war.' She laughed amusedly. We don't have anything to say to one another, Geoff. It's you we wish to speak to.'

She'd hit the nail on the head, he speculated. Whatever could those two ever find to say to one another? Absolutely nothing. She so young, so impetuous, he so old and so temperamental. It was he that loved them, wanted them to meet, interact, enrich him with their presence. They were important to him. But, it was unlikely that outside the dim circuit of his room, they would ever meet elsewhere. And their coming together like this solely for his pleasure quite overcame him. If they'd only get along better, there could be such an identity of attitudes between them. But they were stubborn as mules. We three, he reflected, ought never to part. We must hang together. Consider our eyes, our noses, our stubborn chins. Consider our flying rages, our inveterate, compulsive solitudes. Remember our names, our homes. We are of a piece, alone in the world. Why then can they never agree? Why must I always negotiate between them, the patient, pettifogging pacifist? Why must I look forward to these meetings?

'What's for dinner? I could eat a horse!' she exclaimed.

'Shocking,' muttered Alphonse audibly.

She looked him up and down.

'All your favourites.' Geoff hastened to step in. 'And no extra calories, I assure you. Anyway, you're thin as a rake.'

'Much too thin,' said Alphonse dismissively.

Sheena looked as though she would burst.

'What beautiful champagne!' she sighed, choosing to ignore him.

'Dom Perignon,' said Alphonse, addressing the cabinet. '1952. Long before you were born.'

'It's Alphonse's New Year gift to me,' explained Geoff.

Sheena looked contrite. 'Oh dear,' she said pitifully. 'And I haven't anything for you. You'll say I haven't any manners.'

'Nobody said you had, my dear,' said Alphonse sweetly.

She stabbed him with a killing look. 'But, Geoff, remember, even if I've got nothing for you today, I'll surely get you something next year. And . . . and Geoff, when you're old, and ill, and dying, I'll be by your bedside, mopping up your spittle and closing your eyes and laying you out straight and nice and arranging the wreaths . . .'

'Ugh!' cried Geoff. 'Will you please stop it!'

Her eyes were large and grave.

'I mean it all, Geoff, honest.'

The little perisher, she had him all in a sweat!

'Alphonse and I have some crossword puzzles here that we could not quite work out to our satisfaction,' said Geoff, changing the subject. 'Alphonse thinks you're clever, Sheena. Don't go by his frowning face. But he's got this deep faith in you. "Only she," said he, "can work these out for us." And what Alphonse said, so say I.'

'Well, maybe I can,' she playfully taking a sip, 'And maybe I can't. But I can try.'

And thank God for that, thought Geoff, relieved. Get her busy and keep her wilful little nose out of mischief. There's no knowing what she'll say or do next. Still, there's no getting away from the fact that where she turns up, anything may happen. Too flighty, too fanciful and too ambiguous altogether. She's got this little streak of cruelty too, the little beast. Loves coming up with the sly, the hurtful, the raw-nerve observation. But then, when you're least expecting civility from her, she'll stun you with her absolute tact and good sense. Mad girl, he thought affectionately. Now, Alphonse—he went on, sinking deeper into reverie—is reliable. He's solid and square. You don't like him completely but you know where you are with him. He's got this tough-nut gruffness and stuffiness but a single remark from you can bring mist to his eyes and a quiver to his voice. He won't reveal all his secrets to you but he's by and large forgiving; and where he's not, he'll freely agree with you when you set out to prove your point. There's sound stuff in the old guy and I wish it were possible to have him here with me for good—but it can't be done and more's the pity.

Geoff looked long and fondly at the yellow-tinted portrait on the wall.

'Who's that gargoyle?' broke in her sharp young busybody voice.

'Mind your ps and qs, young Sheena. That's Alphonse as a young man.'

She uttered a little squeal and gazed at the picture with glee.

'Golly!' she cried, her eyes like saucers.

There's mischief brewing in that vile young brain or my name's not Geoff Fernandes, thought Geoffrey apprehensively.

'Portrait of the Artist as a young Ghoul? Ugh.' She took a deep breath. 'I marvel that you can sleep alone in this room, Geoff, with that . . . that thing looking at you all the time. I mean, I don't want to hurt your feelings, Alphonse, you're sweet and all the rest, but I think your present complexion and figure is a great improvement upon your past. The roses may have fled from the cheeks and the lilies from the brow but at least you no longer give one the creeps.' She tittered maliciously.

'You,' rejoined Alphonse calmly, rising to the occasion, 'are no oil painting yourself.'

'Oh, I'm sure I'm not,' she said modestly. 'But I hope soon to be.'

'And that reminds me, Sheena,' interrupted Geoff hastily, before Alphonse opened fire, 'when am I to get that photograph of yours? D'you know, when you aren't in front of me I have trouble remembering your face.'

'You'll have to wait.' She waved an affected hand. 'Till I'm much prettier. I'll send you a blow-up of mine.'

'Gather ye rosebuds while ye may . . .' began Alphonse's wheezing cackle.

'Oh, help!' cried Sheena, rolling her eyes heavenwards.

'And why haven't I a picture of yours?' she demanded, flirtatious, wrathful.

'I . . . I haven't a proper snap yet,' stammered Geoff, confused. 'I don't photograph well—most unphotogenic, you know—I mean there're many snaps of me but I don't think I look like any of 'em. They're—how d'you put it?—they aren't true to the real me, the . . . essential me.'

'Rubbish!' she declared. 'You're a jolly sight more presentable than that . . . that moth-eaten earl there with that . . . that feather-duster of a beard . . . !'

'Oh hell, Sheena, must you now?' protested Geoff feebly. I'll never have these two together here again. What a rotten idea!

To his immense surprise, he opened his eyes to behold Alphonse convulsed with spasmodic gusts which he realized was Alphonse's version of a boisterous laugh.

'Ho! Ho! Ho! Ich! Ich! Ich!' went Alphonse. 'Feather-duster! Oh ho ho ho! Feather-duster indeed! Feather-duster, to be sure. I insist . . .' he turned to Geoff, '. . . on toasting this young lady. I'm proud of her. Young lady . . .' His beetling brows shrank in awesome concentration as he fixed his piercing gaze on Sheena's pouting face. 'Young lady, I'm proud of you and no mistake. I'm proud of your spirit, I'm proud of your speech and I'm proud of your splendid presence of mind. I drink to your health, madam.'

And the Perignon went gurgling down the thin alley of his throat and a drop or two ran down his chin and wet his old beard.

'Why, did I say something wrong?' asked Sheena, bewildered, turning to Geoff.

'He likes you after all, that's all, my dear,' said Geoff. 'And I absolutely join him in this toast. To the New Year and to our own Sheena! For she's a jolly good fellow!' cried he with a flourish and gulp, singing out the last words with abandon.

He wished he could snap all three of them together. What a great photograph it would make, old Alphonse, himself and Sheena. But then, how on earth could he himself get into that photograph? One couldn't shove oneself into the group and without him there in the middle, ordering it all, what would be the point? And, an outsider in their midst, brought in solely to execute the mechanics of camera operation, would somehow break the spell of their three interlocked presences. It was upon a happy note of singing and toasting that they sat down to dinner.

'Mmmm,' murmured she, biting into the pineapple. 'This is splendid.'

'Not bad at all,' wheezed Alphonse, spooning up.

'You've done yourself proud, Geoff!' exclaimed she. 'Candles too!'

'All in your honour, milady,' said Geoff gallantly. 'This night,' intoned he, getting sentimental, 'is no ordinary one for me. May I make bold to tell you, young Sheena, that you look absolutely stunning in that crimson blouse.'

'This one?' she noticed it absently. 'Why, don't you remember it? It's one of Hannah's. You sent it across.'

Geoff peered at it in amazement.

'Well, well, well,' said he. 'You don't say so? Now that you mention it I do remember it on Hannah when she was young. But you've done something to it, haven't you?'

'Oh, I've added a pair of fancy epaulettes and styled it a bit.'

'Most becoming. Perfectly charming, my dear,' said Alphonse with a courtly little bow.'

'And now,' pronounced Geoff when the meal was over, 'will someone kindly tell Alphonse and me who killed Alfred Fletcher?'

'Alfred who?' laughed she. 'I thought you guys had puzzles for me to work out and now this.' She went on after a little pause. 'What d'you expect of me? Who d'you think I am?'

'The hope of our future!' cried Geoff, tipsy and roaring with laughter.

'I'd much rather draw you some pictures,' she said, sinking down on the sofa. 'I'm rather good at lightning sketches—or don't you know?' She looked from Geoff to Alphonse and back at Geoff. 'Ha! Suppose I gave you Alphonse's nose and beard and suppose I gave him your chin and your eyes—what fun?'

'How very extraordinary now,' exclaimed Alphonse, staring at her over the rim of his glasses.

'What?' asked Geoff.

'I too,' said Alphonse, 'loved to sketch and let me tell you, young lady, that which you have just described was one of my favoured pastimes. Interchanging noses and eyes and expressions. It was very, very adventurous.'

Sheena was interested. 'It sure is. You don't mean to say that it isn't my original copyright? You did it before me?'

Alphonse nodded happily, rocking very hard upon his chair.

'I sure am impressed,' she said.

'Oh, Alphonse is a man for all seasons,' said Geoff. 'You've got to know him better, Sheena, to realize how clever and deep and inspired he is.'

'Tut! Tut!' clicked Alphonse bashfully.

It was upon that instant that a loud bang outside the door arrested Geoff's attention. Bang, bang, bang, bang! It was followed by a salvo of blasts; motor horns began simultaneously beeping, fireworks exploding. Skyrockets zoomed off in iridescent tangents, bloomed into giant flowers that broke in the upper air and rained burning petals upon the city. Outside the dark window panes, showers of smashed golden dragons cascaded in the dark air. Geoff rushed to the window. Balloons soared, puffed up, swayed and swung aslant away into the night and a burst of riotous clapping and singing shot out of the TV screen.

Happy New Year! And Happy New Year! And Happy New Year again—they chanted. Standing, beating time upon the rug, Geoffrey Fernandes found himself smiling tipsily and clapping to the music, wishing himself a happy new year again and again and again. That's what one waited for—this moment of the trapped present, this make-believe zero-time, this instant of pause between two calendars of time, a carnival of gilt glory, this tutored fling of music and this lissom excess swaying upon the screen to lend your old bones its own illusion. They did not say anything like 'Peace on earth and goodwill to all men'. The world had grown up. But after half an hour of intensive merriment the compere flashed into view, smiling beatifically as in a vision of indescribable cheer. 'Goodbye and good luck,' she bade him personally. 'And keep smiling.'

It wasn't necessary to utter any farewells. Geoff Fernandes knew that he had thrown a successful party and got away with it. And to throw a successful party when one is all alone of an evening and all alone in the world—well, almost—is no mean feat. To throw a successful party with nobody attending save an old grandad, dead and gone for forty years and more, and a flighty young fantasy of a granddaughter, unborn still and unlikely ever to be born, was, by God, no minor feat. There was no one else that Geoff Fernandes cared to entertain now save past or possible people. Five rich fulsome years in the beginning of one's life spent with the one; and maybe five possible years at the end of one's existence with the other—nobody knew how many significant beings passed one another by in time and could never meet save in him. To get them to meet and be his guests, be it only once, was old Geoffrey's wayward dream. And he'd carried it off, he happily knew, this tipsy New Year's Eve.

The Taste of Almonds

The late Nizam of Hyderabad, it was said, relished burfi made from the milk of cows that had been fed on a special diet of pistachios.

It was a scale of splendour that Nawab Jamaluddin Naqvi, senior baron-in-residence of Sher Kothi, Khoa Mahal, Kanpur, had not been able to match. All the same he had, in his youthful days, devised some modestly comparable approximations.

The decades had robbed Nawab Saab's memory of all redundant details, personal or public, as his progeny had deprived him of the freedom of movement deemed injurious to his well-being. It was just as well, for Nawab Jamal Saab senior's intelligence was now rendered altogether impervious to most demanding subjects. Only the very remote past shone in his eyes with the sharp clarity of a world recognized. That Sher Kothi was now a ramshackle, mouldering structure, moss-covered, vermin-infested, rafters rotten and the roots of the peepuls rending asunder the old stone pavings, made no impression upon his consciousness. And that Khoa Mahal, once the extensive property of Nawab Saab's forebears, was now a filthy labyrinth of dingy alleys, slushy, smelly and inhabited by poor vendors, shop assistants, baker's boys, poor tailors, shoemakers and embroiderers, mattered little to him.

Half a century's close consort with Allah (five interviews a day) and for the last two decades a stern leash upon the errant Iranian blood had refined Nawab Saab's spirit and bent his back. But as age

97

advanced and the cornices and balustrades of his sprawling Saracenic homestead crumbled and gave way, as the world receded in clarity and the very birds wheeled away in ever-fading circles into the sooty sky, the pangs of the palate arose with vengeful spite to torment and to mortify. And the palate, Nawab Saab sorrowfully realized, may not be mocked.

Not for him the strong savours of the common gourmand, all nutmeg and saffron, burning paprika or pungent cardamom. Nawab Saab's savours, like his sensibility, were more sophisticated. To him there came insistently, like the voice of Satan in the Garden, the tender scent of pomegranate, memories of lost Qandahar, cashew nut in cream in ivory bowls and ah! most tantalizing, visions of almond blossom, almond burfi, sweet, delectable almond paste beneath its mantle of shining foil, moon-cool and fulfilling as a draught of spring-water from a rivulet of paradise!

To waken of a summer's morning, obsessed with the feasts of the past and to discover the door of the court unbolted was a happy agreement of circumstances worthy only of Allah's foresight. One intuition alone sustained him. Somewhere down the way, to right and then to right again, beyond the mosque and the tentmaker's, was Nadeem, faithful retainer, sweet sycophant, Nadeem, prince of the palate, sweetmeat wizard, artist par excellence!

So, into the entrails of a hectic teeming bazaar wandered Nawab Saab for an hour and more, asking: 'May the offence be excused, noble sir, but be this the lane wherein Nadeem Khan, the sweetmeat seller, holds residence?'

It was a quest unrewarded. Nobody in that crowded, noisy bazaar had heard of Nadeem Khan. The blazing sun made Nawab Saab's brow sweat and made his ragged kurta and checked lungi cling to the clammy skin. The dust and slush soiled his old nagras where the embroidered peacocks once reposed. Noise, rancid gutters, horse's hoofs and bicycle bells made havoc of his confidence. And a multitude of preposterous shop signs, each more grotesque than the last, confounded his befogged wits. It was a crazy, teasing world. He paused before a stall and read with difficulty (the language of his own time being Persian or a civilized Urdu), the Hindi alphabets: 'Hul-chul Chaat' and above it the pious sentiment: 'This too shall pass.' To the best of his knowledge and belief, 'hul-chul' meant 'hurly-burly', confusion; and why the shop owner should designate his shop 'confusion' was beyond his comprehension, and what confusion should have in common with the observation that all is ephemeral challenged his powers beyond their scope. He shook his head, mystified, and went on. There was another entitled 'Badnaam Lassi' or 'Whipped Curd of Ill-fame', surely an extraordinary style of advertisement, where he was offered two choices, an Amitabh Bachchan glass, to wit, a nine-inch-tall glass, or a Mukri glass, that is, a five-inch glass, allusions which were lost on Nawab Saab's intelligence and did nothing to further his grasp of contemporary things. Declining, he hastened on, only to be arrested by the caption: 'Sold by son but guaranteed by father' over a cart and beneath, in golden letters the name 'Hahakar Kulfi' or 'Uproar Kulfi'. This was Kanpur's mad, boisterous folk culture and it only made Nawab Saab's confusion worse. 'Nadeem, Nadeem,' he muttered to himself, his eyes scanning the bewildering names, sweeping over the wares, darting into the interiors.

And it was at the end of an alley, upon a dingy plank over a drain, that his search was crowned with partial success. A sweetmeat shop, though not Nadeem's, and plying a brisk trade judging by the crowd, almost as numerous as the flies, and above, the piquant sign: 'Welcome and Be Cheated. Asad Mukhtar—Sweetmeat Seller.'

The array of colourful sweetmeats laid out on open trays or piled in symmetrical pyramids upon platters or still sizzling in large iron cauldrons of boiling oil, would not, in their appearance and colour scheme, have met with Nawab Saab's approval. But hunger having given him an open mind and the crowd of customers having afforded him ease of access, he professed himself willing to give Asad Mukhtar, sweetmeat seller's talents a fair chance.

He was not impressed. There were pedas choked with sugar, smashed-pearl laddoos which stuck to the teeth or dry gram-flour laddoos which grated against the tongue. Squares of cottage cheese paste as cottage cheese had no business to be; jalebis too viscous of syrup and too soggy of skin. It will be evident, by reason of Nawab Saab's growing disgust, that he had already given Asad Mukhtar's skills more than a fair chance when at last some milk-cauldron scrapings set in trays brought to the discerning palate a faint, long-lost intimation of the past. And it was precisely at this moment that all hell broke loose.

'Hey, grandsire! What's that you're doing, grey-beard? I saw you, I did, you mangy mongrel!'

His bent back prevented Nawab Saab from drawing himself up to his former height but his eye was austere and his voice admonishing.

'Your pedas are inedible, noble sir,' said he. 'Less of the sugar and more of the milk. Your laddoos have no trace of chopped raisins or walnuts or cashew nuts. And you must not expect me to believe that the medium you use to fry your jalebis in is the best Khurja ghee. There is no silver foil on your burfis, but this I concede, your khurchan is passable . . .'

'Ah-ha-ha-ha!' roared the excitable young man, at a loss for words. 'Oh, God above, he robs me in broad daylight, pays not a paisa, tries everything, helps himself, then spits on my skill!'

A crowd had gathered. Nawab Saab's runaway rhetoric had drawn the masses but his talk of cashew nuts and pure ghee in this humble pocket of Kanpur had provoked their merriment. Clearly in this nautanki, here was a clown to hoot and the Kanpur crowd knows a good nautanki when it sees one. There was immense laughter, many sallies.

'Khurja ghee!' roared one. 'You oil your beard with it, do you, old-timer?'

'I get my retainers to massage my calves with it, sir,' was Nawab Saab's unruffled reply. A shocked silence fell at the felon's smooth daredevilry. At his age and with a back as bent as that and a prayer-mark as large as a rupee coin on his forehead too!

'What I am looking for is some good old-fashioned malai-gilloris. Real cream and almonds.' Nawab Saab sought the crowd's assistance. 'Can any of you gentlemen tell me where those can be had?'

'I'll give you malai-gilloris!' shouted the young man, at the end of his patience. 'Were it not for your bent back, grandsire, your beard would pay for your booty!'

Nawab Jamal Saab stared at the rash young serf, incredulous. His eyes were irascible, his voice dangerous as he intoned the following words:

'Do you know who it is that stands before you? You are addressing Nawab Jamaluddin Naqvi, owner of this estate, this bazaar and a quarter of this city.'

Look on my presence, ye scullions and tremble—his voice suggested.

'What is more, for your inadequacies at your art, I shall have your shop closed down, your vessels confiscated and your back dealt twenty lashes at the very earliest, sir.' His voice was icy with contempt. 'Your place shall be taken by Nadeem Khan, when I can find him, Nadeem Khan, the finest chef in all Kanpur and Unnao and Etawah as well!'

The young man froze where he stood and his face went pale, his fury forgotten.

'Nadeem Khan has been dead these thirty years, sir,' said he slowly. 'He was my maternal grandfather.'

'Nadeem Khan dead? How? When? Why wasn't I told? Ah, Nadeem, Nadeem!' The old man's grief was pitiful to behold. His red eyes filled and his voice was shrill. He sank down upon a wooden bench. 'Ah, Nadeem, my friend. And where can I get my gilloris now, answer me?' He sniffed like a child. 'There are no almond gilloris left in the world. And no friends like you. Quality is gone and fineness too. Ah, the world is too poor now, O Nadeem.'

Some men from the crowd came forward and put their arms about his bowed shoulders and knelt before his form. And one said: 'Ah, do not weep, old master. For those that are gone belong to Him now, says the Book, and presumptuous are we to claim them for our own.' And another whispered: 'Hush, do you know who this is? It's the old Nawab of Sher Kothi, the senile one, the one who's kept locked up.'

A wave of compassion swept over the crowd. Such things do happen. How did he get out? Never mind, he doesn't remember his way about. Almonds and walnuts, was it, granddad? To crush beneath teeth you lost a quarter-century ago? 'For shame, Asad. Salaam him, Asad. Go on, where's your Islamic civility, man? Render unto the old masters the things that were theirs, if only in charade, Mian!'

And Asad came down from his wooden platform, his ladle and boiling cauldron forgotten, and kneeling in the dust, bowed low and salaamed the old one. And said: 'Huzoor, your wish is my command. There, there, now. Gilloris it shall be, though with my last paisa. Almond gilloris, be sure now and no mistake, old master.'

His brother Khursheed brought a charpai for the Nawab to sit on and the shoemaker next door appeared instantly with a fan. 'Be seated, master, be seated,' urged many gentle voices.

Nawab Saab's tears were dry now and he was in his element. This courtesy of fawning and feting he knew and understood. Speech breaks from his lips in an irrepressible wave.

'At my behest,' he is telling the crowd, 'a seer of almond paste was boiled in three seers of sweetened milk in an earthen pot perched upon a slow-burning wood fire. From dawn till dusk it thickened, the cream removed repeatedly, flattened on a platter and chilled over blocks of ice. And when cool, stuffed with cardamom and chips of almonds, twisted cunningly betel-wise, sprinkled with the essence of rose, and folded in foil of silver . . .'

'So shall it be and exactly so, old master,' whispered the old seamstress in the burqa. 'Rest thy poor bones awhile on this charpai and we, thy slaves, shall do the rest.'

So Nawab Saab yawned and, the excitement of the morning having imposed a heaviness on the limbs and a drowsiness upon the eyes, stretched himself, yawned again, sleepily murmured God's name and went to sleep.

And how, they asked of one another, can we poor folk get almonds for him? Almonds sell at two hundred rupees a kilo. And Khurja ghee is hard to come by for the likes of us. Milk for it alone shall cost fifty rupees and more. And no man here but makes a petty sum too small to fill his belly or clothe his own. The poor cannot afford to pay such largesse nor enact such scenes of munificence. Yes, they said, the world for us has become too poor, for was not once this filthy lane a flourishing hive of merchants and do but observe it now.

But there were others that urged: silence, I beg you, consider this old one here. If there is one that is poorer far than we, yonder does he lie and may the Prophet pardon my presumption. To him do we owe that two-and-a-half per cent rather than the ne'er-do-well mendicants that come a-begging at our doors.

And then there transpired a most wonderful gesture, yes, even in that dingy lane. Seamstress, tailor, shoemaker, baker-boy, rickshaw-puller, fruit vendor, holy man and gram woman, barber and butcher, all came forth and said: 'Asad, my lad, take this and use it. Its all I can spare today, may God not shame me for my poverty, but its what I give you for him that lies there . . .' So they came, many more than one may think possible, cultured and fine as only the very poor can sometimes be.

And so Asad sent Khursheed to buy more milk and the seamstress volunteered to buy the almonds and the tailor and vendor brought wood for the fire and the curd man supplied the earthen pot. Nawab Saab slept upon his charpai, the mosquitoes gently fanned away from his ancient limbs by Asad's young wife.

And as the work went on, they stole looks at him and whispered about him. A very holy man he was, they said. A Haji. That was when he was younger, said another. He had the permitted four wives but the only snag in his serenity was that the four devout ladies were given to bickering and spitefulness all day and try as he might he could not maintain equality and accord betwixt them. My father told me all about it as a child. So Nawab Saab grew disenchanted with his women. They say that he fell headlong in love with a nautch girl but when he announced his decision to marry her, a storm broke out. Such moral indignation there was, such turbulent discourses from the Book. All that Nawab Saab said was: 'Why, what difference betwixt four women and five?' But public opinion prevailed and so Nawab Saab renounced his nautch girl, sadder and wiser, and loved no more.

Everyone laughed throwing indulgent glances at the charpai. 'Hush, for shame!' reprimanded the tailor. 'A Mussalman must not gossip nor deride another. Scandal-mongering is haraam so hold your tongues.' But someone else had news to impart. The young nawab, his grandson, has a bicycle shop on Meston Road and locks up the old one personally before he leaves. An old maid cooks and sweeps. The young Nawab's father was a great cock-fighter and the young one is an accomplished kite-flyer and wins all the bouts. This old one wanders about when he can and is brought home by kindly passers-by.

It was many hours later and well into the dusk when Nawab Saab was woken up with the gentle plea: 'Huzoor, awake. Your almond gilloris are ready.'

Sitting on his charpai, Nawab Saab wiped his mouth, cleaned his beard and dried his eyes.

'That was good,' sighed he, a man content.

Asad, the sweetmeat-seller, bowed. Hasan, the tailor, bowed. The grocer, the bangle-seller, the seamstress, the barber, the butcher, the tea-shop owner, everyone bowed low and said: 'The honour is ours, old master.' And a few smiled but a few faltered.

'We regret, old master, that your honour had to wait long for the gilloris to be ready,' apologized Asad.

'Ah, no,' murmured Nawab Saab.' I quite enjoyed my slumber on this charpai. I dreamt of almonds . . .' He chuckled mischievously and looked round for laughter. Everyone laughed politely.

Nawab Saab took off his battered cap and handed it regally to Asad. 'Take that, my man,' he pronounced with solemnity. 'That is a royal cap in recognition of your services. I regret that I do not have any gold on me today, but that cap is far more precious. Show it anywhere on my estates and take anything you want in my name.' Nawab Saab grew sententious. 'Take anything from the world, I tell myself, my men, but pay for it. Take first and pay later, or pay first and take thereafter but pay you must, now or in jahannum.' He swelled with importance. 'Only we, who came as conquerors, took and paid nought, but that was our privilege.'

The shades of night had fallen upon the old blackened balustrades when Nawab Jamaluddin Naqvi, seated royally upon a rickshaw drawn by Mehtab the puller and escorted by a flock of his loyal subjects, was conducted to his residential quarters in Sher Kothi, his palate at peace and his pride most appeased.

And Asad put the cap reverently upon a ledge in his shop, for even with his unpolished sense he knew what it signified. Like the coins of the old water carrier in our history books who was exalted to kingship for three brief days and who insisted on striking leather coins cut out of his water-bag for the citizens to use, be it only for three days, the cap stood for the richness of some delusions and gestures, a gift from the poor to the poor, where all are poor before God.

Goddess of Clay

Whenever old Manik Das shuffled down to Robi Mullick's grocery store in the village for a trifling loan or a bagful of fluffed rice and sugar or a pinch of snuff on credit, great was the laughter.

'What, god-maker?' jested the village wags. 'Can't conjure up a handful of sugar with a mantra? Of what use are all those gods and goddesses in your yard?'

Or Robi Mullick, our grocer-financier, pronounced heartily: 'Ish! The number of loans you've taken this month can only be counted on Ma Durga's fifty fingers, Manik-da, certainly not on mine.'

The wags crowed. 'Ma Durga's given up warfare, no? Counting loans, is she now, ho god-maker?'

'Silence!' roared Robi. 'This is Kali-yuga, my young sparks, so what better use for the ten hands of the holy than counting loans, investments, assets, taxes, interests. These things have their spiritual counterparts in heaven, yes, even taxes, even soap and tea for free, so look sharp, my lads.'

And they hooted and slapped Robi's back and begged him for a bidi apiece to celebrate his wit. Those wags were our village chess players, good-for-nothing layabouts who carried on their intent game, come rain, storm or riot in Robi's corridor.

Old Manik Das smiled mildly. He was a lanky old-timer, vague in the eyes, uncertain in his movements, gone stupid over the years. It was common for all young men of superior intelligence in the village to smile after the old one and tap the forehead to denote complete senility, and they did so now as he tucked the packet carefully into the greasy bag and left.

But he it was that made those clay idols for our village Durga Puja, our Lakshmi Puja, our Kali Puja, even our Vishwakarma and Saraswati Pujas. For, you know, between the monsoon months and the next year's summer our goddesses must be feted. He had his ancient shack down a by-lane and lived in a ramshackle room behind it with two of his sons and a spitfire of a daughter. Forty years he had fashioned the goddesses for our village. And his hands worked miracles. Nobody could give our Saraswati's face that tender thoughtfulness or Kali's that dark rage. He was even better than his father, Nimai Chandra Das and his grandfather, Abani Shankar Das. Great pains he took procuring his material. River clay and paddy husk, the firmest, most supple of bamboo shafts, old paper, shreds of cloth. He did not like these modern moulds that made the goddess look like a simpering starlet or an overblown matron. He patted out each separate face, rendering it lyrically with his leathery hands. He lingered long over each arching brow or slope of cheek or bridge of nose or curl of lip.

And he did not like being watched. The children used to gather outside his shack. The old one was too mild to chase them away, but his creaking song ceased abruptly, his fingers faltered and his face grew tense and ashamed. A little later he abandoned his work, lit a chillum, slunk into the room and waited for them to leave.

Naturally his work was slow. He took weeks to finish each Durga idol. 'Hurry, hurry, Baba,' urged his sons. For in the time that old Manik Das took to complete a single idol, other clay modellers would have finished six. But the old man was roused to one of his mad fits of rage.

'Ho!' he fumed wrathfully. 'Does one stand before a blest woman before the nine months are done and shout! Hurry, hurry, deliver before thy time?' And his sons knew there was no arguing with him.

The old man would stand, lost in introspection, drape his fingers lightly over a clay wrist or ankle, think deeply, hum a verse from the

'Song of the Goddess', add a dimple, soften an angle, bend a little finger and that was that. He never seemed to realize how little he earned. For with Manik Das it was the verse no less than his hands which wrought the perfection of the fiery woman, the lady of the lion. Shail-putri, daughter of the mountain, he mumbled. Brahmacharini, chaste one. Kal-ratri, night of the aeons, protectress of the ten directions. Each attribute, each utterance, surely left its impact upon the clay. The beauty of her names! Chhatreshwari, he whispered, giver of shadowhood to the shadow; bearer of the virtues of ego, mind, intellect, bearer of the thunderbolt of the five breaths; adorner of well-being; Yoginidevi, of all essence, form, fragrance, word, touch; Narayani, to the three gunas; protectress of dharma; Swar-rupa, she whose very shape composes the subtle stuff of sound!

He stood back to survey the work of his hands.

'And does one stand before a blest woman and say! "Hurry, hurry, die before thy time?"'

Manik Das's hands shook.

'What's the matter, Ma?' Of all his six daughters, this one, Uma, was the worst.

'Matter? Ash in your eyes if you still can't see!' She leaned against the wall in bitter melodrama and addressed the clay idol with scorn: 'He lets me grow into a dry old crone, dry, dry, dry as the sugarcane stick when all the juice has been crushed out! Then he looks at me as tho' butter will not melt in his mouth, no, neither butter nor jaggery, and he asks, "What is the matter?" Huh! How long will I go on stirring his rice, ha?'

Manik Das shook inwardly. What was the vixen's problem? True, she was an abandoned woman and her husband's folk had cast her out, but she didn't want for anything. He had brought her back and willingly. And here she sat and accused him day after day. He was the usual victim of her tantrums and her perversity knew no limits.

'Ha!' she scoffed, delighted with his shock and dismay. 'See the way he lovingly carves those full arms and buttocks. And he has the nerve to ask me—"What is the matter?"'

Manik Das trembled. 'For shame, daughter, have you lost your mind?'

With a wild sob she rushed out. A daily scene this, reflected Manik Das helplessly. He could not work with a mind so troubled. He lit a chillum.

The village wags knew what the matter was. So did our women, beating their clothes at the community pond. Between them, our wags and our virtuous women could render accurate accounts of the contents of your coffers and your conscience both. A woman on heat, and not even worth your lechery, held the young sophists at Robi's store. Dark as night, a belly like a rice pot and a skin like a toad's, a shrewish tongue and no morals to boot. The women at the pond did not blame her husband for throwing her out. After all, Somesh Chandra of the next kasba belonged to a proud family, had a large patch of land of his own. The women of his household had skins white as milk or turmeric-pale. Heavy gold bangles they wore. Why he should have married that spitfire, no one knew. For Uma it was relentless war.

'I heard what you just said, Aunt. And why should I put vermilion in my hair and why should I wear a shell bangle? He threw me out, didn't he, the swine? He's dead for me, that son of wanton birth!'

Mark how she flings her pitcher into the water, muttered the good women at the ghat. At least maintain a decorous silence about your situation, my great lady, held those moralists. At least maintain that your husband has now got a job in Calcutta or Ranaghat or Burdwan and that's why you're here. If you don't please him, my queen, he has the right to give a kick on the buttock! Brazen hussy! Dirty slut!

'Go, sit in a balcony with flowers in your hair if you're that desperate,' teased the wags. 'But do, do let us know when you're taking to the anklet bells and we shan't fail you, madam, for old times' sake.' And no less than a dozen brave men made their claims and narrated the incident and all the ladies, listening behind the scenes, shook their heads and affirmed that they'd always known that she was a bad lot. Each day Uma raced away from the pond in a whirlwind of hysterical confusion, mouthing venomous imprecations, sobbing, like one possessed.

Old Manik Das still sang as he modelled the day. She is the victorious one behind, the victorious one before, unvanquished to the left, unvanquished to the right. Udyotini, her crown illumined, her forehead bears a garland, the renowned one where her brows are, the three-eyed one, she, the breath of whose nostrils gives birth to time, conch-shaped between the eyes, inhabiter of the doors of the ears, Kalika, of the cheeks; fragrance at the nostrils, speech at the upper lip, immortal nectar at the lower lip, Mahamaya, at the palms, Bhadrakali, at the throat, bow-bearer at the spine, bearer of the thunderbolt at the arms, Mahadevi, at the breasts, grief-queller for the mind, Kamini, for the navel, granter of all desires, Mahabaladevi, at the thighs, Vindhyavasini, at the knees, oh, she, possessor of the lion-force at the ankles, lance-bearer of the heart, rider of the buffalo . . .

Uma's lip curled in scorn. Sullenly she turned her back to him and strode into the inner room.

Uma stared at her reflection in the cracked mirror. Kalika, of the cheeks, she muttered bitterly; fragrance at the nostrils, immortal nectar at the lower lip, Bhadrakali, at the throat, Mahabaladevi, at the thighs! She looked at the mirror and her own ungainly form in rage. If I flung this pitcher into that wall the crash might stop his crazy chanting.

She lowered the pitcher down beside the earthen hearth and thought, 'I shall carry this ugly face like an evil karma till I die.'

'Hurry, Baba, hurry,' urged the sons. 'The third day of the goddess's advent and still a lot of the paint remains to be applied, and what if it rains? You waste time singing and dreaming. If, for instance, you let me apply the paint on this order, Shubodh can attend to that Kartika there while you rest in the afternoon.'

But the old one would have none of it. He was possessive about his creations. Each year they noticed the madness that claimed him as the ten-day advent advanced. His absent-minded concentration and his irritability grew, so did his senile murmuring. He helped drape the folds round her form, arranged in her ten hands the conch and the discus and the club and the hatchet, the lance, the massive bow, the trident.

'He who wears the armour of your name,' he whispered softly to himself, 'in the three worlds shall he be blest. Desires fulfilled, all victory his, disease, all ghouls of the sky, sea-travelling powers, female spirits, movers in space, destroyer forces, all, all cast away. For him your ultimate sanctuary, Mother, for him shelter in your form beyond which no form exists.'

On the fifth day they came with their carts and took away the idols, shouting, clashing cymbals, blowing conchs, beating drums and dancing. The sons stormed and haggled themselves hoarse.

'Thieves!' roared Proshanto. 'You'd cheat your very mothers of their last drop of Ganges water! Not Brahmins but Shudras in soul are you!'

'Next year take an advance!' shouted Shubodh and followed it up with a string of profanities. Manik Das watched her borne away in silence, not seeming to mind anything, not the broken assurances of full payment, nor the lying and the ribald abusing in her sacred presence.

Early on the sixth day he stood outside the festive tent, watching from afar. The lamps swung on their chains, dense fragrance rose from the censers and the dizzy drums thundered. Armed with her weapons, she towered astride the writhing demon, no longer clay, and her scorching eyes raged with an intense cosmic wrong. Every year Manik Das witnessed the miracle, a mood that was not of his making emanating from her face and a different expression each day.

Armed with the celestial weapons, mounted upon a lion, Durga emitted a blood-curdling cry. The seas trembled. The earth shook. The mountains rocked. Mahishasura's heart skipped a beat. I have come to fulfil Brahma's boon, she said. You wished to die at the hands of a woman? So be it. And as she breathed, thousands of soldiers came into being and fought at her side . . .

'Kanto!' cried Uma, catching up with him, gushing winsomely over the handlebar. 'Fancy seeing you here! Father and I were speaking of you just the other day. Why do you neglect us so, you forgetful thing? With these eyes I saw you cycle past our door and not a thought you gave us.'

Head inclined coyly upon the shoulder, Uma's voice is teasing music. 'Too learned for a tailor-boy, yes? Too big for your friends? Fine new clothes too. My!'

Suddenly she reached out and gripped his arm. 'Come!' she laughs gaily. 'Today is Shoshti day. Won't you come to sweeten your mouth and touch Baba's feet? Won't you measure me for that new choli you promised me?' She winked naughtily. 'I simply won't let you off.'

Kanto recoiled, filled with revulsion and panic. He shook her importunate arm off, a deep frown of disgust upon his swarthy face. It may have happened twice before, he scarcely knew how, but never, never again. He shuddered at the memory.

'Listen,' he spoke hurriedly. 'D'you know who saw me at the shop recently? Your brother-in-law, Ashit. "Look after your health, tailor"—that's what he said. Everyone is afraid of Somesh, your man. You know what he did to Milon Bose when he gave you money? I wish you would not come after me and insist on this thing going on. There was a to-do at home too. I don't want any trouble for the family . . .'

She could have slapped him hard. The screaming words exploded shrill and hot upon her lips. 'After what happened in the boat and the riverside reeds, you're on Somesh's side too? You hang together, you men? Burnt face! Field mouse! Stinking mole!' She was aware of herself racing away in that old primeval flight away from all people and things. She was aware of the tempestuous thoughts. And to think I almost bore this guttersnipe's child! This worm's! Oh, thank the goddess my womb burbled forth its refusal today! Only another woman could soothe and in this hellish village all the women hated her, the bitches! Except one. It is only in the festive tent of the goddess that she could find something for herself. So she stood in the corner and seethed with rage.

And the goddess told her what she had to do.

It was with grim decision that she sought him out.

'One minute,' she stepped in his way. 'There is something I would have you know, dear Kanto,' she said sweetly. 'There's something you must tell them all from me—it has festered too long inside me! "Everybody's afraid of Somesh, your man,"' she mimicked in bitter mockery. 'Not everybody, my little snivelling prick! And never call Somesh my man, ever again. There was a man who wasn't afraid of Somesh and his filthy clan and I bore him a son! Yes, do not think that I am alone, tailor-boy. His hands hacked off the heads of goats—phut, like that, and snapped the chickens' necks in two, so look sharp, tailor.'

Kanto gazed at her in horrified suspicion. 'Waseem Khan, the cobbler?' he whispered. He'd heard it before. A caste woman too.

Her eyes glittered in malice. 'Yes,' she announced recklessly. 'That was a man made of beaten gold like Kartika, with sinews like Durga's lion. And a face as compassionate as the goddess's and as thoughtful as Saraswati's. He fed me the nameless meats of his poor hearth when, bruised and broken, I crept to his door. Do you know the bride-price Somesh gave me—beatings and beatings, red weals and blue-black bruises, hunger, insults and filth. Not he alone but also his vile father and his foul-mouthed mother. Barren, they called me, barren and ugly and poor. Waseem Khan never called me ugly or barren. He applied turmeric on my bruises and told me the story of the Prophet and the man who was beating his slave. Do you know what the Prophet said to the man, tailor-boy? "You should know, Abu Masood, that God has more power over you than you have over this slave." He sent me back to Somesh with another story out of his big Book. The Prophet said to Abu Jandal: "O Abu Jandal, have patience for God will soon show you and your kind a way out of your suffering." "Go," said Waseem Khan, "and weep not. If man only foresaw the hopefulness of tomorrow, he would never despair over the defeats of today."'

She frowns into the distance and suddenly, in her abrupt, vicious way, bursts out laughing. 'To remember all that rejoicing in Somesh's household when my womb filled. Somesh, gloating oaf, so proud of his virility! And as my belly grew, they fed me milk and fish, nuts and festive sweets, I, their starveling! I stole away each day to see him in his shoemaker's hut and he gave me new mangoes for the palate and meats of many kinds for strength, talismans against spirits and sacred stories from his Book. "Do not spend so much on me, cobbler. You're a poor man yourself, you know," I said to him. But he had a pious answer for everything, that man. "What should I do with my earnings, girl? Hoard them up! No, by God, for the sake of tomorrow, I will not disobey God today." The Prophet said that God told him: "Mankind, spend and you will be spent on." To think that I betrayed a man like that for a snivelling like you, may I be punished for that, slut that I am, may I be punished for a hundred lifetimes!'

'Why didn't you go to the fellow for good?' Kanto's outraged honour smarted under the lash of her tongue.

'I did, many a time,' replied she and there was now no sting in her voice, only a boundless nostalgia. 'I took the child for him to see even before the forty days were done. I took him flowers and coconuts and sweets from my goddess. And I bent and touched his feet, for my gratitude knew no end.'

'And Somesh let you go?' Kanto's sneer was lost on her. She herself was lost to the world and enclosed in her own story.

'He did not know. I lied to him. I'm a cunning one—doesn't the entire village know of my cunning and my shamelessness, eh, tailor-boy?'

Curiosity had long overcome all of Kanto's fears. He drew closer, goaded her on with searching questions. A pretty story for the village this would be. Nothing like this had ever happened.

'I touched his feet,' she recalled in a dream. 'And he chided me and said: "Don't do this. This is kufra and it may not be done. Man must not bend his head before man."'

'And then?' prompted Kanto.

'Then I burst out laughing and said: "But I am a woman, dear cobbler, and a woman must bend before man, must she not? Keep telling me nice stories out of your Book. I like them but keep your way for yourself and leave mine for me and please do not preach. I have brought you some prasad." And he laughed and took the coconuts and I said: "May my goddess bless and protect you from all harm, good cobbler. I shall ask her for it every day of my life for you have done me a great favour. "'

'Oho,' taunted Kanto, insidious. 'Why didn't you go wed him, then? He'd have put you in a black burqa and pyjamas and done you the same favour year after year and you could've peopled the village with your brats. Everyone knows how they breed.'

'I wish I could, I swear before all!' cried Uma fiercely. 'But Somesh would have cut my throat with the kitchen bonti, yes, beaten me to pulp with the iron pestle. I have many marks and bruises on my body and they aren't the marks of love, be sure. So I left him and returned until . . . until they finally threw me out some weeks later.' She closed her eyes and was silent. Then she opened them and they fell on Kanto's surly face and a passion of fury swept over her. 'Go, worm, and to hell with you!' she screamed. 'Go, tell them all. Be my tale-bearer—that's all I ask of you. Tell them that the god-maker's daughter has gone to find her son and her paramour and may all of you rot with my curses!' She gave him a little push. 'Go!' she hissed.

In the pandal a deathly conflict was in progress. Enraged Mahisha leapt upon the lion and rushed at her but Durga soared over him and pinned him down. Mahisha struggled to free himself. As half of him emerged from the mouth of the buffalo, Durga raised her sword.

That was the first and finest woman and only she could be of help against the wretches who took away her son, her trunk of sarees, her gold jewellery, her good name. Uma cast a shamefaced look at her faded saree, her bare arms. She looked around. Today was a day for Murshidabad silks, gold-ridged combs, Dhaka-crisp cottons, tinsel-tasselled braids. It is the eighth day of the goddess's cycle and the third day of mine!

And when Manik Das, lifting the rice to his lips that night, queried: 'Ma, what ails you?' she said nothing, just sat, head in her hands beside the extinguished hearth.

If, she thought, I take the Tentul-tola bus, I'll have to pay a rupee. If I take the boat ferry, boatman Dulal will recognize me and open his big mouth in the village. So Uma resolved to walk all the way. Carefully rolled in a bath-cloth, she carried her only presentable tussore silk and knotted up in a kerchief a tiny pair of earrings. Not as a pauper but as a conquering lady would she appear at her worthless husband's doorstep. Give me back my trunk of sarees, she would demand. Give me back the gold mango collar and the thick bangles I wore at my wedding. Give me back my little son for he is mine, not yours, and the time has come for the truth to be told at last. Her rage was weapon enough to quell an army of demons. By the oath of Goddess Kali, this Oshtumi day was the last one in my life that I went to the puja pandal clad in rags.

With a blow of her sword she felled Mahishasura. Victory, victory unto you, goddess! Bearer of all the energies! From Shiva you received your mouth, from Yama the tresses on your head, from Vishnu your arms, from the moon your twin breasts, from Indra your katibhag, from Varuna your thighs and calves, from Brahma your feet, from the sun your toes. From Agni came your eyes, from Sandhya your brows. From Shiva you got your trident, from Vishnu the discus, from Vayu the giant bow, from Indra the thunderbolt, from Yama the celestial staff. The sun fed you with his flames. Mighty Kal gave you the sword and the shield, Himalaya your lion, the Ocean your garlands, your lotus and your gems. Victory unto you, Shakti, Upholder of Dharma, Mahavidya, Mahamedha, Mahamaya, Mahasmriti, Mahamoha, Mahadevi, Maheshwari . . .!

Today was her tenth day of conquest. No longer did Manik Das discern clenched rage in her painted face. Today there was soft regret, a speechless transfiguration of leave-taking. Her eyes shone limpid, unusually bright. Thus did a woman leave her father's hearth for her spouse's, reflected the old man, quite carried away. Today she must go. And Uma, after her mysterious absence, was back again.

Today the battle was over and won. But Uma stood alone, her lower lip cut and swollen, her hair disarrayed and her eyes smoking. What a victory there was, she addressed the goddess in the strangest of personal prayers. Your worshippers desert your tent for their own celebration. Only I, forbidden menstruating woman, dare enter and defile your tent with my impure body. But of course you do not bleed unholy blood and you do not shed human tears, Great Cosmic Woman!

Quickly she pulled the fringe of her saree over her cheek and bent her head lest the mark of shame become visible—Somesh Chandra's five flat fingers, still stinging upon her cheek.

And Waseem Khan, that man of honour, that icon, that god among men with the face of a lyrical sage and the words of the valiant defender, sat busy in his shop when she came in.

'I have come to you again,' she said simply. 'Please help me.' He looked up at her and a shocked, suspicious alarm appeared in his face. 'Why have you come?' he asked.

He threw a hasty look towards the interior of the shop and spoke aloud: 'A pair of slippers for mending, sister?'

Ah, she thought, how very fitting. A dangerous sweetness stole into her voice.

'Why, no, dear cobbler. Don't you remember, I never, never wore slippers when I came to your house. They made too much noise in the night so I left them behind.'

The panic in his expression changed to desperate sternness. 'Be quiet,' he rasped and resumed in his normal voice: 'A pair of shoes for your little one, sister?'

But Uma was not to be outwitted by a mere man today. 'Our little one, you mean?' she asked loudly. She sat down cross-legged upon the floor and put her bundle beside her. 'And how is he now, cobbler? Surely you see him in the village often? I am going to bring him here soon, this very day, in fact . . .'

Alas for Waseem Khan, that lion among men. His terror before his holy Islamic wife, his shame before his four legitimate brats, was a sight to remember if only it were not so demeaning. 'This is an insane woman, begum,' he pleaded. 'Believe me, O Farida Khanum, truth and falsehood are one to her; can this creature be the landowner Somesh Chandra's wife, tell me? And what would I, a cobbler, be doing with a pious Hindu woman?' And more to the same effect . . .

'Who is this funny woman, Mother?' asked a little boy of a young lady outside Somesh Chandra's homestead.

'Hush, the woods here have a rakshasi, a demoness who comes to take away children,' answered the lady.

Manik Das had never missed a single immersion. He tramped the seven miles to the river's edge, ahead of the crowd and the bullock carts, and waited by the promontory above the mango orchards. His emotions were mixed. An immersion put an end to what was begun and wrought with love, a death-rite against the setting sun with the river as witness. What a din and clamour, blowing of conches, shouting and beating of drums. Dancing, clapping, burning incense, they carried her and her attendant gods far downstream before they let her go and the boats returned.

Above the Tentul-tola bridge, Uma spoke incoherent words into the air. 'See what they do. They're careful to remove all your silks and your gold and your weapons, your sword and your lance and everything else, before they cast you away. Another goddess shall get them, come next year, a younger goddess. Stretch out your ten naked arms to the sky, Goddess Durga, before the dark waters receive you, for such is the forgetfulness of man . . .' There was much else she uttered. A crazy woman often makes speeches to the gods or to the empty air.

And Durga's billowing tresses spread out on the water. On the Tentul-tola bridge a passing carter thought he heard a splash.

Honourable Mention

Do you see that man there, hunched upon that microscope? His name is Abhijit Das.

You have heard of success stories. I shall tell you a failure story. That is my teacher and my friend. He taught me all I know. Of course, I superseded him. I do not know whether what I feel for him amounts to detestation or devotion but I can't get him out of my system.

There isn't a bus he hasn't missed, an opportunity he hasn't lost or a promotion he hasn't been denied. And, what enrages me most is his endless justification, his declaration that every failure was of invaluable profit to him. I have never known a man who so emphatically defended loss. This supercession is, in the ultimate analysis, very good for me, Ramendram, it will stop me exerting myself so much and I shall have time for my photography. This setback is just what I needed, Ramendram, it has prevented my blood pressure from shooting up—success can be so tyrannical, so demanding, you know. This rejection is a blessing in disguise; who knows, maybe it has saved me from becoming a crashing bore. I can see my own limitations better and hope for excellence next time. This lost promotion is, in the ultimate sense, a great asset—at last I have come to terms with injustice, a formative growth, you'll agree. And, most absurd of all—this heart attack has actually proved so good for me, Ramendram, its shown me the worth of life in its broadest perspective, revealed to me the time wasted, given a new focus to my vision, Ramendram. 'In the ultimate analysis', 'the broadest perspective', 'when all things are taken into consideration': those were Abhijit Das's favourite phrases. Everything was *sub-species aeternitatis*, we mocked. I never saw such an organized and resourceful philosophy of escape.

I was his junior research assistant for seven years and I am now his senior, I, Ramendram of the swarthy face and the lantern jaw, penniless rationalist from Madras, who admired Abhijit Das passionately, baited him with a ferocious joy that was keenly akin to scorn, young, ironical, hostilely defensive about my ardent disbeliefs. I was by his side when Abhijit Das, fifty, class two and desperately unfulfilled, threw in his last stake. Those were the most meaningful years of my life. I remember that day of discovery, the only scientific miracle I was ever privileged to share. Wet Calcutta, August 1978, it was.

He must have missed at least half a dozen buses and stood shivering in the rain at the bus terminus that morning. I can see him even today, soaked wisps of grey hair, a battered briefcase under his arm, myopic eyes straining searchingly through damp spectacles and the fine-spun rain to discern the numbers on the buses. Do you know Calcutta in the monsoon? The streets are roaring ravines; the buses squelch past, crazily tilted, cruising round the corners, gorged with clammy humanity, men sealed tight in steamy interiors, clinging to window bars, balanced upon mudguards, spilling out of the doors. Flogged and spiritless, the chilled palms dangle ragged fronds, drip slow, slimy drops. A sky choked and tense with rain. Umbrellas an oily black retinue toiling up the avenues. Drenched trams rattle past, jammed with men, reeking, humid flesh and shivering skins, one arm clutching the bar, galley slaves chained to the oars upon a wearisome voyage. Waiting for the bus, Abhijit Das could so easily be elbowed aside by the first flashing-teethed, mahogany-faced youth. 'Sorry, dada!' The lad would have waved a mirthful hand as the bus growled off. Did he smart at the effrontery of the young or lapse into the thousand natural self-pities that late middle age is heir to? I honestly do not know. Somebody gave him a lift, I guess, some acquaintance from better days. I can just see Abhijit Das sink timorously back upon the cushioned seat in relief, saying: 'How lucky to miss that bus, after all! I can now reach the institute much earlier in your car.'

I have no patience with negative philosophies. But here was a man who doggedly translated every negative experience into positive deductions and congratulated himself constantly. I thought Abhijit Das did protest too much and I told him so.

And what an exasperating fool he could be sometimes. Absolute strangers were detained and compelled to listen to his eager babbles. I can visualize him in the car, wagging his large head, eyes shining, gesticulating in passionate self-absorption, talking, talking, while his unfortunate benefactor with an expressionless face, steered through the raging traffic.

'Do you realize what that implies? Can you guess at the tremendous possibilities? It can only point at some sort of botanical individuality, even within plants of the same species. Not determinism but botanical decision. Individuality with all its attendant implications. We have experimented on FS with as many as 150 different species. A hibiscus, for instance, has been proved to register higher FS than, say, a carnation. One may suspect that some connection exists between higher pollen productivity and higher FS but we have no conclusive evidence yet. Nature is not single-minded, I frequently reflect. Everything does not revolve round fertilization. There is room for the lawless, the erratic. You have heard of Heisenberg's "uncertainty principle" perhaps in the domain of physics? Ah, no, I recollect that you were not a science student in the old days. Well, to return to the subject in hand, we have stumbled upon an unfamiliar dimension, sir. The electrograph has some very interesting data to offer. Exciting, to say the least . . .'

And his audience so frequently responded with a polite, well-intentioned query like: 'What is your basic salary at the institute?' or 'What upward mobility can you expect in your particular line?'

And Abhijit Das's voice would suddenly die away.

On his pedestal the Marquis of Hastings sat drenched aloft his prancing stallion, one hand strained upon the reins, the other shading carved, empty eyes which sought something indiscernible behind the troubled rain.

What a despicable, babbling old romantic!

The Institute of Botanical Studies loomed vast, Georgian-beige, large ornamental gateway with brass eagles and victorious crossed bugles, the triumph of science over superstition. The paved drive was washed clean by the shower and the hedges so sharply green that they shocked the eye. Round the corner went he, past the old moss-blackened fountain, into the porch and up the stairs. The lab was on the second floor on the southern face. He opened the white door and stepped silently in. That morning the windows were shuttered against the slanting shower and the eucalyptus turned and tore forlornly against the shut panes. We had all the lights on.

'You're early today, sir.'

'Yes, I got a lift. Do I see you entering yesterday's readings?'

'It's that Discus Allegoria we did yesterday.'

'Let's hear it again.'

'30 and 16. PLT 12 in the first round. 45, and this is amazing, sir, actually an FS as low as 4. Then a fairly stable return graph. Last month when we were doing those projections the same thing happened. The electrograph kept swaying round to the most absurd counts and all my calculations were upset.'

'Can petals wince under sound frequencies, sir?'

He would take that sort of dubious sally with such grotesque gravity.

'You wretched pundit, you botanical buffoon!' I took such liberties with him, so long as I did it in the Queen's English. I object to all these poetic vapourings! Wake up, you shabby slob! What are you trying to construct? A philosophy of Botany, here in a third-rate government institute, here in our jaded lab?

A quarter of this I spoke aloud, sirring him between breaths; three-quarters my voice implied. He only laughed meekly.

'Ramendram, spare me your onslaughts. Mridula, we shall have to go over those reactions again.'

And yes, there was that girl whom Abhijit Das endlessly watched with strange, mellow eyes, to our secret merriment. An ugly girl, some would have said, with her still, abstracted eyes behind thick school marmish glasses and her hair gathered into a severe braid. She could not have been more than twenty-seven or thereabouts but she always dressed in those stiff whites and greys and browns, a woman one could never picture in scandalous pink or an explosion of orange. I guess that was a gesture of defiance or despair. An unattractive girl who had pledged to leave beauty alone. And I guess Abhijit Das, doddering old knight-errant, fancied failure above mere beauty. But her hands as she wrote were startlingly exquisite, calm and impersonal and complete. She was Abhijit Das's Girl Friday at the Institute. She was also our Ashok Mohapatro's fiancée.

Abhijit Das never drank so that a single beer had him dithering. Oh, help, now the confessions come pouring out in true Augustinian self-laceration, with me for Father Confessor! Who wants to listen to your sordid fantasies, you slime?

'Sometimes, Ramendram, I wish I was born twenty years later.'

'You mean, circa the year two thousand?'

'No, no.' He wagged his head vaguely. 'I mean twenty years after I was born. I have missed a woman by about twenty years.' Mercifully for her, thought I. No names but I grasped all.

But A. Das had more to reveal: 'When I was fifteen, Ramendram, I desperately wished I was about thirty. Maya was about twenty-five then, a cousin, and I was a callow school-going lout. Strange, isn't it?'

'Very. And your wife? Have you aired these hopes in her presence?'

'Hopes?'

'Twenty years younger or twenty years older . . . ?'

He sighed. 'I wish I had. Anyway, I wasn't the one she was supposed to marry. She was engaged to my elder brother. And what were the recordings on those *seboria eltonias*?' From mawkishly personal, he could turn briskly professional.

'When I switched on the Gama screen the graph appeared very uneven. Sylvan high-sap pressure.' I essayed to laugh.

'And by the way, Surendranath plans to attend that Seattle conference in February. He told me to get on with my FS paper. He intends to read it at the conference. Oh, I knew you'd rear like a cobra, Ramendram.'

'Like hell he will! I shall find myself sabotaging all our apparatus if that old skunk is planning to steal the show.'

A. Das held up a warning hand. 'Noblesse oblige. After all he is Director. So we stay in a couple of hours extra and work, full speed ahead. In any case you're leaving in October.'

'I'm not.' I scowled, 'I flunked the exam.'

'What a pity.'

'Missed by three marks.'

Something in my deadpan voice made Abhijit Das melancholy. 'I must now be infecting all those who come in touch with me,' ruminated he. 'There's a pattern in these things. I don't know if I pursue the pattern or the pattern pursues me but I have come to recognize the symptoms all right.'

The last thing I wanted was philosophic consolation. But A. Das grew reminiscent. 'Three attempts at the pre-medical test, all missed by a hair's breadth. For eight years I missed everything I tried my hand at by the narrowest margin possible. Earlier in school, sometimes the headmaster's son had to be given a promotion in my stead or a bout of flu on the day of the exam. A careless examiner or an irritable interviewer or a theory unknown to the expert himself. The proudest and saddest moment of my life was when I bagged the second position by a single mark, mind you, in my B.Sc. . . .'

I listened patiently, my thoughts busy elsewhere. There was nothing I wouldn't do for this empty old anti-hero, even kick him up the ladder if I could. Overtime we would work, we fifteen research assistants, and that paper would not go to the Seattle conference first, I suddenly resolved.

She was a bird of passage in his uneventful life or some such horrendous piece of shabby poetry. Ashok Mohapatro was our brilliant engineer.

'You're very painstaking, Mridula.' The silence was getting oppressive. In my own corner of the lab I bent over my ledger, my face expressionless.

'Ashok is leaving for Connecticut in November, isn't he?'

'Yes,' said she tonelessly.

A. Das, I saw out of the corner of my eye, concentrated tensely upon the page before him.

'I do hope the project is complete by then. We don't want to lose both you and Ashok before that. Where would the team be without you?'

'If the unit needs me, sir, I can't think of leaving.'

When Abhijit Das spoke it was in a hearty rush. A bogus paternalism, a phoney note of disinterested patronage, sounded false and unconvincing, in his reedy voice.

'Come, come. Cut out all that dedication stuff. When was it decided?'

Her voice was low. 'Very recently,' said she evasively.

'Listen,' spoke he and there was now nothing phoney in his headlong appeal. 'Don't be indecisive about important things. Learn to arrange your priorities wisely. Don't keep things waiting. I know our work here matters to you but I don't want you to go the way of Ramendram or Bhupen or, for that matter, myself . . .'

Oh, I could have thumped him on the back, this Hamlet turned Polonius, for his crisp delivery, his precise prescriptions. His performance couldn't have taken in a child, let alone an intuitive woman. And, when he tried to be jocular he was positively outrageous. 'I give you these flowers of middle-aged wisdom, etcetera, etcetera, etcetera.' 'Congratulations, A. Das!'—was what I was tempted to shout across. 'What a succinct, clear-sighted philosophy you have just enunciated!' Flowers of middle-aged wisdom!—I almost choked. 'Go,' said he to her. 'Or you'll miss your bus tonight.' And she left.

September and our endrometer whirred incessantly. The tapes raced, wheels turned, the dial turned green, the magnetic needle slid on and off the rotating drum. The silence in the lab was intense. On the table Bhupen spread out the graph sheets while Mridula worked upon the slides and I recorded the shock pulses for the month-old *Arboria rexus*.

'What I fail to understand,' mused A. Das, 'is why the counts are so unbalanced between the synclinal swings and the anticlinal stops . . .'

Change the plates. With a dim roar the E.G. started again, clicking rhythmically. The lights in the lab switched off, the dial turned a slow, burning green.

'Stop!' cried A. Das. 'The readings again.'

'A-52, lapse 200, A-40, lapse 196, A-42, lapse 203,' read Bhupen.

'If the speed of the drum is lowered, sir . . . ' suggested Mohapatro.

'We must pursue the speed of a phenomenon we cannot yet define,' ruminated A. Das. 'Speed. What a questionable word in this context. Lower the speed to record frequencies of what? I am often suspicious of all my primary hypotheses.'

An obscure process shaped itself under our very noses, and, try as we did, we failed to keep pace with it. Our artefacts told us some things which our recordings affirmed; on the glowing dial the needle swung, clicked, hesitated, swung to higher figures and then, unaccountably, dropped. The magnetic needle jumped once, twice and then the dial went dead. The lapses between the anticlinal and synclinal readings barely averaged a hundred. I thought, A. Das would explode in frustration.

It was a bleak, windy October morning. We had worked all night. Mridula cleared away the mugs of tea and I lifted my heavy head from the table, sleepily protesting, when Das, who had continued working while we snatched a catnap, suggested that we resume. Then I noticed that strange, taut spring in his voice.

'Look . . .' said he, and in the middle of a pin-drop silence we saw the dial turn dim green like the eye of a jungle deity. The two arms circled slowly and swung to a stop. 52 and 52. 52 and 52. 52 and 52.

'As I always suspected,' was all that Abhijit Das could trust himself to utter. 'Ashok, the dimensions of the magnet had to be altered. That's all really . . .'

Nobody spoke. Then suddenly the shell of silence cracked. Bhupen gave vent to a loud whoop and Mridula drew in her breath sharply. As for me, my first impulse was to hoist A. Das upon my shoulder, footballer that I was, and hurrah him down Roy Choudhury Avenue! 'You blithering priest of science! You've done it!' somebody was roaring incessantly in my ear and I rather believe it was I. But, A. Das, I recall, only pulled out a chair and sank, exhausted, into it. Then he remembered. 'Now to formulate the findings in a paper for the Seattle conference,' said he wryly. 'Surendranath is worried, you know.'

Formulate the findings in a paper we did, all fifteen of us, and much good A. Das's dutiful dedication to the Director did him. He never suspected a thing. If Surendranath received his copy in early November, ours was dispatched a good three weeks earlier. It was I who sealed the envelope, Bhupen who drafted and typed out the covering letter and it was our Mridula of the bird-like hands who forged, yes, marvellously duplicated Abhijit Das's meandering signature! And when we stood outside the GPO, the operation complete, we felt we were the self-appointed arbiters of fate, titanic agents of a superior destiny, who had craftily outwitted our teacher's objectionable habit of surrender.

So when Abhijit Das received that large blue envelope a month later and perplexedly fussed over it, turning it this way and that, now studying those American stamps, now rereading that typewritten address as the truth slowly dawned upon him, all work ceased in the lab and one by one we stole around his swivel chair, triumphantly awaiting the belated decision of fate.

The long sheet fell out.

My dear Dr Das,

We are happy to receive your paper entitled, et cetera et cetera. We invite correspondence on the subject, so on and so forth . . .

And then, unspeakably, damnably, the words which fifteen pairs of eyes devoured with a growing sense of the impossible:

Of course it must be made known to you that your interesting theory has almost wholly been anticipated by Doctors Klein and Humboldt of the University of Berlin only this July. Your findings happily coincide with theirs . . . The Klein–Humboldt formulae have recently been applied and found valid in all our institutes . . . We are dispatching our quarterly journal containing the Klein–Humboldt paper printed this September . . . et cetera, et cetera.

Yours sincerely, damn and blast!

It was then that Mridula, who was late that morning, appeared upon the threshold. Her face lit up at the sight of the envelope and with a bound she was by A. Das's side, eyes sparkling, voice asnap with excitement.

'Washington! Oh, what does it say, sir?'

'Thank you all,' said Abhijit Das very slowly. 'It says in short that our work deserves an honourable mention.' He handed her the sheet and turning, passed a hand over his forehead and looked away, shading his eyes, out of the lab window, past the Marquis of Hastings and the distant grey warehouses, at the murky, unmoving river.

So we walked by apparent accident alongside him that evening, tense and speechless, and a little awed, yes, even I, noisy Ramendram. We queued up for the Thakur Pukur bus, and, as always, when the milling crowds jostled and fought for a foothold or a handhold, A. Das just made no effort, and stood listlessly by, and we, who could push and shove as well as the next man, for some unspoken reason, chose to stand unresisting by and miss the bus with him. If A. Das understood, his face registered no response but inevitably the situation oppressed him into inane talk.

'Look,' said he, 'are all of you coming home with me? Don't. Mira is away and what with the load-shedding and the mosquitoes, my house isn't exactly a picnic in the evenings. Besides,' he continued, 'we must separate at the Taratalla Crossing. I go straight down Diamond Harbour Road, you know, but all of you go different ways. No point walking me home and then walking back. You'll only waste time and it'll be dark by the time you get home.'

Nobody agreed or disagreed. This was a collective experience and nobody knew quite how to explain or understand it.

I still don't know what to make of that day, whether some science simpler and superior to our own intervened to tutor us in fate's complexities or whether the complexity was speedily taken out of our taxed wits with a curious, brilliant and brutal twist of resolution. Life is full of such constant allegories. For, half an hour later, as we approached Taratalla Bridge a ghastly spectacle met our eyes. I have never forgotten that scene, police whistles shrilling, the bottleneck that had developed on the flyover, the surging crowds, the noise, the shaken, eyewitness narrations, and above it all the wailing siren of an ambulance and cries of pain, death in the air, the confused buzz of voices and vehicles wreaking silence upon our shocked senses.

It was A. Das who spoke first. 'Bhupen, look! It's that Thakur Pukur bus we just missed. Number 69, I distinctly remember. Ah, poor souls!' And his hand went involuntarily to his head in an old-fashioned, instinctive gesture of respect for the dead, the dying and those who would die.

Not that we were superstitious but the day's developments were too concentratedly significant for our threadbare control to endure. We did not actually shake but some sense that was already disarrayed, revolted within us, totally dashed in the face of an ironic enormity.

'It could have been us,' was A. Das's inane afterthought. 'Had we not missed the bus, Ramendram. Oh, God!' He mopped his brow, smiled wearily at us, a smile of pity and terror, of relief and thanksgiving, above all, of a curious new release from complaint or secret inner argument.

Abhijit Das had found a reason, made order out of chaos, I slowly guessed, made his own version of sense of the pattern, made peace with it and accepted its reckless terms.

'Go home now,' said he to us. 'Be grateful you missed that bus today.'

The Second Attack

If you haven't actually watched cancer devour somebody close to you, you know nothing about it. Believe me, it isn't a pretty experience. I know. I watched a mother die of it. And she a woman with such a keen sense of fun.

Carcinoma of the left breast. Something in her body betrayed her, treacherously gave her unknowing consent, and the large sluggish cells began multiplying in their millions. When diagnosed it was already too late. The breast was removed. The wound healed well. There were many visits to the hospital for radiation and chemotherapy. But with awesome inevitability the strings of wicked reddish nodules reappeared like beads upon an evil rosary of death. Don't they say once it's there in your system, nothing, no, nothing can get it out? Metastasis, they call it in medical parlance, or relentless migration, relentless recurrence. This and a second heart attack.

It was then that I saw her performing those many ceremonies of self-immortalizing. She used up all her prized perfumes. (The terrible association of the thought—for later when the stench of her sores grew intolerable we burnt incense round her bed for twelve terrible days! Can you picture it? Funeral, sweetish incense round the bed of a living person?) She wore out all those seldom used silk sarees, sent for the gold ornaments in the locker, dressing up for those radiation therapy sessions at the hospital as one normally would for a festival. She had the backyard cleared and fruit trees planted—guavas and Chinese oranges, lemons, even an apricot and an almond. And when those first awful bunches of hair came off upon the comb, the inescapable side effect of her chemotherapy, she rushed to the photographer and posed for three glamorous portraits, decked out in her best, a fixed, studied smile of cool graciousness upon her face. It was a prolonged gesture of denial and defiance. And it could not last long. Her hair went in exactly four days—all of it.

Then came those terrible black days when she lay in a dirty housecoat, quite bald and absolutely shrill and fretful, disbelieving our cheerful assurances, our wretched baby-talk. Everyone had come to be with her, her brothers, her many children, their spouses and their children. The house was packed to capacity, some of us even spreading our bedrolls on the floor. It might have been a marriage or a thread ceremony or a child's head-shaving feast! There was even room for quips and cracks and solemn games of chess and long speculative political discussions late into the night, for everybody was meeting after a long time. The last wedding was six years back.

Alone in her corner room, attended by two or three people by turns, Mother became a different person. She was no more the good-natured woman we had always known her to be. She uttered bitter, spiteful words. She told her two daughters-in-law how much she detested them. She told me and my brother how casually we had always taken her. And as for my father, she had no words in which to express her abhorrence. Her earlier anxiety lest she should utter damaging words upon the operation table under anaesthesia now changed to imperious contempt. 'Oh, go and wear your hearing aid, Mr Bose!' She dismissed him with a wave of her hand. 'You can neither hear nor understand me. Not that you ever did, of course . . .' She found us all a set of selfish brutes and had so many things to denounce us for, so many accusations to make. The tantrums began at daybreak and continued all day with a brief respite after lunch when, mercifully, she slept. We were at the end of our tether. We had no idea she hated us so much.

It was the same with visitors. Friends and local relatives came to see her and she lashed out at them, raking up old quarrels, pouring scorn over everybody. She seemed to derive a peculiar joy in being perverse. We stood around, our faces crimson, and didn't know what to do. When the visitors left her sickroom, Father apologized, saying that Mother was now no longer herself. Why did she do this to us? It seemed that now that she was more or less certain that the end was near, she felt released from all social discretions, all worldly bargains, equations and observances. She was tasting a new sort of freedom in her self-expression and liking it. It seems to me that our terrible emotions are valuable props and there are circumstances when hate and bitterness serve one's vitality. It now seems to me that she derived a certain strength from them and used them to nourish her will to continue.

One particular day continues to trouble my memory, a month before she went.

She had woken up in a peevish mood, refusing to eat, being difficult and tearful and sarcastic by turns. Several visitors came to call and she excelled herself in general rudeness. With old uncle Pitamber Nath Ghoshal she brought up that twenty-five-year-old matter of the loan of two thousand rupees that he had refused to advance her when her younger sister, our Aunt Mohua, was to be married. With Aunt Shefali she had bitterly recollected the details of the time when the latter had done her little bit in getting my earlier engagement broken. To our neighbours, old Mr Shantanu Dutta and his wife, Mother narrated all the nasty things about her that they had regularly told our common servant. She made it clear that she neither forgave nor forgot. The morning wasn't exactly a social success.

Naturally, therefore, when the doorbell rang yet again late in the afternoon we looked at one another, agitated. Who was it now?

It was my father's friend Bijon 'Jethu', or elder uncle as we say in Bengali, and Aunt Juthi, his wife. Bijon 'Jethu' and his wife used to be frequent visitors at our house when we were kids. We feared the worst. Especially as there had always been an unexpressed dislike between Mother and Aunt Juthi.

To make matters worse, Aunt Juthi had remained youthful and sweet-tempered after all these years, still slender and attractive, tastefully dressed and her hair still raven-black while Mother lay there bloated in her dirty housecoat, bald as a husked coconut. No wonder we were subdued as we led them in. I escaped into the kitchen where my wife was making tea.

When I returned I was surprised to see how smilingly Mother spoke, how she laughed, how she talked of the old days and the fun they'd had at so-and-so's wedding and on such-and-such a puja. Her sharp eyes took in Aunt Juthi's elegant clothes, the bangles on her wrists, her neat, sleek hair, her unwrinkled face and her gentle good-natured responses. Aunt Juthi had brought a box of sondesh for Mother, which, of course, she could not eat. But she laughed and lied: 'Of course I can have them. There's nothing much the matter with me. There's this physical disorder but it has nothing to do with me. I am not ill.'

I laughed uncomfortably. 'We daren't call her ill, Jethu,' said I. 'She isn't ill. Only her body is.' That's the way we put it in colloquial Bengali—'my body is bad'. Not I.

To Uncle Bijon she said not a word. After they left Mother became very silent and very sad.

The next day she called me and said: 'Son, will you do something for me?'

'Of course,' said I.

She hesitated. 'Will you . . . please tell your Bijon Jethu that I'd like him to come and see me again soon.' She looked afraid. 'Don't even tell Maya,' she added. (Maya is my wife.)

I said I'd get in touch with him.

That evening Bijon Jethu came, as reserved and subdued as before. I had an impression that the visit was unpleasant to him, an unavoidable evil.

'You asked me to come?'

'Yes,' said she. 'Yesterday I could not talk to you.'

And then she began talking feverishly. She talked and talked. She talked without logic or continuity. She narrated how her mother-in-law had taken away her gold mango chain. She spoke of her terror of losing me as a child. She related her thwarted hopes of getting a teachers' training certificate. She spoke of acute headaches. She spoke of the time Father retired and we lost the bungalow and the servants, and the vintage car was sold. She described the second heart attack. She seemed to be rendering a comprehensive account of the years, compressing all the backlog of suffering into that feverish trivia.

But Bijon Uncle uttered not a word. And, when I pushed open the door, helping my wife with the tea tray, he had just put his first cold question:

'Why did you ask me to come?'

I retreated discreetly behind a screen.

'I must return something to you,' replied Mother in a small voice, chided by his coldness.

He looked at her questioningly.

'A book in manuscript. Yours. Do you remember that one you wrote? "A Boat Across The Hoogly"?'

Suddenly he gripped the arm of his chair, consternation in his face.

'I do not understand,' he muttered.

'How can you understand?' she mocked indulgently. 'It was the most intelligent deception of my life! Don't you remember? You persuaded the Tollygunge Sanskritic Patrika to serialize it. You never heard from them, did you? I intercepted their acceptance letter. Yes.'

She was smiling in triumphant glee now. 'I went to our little post office and even intercepted the manuscript when you sent it. And that pleading little epistle you wrote them a little later. Postmaster Choudhury's daughter was my friend and I often carried his lunch for him and waited in the office whilst he went to wash his hands and gargle at the tube well in the yard. That's how. You waited, alas, poor Bijon, so pathetic, ah, the failed disappointed poet, ah, the unrecognized genius, upon your terrace. Weeks and months and no reply! Ha, your lovely Bengali calligraphy, poor Bijon! As I waited behind my barred window across the lane . . .'

The light fell upon her face and I saw an expression of unbelievable pathos and rage in her wasted eyes.

'Maybe,' she said insinuatingly, oh, ever so malicious, 'maybe you could have become famous, a writer, a well-known writer like our Sarat Babu or our Bimol Mittro, instead of a petty accountant in an insignificant tea firm, eh Bijon?'

What sophisticated revenge shone in her eyes. Truly, hell hath no fury . . . and this was, Oh God, my old mother!

Then suddenly her face set in a waxen mask and her eyes grew limp, imploring.

'Do you remember those little Calcutta papers, Bijon? And the things we used to scribble and send? You wrote very well, you know. You had what it takes. Do you recollect how you corrected my little verses on champak blossoms and joba flowers? Do you remember that Puja play in which you were Maharaja Harishchandra and I could not read Taramati's lines well enough? Ah, Bijon, do you remember that flock of herons in the paddy field in New Jalpaigudi? And the way the blue mist boiled up from the valley in Darjeeling that summer our theatre group went there? 1949 it was—just after the war. Do you remember the pink plume of cloud upon Kanchenjunga's crest . . . ?'

But Bijon could endure no more of it. Eyes glazed, he sprang to his feet.

'Wait,' she called after him. 'The manuscript. "A Boat Across The Hoogly". It's lying in my old chest of drawers. You don't want it back?' Her voice shook, a little shameful.

'No,' hissed he in a low snarl and made for the door.

After he left Mother lay down very quietly, her face to the wall, and took no notice of us. Only Father looked upset and angry and said: 'Why did you let her babble so much and tire herself out? You should have barged in and told him to leave and let her rest.'

I chose to say nothing to that.

That was my mother and the confusion she wrought in my filial picture of her.

I refuse to call hers a failed life despite the excruciatingly painful death God gave her, despite the great unsuspected disappointment of her life. If success is a positive feeling about things, I always looked on her as one of life's anonymous successes. What else can be said of a woman who admitted to physical breakdown but denied that she herself was ill? And, what better can be said of a woman who even when she lacked money, never called herself poor. In all my life I never knew her to read a line of poetry, real or fake. She loved her little morsel of malice. And, I don't think she ever had a profound thought in her life save the saws of inherited folk wisdom. Her photographs are now upon the wall. And, the fruit trees in the yard are all abloom. What is there to do but nurse her in my mind and the memory of that strange evening? What is there to do now save put her behind me and go on, striving to make sense of what remains of life?

I have now integrated her two big defeats in my understanding in a dim conjecture of what appears to be one of God's many formulae. I step into her garden and intuit its perennial laws. To make a plant grow well you must feed it and sun it and water it. You must encourage it but you must also disappoint it regularly, cutting down its shoots mercilessly after all its laborious growth, denying it judiciously, slashing out the leaves and the hoary old stems so that the energy that sustained them be renewed for other, younger ones of its kind. There are those which are cut down by the wise gardener; there are those which drop off naturally on their own; and there are those which are irreparably ravaged by disease and suffering as they decay. And, new leaves everywhere. Metastasis and metempsychosis—the truth of the garden.

I could make a second-rate poem of it to send to a little Calcutta paper as my mother did in her youth. Now I never will.

Grey Pigeon

Those were the days when a single breadwinner supported a horde of children, a wife or two, some odd brothers and sisters and frequently half a dozen cousins and mates of the village, all on a salary of forty or fifty rupees a month. All were welcome and all were accommodated, for did not milk then sell at a paisa a seer (and that included a crust of cream, one-finger-thick), and silk at a rupee a yard, and a pair of the finest Flex shoes at five rupees a pair? Did I say 'welcome'? Forgive me, in our house there were some that were not. For when Bade Chacha Imam Bux came to stay, quite without notice and for months at a stretch, it was only we children who rejoiced.

An ancient musician was he, stooped, wiry, tapping his stick down the wet alley, shooing away the chickens and the curs. I can still see the discoloured, quilted jacket, out at the elbows, and the gathered trousers, grey with dirt.

My sister, Afeera, nudged me. Together we peeped through the trellis on our mouldy terrace. Afeera's eyes shone. An evening of fun! But I was doubtful, for whatever would our Ammi say?

Ammi had a lot to say. Her eyes snapped dangerously, her two-dozen bangles jingled furiously on her wrists as she rolled out the dough and slapped the muslin-fine bread on to the skillet.

'Now do be silent, mother of Ilyas!' shouted my father. 'He'll be here any minute.'

And no sooner were the words out of his mouth than Bade Chacha seized the heavy doorchain and hammered upon the door. 'Abdul Hamid!' he roared. 'Open up! This fakir is here again!'

Ammi bristled, bent over her wood fire. Fakir, forsooth! She was ready to bet her seven-tola anklets that his crafty eyes never missed a comely wench! 'Afeera!' she hissed, commandingly. 'Stay inside. You're a big girl now.'

But my brother, Ilyas, and I crept into the courtyard where Bade Chacha Imam Bux had made himself comfortable on the divan, drawing up his dirty feet on Ammi's precious coverlet and reclining sideways upon her embroidered bolster. He pinched my cheeks: 'Aha, little two-anna-bit!' cried he, addressing me by his special name. 'And how many teeth have you lost, old-timer? Abdul Hamid, Allah grant you of his bounty, and will it please you to pass me that handsome hookah there. Also that beauteous spittoon and give your Ammi my salaams, and will she send for a clutch of betel leaves?'

He poked Ilyas in the ribs. 'And what has your Ammi made for dinner?' he asked cheerfully. Then he motioned to my agitated father to be seated and, taking off his muslin lace cap, ran a grimy hand through his shoulder-length hair. He took a long pull at the hookah, a man content.

'What does huzoor fancy?' muttered my mother spitefully. 'Lion-meat roasted in saffron or a peacock in almond gravy? Hish!' she sneered, venomously tossing her yard of tinselled veil over her shoulder. 'Lived all his life on a flake of garlic and a bunch of dry loaves like a yokel and comes here demanding a white-sheet feast!' But she sent me for the betel leaves all the same and I ran down the wet lane, clutching the coin in my haste not to miss out on Bade Chacha Imam Bux's oratory.

For Bade Chacha Imam Bux, ne'er-do-well, up-to-no-good, ancient rolling stone, call him what you will, was a prince among storytellers. The pigeons came crooning down under the dark cornices, the sky grew dim, a flimsy rag of shadow lapped and fluttered about the lantern base, and behind a pillar even Ammi flopped down on the last step of the staircase and listened, suppressing a laugh or announcing her scepticism with a snort.

Many were the tales we remembered. There was the eerie adventure, with its numerous artistic variations, upon the dark road that ran from Faizabad to Lucknow and along a cemetery notorious for its vengeful denizens. There was the chilling demon-drama that occurred in the lane-mansion of Ashraf Ali—'the same Ali who went to madrasa with your esteemed father, Abdul Hamid'—in which the intimate proximity of the Evil One and his cohorts made us hold our breaths and steal closer round the lantern. All night long, through the hours of peril, curtains caught fire; filth descended on the courtyard; chandeliers exploded; gilt mirrors fell off their nails and terror reigned until dawn, at the hour of the first tremulous minaret call that went searching the tall sky in quest of God, the holy words scattered the evil spell. The Devil was very close to us these days and Bade Chacha's profound understanding of the dreaded one's ways filled us with deep respect. And so it happened in every tale. Sceptics came, dissenters, heretics, and questioned the Evil One and the Evil One responded with resounding smacks, with clods of excrement and the women fainted. Only the renowned Pir of Rehanabad, he that spent his leisure hours, a-twirling in incommunicable ecstasy, did the Evil One hold in some respect, and thus did the holy man arrive, with many tangled incantations, and amulets and exorcisms and seven nails were driven into the musty walls and joss sticks lit to sweeten the soul and the Evil One questioned, gently at first, then with ringing authority, upon the nature of his grievances.

But this evening Bade Chacha seemed to have lost his flair both for the sensational and the supernatural.

'Oh, to have fallen on evil days, Abdul Hamid,' he sighed in uncharacteristic melancholy, thoughtfully seized a leg of chicken and tore at it with his scanty teeth, meditating on the trials of fate. A trickle of gravy crept down his chin and he mopped it with his sleeve.

'My father was Quanungo. From Patwari to Quanungo, from Quanungo to Naib Tehsildar, fate took him, so sweet was his flattery and so winsome his wit. And his father?' He looked down gravely at my brother, Ilyas, who hung upon his words. 'His father was dewan to the Emperor Aurangzeb.'

I heard my mother mutter something behind her pillar and Afeera tittered, but we? We believed all, my brother and I, so willing was the suspension of our disbelief; we'd have believed him had he told us that his great-great-great-grandfather had been dewan to Allah himself!

'I, misguided wretch, sought to be a musician,' said Bade Chacha. 'Fourteen years I offered up, practising those tangle-throated tricks. The tremolo that is like an echo revolving in a brass bell. The cadence that is like a note swooning down a veena string. And the regurgitating cascade that is like water emptying out of a broad-mouthed earthen pitcher. Ragas of the morning, ragas of the evening and of the deepest night. The difference between the "re" of Marwah and the "re" of Poorvi. I was, I do not blush to say, Abdul Hamid, a local celebrity, a prodigy of unparalleled versatility. Thumri, ghazal, dhrupad, khayal, all were my province! And truly, my teacher's teacher, the illustrious Barkat Ali Sanvaliya, was descended from a long line of maestros, yes, from the durbar of the ill-fated Muhammad Shah Rangila himself. Now when the invader Nadir Shah sacked Delhi and withdrew, our sad king, the colourful, music-loving one, our Muhammad Shah, grew disenchanted. Wherefore this music, asked he, wherefore this art? Never more shall the strings sound and the drums beat in these portals. And, he sent away all the songstresses, the flute players and the fiddlers. Then it was that the two old masters, Mian Jani and the shining Ghulam Rasool, sought refuge at the court of Asaf-ud-Daula of Lucknow. Well, we soft-souled ones, we musicians, you know how tender is our temperament and how quick our ire. Ghulam Rasool left Asaf-ud-Daula's court, slighted, I never learnt why. To cut a long story short, his pupil, my master's master, Barkat Ali Sanvaliya, became durbar musician to Nawab Hashmat Jung, the "Baawan-hazari", the fifty-two thousand one, and the Farrukhabad gharana was born. And what a patron he had, Abdul Hamid! One of his servants, a Maghru Khan, sang Raga Des as only Allah's minstrels can.

'My own master, Barkat Ali Sanvaliya, was presented with a baby elephant and a golden shawl by the nawab. Alas for him, a grey beard will not teach one anything. One cold night, returning from the nawab's court and beholding the famous tawaif, Munna Jaan, warming her hands over a wood fire, our master gallantly offered her the shawl. Words passed, I know not what, and the shameless hussy angrily cast the precious shawl into the fire, crying, "There, that much for your fine words!" That was the year when the first railway line from Farrukhabad to Kanpur was opened.

'Another one of my teachers, Nabi Bux, received five thousand dhrupads as his holy wife's dower, secret notations of sound and style, family formulae preserved for nigh three centuries and more precious than all the gold in Hindostan to the music-loving one's eye. Twenty children the couple begot, each one a musical prodigy. Then, true to the law laid down in the Book, nikaah was read out and the old couple united in matrimony anew, and lo! two more children followed, twins, then the good lady died and Nabi Bux composed the most memorable mausoleum in sound to her memory, which did perish with him for no son of his approved of it on grounds of classic purity though all who heard it felt it clutch the heart in the simplicity of final woe; yet the maestros reluctantly agreed that certain combinations in it were just not permissible, and a debate did divide the sons for two decades and more.

'I was born during the great famine, they say. That year Mallika Victoria died and a song went round our lanes—"Ah, the Mallika is gone, alas for us, our shops are closed."

'I was born with doom writ in these palms, you see. Music, Abdul Hamid, has proved my undoing. It took me to seek my fortune at the durbar of the nawab of Santoor. Truly a man of feeble wit. Fourteenth scion of a noble line, titular head of a tiny state, a one-cannon, four-elephant state, a kerchief-breadth of barren land. A man who saw phantoms everywhere, tossed and puffed upon his brocade bed all night, wrestling with direful anxieties even as Yaakoob in the Holy Book wrestled with the Unknown Stranger. But the begum was a veritable queen; she revealed her proud blue Persian blood in every measured utterance and every chiselled movement.

'The nawab affected to like music. He preferred the coquetry, the teasing flirtation, the sweet, strong passion of thumris. Songs of the rain, songs of the swing, songs for the wearing of bangles, yearning love songs, wedding ditties, songs of complaint and accusation. The begum, alone in her villa, listened to pure, speech-less music, long, melancholy meanderings of mood, subdued and reflective. One evening as I let my voice loose in a cascading welter of trills she interrupted me. "Maestro," said she through her veil, "give me something quieter." I bowed my head. I thought a while. Then I began a smoky Aheer-bhairava.

'Ah, the ultimate loneliness of Aheer-bhairava, Abdul Hamid. The notes lit up slowly like lamps in the dark. Each note flickered like a flame blown upon. Then it moved away, lone, silver-chill, into stellar dimness. She sat very still. I knew everything, or so I thought, about the misty terrain of this raga, how to shade a note, inflect it and hold it steady; mute it, and, placing it effortlessly upon the air, argue beyond it, impelled by its own classic logic, how to set each note with infinite perfection, symmetry and finish.

'Thus I ended, extinguishing each exquisite phrase slowly. Never had I sung thus. "Now you, sir," said she, turning to my old master.

'Now old Sajjad Ali's voice was long past its prime. He opened wide his jaws. He made monstrous faces. He emitted raucous, cackling trills. He slapped his thigh. He flung one trembling hand into the air, drawing it this way and that as though 'twer a kite at the end of a string. He clapped the other hand to his ear.

'My face went red. What shame! What was wrong with the old man? He was trying so hard to outdo me. I never realized he was so bad. And he had taught me all I knew. I sat embarrassed. The ladies covered their mouths with their dupattas, yawning genteelly. But the begum sat listening intensely with her deep, grieving eyes. I could not understand her concentration. What was the old man uttering and what did she understand? It has taken me thirty years to grasp that, Abdul Hamid. She presented Sajjad Ali with a ring. She gave me nothing, not a word of praise. I burned in indignation.

'She must be dead. A very strange woman. She detested her husband though once, it was rumoured, she had poisoned one of his courtesans. She cared not a whit but when he came she bowed low and touched her fingertips to her brow and offered her salutations in reverence or irony or both. It was good to hear the sharp thrust and parry of their repartee. Tablas, veenas, fiddles stopped, fan-women stood, transfixed. (Here Bade Chacha flung himself into mimicry. He enacted it all, the low bow, the sitting down with billowing trousers daintily gathered on the ottoman, the offering of paan.) "It is my good fortune that sire has crossed my humble threshold."

'"The good fortune is mine, Begum."

'"Your lordship has become for us as rare as the moon of Id."

'"I can no longer ride across as I was wont to do, Begum. That fall from the mare cost me four ribs and the ache never did repair."

'"A paltry loss, sire. Allah shall fashion of each rib a fair maiden for sire's paradise."

'"You jest, Begum. They say Mother Eve spent her leisure counting Father Adam's ribs to ensure that no new maiden trespassed into Eden. Mean you to do the same?"

'"Allah preserve us all, sire, finding a single rib in your gracious person would then be like seeking a pearl in the waters of the Jordan."

'The nawab probably swore—"Perdition take the woman!"—but on the face of it he smiled. "God be praised, Begum, but your tongue is like the magic staff of Haroon, a fragrant flowering shrub one moment and a lashing serpent the next." Oh, she could reduce him to nought, he with his timid, dissipated face, his endless poor lusts, his elaborate forked moth-eaten beard. Oh, she knew how to use her

voice and her face, to narrow her eyes or leave them veiled; she knew
how to lift her haughty brows in disdain, to make the rage stand tall
in her eyes and a fierce, black flame shake in the depths of the pupils;
and she knew how to avert her face towards the filigreed screen, her
lips atremble, her fine eyes fuming over, and ere the instant passed,
they were veiled again and she played with the long, dangling emerald
in her earlobe. A most mobile and splendid face, a noble work of
great perfection though all her beauty was over. And she knew how
to clinch an argument and bring the blush to the nawab's florid cheek
with a choice quatrain or a couplet like, "Grey pigeon, for thee the
still minaret, for thee the lonely sky. Leave to the bright bulbul the
amorous flowers of paradise."

'Alone in his chamber with his minions he flew into his famous
rages and declaimed upon his authority, his royal lineage, his prowess
in love and in war. See, we whispered, the sun has set on them, these
little three-copper-sovereigns. Now even the khidmatgars do not bow
quite so low when, earlier, a mere frown could set them ashiver like
the twin minarets of Siddee Bashir.

'Do you know the ravenous rage of a king who is losing his
kingdom, be it ever so petty? Or the power and the poison of a
woman who has lost her beauty? Or the acrid lasciviousness of a man
who has lost his manhood? For true, it was whispered, he was now
no more a man, yet he did seek out the youngest, most delectable of
maids, so subtle and strong was his lust, so deep his insight into the
secrets and nuances of love. Such is the drama of decline and loss,
Abdul Hamid, for can anything be more wondrous-strange than
that which is laboured over with love and with art, that which is so
fine and important, that which is cherished, polished and perfected,
should perish without fail? And the mad pir, he that was ever loudly
mediating betwixt God and the Devil, sang riotously beneath the
banyan tree: "Dry, dry, dry, dry the well, hush! The empty pot doth
hang upon its noose. And why did he fill a carcass with wine? To cool
the street, ha?" And he roared gleefully and brought up the refrain:
"He laughs, he laughs, he laughs, he laughs!" And no one dared ask

him who laughed, God or the Devil or himself or all three, for he
flung his wild locks back and piercingly demanded: "Tell me, doth
the enchantment lie in the bottle? Why then doth not the bottle
swagger and sing?"

'You want to know what happened? Can anything more
remarkable have happened to me than that everyone I grew up with
is dead? The nawab listened to his thumris. His beard grew darker
with more henna, his brow more creased. He lost to those comic,
pink-faced sahibs. He found new dancers. There was music for every
season, for springtime, for the season of falling leaves, music for the
day of lamentation when the procession sallied forth and men smote
their breast and walked the fire and wept and wept in an ecstasy of
grief. O Hazrat Ali, O noble martyred one, O brave, loyal ones, alas,
cheated of all, duped, done to death, treacherously, treacherously,
killed, killed! I was the one who composed the saddest songs, who
wept the most burning tears. It was a skill, God-given. Sorrow was
with me an art par excellence, elegant, acclaimed, a lavish abstraction.
Ah, woe, woe!—wept the men. Alas, alas!—groaned the women.
Now with age I have lost that joy in weeping. Sorrow is but sorrow,
without exaltation, without cure. The nawab in his balcony sat
moist-eyed, till the season of mourning was over. One day he died
and we musicians dispersed.

'Ah, Abdul Hamid, an old man carries many aches. Many were
the gold mohurs I won from rai-bahadurs, khan-sahibs, khan-
bahadurs, nawabs even. Courtesans came to me to be tutored in
singing. Nobody wants a musician of that kind now, for an age has
just died, don't you know? I am my own audience now. When I sing,
each note thrills me and with a shock I realize that it has achieved
its ultimate shine. It dangles, polished, like a gold mohur I give to
myself. Sometimes Rahmatullah, my young nephew, begins laughing.
"Bade Mian, your voice is cracked like a split bamboo and can barely
hold a tune!" he scoffs.'

Nobody asked him to sing but Bade Chacha Imam Bux closed
his eyes and sang. A raga, so the classics say, that mourns for a wife of

many years. He croaked horribly. At high notes his voice squeaked. Even our Afeera sings better. Ilyas and I counted his dirty teeth. At last he stopped. llyas nudged him impatiently. 'But where was the Evil One, Bade Chacha?' And the *pir* with the incantations and amulets and cures?'

'Only a maulvi can tell, child,' sighed Bade Chacha. 'Perhaps not even he.' He raised a feeble hand to his throat. 'My Evil One lurks here,' said he. 'I once heard the maestro Faiyaz Khan say, 'When one's art has attained exquisite youth, one's voice is reduced to a wretched ruin because seldom the twain do meet.''

Major Event

For the first time in years, Vasant Panchami had fallen not only on 31 January but on a Tuesday as well, announced Badal Kaka. We all roared and thumped Grandfather on the back. And when Grandmother opened her mouth to speak, Shubho popped a sondesh into her mouth.

'Fifty years of marriage, Grandfather, and to such a spitfire, heavens!' gasped Probhat Kaka, putting an arm affectionately around Grandmother's shoulders.

'But I dealt with her, ah yes,' chuckled the deaf old man, shouting fit to raise the dead.

'So we perceive, Baba,' said Bimol Kaka with a wicked grin and a wink at all of us. 'There's the eight of us standing evidence of how well you dealt with her.'

'Hush, you rascal,' hissed Aunt Bithika, pulling Bimol's ear. 'Take no notice of this young scapegrace, Baba. Times are different now.'

'No different!' roared Grandfather, mishearing again. 'It was Saraswati puja day and no different.'

In those days we lived in a distant suburb of Calcutta which lay within the 24 Parganas. The vast city hummed in the background but where we lived the sea breeze came thrashing in, bending the palm trees low. All the shadows which stood still in the green ponds went sliding across the mirror-dark water. And in the twisting lanes a dark young woman went balancing her pitcher with a plaintive melody of Bengal on her lips:

Tree-like I catch my fingers in your clouds.
Undo these bones, unfasten these thoughts,
For my heart is full; ah, do not touch me, lord,
Lest a shock of tears shakes out of me . . .

The areca nut trees thrummed their dry green leaves like taut, vibrating strings under the chilly wash of wind.

Do you know what Saraswati puja day meant to us in those days? We awoke and saw the pale fumes of light collected in a corner of the sky. For half an hour the day seemed dazed by that dazzling fuzz of light and the morning was a shimmering fabric blown across the land. Then a sharp, crisp sunlight came and thawed the masses of cloud. Out in the open in the little tents, the slim white goddess sat on her swan, her long fingers curled upon a celestial raga. Little girls and boys, clad in yellow, learnt their first alphabets at the feet of the goddess and the bare-chested old priest lifted aloft the bowl of smoking incense. On such a day there was music everywhere.

And on that Saraswati puja day the eight sons and daughters, the sons-in-law and daughters-in-law and we nineteen grandchildren assembled to celebrate the golden jubilee of our grandparents' marriage. Nobody enjoyed the pantomime more than the old couple themselves. Grandfather sat on the old canopied four-poster dressed in his crinkled white dhoti and white Panjabi with gold studs, eating sweet rice paste. And Aunt Bithika draped her rich Benarasi silk round Grandmother's portly form, laughing at her protests. The treasure box was unlocked, the gold peacock pendant hung round Grandmother's neck and the heavy bangles forced on to her dried-up wrists. Then young Mita ran and fetched the blue gauze veil from her dance costume, never mind if it did not match. And Aunt Minoti rubbed sandal paste and drew a pretty ceremonial pattern on Grandmother's creased forehead. Grandmother scolded and laughed in confusion, hustled about by the crowd of rollicking youngsters. Nobody listened to her. But Grandfather sat with a twinkle in his eye, his hearing aid plugged into his ear. Only the headgear was missing. And Probhat Kaka ran and got down the dusty white, conical topor and matching coronet from the kitchen loft, left over from Bithika's wedding.

'A little crooked, but it'll do,' he said, blowing on it as he placed it carefully on Grandfather's bald head. A roar of cheers and laughter went up. Somebody produced a marigold garland. Somebody thrust a box of sacred vermilion powder into Grandmother's hands. Somebody blew on the conch and in unison, rolling their tongues in their mouths, the women burst into the shrill *uloodhvani*, laughing. Sondesh was passed round and even the two dogs got one each. 'Camera!' shouted Badal and old Mr Roy, our neighbour, appeared with the battered box camera.

'Not so far apart!' he shouted. 'A little closer, a little coy, now smile.'

And the old man put his arm around Grandmother's shoulders.

'That's the spirit!' cried young Mita, clapping. 'Now another one.'

Little Sumana wanted to sit in the middle, near Grandfather.

'Hush, child, people will get confused as to who the real bride is. They'll think Sumana has married an ugly old man.'

'Ho, Grandmother, don't let him hear you!'

She smiled, her mottled face puckering up in impish glee. 'He can't. That's the fun of having a stone-deaf husband.'

'Speech! Speech!'

By a miracle the old man heard. 'Why do you shout, young fools? Nineteen twenty-two!' he roared. 'I drew my salary from the British exchequer.' He glared round importantly.

'Stop him,' someone groaned, 'before he launches into Burke's speech at the trial of Warren Hastings again.'

'Our Collector sahib said at a wedding, "Marriages are made in heaven."'

'And broken on earth, Baba?' piped up Mithu. The aunts shushed him and he subsided.

'Marriages,' continued the old man pompously, 'are made in heaven.' We asked our Collector sahib, "What, sir, is the secret of your happy marriage?" "Listen, gentlemen," he replied. "I shall let you in on a secret. On our wedding day we decided, memsahib and I, that all major events were to be in my charge and all minor events in her charge. The secret, gentlemen, is that not a single major event has occurred in our life!'"

A commotion of merriment filled the room. 'In my own case I have been, alas, in the same unenviable situation as our revered Collector sahib. Not a single major event has occurred in my life.'

Shibu Kaka rolled his eyes at his brothers. 'Well, here we are anyway, Baba, your eight minor events!' And everyone rocked with laughter, Grandmother loudest.

'Marriage,' said the old man, 'is the everlasting companionship, the imperishable tie. Whom God hath joined together none can draw asunder.'

'Oh, oh . . .' said someone faintly.

Grandfather went off into a long rambling Sanskrit passage. 'Amid the most transient things,' he translated, 'a happy marriage is proof of the permanent. On this day we thank you, my wife and I, for being present and celebrating this day with us. Thank you.' And he looked grave and sombre, quite edified by his speech.

That Saraswati puja day is vivid in my mind. Its pellucid laughter throws into bold relief the stark drama of the following day.

In the grey light of dawn Aunt Bithika went slowly up the dark staircase with a mug of tea and softly pushed open Grandfather's door.

'Your tea, Baba.' The old man slept with his back to the door. By his pillow lay his string of prayer beads and a closed book. 'Baba,' called Aunt Bithika and then a strange terror leapt into her voice. She swiftly crossed the room. The old man lay with his eyes wide open, staring in amazement at the far corner of the room.

She shook him and shook him, then ran calling, 'Badal, Badal!' down the stairs. Her husband stirred in his bed. 'Badal, come! Baba!' She burst into the room.

They stood by the old man and Badal closed the eyes with trembling hands. 'All that excitement yesterday . . .' he murmured. He looked up at his wife. 'Let us wake them up . . . tell them Baba's major event has occurred at last . . .'

'Oh, Badal . . . Ma! How shall we tell her?' And they thought of Grandmother asleep peacefully downstairs, an arm round the youngest grandchild, rising and falling gently with the child's living breath.

Bithika looked at her husband and clutched him by the shoulders as though assuring herself that he was there with her. And as they gazed at the old man, then at one another, the first terrible tears began shining in their eyes.

Coming of Age

The seventeenth of March promised to be more of a homecoming feast for his mother and a requiem service for his father than a birthday celebration for him, Edwin reflected. It was to be a grand symbolic event in the history of their family.

The Watkinses had been a more or less nomadic family for well over two decades now, building provisional homes in sundry small and large places across the length and breadth of northern India, from Cossimbazar in the east to Rawal Pindee in the west. When the late Colonel Vernon Agnew Watkins was alive it was places as diverse as Umbala and Meerut, Cawnpore and Allahabad, Dehra Doon and Sialkote, Jubbalpore and Fyzabad. After his death the memsahib, her two daughters and son drifted from one place to another in the north-west, Punjaub, Oude and Behar, sometimes staying with friends, sometimes setting up residence on their own. The memsahib dabbled in missionary activity for a while in the hamlets of Jounpore, Azimghur and Goruckpore, distributing Bibles, tending the old and the sick; but her efforts at converting the heathen, though conducted in a spirit of the utmost sympathy and well-directed industry, accorded ill with her general disposition and it was not long before it was amply clear to her that to be an ambassadoress of Christ was not her natural *métier* in life. Thereafter she took up schoolteaching and holding piano classes for young ladies of genteel families and finally—and most lamentably—going into the millinery business.

This loathsome party was to be his mother's greeting to Calcutta and her farewell to hard times. Now that he was shortly to come of age and the solicitors in London had released the papers, the memsahib looked forward to moving in superior circles again. If his mother's protracted planning was anything to go by, it was to be a sweet, uplifting, cheerful-tearful occasion for family and guests alike.

The Colonel Memsahib, as she was known to the native bearers, had spent twenty years in genteel deprivation, living on her late husband's military pension and her own meagre earnings, concealing her reduced means behind a mask of cool Christian austerity with the demeanour of one who espouses want rather from choice than from misfortune. But the great occasion to come was evidently designed to give free expression to any dormant cravings for pomp and splendour which may have lurked in her gentle bosom. Left to himself, Edwin would much rather have beguiled the day alone with Mr Dutt, talking poetry and philosophy and world affairs and matters fantastical and no fuss at all. But Colonel Memsahib and the two girls gave vent to such an outcry at this mild suggestion that he let the matter go.

'Fancy!' cried Rosalie pettishly. 'Our only big party and he says he'd rather not! And I've told the Parker girls all about it and the Kelly girls and the Rickettses. And I've lunched with them all and they'll soon be off to Simla and I may never set eyes on Major Norton again. And whatever for have I been practising my music till my fingers and thumbs were ready to drop off?' she demanded plaintively.

'Rosa, Rosa,' murmured Colonel Memsahib reprovingly. 'Pray do not pout and frown so. And recollect—a lady doesn't ever allude to a gentleman—be he ever so much her senior—as though she cherished—er—expectations from him.'

'I beg your pardon, Mama!' shrilled Rosa tartly. 'Whatever do you mean? I have the impression—if you'll forgive my saying so—that the expectations have been entirely on your side . . .'

What a cosy family, reflected Edwin, and how delightfully chummy!

Shortly after her arrival in Calcutta the Colonel Memsahib had let herself go, stinting herself nothing. She rented a bungalow on Bentinck Street, Bungalow No. 11, lately occupied by Major Burney and consisting of six rooms and two bathrooms at the handsome rent of fifty rupees a month. She purchased, after much deliberation, a very handsome park phaeton with moveable coach-box, beautiful English lamps, cushions and rugs, polished steel driving rail, pole, bar, shafts, and, to complete the outfit, a very presentable grey mare of about fifteen hands, advertised as 'quiet to ride or drive, guaranteed sound and hard-working and about nine years old'. All for the colossal sum of eight hundred rupees. Oak wood chests, bedsteads, teak bureaux and dressers, settees, rocking chairs with embroidered antimacassars. A complete service of plates, a selection of the latest books and music, furnishings and drapes, punkah-protectors, fire screens and paper shades, pots of geranium, verbena, fuchsias and violets and, as final necessities for social acceptance, a handsome chandelier by Defries of London, fitted with three plated Argand lamps, and a Brodwood's grand, square piano, almost new, with tuning fork, hammer and tin-lined case. From a Signor S. Barsottelli she purchased a very choice collection of classical alabaster table ornaments, mosaic tables, marble vases and diverse fancy articles. Into her and the young ladies' wardrobes went a quantity of grenadine, muslin, organdie-trimmed muslin garibaldis, Alexander sashes, lace Berthes, cambric and lace, handkerchiefs, collars, cuffs, bonnets, shawls, wooden bustles, whalebone stays, velvet knots with fancy combs, ribbons of different widths and colours, corsets, feather fans, steel skirts, hair pads and nets, parasols, hats, stockings and fancy boots. Into her sideboard went a dozen each of table forks and spoons, dessert forks, teaspoons, gravy spoons, fruit knives, fish knives, soup ladles, milk ladles, a pair of muffineers, decanter stands, knife rests, wine glasses, tumbler covers, butter pot, jugs, sugar urns, coffee mill, salting machine, ice machine. Upon her shelves went an array of the newest novels—*Beatrice* by Julia Kavangah, *Luttrell of Arran* by Charles Lever, *Mercedes* by Sir C.F. Wraxall, *Bart* (in three volumes), the fashionable *Behind the Curtains* (in three volumes). It was absolutely *de riguer* to have also some illustrated books for dismal evenings, hence there was *Hyperion,* with twenty-four photographs of the Rhine, Switzerland and the Tyrol; *The Lake Country* with hundred illustrations; *The Stones of Palestine—Notes of a Ramble through the Holy Land* by Mrs Mentor Mott; and finally *The Life and Lessons of Our Lord,* unfolded and illustrated by the Reverend John Cumming. Upon the music rack went *The Standard Song Book* and *The Great Comic Volume of Songs, Moore's Melodies* and her old collection of Schumann, Schubert and Chopin. Into her cellar went the best brandy, port, sherry, champagne, moselle, claret, hock, gin, porter, noyau and beer.

It is but just to suppose that consequent upon her stupendous refurbishments, the memsahib felt amply equipped for civilized and gracious company, the joys of human friendship with equals, the niceties of culture, high thinking and living. It was a pity, though, that culture relied so heavily on the purse and the esteem of equals depended greatly upon appearances; nevertheless the memsahib now deemed it opportune to front her old circle again in a spirit of graceful elegance.

There were the girls' prospects to consider too. There was such a surfeit of eligible bachelors now in Calcutta. Even her own excessive adherence to form and her often unreachable standards of breeding and family could not fault some of the aspirants. But what with the closure of the Company and the recent takeover by the Crown, there was a collateral influx of fresh young adventuresses from home to outweigh the advantages of having so many new ranks of young officers and civil servants. Now was the time to cast herself in a role that ill-beseemed her—that of an astute lady mother. The party would have to be on a large scale.

But the Colonel Memsahib had, in her own way, bestowed a touch of soul to the proceedings. For the lady had long learnt the fine art of commingling the banal and the beauteous in her two decades of strife to maintain a semblance of aristocracy in her straitened circumstances. It had to be conceded that she did it exceedingly well. The memsahib had retained her lavender-fragrant presence, like an angel from heaven drifting about on an earthly mission of cleaning house, doing the flowers, giving music lessons and administering quinine to the servants with a gracious head perpetually bowed, if not in true subservience, at least in a token modesty which added a pleasing piece of artistry to her well-modulated person. Given to many excessive notions of form and propriety, situation and style, the gentle lady was a law unto herself and already something of an oddity in the city with her many little dated insistences and observances. To the two girls' little perplexities, to Edwin's unsure, protesting self, the Colonel Memsahib had adopted a habitual air of gentle remonstrance and patient admonition. Speaking in a low, tuneful sing-song with a mock-rational tone of balancing alternative propositions of unknown absurdities which it was her sad lot in life to quell, swaying her head from side to side, a vague, abstracted expression upon her face. Thus did her cultivated voice ascend and descend the complete musical scale from reprimand to reassurance, from reasoning to persuasion to command. Some day when the girls found husbands and Edwin a calling, she would be free in a lucid world of reason and music and crystalline propriety of word and gesture and act and that was the Colonel Memsahib's dream.

Edwin had only the vaguest inkling of the stupendous spiritual scale on which the evening was being planned. There was to be plenty of music. Valerie and Rosalie were at the newly purchased piano all day, one hammering insensitively away in thunderous passion, the other stroking the keys in an excess of syrupy sentiment until all his nerves were on edge. There were to be readings from the Bible by Father Basil and a brief, presumably ennobling sermon. There was to be the cutting of the cake and the toasts and then he, Edwin, was to be ceremonially presented with his father's watch and gun which had lain awaiting this day for many years. The watch was a fine gold, engine-turned hunting piece by Barraud and Lund with a gold Albert chain and key and a gold guard chain to match. The gun was a highly finished single rifle by Henry of Edinburgh, bore 451, length of barrel thirty-one inches, in a fine case complete with Vernier match and a Rob Roy ammunition box. There was also a letter from the late Colonel, sealed with his ring and addressed in his unpolished, soldierly hand, which had rested these many years embalmed in a locker. Upon receipt of these ritual gifts, he, Edwin, was duly to retire into the morning room to unseal and read the letter. The guests were meanwhile to regale themselves with a fulsome repast followed by convivial conversation, songs and dancing—this last in view of the girls' prospects—after which Edwin, duly overwhelmed and uplifted, was expected to make an entry and utter a few charged words which would bring tears to many an eye. More dancing, more singing, more conversation and the guests were to leave in a mist of heartwarming emotion, gladdened and grateful to remember an exalting evening for evermore.

'We must have Christina and Lavinia Dithers,' said the Colonel Memsahib drawing up the invitation list. 'And Mr and Mrs Courteney Rawlinson-Smith. The Pages, the Parkers, the Lawrences, the Philipses, the Hamiltons. Young Master Jacob, Major Norton, Majors Burnett and Hyde, Brigadier Daniels, Mr Morris and his friends at the Saturday Club . . .'

'And Uncle Chris and Aunt Lucille,' prompted Valerie. 'And Father Basil, of course.'

'I'd like to ask Edwin if there's anyone he'd care to ask?' murmured Colonel Memsahib, more in a correct observance of domestic courtesy than any serious expectation of dissent from his quarter.

'Edwin, my love, is there anyone you'd like to call?'

Edwin shrugged. 'If you really wish to know, Mama, there's my friend, the poet, Mr Michael Madhusudan Dutt.'

'Oh dear!' sighed the memsahib.

'A local Bengalee!' cried Rosa.

'Edwin, dear, do be sensible. Your Mr Dutt, I grant, may be a very fine man but shall he be comfortable here?'

'Mr Dutt writes English poetry, Mama,' said Edwin stubbornly as though that fact alone were sufficient to waive aside all social unease. 'His poem was noticed by the *Athenaeum* which said that he was akin to Scott or Byron. And he's the best neo-Milton this side of England. His "Captive Ladie" is like a piece of medieval minstrelry.'

'Dear me,' said Father Basil, unimpressed. 'What did you say his name was?'

'Michael Madhusudan Dutt.'

'Michael-eh? The devil's own name,' muttered Father Basil. 'And Madhusoodun—that's no Christian name.'

'I suppose we'll have to call him if dear Edwin insists,' sighed Colonel Memsahib. 'And is there no one else?'

'No one else,' said Edwin shortly.

'That's the one that made the native Bengalee boys chant verses from the *Iliad* and the *Odyssey* in their heathen temples?' ventured Father Basil conversationally. 'And all that to-do about ham and beef?'

But Edwin was in ill humour. 'That,' rejoined he curtly, 'was Derozio. Dead.'

There was a long uncomfortable silence.

Edwin had not seen his father, the Colonel, that hero of Sind, that military legend, the Colonel Sahib having died soon after Sind. But nowhere in the memsahib's allusions to him was the past tense ever used. The Colonel Sahib might have been out on campaign down south or up north-west. Or else he might have stepped out of a pleasant morning to the Golf Links or the polo ground or the club. The Colonel Sahib's opinions still guided all moral questions in the household. His axioms were law and his decrees unconditionally binding. The memsahib, it was clear, was merely biding her time while her lord and master was out of town, soon to return and handle things as of yore. Meanwhile, she wanted him to recognize, when next they met, the worth of her contribution to the home. Edwin retained no recollection of his celebrity father but had constructed his own version of his grandeur. He saw, in his mind's eye, a short, sprightly, bewhiskered being with a scrubbed and freshly laundered look about him, a man who seemed to sparkle in every fibre of his person—his glasses, his cuff links, his gold collar stud, his buttons and medals and decorations, his pen and watch and buckle, his diamond-hard eyes, grey and cold, like a Scottish loch in mid-winter, his crisp, blond hair, his robust cheeks and smooth, ironic brow. There was invincibility in the man and all the radiance of mythology—a man who seemed to go about on padded feet, specializing in stillness and the sudden spring. That was his style—in repartee, in wit, in battle and in love. Whether Edwin's personal picture of his father corresponded to his historic progenitor, Edwin had no means of confirming. Father was everywhere, like God, and no family occasion could dream of excluding him. Father was the ultimate arbiter, the final court of appeal, the maker of family norms and forms, relayed through the utterances of their mother. And that letter in the locker awaiting his attention was his recognizable voice, heroic and ineradicable in their midst, conferring solemnity on the occasion and a higher continuity to their small personal histories. The high moment of the evening was naturally the presentation of the letter and the rest of the evening had to be worthy of that instant. Thinking of it, Edwin felt a shiver of suspense and emotion as though an invaluable key to an emotional mystery was to be handed him.

So it was that the parlour was painted and the carpets sent for cleaning. Dust sheets removed, the furniture polished till it shone. The giant cake, ordered at Goolam's, a massive eight-pounder with twenty-one ornate keys iced upon it, and candles, buntings, streamers aplenty. The durzee was in all day, sitting cross-legged on the mat, busy with bales of mull and organdie and light summer-worthy silks, sashes and tuckers and frills. His own camel-hued suit of Russia Duck was ordered at Wazirully's.

From old habit, Edwin surrendered, living as he did in mortal dread of his two sisters. For years he had maintained a constant critical watch on all their little pretences and airs and graces, their polite jealousies and rivalries, their genteel gibes, their mutual hatreds and false amities.

Valerie was the family saint, a self-absorbed saint of trance-like passivity, eyes lifted and all conscious expressions operating upon a high plane of sublimity. Edwin could never resolve in his mind whether Val was a very fine being indeed or just a wonderfully gifted humbug. Everything she spoke or did was sweet and equivocal. She had sad eyes which she continually put to good use, but burning, suppressed, furtive eyes too which had been trained to look soulful while they took note of everything. She had a face like a jaded madonna's, with hollow cheeks, lank chestnut hair and a too-thin form. Of it all she made ingenious use, maintaining a certain cultivated silence and promise of depth and mystery as her most attractive feature.

Against Rosalie's rash, buoyant charm Val advanced her patient humility. Against her quick, sharp wit, she matched her mock-refined, non-committal reserve. Nobody knew what Val ever really thought but Edwin suspected that an elaborate little manufactory of schemes and subterfuges, submissions and strategies was active within her, carefully rehearsing while she sat with pliant, pensive mien at the piano, ostensibly carried away upon a flood of soul-stirring music.

Rosalie was flighty but very consciously so, specializing in a certain charming indiscretion, a flair for the rash and the unreasoned remark, the sudden, dimpled smile, the innocently hurtful, the naïve apologetic little schoolgirl memsahib who said all the wrong things of sheer unworldliness. For ten years the family had been obligingly laughing at Rosa's quips—she expected it of them. She was confirmed in the role of the talkative and bantering naughty little missybaba with the ringlets and bangs, the small ankles and waist and the ever-jingling earrings.

'Have I said the wrong thing, Aunty Lucille? I mean, your silver locks do really become you and go with this silver-grey gown so elegantly. It wasn't so good some years back when the colours of the gown and the locks of hair were both stronger. Oh, oh, don't look like that. What have I said, oh dear me?'

'You mean it well, I'm sure. Now go, there's a dear.' And Rosa, eyes wide in innocent astonishment and contrition, all ablush in shy, endearing confusion. 'That young lady,' one almost heard the late Colonel's voice, 'deserves a good wallopin o'er her britches!'

And Valerie, the great actress, all the while marvelling at her baby sister's wit and charm. And with an insidious simultaneity enacting her own perfect little tableau of superior modesty, demure reserve and cultured humility. She, the shrinking, sensitive soul, the flower wasting its sweetness on the desert air, throwing into sharp relief all Rosalie's brash, graceless speech, her rough, flaunting ways, her loud laughter, her squeals and her swagger. What a sweet, vulnerable maid, thought Edwin dourly. Practising to perfection the fine art of ingratiation. There were two kinds of memsahibs, reflected Edwin. There was the loud, indomitable one, shrill and authoritative, ready to expound a point, ready to grab everyone's opinion as her own, ready to tell you what to do and how to do it. That would be Rosa in twenty years. There was the other type. Vague, wandering, evasive, with a feeble sort of sincerity and a wavering goodwill; a woman who fades gently away, degenerates, and whose opinions become more and more complicated and unsure. She has a sad, unstated accusation against someone, who, one never learns; she has been wrongfully sacrificed for someone else's happiness and a sterling modesty forbids her speech. In everything she does there is graceful self-denial, quiet service. That would be Val's performance in another twenty years and Edwin was sure she'd perform excellently.

How it happened so suddenly Edwin never knew. A whole month the dreadful party was being planned and then, here was he, confused, in its very centre, turned out in his fine new suit of Russia Duck with a gardenia in his buttonhole, and a constant twitter of voices about him and the dazzle of dozens of candles, the very air starched with frosty light and the fumes of flowers and perfumes, pomades and potpourri.

The gentlemen were all in good voice and in excellent spirits, to judge by the babel of conversations severally raging in the over-crowded chamber. A dark brown thoroughbred, sir. He's called Charlie—sire Sir Hercules and dam Black Bess; fifteen—three tall, rising seven years, the very cut of an English horse, take it from me, sir! The vessel *Saladin* left London on the nineteenth of December and with a hundred and seven days out you can expect her any time. Eunice arrived from Melbourne, God help us all, on the *Queen of Australia*—I received the foul news by this morning's dawk from the dawk-khana. It shall be my pleasure, Mr Bunting, to present you with a selection of the finest brandy—Exshaw No. 1— I, and Todd and Heatley's champagne for Mrs Bunting. Or assorted French liqueurs if you prefer. Or Marcobrunner hock or Graham's Geneva gin. And, I may tell you, that I have received a consignment of numbers 1 and 2 Havana and Manila cheroots and tobacco of various kinds, cut and uncut. That's a very serviceable grey mare I got, sir, goes perfectly, in buggy, gharry and saddle, and a set of Cawnpore-made plated harness as good as new—all for a hundred and forty rupees. Enough, say I! I sail next month. I've written to the Calcutta Shipping Intelligence and booked my passage on the *Aberdeen*. Allow me, then, good sir, to recommend that estimable volume on *Our Tropical Possessions in Malayan India* by John Cameroon, Esq.—I trust that it shall acquaint you with Singapore, Penang Province, Wellesley and Malacca, their peoples, products, commerce and government long ere you land. About four thousand acres of waste land, Mr Lawrence, in the district of Lukeempore close on Nynee Tal. It adjoins large villages of the Shahjehanpore District and the soil is good and at eight rupees an acre my mind is made up and I mean to write to Mr McBarnet of the Simla Bank Corporation by the next dawk.

The young maidens were meanwhile in a twitter over the words of the songs in *Christey's Minstrel Songs,* trying them out on the instrument or else in fits of laughter over the grotesque verses in the *Great Comic Volume of Songs* as sung by Sam Cowell and Co. or else in raptures over somebody's white embroidered muslin, somebody's trimmed organdie or somebody's fancy silver buttons.

Away in their corner the old ladies discussed heartburn, dyspepsia, pain in the right side and shoulder, habitual costiveness, depression of spirits, oppression after meals, nervous and general debility, and examined the medicinal virtues of Dr E.J. Lazarus's Essence of Chiretta, created by the baids and hukeems of Hindoostan for centuries and now being advertised in the papers. I strongly urge Gregory to adhere to magnesia water or seltzer or potash water but all he retorts is: 'Deuce take it, Mama, or do you actually see me tippling orangeade at the Club?' And have you seen my new fuchsias and my new violets, Clara? This miserable climate kills my nasturtiums a month too soon but it can't be helped, can it? Toilet and smelling salts, pomades, otto of roses.

'Well, well, well, Martha Parker, I scarce knew you!' Charming Leslie smiles a challenging little smile, eyes narrowed in quizzical glee. 'Admit,' her eyes commanded, 'admit, Martha Parker, that time has been kinder on me than on you though we're fifty if a day. Admit that I have had a better deal in life, that fortune has favoured me with strange preference and you, ah you, poor thing, though you did happen to be a general's daughter . . .'

'Indeed?' Martha Parker smiled. 'But I knew you at once, dear, and so little changed from the night of the Darjeeling Tea Planters' Ball back in '36. Let it go, her resigned expression wearily surrendered—some are granted more than others, some that least deserve; and some are denied that may with justice claim their due. Too late to eat one's heart out—I have long consented.'

'Dear Uncle Chris, and how may you be?' Going up to him with both hands extended was Valerie. Leaning forward on an impulse, she whispers something in his ear. 'Bless my soul, bless my soul!' rumbles the old gentleman, roaring with laughter. And Aunt Lucille saying; 'That girl o' yours needs awatching, Charlotte.' Catching Rosa's eye across the room, she bows and throws her a kiss, then sinks down upon the blue settee and watches with bitter eyes and deprecating mouth. 'Behave yourself, miss, the missus is a-watchin'!' reprimands Uncle Chris with a twinkle in his eye.

And the Colonel Memsahib bowing, bowing, smiling, extending her white gloved hand, a band playing in the lawn. Upon the chintz-covered armchair nigh the piano sat Father Basil, that lumpy personage, quite bald, quite rotund, eyes habitually falling shut whenever he ruminated a point a long, long instant before he hazarded an answer, fingers entwined above his enormous middle. All the vases filled with tearoses, platters of potpourri on tables, clumps of late blossoms arrayed along the walls. The Parkers, the Lawrences, Matilda and Emilia O'Brien in light summer dresses of mauve and primrose. The bluff old army veterans bending gallantly to kiss the Colonel Memsahib's hand.

'What a rude, rude man!' frets Valerie. 'Oh, there you are, dear Major Norton!' The Major sank jocularly down upon one knee and Rosalie hid her face, the bashful belle behind her ostrich fan. And the Major's unstoppable flood of utterance, each full-throated syllable pounding richly forth with an air of jocund and indisputable authority. What an apoplectic face had he, the Major, and the full eyes of yesterday's lover and today's drunkard.

Edwin was confused all through the evening. There were bursts of melody from the fiddles and trumpets in the lawn. The long drive was lined up with buggies, dog carts, gharries, phaetons, barouches . . . The buzz of many voices, luminous swirls of muslin and of silk, smiles, smiles. Outside, the punkah-pullers swung and the large fans undulated slowly, lapping up a warm breeze above their heads. He was aware once of Mr Dutt's presence and remembered crossing the chamber quickly to welcome and show him in. He seemed to recall that nobody spoke much to Mr Dutt or looked at him. But Rosa gave vent to an utterly uncalled-for titter over something the Major muttered. And Valerie studied him cautiously with that measuring, surreptitious eye that old spinsters have. The Colonel Memsahib, on being presented with her new guest, gave him two fingers to shake, allowed a frosty smile to hover a second about her seraphic face, murmured scarce audibly: 'Mr Datt-er—to be sure—please to step into the parlour.'

And then he was aware that a profound silence had fallen and the Colonel Memsahib was beseated upon the piano stool. The Colonel Memsahib played well. She had a way of addressing the keys with reverential reserve, touching them gently and a rustle passed through the room as though an enchanted hand had made a magic pass above their heads. Her fingers yearned upon the strangest melodies, pausing with infinitely restful reluctance before deep spells of stillness. She commenced with selections from Schumann's *Nachstucke* and a troubled music filled the air. Dark feelings and images, sinister funereal fantasies, tumbled out of the instrument. She followed it up with portions from Schubert's *Moment Musicaux* and a limpid coolness swept in, becalming the earlier agitations.

The she took up Chopin's *Raindrop Prelude*. The rain fell softly as it falls unseen at some incalculable hour of darkness or of dawn, as it falls, drip by unheard drip, outside the marges of the deepest sleep, until one does not know if one dreamt of the rain or the rain dreamt of itself. Such rare restraint and delicacy had she and so unlike Valerie's rapturous emotional playing and Rosa's tempestuous rhapsodies.

The Colonel Memsahib held her back very straight as she played and her head uplifted and looked, unseeing, into the candlelit distance, with an indrawn face which brooded upon precious perceptions won with strife and in pain, which saw into clarities and visions that made it plain that happiness, too, was no answer to human suffering, that love and loneliness had their extent and also their limits and which chose, wisely, a glorious self-forgetfulness.

So now she was adrift, pennants flying upon a shoreless sea, carried without effort before a northern wind, working her intricate, unhurried way alone through Bach's straits and channels. Lofty transports of contemplation became renderings in notation, high seriousnesses, orders and hierarchies known to light and to earth, to sky and to water, uttering unpronounceable symbols and simpler, superior solutions; then, giving way, acceding to its own impersonal rejoicings with the serene composure of the most high. Then, interrogating itself again in new ways and answering itself in many celestial idioms, all uttering the same changeless thing. And the listening heart stopped in speechless recognition of an old reassurance with each repeating reply. And this interior dialogue, this absolute geometry, saved from being mere debate by the complete tenderness with which each feeling phrase of the divine argument was addressed.

Then she dipped her head, consulted the conclusive theme again, listened deeply, conferred with another octave, crumbled a few final bunches of notes and a flight of ultimate sounds fluttered up and scattered upon the carpet and lay still.

So profound was the hush that for a long while everyone forgot to clap. Then the applause burst, Mr Dutt clapping louder and longer than anybody else. She stood up and bowed gracefully. The way Valerie ran forward and kissed her mother's hands, Edwin was sure she was consumed with intense jealousy.

'But my dear Charlotte, this was absolutely marvellous!'

'Breathtaking, madam!'

'Perfectly ravishing, my dear!'

'Madam, allow me,' and the old Brigadier seized Colonel Memsahib's hand and languished his lips upon it.

'They're all Vernon's favourites,' said the Colonel Memsahib abstractedly.

Nobody could quite define the unease but the awkwardness of the moment was sudden. A dead man was the recipient of that soul-offering not a chamberful of living men and women. For they all realized they did not exist for her as she played. That music was for Vernon's ears who lay buried somewhere in the north-west.

Many of the guests felt that the Bible reading and the sermon was not of a piece with the rest of the evening and served to impose an unnecessary ecclesiastical tone upon the evening's gaieties. But the memsahib was adamant on this point. This was more of a sacred occasion than a mere birthday celebration. Hence Father Basil and his New Testament, and on the whole the guests bore with it in good grace. Charlotte was known to be strange in some ways.

A special lectern had been placed in a corner of the parlour, betwixt two clumps of white chrysanthemums in painted pots and this was to be Father Basil's pulpit. Thither went Father Basil, plump and pontific, the picture of priestly poise. Long years on this subcontinent had brought out in Father Basil a native priestly strain, that of dining well on most of his spiritual and temporal excursions to the homes of his flock, and but for the uniform of his calling and the nature of his faith and the colour of his skin, he might have been a local Brahmin priest to judge from his form. His was a well-oiled, well-dined and well-wined voice, rolling rhetorically forth as though each phrase were a special tasty morsel he turned over in his mouth with relish and each period a good, soul-satisfying gulp.

'"And whither I go, ye know the way." Thomas saith to him, "Lord, we know not whither thou goest; how know we the way?" Jesus saith to him, "I am the way, and the truth, and the life. No one cometh to the Father except through me. If ye had recognized me, ye would know my Father also. From now ye are recognizing him and have seen him." Philip saith to him, "Lord, show us the Father, and it sufficeth us." Jesus saith to him, "So long a time have I been with you and hast thou not recognized me, Philip? He that hath seen me hath seen the Father. How dost thou say, 'Show us the Father'? Dost thou not believe that I am in the Father and the Father in me? The words that I say to you I speak not from myself, but the Father who abideth in me doeth his works. Believe me that I am in the Father and the Father in me; or else on account of the works themselves believe me."'

The text had been chosen by the Colonel Memsahib and Father Basil, eyes half-closed in his ruminative exertions, launched forth upon his discourse, drawing trails upon trails of theological niceties like magic ribbons out of the great cavern of his mouth: 'Brothers and sisters in Christ! The destination of man is unknown to him except in its formal accounts. We are told that the Christian must seek Heaven and perfect fellowship with our Father. But it is a Father we have never met and the phrases that describe him are beyond our faculties to grasp: "Things which eye saw not and ear heard not, and which entered not into the heart of man, whatsoever things that God prepared for them that love Him." But though the destination be not known and be unknowable, brothers and sisters in Christ, yet the Lord pronounces unto us that each of us knows whither we are bound. We are daunted. Like loyal and literal-minded Thomas, we ask how this may be. But reflect, my brothers and sisters, we do not go to a coaching inn and ask the innkeeper to recommend a direction and a coach—it is only because we know something before we commence the journey, because we know whither we mean to go, that we even ask how to begin. "Whither I go, ye know the way." "I am the way," saith the Lord. The way is well known because the way is the Lord Himself. The Christian must pass through the veil, must pass through the flesh. We must eat the flesh of the Son of Man and drink His sacred blood so that our being becomes one with the substance of His divine nature, so that we are united with Him and discover the deity indwelling in it. We become "very members incorporate in His body" and come to the Father through Him and thus does He become the way.'

The punkahs lolled upon the still air hither and thither and the flame of four dozen candles shook and swayed with every pulsation; upon the pale walls faded shadows flapped in gentle waves as though the very room breathed softly to itself, inhaling the thoughts, the scents, the words that bred within.

Lizzie Lawrence yawned gently and whispered something to Rosa. And when Father Basil uttered the words 'eat the flesh of the Son of Man and drink His blood,' his bulbous eyes dilated in such threatening emphasis and his jaws worked up such a peculiar chomping motion that it sent little Lucinda Parker helplessly agiggle despite the desperate pinching of her lady mother.

Edwin sought the room for Mr Dutt. There he was, sandwiched between old Mrs Page and Major Norton, nodding diligently, the picture of sympathetic catholicism.

'Truth is a personal being apprehended in the only way in which personality is ever fully apprehended . . .' the venerable pastor was holding forth. 'This is the only way in which spiritual and divine reality can be expressed. What is personal can only be expressed in a person. I grant, brothers and sisters in Christ, that this invaluable truth is made use of by most heathen institutions which, if anything, are composed of hordes of barbarous personalities of monstrous and questionable divinity . . .'

'At the very earliest opportunity I must get to speak to him alone,' thought Edwin anxiously. There was a lot that Edwin had shyly saved up for this evening. Questions of great import awaited Mr Dutt's judgement. Poems of his own composition waited to be assessed by the great man's discerning eye. Bookshelves to be displayed. But when the pastor had finished, Brigadier Daniels it was, grating out one of his sensational stories. And Edwin blushed for him and wondered what on earth Mr Dutt thought of the bluff, beefy British company present. Even when the company stood up to sing 'God Save The Queen' the words inspired acute embarrassment in Edwin's heart. And when they came, roaring roundly down to the words:

> O Lord, our God, arise, scatter her enemies.
> And make them fall! Confound their politics,
> Frustrate their knavish tricks, on thee our
> Hopes we fix, God save us all . . .

Edwin did not know where to hide his face. It was obvious that the God being thus invoked was an Anglo-Saxon god, down from the Norse seas in his Viking craft, winged helmet, hatchet, eyes of ice and nostrils breathing fire. Edwin would have given anything to divine what Mr Dutt was thinking even as he stood, head bowed, with the carolling crowd.

'Ladies and gen'lemun!' The Brigadier's voice ground the silence to dust and his tale trudged down the air on martial boots. 'We have just given voice to our estimable anthem, a song of ancient glory and renown, a song to o'erwhelm each true-born Englishman, be he a languishin' in 'eathen barbary, beyond the wild ocean.'

The Brigadier's narrations—no matter what their literal content—were usually delivered in tones of macabre gloom.

'This song, dear ladies and gen'lemun, forms the subject of the experience I am about to narrate to you. I owe to it not only my position but my very life, such as it is, as sure as my name's Daniels, as sure as I am a-standing before you now. I ask you, gen'lemun and ladies, to envision a small group of us, British officers, staunch, tried-and-tested men, scarce ten of us and two faithful Gurkhas, lost in the tortuous ravines nigh Jhansi, whither we had followed in the wake of the forces of Sir Hugh Rose. I ask you to envision the rebellion of fifty sepoys, men we had drilled and trained in battle-craft and that now uprose 'gainst us in dastardly betrayal.

'It is but just to admit, in fairness to the poor devils, that they escorted us to a place of safety, yea, saluted us and all, ere they decamped with their arms to join the army of the militant Ranee.

'A pretty kettle of fish. But, as I always say, 'tis easy to bait a native. Play on their ruddy emotions, I say. Pat 'em and coddle 'em awhile. Call 'em by their nicknames. Ask after the missus and the brats and the tribe. Send him a gew-gaw for the bambino. Ten British officers and fifty sepoys turned rebel! On the very march to Jhansi! Sir Hugh would have the hide off our backs and no mistake. But we got 'em back, yessir, that we did and it was the brain of my bright young Gurkha lad, Man Bahadur Thapa. Egad! Did it please the feller-me-lad to be called "Man" by me, for sure he had the countenance of a lemur and there was I, Robinson Crusoe!

'You don't know those ravines. God bless you, sirs, that's where those devils, those thugs, plied their trade. In next to no time the infernal noose'd be round your neck, without so much as a by-your-leave, and next thing you know, twang!—and you'd given up the ghost and pretty silly you're feelin' then!

'Well, here we were, lost, and the nearest settlement a village of former thugs that'd taken to farming. But, as I say, once a thug always a thug and not to be trusted! Six miles of tramping in the dark and there we were amongst crowds of thugs—a most unlovely situation, let me tell you.

'"Those're no perishin' thugs," said I to myself. "There's something regular in their march, their backs are too straight. Those, my lad," I said to myself, "are rebels and no mistake, as sure as my name's Daniels or I'll eat my hat."

'They welcomed us, every man Jack of us, and gave us food and shelter; and no man amongst us but had his hand to his holster. Two hundred or so thugs and fifty of 'em our men. And how in the name of Mike were we to tell 'em in the dark? And how get 'em to return, much less show us the way? Any moment and the devils would decide that enough was enough and we'd be partin' company with our immortal souls.

'"Twas Man Bahadur Thapa saved the day with that bright thought of his. And here's what we did, ladies and gen'lemun: we built a campfire and, beseated round it, we forthwith burst into song. Aye, yes, we sang fit to burst our vocal cords, fit to raise the dead. You wouldn't take me for a lusty carollin' choirmaster—hey? I give you my word for it, I'd ha' outdone the entire chorus at Canterbury Cathedral that night. We sang "Now Are We Met" and "Home, Sweet Home". And "The Soldier's Farewell" and "The Departure For Syria". Yea, and "Bonnie Dundee" and "Go Where Glory Waits Thee".

'There's no one to beat 'em natives for good, wholesome curiosity. All round the camp we grew sensible, presently, of waiting, listening figures, asquatting upon the rocky ground. Some of 'em, poor blighters, even beat time and one of 'em brought a little two-faced drum and beat his native tattoo 'pon it to speed our singing and we made a very pretty company indeed, very cosy and chummy, take it from me. Then when the singing and beating time was well under way and every man of 'em rocking and swayin' to our singin', we changed tune of a sudden in true defence strategy and commenced that most glorious anthem "God Save The Queen".

'You guessed it, fair ladies and gentlemen. That did it. Fifty men were 'pon their feet, saluting silently, quite, quite carried away, all thought of mutiny clean forgot. That's how I drilled my men, sirs. Fidelity and iron discipline. Why, they'd rise from the very grave to hear the anthem, but the poor blisters haven't any graves to speak of, curse 'em!

'In scarce an hour we were marching back through the wilds of Boondelcund to join Sir Hugh. So say I, my good sirs, the native's got his heart in the right place. He may get the heebie-jeebies and may up and rebel awhile and may work 'imself up into a fidget o'er ham and beef and the purdah o'er a woman's face and tripe like that but he knows what's good for him.

'"God Save The Queen!" say I. God saved me that night and all for that song. You know the phrase "bought for a song"? Our lives were bought for a song that night and no mistake!'

There was to the Brigadier's deductions on native psychology a general outcry, the subject being dear to every spirited English heart. The morality of the native, his maturity or absence thereof, his secret wiles and wishes, was something that most of the company present held strong opinions about.

A babel of voices rose into the air, a general hubbub of political discourse, all very familiar, all very predictable to Edwin. For six years now, when Englishmen met in India, they discussed the mutiny, the native atrocities, the takeover by the Crown. Every aspect of the epoch had to be religiously gone over upon each possible occasion. Whether Napier was the superior statesman or Dalhousie. 'Statesman?' shouted an angry voice. 'I beg your pardon! Tradesmen! Mercenaries! Nay, sir, be not overheated. Neither statesmen nor mercenaries. The proper phrase to employ is "strategic sportsmen" and strategies can oft run amok. I appeal to your forbearance, sir, but Napier's missives bear scant vestige of strategy. Do but consider his brash memoranda. The Marquis of Dalhousie, contrariwise, seemed in absolute control of the situation until 1956. Had Parliament appreciated the import of his repeated requests for more European troops, history would have transpired otherwise. Deuce take it all, sir, not a single European officer to command our sepoy armies betwixt Allahabad and Calcutta. Scandalous! Why, what is it but asking for trouble? It's serving mutiny to them on a silver platter—only a dolt wouldn't help himself. And the native is no dolt, whatever some of us may be disposed to feel. The man of salt was Lawrence, gentlemen. He alone, if I may say so, had the vision and the political sensitivity to foresee the disaster. Witness the way he provisioned the Lucknow Residency in anticipation of a long siege. That was a man of a different stamp, yea, built of sterner stuff. 'We didn't have postmen then to run our affairs, sir. We had generals and men of mettle.'

Edwin thought it very bad form to attack poor Lord Canning for his past calling. 'Well, he was Postmaster-General—that makes him general enough!' scoffed the lively young voice. More laughter rocked the company. 'Poor Clemency Canning and his pettifogging policies, his pussyfooting pacifism, his endless pardons.' 'Pardon? Shame, shame! The native has known no peace for fifteen centuries, sir. Pardon, freedom, peace, are things he cannot apprehend emotionally. Why, let 'em run the show for a year and see the godawful mess they'll get it into. You can't run a country on baksheesh, sir. The baboo had better stick to his baksheesh. Moreover, the native philosophy of honour isn't the same as ours. Honour here is amoral. This country, sir, has never known a republic.' 'Nay,' uprose the youthful dissenter, 'I cannot concur with you, sir! Consider . . .'

It was time to draw Mr Dutt away, decided Edwin. He found Mr Dutt holding polite converse with old Mrs Page on, presumably, the breeding of roses in Indian climes.

'But, Mr Datt,' protested she, 'when you breed the English tearose and the native variety, it is to be seen that the native strain often overwhelms the English strain. And what began as a warm, peachen blossom turns into a miserable tiny crimson bloom. The native strain,' she said acutely, ' is a nuisance.'

'Not entirely so, my lady,' was Mr Dutt's meek answer. 'For your potpourri, recollect, native petals are best.'

Edwin plucked at his sleeve. 'One moment, please,' he whispered.

'Mr Dutt, sir, I particularly desire that you behold my room. There's something I must sound you on and I'm afraid it isn't very congenial here.'

'As you wish, Mr Edwin,' readily agreed Mr Dutt.

'This way, please.' Why did Mr Dutt persist in addressing him as Mr Edwin—only servants did that! Edwin felt belittled by that tone of natural respect that stole into Mr Dutt's voice whenever he spoke to him.

'A very extraordinary room, in sooth, Mr Edwin,' observed Mr Dutt, looking around with interest. 'It is as though two men dwelt herein, not one.'

'It used to be Father's room when I was little,' explained Edwin, trying not to be amused by the other's quaint turn of speech. 'Those are two of his tigers.' Edwin pointed at the two striped pelts asprawl upon the far wall above the bookshelves. 'Yonder are his war trophies. He was the hero of Sind, you know. And that is his native sword collection.'

'And these books?' enquired Mr Dutt.

'Mine,' said Edwin bashfully.

'The chamber of a soldier and a man of letters! Remarkable!' pronounced Mr Dutt precisely in his too-careful English. 'Sophocles, Plato, Augustine, Hume, Spinoza. And this I perceive to be literature. The complete works of Shakespeare, the complete Pope, Blake, Gray, Spenser. Scott and Mr Wordsworth. Even, dear me, the melodious Mr Tennyson's newest lyrics. This, Mr Edwin, is impressive. And you have read all these volumes?'

'All of them,' replied Edwin.

'And reflected upon them?'

'I have endeavoured to—in a modest way, of course.'

'You do not seek to be a soldier like your estimable father?'

'I believe I have a singular want of aptitude in that direction, Mr Dutt. There are other areas of usefulness in which I aspire to render such small service as I am capable of.'

'Such as?'

Edwin drew a deep breath. 'I wish to write, Mr Dutt.'

'Ah,' was the non-committal rejoinder. 'Poetry?'

'Well poetry . . . and . . . and things speculative. I . . . I have thought generally upon things a bit and put down my . . . my views.'

It sounded so preposterous, so presumptuous, that Edwin was constrained to blush. The words came in a rush. 'I am putting together my very first volume, sir. If . . . if you'd care to examine it . . . I'd be most obliged to you.'

'It would be a pleasure, Mr Edwin,' responded Mr Dutt suavely, beseating himself.

How that hour flew past Edwin scarce knew. Not all the questions he had accumulated in his mind found satisfactory answers. Some sounded downright silly.

'Mr Dutt,' he asked gravely, 'why are poets unhappy men?'

'I don't believe they are, Mr Edwin,' replied Mr Dutt with a twinkle in his eye. 'Many of them, I find, have proved themselves singularly churlish and not one whit different from other men. Much of the unhappiness, I'm disposed to believe, comes from a formal tone of voice. Men of thought and feeling, it is commonly presumed, must of necessity be of a melancholy disposition and the minor poet makes it a point of honour to be distressed and world-weary. I beg your pardon, Mr Edwin, have I uttered aught that is amiss?'

'How do you tell a minor from a major talent?'

Mr Dutt smiled disarmingly. 'In me, Mr Edwin, stands before you an example of a contented minor poet. And I pray that I may ever stay so and never have too big a price to pay the Muse for what she may choose to bestow upon me.'

'I do not altogether understand.'

'I'd rather have bread and peace than poetry, Mr Edwin.'

'But the . . . the search, Mr Dutt? The prophetic mission, the special destiny? To utter, to know, to show the way, to find words for things?'

Mr Dutt shrugged and said with a very straight face, 'Allow me to offer an opinion, Mr Edwin. Actually there are no words for things. The only language is analogy. There are only roughly similar resonances. The poet strives to reconstruct a similar vibration, that's all.'

'But there is the simple truth in a line—like the cut of a knife, like the taste of water . . .'

'There you are,' smiled Mr Dutt. 'Analogy again.'

'You think my compositions lack complexity?'

Mr Dutt reflected. 'On the contrary, Mr Edwin, they abound in compound visions. Where they fall short of ideal expression, if I may be excused for saying so, are the places where a natural simplicity is deliberately avoided in preference of a tortuous complexity.'

He picked up Edwin's leather-bound notebook.

'I see that you are indeed a good nature poet,' pronounced he kindly. 'Consider this line—"the tipsied, twinkled tremor in the trees" and "the white sky streaked with silver scales". Excellent alliteration. A very vivid flash of observation, a very arresting expression. And this image of the world blowing out of the sun in a broad, smoking beam. Very striking. And this phrase about "a wisp of a river folded up in sky". And "the heavens crumbling up into creased clouds". Very moving. But, Mr Edwin, the stanza I like most is the one about the birds. You speak of their "long discourse, long, shrill narrations, long tuneful exclamations". And then there descends this lovely rain of words—"bat, soar and flit, dip, twit and quip", followed by that sudden brake to the speed with this beautiful visual image of the single raven marooned upon a pole in a grey sky! This is indeed well expressed. Yet, say I, the vision you beheld was simple, and the expression you construed of it is compound. Truth moves in one direction, these lovely phrases move in another.'

'But don't they meet in some real images, sir?' asked Edwin anxiously.

'That they do, but whither are they bound? Are these pictures ends in themselves? If so, there is no more to be written or said? Or do they correspond to some state in you which you must infer? Some phrases go round in a circle and meet at the far end of the circumference, as it were; the sense must wait for the picture to form. Which is why you must use natural metaphors, not conceits, Mr Edwin.'

'And this one entitled "Hymn"' went on the great man. '"Lord, cool my soul with showering rain. All nature trapped in a dewy net. Swarms of trees, streams of breeze; shoals of cloud, flowers wading wet." In spite of the questionable grammar and the confused movement of the lines, I find a general freshness, a monsoon wetness, a washness—and the idea of fluid mobility is put well across. A little cleaning up and it shall be a fine verse yet.'

'I . . . I rather believe that the first two lines are bad ones and sort of . . . stumble into the next two lines which are reasonably good . . .' Edwin endeavoured to expound his personal assessment of a verse which had troubled him much.

'If you are inclined to consider it that way, yes. There is a distinct rise and fall of inspiration, as it were. Excellent expression and bathos. To speak of trees a frisk in the sun and tricked out in trinkets of the sun is surely pretty phrasing but to the punctilious maker of phrases it may well appear an overdone alliteration, if I may say so. In inspiration too there are alternating pulses of action and rest. Actually I don't think one may speak so simply of good lines and bad lines, Mr Edwin. There are lines which follow the contour of observed and felt reality and lines which stray and lose themselves. In a poem, as in battle, one trusts to the unknown accident.'

It was at this point in the dialogue that tripping footfalls sounded just outside the door and a mirthful voice shrilled wickedly in the corridor without:

Follow my Bangalorey man
Follow my Bangalorey man.
I'll do all that ever I can
To follow my Bangalorey man!

Edwin knew the rest of that absurd ditty: We'll borrow a horse, and steal a gig, and round the world we'll do a jig, and I'll do all that ever I can, to follow my Bangalorey man!

The rhyme ended on a high, affected operatic tremolo and Edwin rose hastily and threw open the door.

'Oh, there you are, Edwin dear! Its naughty of you to hide yourself so, Mr Datt. We're going to sing and you must promise to give us a song,' dimpled Rosa with mischief in her eye.

'I . . . I'm afraid I don't know any English songs, Miss Rosa,' said poor Mr Dutt, confused.

'Oh, come, come,' twinkled the charming young miss. 'You can surely give us a Bangalorey song—or a Bengalee song!'

Edwin gave her a savage, scorching frown which she blithely took no note of. 'And you're not to run off again, Edwin dear. Matilda O'Brien's pining to sing a duet with you and she simply won't let you off.'

The grand Brodwood piano was now thrown open to the guests, more candles brought and everybody seemed in good voice from ancient Mrs Page and Brigadier Daniels to wee Emilia O'Brien. Chairs were pulled up and cake and fruits passed round, the native bearers moving hither, thither and yonder like mute, impersonal puppets.

Majors Norton and Perkins led the singing with a gruff, hearty rendering of "Before All Lands In East Or West", with Brigadier

Daniels adding his rusty baritone to the snatches which pleased him most.

> *Be-fore all lands in East or West, I love my na-tive land*
> *the best,*
> *With God's best gifts 'tis teem-ing.*
> *No gold or jewels here are found, yet men of no-ble*
> *souls abound,*
> *And eyes of joy are gleam-ing*
> *And eyes of joy are gleam-ing.*
> *Be-fore all peo-ple East or West, I love my coun-try-men*
> *the best*
> *A race of no-ble spi-rit.*
> *A so-ber mind, a gen'rous heart, to virtue trained, yet*
> *free from art,*
> *They from their sires in-her-it!*

Then followed a long, lank, listless lament by the old and young Mrs Pages—"On The Banks Of Allan Water"—which retold the tragedy of the dead miller's daughter. Then another patriotic effusion in the form of "The Red, White and Blue" rendered by the three rollicking Lawrences:

> *Bri-tan-nia, the pride of the o-cean,*
> *The home of the brave and the free,*
> *The shrine of each pa-triot's de-vo-tion,*
> *The world of-fers hom-age to thee,*
> *At thy man-dates he-roes as-sem-ble,*
> *When Li-ber-ty's form stands in view,*
> *Thy banners make ty-ran-ny trem-ble,*
> *When borne by the Red, White and Blue!*
> *When war spread its wide des-o-la-tion,*
> *And threat-en'd our land to de-form,*
> *The ark then of free-dom's foun-da-tion,*

Bri-tan-nia rode safe through the storm.
With her gar-lands of vic-t'ry a-round her,
When so no-bly she bore her brave crew,
With her flag float-ing proud-ly be-fore her,
The boast of the Red, White and Blue!

So catchy was the melody, so well harmonized, that all the guests joined in and the chamber rang with the glad throb of many voices. A deep, charged silence fell as the last bars died away and it was now the Colonel Memsahib's turn to sing. True to her general strangeness the lady chose an old Scotch air, "Wae's Me For Prince Charlie". She rendered that old Jacobite lament with such intense sadness, such personal meaning, her lone, fluting voice seeking old resonances, that many a lace kerchief was applied to the dewy eyes of the auditors and many a manly throat cleared in nostalgic memory. A great wrong, an ineradicable sin still commanded penance and expiation. And when she came to the final words:

Bonnie, bonnie bird, The tears cam' drap-pin' rare-ly,
I took my bon-net aff my heid, for weel I lo'ed Prince Charlie.

and then

O this is no' a land for me,
I'll tar-ry here nae lan-ger . . .

A distinct sniff from the old Brigadier drew the attention of all, young and old, to an indefinable misery they all felt. A loud encore received the closing bars and this time the memsahib rendered two choice old pieces composed by Sir Thomas Moore, "Silent, Oh Moyle" and "Oh! Breathe Not His Name". And yet again the sheer poetry of the haunting words was pregnant with that curious evocation to a personal lover:

Si-lent, oh Moyle, be the roar of thy wa-ter,
Break not, ye bree-zes your chain of re-pose,
While mur-mur-ing mourn-ful-ly, Lir's lone-ly daugh-ter
Tells to the night-star her tale of woes . . .

And as she slowly sang the last words it was as though an ultimate human sorrow, so simple as to be unutterable in the history of human emotion, had at last found musical relief.

Oh! breathe not his name, let it sleep in the shade
Where cold and un-hon-ured his re-lics are laid!
Sad, si-lent and dark be the tears that we shed
As the night-dew that falls on the grass o'er his head.

The lady had an ineffable air of profound tragedy and immense refinement blended together in a strangely striking aristocratic brew. The awed silence which received her words, her playing or her singing was an extension of her powerful presence. She had a masterful sense of volume and time and pitch. And yet it could scarce be overlooked that this tremendous, tragic, tuneful eloquence served to oppress the spirits of the light-hearted. Some of the younger guests essayed to enliven the spirits of the company with that lively old air: "Come, Let Us A-Maying Go" and the popular ballad "How Should I Your True Love Know".

Suddenly Rosa, laughing mischievously, all a-twinkle and a-sparkle, with a dangerous shine in her smile, pranced up to the piano stool, flounced down upon it, struck a few random bars and playfully announced a duet.

'And for my partner,' she proclaimed gleefully, clapping her little hands, 'I must have our Mr Datt and no other. Come, Mr Datt, be a pet. I absolutely insist and I won't take no for an answer.'

Mr Dutt's brown face all aflush with embarrassment, he half rose out of his chair, vainly striving to preserve his composure.

'Oh, but Miss Rosa, I told you I know no English songs. I beg you, let me off.'

'Dear me, how very ungracious,' retorted she. 'In our parties everyone does as we do and we brook no excuses and no exceptions.'

'Oh well,' sighed poor Mr Dutt. 'I must look a fool then before all the company. I appeal to you, ladies and gentlemen, to bear with my singing. I know no English songs and I can't read music, but the lady insists and gallantry demands . . .' He made a feeble bow, and charming Rosa struck a comic pose. This was to be the comic sequence of the evening. Edwin sat, glowering and incensed, in his armchair, truly alarmed at Rosa's frivolous malice.

By some curious stroke of chance Rosa began 'Hark, The Lark', glancing wickedly out of the corner of her eye, with a dimple in her cheek, at poor, awkward Mr Dutt. But, to Edwin's immense astonishment, Mr Dutt was proving neither poor nor awkward. No sooner had Rosa given melodious utterance to the first two lines:

Hark! Hark! The lark at heav'n's gate sings!
Hark! Hark! The lark at heav'n's gate sings!

than did the surprising Mr Dutt nimbly follow with the next two lines:

And Phoebus 'gins a-rise his steeds
To water at these springs.

Nobody could help remark this extraordinary situation and everyone stopped speaking all at once. True, Mr Dutt sang a melody all his own but he had a rich, bass voice and the strange tune he improvised, while nowhere near the original melody, was by no means wanting in pleasing notes or surprising contrasts and was, moreover, a just and appropriate development of the first two lines. More amazing was his obvious knowledge of the words of which even

Edwin retained but a faint recollection. He wasn't reading them in Rosa's songbook for he stood by the side of the piano, looking away at some potted ferns to the left. And such an expression of delight seemed to play upon his swarthy face. And when they came to 'My lady sweet, arise, arise, my lady sweet, arise . . .' he chanced to smile upon his young tormenter with such comic meaning in his face, pulling such an expression of tender distress and woe that the tension relaxed of a sudden and laughter filled the room, and clapping, and many cheers, whereupon Rosa, suddenly aflame, pounded a loud, discordant chord upon the instrument, rose sharply, and closing the lid with a bang, strode haughtily away, leaving poor Mr Dutt in mid-bar, looking astonished, dejected and injured.

Never had Edwin applauded his mother more. The Colonel Memsahib stepped smoothly forward, and, taking Mr Dutt's arm, smiled coolly upon the company.

'But what a pleasant surprise, Mr Datt! That was an impressive rendering, Mr Datt. How do you know the words so well?'

Mr Dutt blushed. 'That was Shakespeare, madam,' he replied simply as though he were speaking of an old friend. 'Miss Rosalie happened to pick up the serenade to Imogen in *Cymbeline* . . .'

'Ah, so it was, so it was,' murmured the Memsahib.

She turned to her guests. 'Gentlemen and ladies,' spoke she in her clear, soft voice. 'Will it please you to move into the dining room? Dinner is laid and the time has now come to present dear Edwin with our gifts. And,' she added, smiling, 'Mr Datt being our Edwin's chosen friend at this gathering, it is only meet that he join me in offering my late husband's gifts to Edwin upon this happy occasion. Mr Datt?' And still lending him her arm, she conducted him regally into the dining room. Good form and grace saved the day for Edwin and it was with relief that the company rose to accompany their hostess to the dining chamber.

'Gracious heaven!' he heard Rosa tell Matilda O'Brien as, arm in arm, they trooped into the dining room. 'Whatever can Mother be thinking of! And who would've thought the Bangalorey man could sing our songs?'

'But doesn't it come out all funny?' was the whispered observation. 'I mean, doesn't it?'

In the sombre dining room three extra tables had been accommodated to extend the length of the one massive mahogany and the guests, beseated at the four tables, drank Edwin's health, the late Colonel's, the memsahib's and lastly, the glorious Empire which had occasioned their presence together upon this glorious evening.

'Honoured ladies and gentlemen!' Mr Dutt apostrophized the assembled company in his best ceremonial manner. 'I stand before you tonight charged with a right sacred duty for which I am much beholden to my gracious hostess.' Here he made a stiff little bow in the memsahib's direction. 'Dare I express my appreciation for the immense honour that your hospitality, trust and fellowship have conferred upon me this evening, an honour I can with certitude say I shall never efface from my memory in all the years to come. In bestowing upon Mr Edwin, on his twenty-first birth anniversary, this missive from his late father, the heroic Colonel Vernon Agnew Watkins, may I prove the bearer of messages bringing good cheer and solace to his young heart and hope and meaningful commitment to his young years. This invaluable gift do I, in the presence of this august company, offer unto Mr Edwin in the name of our Maker and as Mrs Watkins's humble agent and friend, now and evermore.'

'Hear, hear!' cried Major Norton as Edwin rose to receive the sealed paper packet.

'Hear, hear!' cried the young ladies and clapped their gentle hands. And Mr Dutt made his odd little bow again, smiling all over his face, touched, confused and quite, quite overwhelmed.

An abrupt silence fell as the Colonel Memsahib rose to her feet, bearing a well-wrapped and oddly shaped parcel.

'On this happy occasion I have pleasure in presenting the gun used by my beloved husband in his numerous military engagements.

It bore him company full many a year and with my best wishes I do hereby confer it upon his son and heir, Edwin Reginald Braithwaite Watkins, and express the hope that, as of yore, it may be used well in the service of his country and the service of his fellow-men with justice and honour.'

With this short address she turned to Edwin and laid the heavy inheritance in his awkward hands.

'Give um a big hand, gentlemun!' roared the old Brigadier and the next moment, as though by clockwork, everyone was on their feet, singing 'Happy Birthday, dear Edwin!' raising their glasses, smiling warmly, and two bearers, sashed and turbaned, slid in, bearing the large twenty-one-key cake and the beribboned silver knife upon a salver.

The younger guests had every intention of dancing all night, the older ones, of sitting over horrific dawk bungalow tales. The hall was cleared and the band installed behind a screen of potted ferns. Dinner over, the music struck up anon and away floated the young ladies in the arms of the young officers and even the gallant old Brigadier sought out old Mrs Page and offered her his hand with a deep, old-fashioned bow.

The door slid to, muting the music of the band, and Edwin was alone with his father. The seal gave way with a reproachful crackle and Edwin found himself confronting what appeared to him a curiously familiar countenance beheld in a crowd.

He had the impression of knocking upon a door which opened to admit him into a stern, military chamber. Behind the green baize-covered table, beseated magisterially betwixt the maps and the globe and the almanac, was a man. A stiff, formal voice accosted him: 'Major Vernon Agnew Watkins,' said the man, rising cordially and his grip was firm and staunch upon the hand. 'The fifty-eighth regiment under General Napier. Elevated to Colonel after the takeover of Sind, having rendered gallant service in the engagement of Imangarh.'

The ink upon the yellowed sheets had paled with the years. A small, impersonal hand and a distant, unimaginable voice addressed him. Yet there was a ring in certain lines and a real person it was that uttered those careful words into the formless future. And a strange thought occurred to Edwin: just as this father, this voice out of the past, was a myth for him, so must he, Edwin, a babe in arms, a future auditor, be a myth for this father.

'My dear Edwin Reginald Braithwaite Watkins,' the handwriting addressed him by his complete name, as one man apostrophizing another. They were confronting one another, man to man, save that one man sat upon a chair and the other stood to attention. It may well have been 'My dear Sergeant' or 'My dear Corporal'.

'My dear Edwin Reginald Braithwaite Watkins,

'It is with the utmost affection and pleasure that I take up my pen to greet you, this day of the future, 17 March 1865, upon the twenty-first anniversary of your nativity.

'Endeavour as I might, I find it beyond my powers of conjuration to envision you, though you do stand before me, a phantom of my brain. I undertake this extraordinary enterprise of writing to you in person because it is my apprehension that I may not outlast this melancholy year, labouring as I do under sentence of death from a tribe of Afghans which, in no uncertain terms, has spelt the fate in store for me. To Napier I owed a debt of gratitude and duty which I have abundantly fulfilled. To you I am accountable as is a father unto his son, as is the past unto the future. And to my Maker am I responsible for the honour of my actions and the truthfulness of my confessions, so help me GOD.'

Edwin felt the unaccountable command in the air, as though he were obeying the fantasy of another man, twenty years in the past. It was the voice of a self-conscious stranger, choosing his words with care. Large spaces of self-debate and deliberation divided the phrases; the laboured sentences tentatively offered up their arduous clauses, eked out the formal niceties with genteel caution. There was unease in the lines of this uncomfortable monologue wherein the speaker sought to measure the response upon a phantom countenance ere he ventured further. What was it that one generation had to tell the next about itself, wondered Edwin, searching the lines. What was it that it could not bring itself to utter despite the pleasing formalities, the many parentheses, digressions and deletions. The half-truths were articulated in the lines, the whole truth hid somewhere in the deletions and pleaded for understanding and absolution.

Now the tone was grandiose, self-congratulatory, twisting moral meanings this way and that to uphold a personal assertion. Now it was pompous, vainglorious, officious, false.

'My place in history,' wrote the myth, 'is of necessity tied up with the province of Sind, the name given to the country lying on both sides of the Indus south of the Panjaub and extending to the sea. The river gives it life and fruitfulness. On the west and east are barren deserts. This was the cradle of the most ancient civilization, this the route taken by the venturesome invaders of history, the Aryans, the Macedonians, Mahmoud of Ghazni, the Huns, the Mongols, the Turko-Afghans, the Moguls. Sind accepted the supremacy of the Great Moguls and submitted to the plunderers Tamerlane and Nadir Shah. Against the design of history, it was but meet that Sind be claimed by British conquest. History demanded it; the natives foresaw it. "Alas," wrote a Sindee native, "Sind is now lost to us since the English have seen the river!"'

'It may justly be asseverated that our policies in Sind were nobly in accord with the traditions of British rule in India and that any lapse on our part may ethically be indicated to our complete satisfaction by reason of our disinterested intent and by our earnest aspirations of extending the incalculable blessings of British administration upon a province unremarkable for any native ability of government. If it be charged by posterity that our action in Sind did not err on the side of indulgence to the susceptibilities of the native population, and if, unfortunately for our national credit, British performance in India fell to a lower level of unscrupulousness than ever before, I have this to advance: that there is for me no insurmountable necessity of seeking for any moral justification, the peace and progress of the state achieved by the talents, the energy and the ability of Sir Charles Napier, our general, being altogether admirable and deserving of the approbation of history. Indeed, it is my conviction that our conduct in Sind was ever marked by a strict observance of propriety and fair play, the previous Governor General having justly refused to consider the proposal of the Maharaja of Panjaub, Ranjit Singh, that Sind be partitioned betwixt himself and the Company . . .

Edwin read on, scanning through several pages in the selfsame style of narration. It could not be mere suspicion. There was, he thought, some confusion in that military tone. Halfway through the epistle he met a new, unbecoming, ingratiating tone of voice, almost appealing, almost imploring, a crop of phrases alien to the style: 'It is in a moment of the utmost trepidation', 'the forbearance and forgiveness of the years to come', 'endure my words with patience and fortitude . . . ! 'You,' wrote the myth, 'are young and possibly enjoy the privilege of not having yet been vouchsafed opportunities for misconduct.' 'You,' mused the voice, 'may yet be innocent of the discord betwixt intention and act . . .'

The Colonel was no longer sitting. He stood up, ceremonially peeled off some of his decorations and met him as a man, older and weaker, and on his side were youth and judgement. Centrally dividing the letter was a dissent of voices, a contest betwixt conscience and convention.

'There are occasions,' wrote the voice, 'when I am disposed to entertain the speculation that the treatment of Sind, however expedient politically, is somehow personally disconcerting to me. There are times when I am prone to review it as indefensible—the flagrant violations of treaty, the formal announcements unto the weaker foe that we honourably intended to violate such provisions of the treaty as suited us. "The article," wrote we in the utmost courtesy that language is capable of, "must necessarily, regrettably be suspended." We benevolently warned our enemy, in all justice and fairness, that neither the ready power to crush and annihilate them nor the will to call it into action were wanting if it ever appeared requisite, however remotely, for the safety and integrity of the Anglo-Indian Empire or frontiers. I recollect the sums of money exacted under threat of advance, the use of intimidation, the astonishing course of marching upon the desert fortress of Imangarh—literally "citadel of honesty"—without any declaration of war and razing it to the ground. No one shall ever deny Napier's brilliant generalship and the valour and devotion of our soldiers. With a small force of 3000 we utterly routed, against tremendous odds, a large army of 30,000. If Napier alone made 70,000 pounds from the plunder of Hyderabad, well be it known that he deserved every penny of it for his estimable artifice, endurance and strategy. Of his benevolent intentions he alone is the best judge, though his words to the effect that we had no right to seize Sind and yet we did so and made of it all "a very advantageous, useful, humane piece of rascality" has occasioned me no little disquietude . . .

'It fell to me to plant the British colours upon the ruins of Imangarh, a duty of no mean honour and credit. The recollections of that spirited triumph are none too distinct. Suffice that Davis and I led the uphill assault, cheek by jowl, and Davis it was held the British standard. And Davis it was fell, shot from behind and mine was the hand that planted the British flag. Only one other man did witness how my comrade Davis fell, Captain Andrewes, and he lived not long enough to give tongue. No one knows how Davis fell. I do, my son. Imangarh made of me a war hero, a Colonel, and Davis my friend a dead man . . .'

Edwin was conscious of a curious breathlessness and panic, a constriction of throat, a dryness of mouth. The words struggled out of the yellow pages, gracefully overstepping the hurtful truths, but leaving a bizarre welter of possibilities to the imagination.

'Pir Muhammad,' went on another paragraph, 'was more than a bearer. He was a devoted admirer, a fervent follower, staunch and true, a man in whose eyes I could do no wrong. I ask myself ever and anon: what else was there for me to choose? Invaluable information was promised forth and all I had to give up was the native spy. I sent up Pir Muhammad, my servant, my friend, the only native in my camp that night. A hostage for a day, I assured him. The British army would not permit the barbarous Baluchs to injure a hair on his head. Pir Muhammad would not doubt his master to save his soul. We decamped that night under cover of darkness, carrying back with us the secrets Napier needed. No one ever found out what happened to Pir Muhammad. They gave him, I presume, a horrific end when news of the flight of the British regiment got abroad. Imangarh fell and then Hyderabad. But I beheld, one evening, a carrier pigeon a-hover above the eaves of the homestead wherein we were billeted. The note was brief. "We punish dishonour with death." I can no longer pretend ignorance of the act alluded to. The vengeance of the barbarous tribes of these hills is well beknown. My soul is now reconciled to the unknown end in store for me. I entrust unto you the truth, my son: not upon a field of battle did the hero fall, nay. Mayhap in the dead of night shall the coward be felled, the hero of Sind, stabbed in the back with a poisoned dagger, as is the way of vengeance in these parts, the code of honour among the hillmen here. For my part, my son, I have long learnt that the world is not run on principles such as we believe. The world is run on principles other than honour, my son, and wisdom comes with this dire knowledge. Yet one who is raised upon a tradition of honour can but seek to guide himself by a rough imitation thereof in a dishonourable world. Honour is not dead. Honour has just never existed, my son. And if it does exist, whither is one to look for it? I must search my soul for an answer and herein do I find it: witness the honourable confessions of a dishonourable man. My disconcert disproves me. I rejoice in my fall for it proveth me wrong. You have heard of the parable of the Prodigal Son. I bring unto you the parable of a prodigal father . . .'

The exigency of self-vindication dictated such enormous feats of adaptation, the old yardsticks being twisted and tormented into new applications. Suddenly there was naked sincerity, raw appeal, confession of wrong done and waiting to be expiated. Suddenly

Edwin had the impression of being down there in the chair with a troubled, shabby man across the table, a man with a care-worn, anxious face, with a shrinking eye, a question in its expression, a plea for merciful judgement writ upon his countenance. No decorations, no medals, no epaulettes, no sparkle or rasp or repartee, no bark in his voice, no sting in his words.

Many cancellations occurred upon the troubled pages, crossed out but evidently meant to be read as though they were the dictate of a conscience not weak enough for silence and not strong enough for speech. The personality founded upon the cancellations alone was a full-bodied one, consistent and convincing. This was not the picture he had constructed of a hero but a dark negative image. Edwin read on, read over and over again times without number, until the account wound up with the ultimate words: With which words the author of this missive humbly solicits that he be compassionately remembered and that his name, however unworthy, be not omitted in the prayers of his son, Edwin Braithwaite Reginald Watkins, in whose safekeeping be entrusted the legacy of truth herein recounted and that the mercy of his progeny be vouchsafed, commending the soul of their sire, Vernon Agnew Watkins unto Jesus Christ, Our Lord, Amen.

Edwin never knew how long he lay thus, head down upon the table, weary beyond words. Many a time he looked, uncomprehending, from the gun to the faded sheets before him. Only two truths struck him as conclusive—violence and words. Edwin had the sensation of being somehow edged, weightless, in an inverted world at an awkward slant, of looking down from a great height upon a curious, oblique landscape of treetops, the geography of which had not been plotted out and for which the old cardinal directions were useless. And winding betwixt them a thin white trail of a path that was not composed of land but was a shred of empty sky. A panic seized him that he might never find his footing again, overstep the safe confines of firm land and step into that insubstantial space that led nowhere beyond itself, that dissembled as solid earth but was composed of treacherous perspectives of nothing. Nobody, resolved Edwin vaguely, must see that letter. And yet its contents awaited his evaluation. His judgement had to be framed and privately pronounced, his face set in a decisive expression ere he left the chamber and met them all without. A great fatigue overcame him. In what way, other than physical, was he connected with that man? Why should his judgement matter at all? Why was it assumed by that long-dead man that some moral continuity was necessary and natural, that errors long ago committed merited assessment and allowance, that confessions conferred integrity and release from guilt? That man had fallen in his own eyes and he now waited to be reinstated in dignity by an act of emotional surrender, twenty years late. Suppose, reflected Edwin, I were to decline this honour, deny this responsibility? However could one resume one's own continuity bereft of so many favourite ideas? Too much had to be redefined before he could look another human being in the face unashamed. What an ungracious birthday gift to confer—a lexicon gone suddenly bankrupt!

A bonfire had formed no part of the memsahib's plans for the evening, yet she was presently amazed to behold a glorious bonfire ablaze on the drive with Edwin rallying up the visitors to partake of the pleasures of the night air with an elation altogether out of accord with his sombre cast of mind. And when, led by an aghast Colonel Memsahib, the guests assembled in a confounded bunch upon the porch, Edwin lurched out a piece of hectic oratory, the merriment of which was absolutely at odds with the senselessness of its words. Only a smattering of phrases reached the ear in a grand, garbled delivery:

'Gentlemen and ladies!' cried Edwin. 'As part of this evening's delights I am required to make a speech upon perusing the memoirs of the late Vernon Agnew Watkins, unhappily my father. I wish to bring to your kind notice, ladies and gentlemen, that the posthumous confidences which the late Colonel thought fit to repose in me this evening of evenings, lie rightly reduced to cinders at the bottom of yonder bonfire and I defy any to induce me to utter a word respecting them now and evermore! I wish to draw your attention, ladies and gentlemen, that this is no ordinary bonfire. Into its making have gone the thoughts of Spinoza, the sonnets of Shakespeare, the reflections of Marcus Aurelius, yes, all the prized books of my library, all the prized preoccupations of my brain. Into it have gone my petty compositions, my shabby speculations . . .'

'Edwin!' cried the Colonel Memsahib, aghast, hastening forward and laying an arm upon his. 'What's all this, Edwin? Speak up, my son. Pull yourself together. Compose yourself, do.' She stared up in shock and dismay at his strange, glazed eyes, his working jaw.

Edwin shook her off. 'Farewell!' cried he in derision. 'Goodnight, gentlemen. I have now come of age and enjoy the privilege of granting you leave to tread the measure all this lovely night through. I, for my part, shall advert to my chamber, alas, empty of all I cherished, and leave you to your joys!'

Oh, heavens, the scandal! Rosalie was in tears and the memsahib tight-lipped, took in the situation. Already there were delighted whispers being exchanged. However would they ever live it down? All Calcutta would hear . . .

Commotion reigned in the ballroom, cries and exclamations, queries and bewildered exchanges. The servants peered from behind curtains, their black eyes shining in excitement. Nothing like this had ever happened before—a sahib gone berserk and without a drop inside him!

Knocking on Edwin's door, calling out and pleading having proved of no avail, it was Mr Dutt the hostess quietly sought out.

'Please, Mr Datt, we shall be infinitely beholden to you if you endeavour to exercise your influence upon Edwin . . . remonstrate with him to behave himself . . .'

'I shall endeavour, madam,' said he.

And when the gentle knock sounded upon Edwin's door and Mr Dutt's low voice responded from without, the guests were intrigued to behold the door slide open, admit Mr Dutt's slight form and close behind him.

'Mr Edwin,' ventured Mr Dutt quietly, 'why was all this necessary?'

The boy raised tired eyes into his face and an expression of shame and misery filled his countenance.

'I don't know,' stammered he. 'I had to do something. An act . . . a gesture . . . to mark the break.'

Mr Dutt nodded. 'May I sit down awhile?'

'I earnestly ask you to,' cried Edwin.

Mr Dutt complied. 'That letter upset you?' asked he simply.

Edwin looked away. 'I cannot speak of it,' said he, sullen.

'I do not ask you to,' said Mr Dutt. 'But one thing intrigues me, Mr Edwin. What were Shakespeare and Spinoza paying for?'

Edwin hung his head.

'You must needs make your spiritual fathers pay for whatever you hold your fleshly father guilty of?'

'Please,' begged the boy irritably, 'don't ask me anything. I know nothing now save that everything is wrong. Everything is different. It's always been so—and I never knew it. Somebody has been wrong about things. Has ever been wrong. A . . . a chronic error somewhere. A most godawful misconstruction!'

Mr Dutt let him speak. Edwin rose and walked the half-dozen short steps to his now empty bookshelves.

'All these years,' he spoke up with some difficulty, finding himself slowly as he uttered. 'All these years I've been teaching myself, preparing—for what? There's nothing to say and nobody to speak to. No more words for me, I say. No more expression . . .'

'But one who is trained to render in words will go on doing so, speaking, if necessary, to the vacant air,' put in Mr Dutt. 'You shall go on doing what your soul is trained for, God alone knows why. The spirit has its habits as much as the body.'

'You saw this terrible evening, sir. People, music, singing, sermons, speeches, stories, natter! Do you know how much money my mother squandered—to make herself estimable in the eyes of these . . . these fakes, these boors, this empty, unkind lot. What are they capable of even at their best and brightest? Did you hear them speak? Buying, selling, conquering and imposing! Did you notice the manner in which they meet old friends? What haste they are in to render an account—their station, their emoluments, the number of baboos they command! They judge of fineness by a chandelier or a dinner service. They judge of a man by his rank, his decorations. I would I could ask some of them: "But where are you now, sir? Whither have you reached? In yourself?" I daresay they shall answer: "I began as a grocer's boy and look at me, I am the Viceroy's bootblack now and wear the livery of the Government House!" Oh God, oh God, I'm through with it all, I say. That's why I burnt it all up—let them squeal! Men aren't creatures of such excellence that their approval should matter any more to me! I hate these successful people! I love the world's great failures—I wish I knew 'em all!'

He sank into the chair, clasping his head, overwrought. 'My head aches. My head aches with it all! I'm through with this natter, this cunning speech, these crafty ideas. I would I could cross 'em all out of my heart—as one crosses out a wrong line of verse! I will not play this lying game. I . . . I decline. I . . . resign my membership of humankind. I shall never read or write again. I shall not pay for my term on earth in counterfeit coins. I want a . . . a real language, or no speech at all!'

'Wait,' interposed Mr Dutt. 'You are uttering a real language, son. And if you have not noticed it so far, let me make you wise of the fact that you are speaking the stuff of philosophy even when you do deny it. And were you to write it down you would realize that this is your first real poem . . .'

'No, no, no, no!' burst out Edwin. 'To trim lines again with garden shears! Never, never again! I'd rather be a cook or a carpenter!'

'I often wonder,' said Mr Dutt, ignoring his companion's ravings, 'what life would be like to those who need not utter anything about it, who need no language. But you, my son, are one who must ever render things constantly to himself? Even when you abuse it. You shall never be free from the imperative to express. Some day you shall write it down—in a different form maybe . . .'

'Some day!' said Edwin bitterly. 'And meanwhile I am left clutching a gun and a story of deception. General falsehood, death. The whole pattern is wrong and why were we wrong?'

'Not the whole pattern,' said Mr Dutt. 'But a few parts thereof . . .'

'But if,' argued Edwin, 'if a single part seems right, do you accept it with equal force?'

'If you piece it out, son, you are disposed to notice that there are more things that seem right than seem wrong.' He fell silent, reflecting. 'One excellent line of verse can save an entire poem. And recollect: one man's blood expiated for the sins of generations . . .'

Edwin looked up, confused.

'The good thief, recollect, was exalted to heaven on the strength of one act. It's a mixed world—a game of noughts and crosses. You must needs plot it out as you see fit, make it work as you deem right, let the noughts overwhelm the crosses or the crosses overwhelm the noughts—but for every nought there is a cross. I suspect that every wrong has a corresponding right somewhere in the world.'

'And honour?' asked Edwin. '"The world is run on principles other than honour." That's what he wrote.'

'Edwin Reginald Braithwaite Watkins,' spoke Mr Dutt and there was a note of paternal command in his voice that made Edwin look up in slow comprehension. 'I ask you to believe me. Honour is never dead, my son. Human honour may yet be found among the world's fools and failures, spread invisibly all over the world and usually anonymous. Look for it still. Look where you least expect to find it. Be not misled by birth or breeding or speech or style. Fineness occurs oft in the most unrefined. Even when we act in utmost dishonour we know full well what honour is. Even when we do lie most flagrantly we know in our souls what the truth is. That's how goodness continues even in the foulest of acts.'

'Ineffectually,' said Edwin.

Mr Dutt shrugged. 'I wonder,' said he.

'"These are the honourable confessions of a dishonourable man,"' thought Edwin. 'He wrote that too. He knew all along. And one good line of verse can redeem an entire . . .' There were now no clear definitions, no cut-and-dried solutions, no straight causes; there were complexities, qualified situations, flexible yardsticks. But still the old words existed, if no longer absolute at least adaptable and living, still living.

'And, Mr Edwin,' said Mr Dutt, smiling, 'when you order a fresh stock of books for your shelves, dare I hope that I may be present? You shall, I am sure, read the old books again, once you have refurbished your library.'

Edwin rose sheepishly, still confused, but nodded.

'And now come, my son,' said Mr Dutt. 'They await you.' And Edwin followed.

'Your son, madam,' said Mr Dutt.

'Where is the letter? Oh, you burnt it! How could you? What did Papa write?' cried Rosa.

'Hush!' warned the Colonel Memsahib. 'Don't speak of it. He is a little disturbed. It's all been very trying for him.'

'Nay,' said Mr Dutt. 'Edwin has come of age. Some claret for Mr Edwin, madam.'

'Who in heaven's name is he?' sniffed Miss Parker. 'The life and soul of the party, bless us all!'

'Some sort of a native English poet,' whispered Rosa.

'Nay, Miss Rosalie,' smiled Mr Dutt, hearing. 'A Bengalee poet is what I am now. Like Mr Edwin here I have—how do you say?—come of age.'

Emilia O'Brien came and led Edwin away. He strove to remember the steps of the waltz. And did. The band began playing "Leezie Lindsay". The empty floor began filling up again.

Winter Companions

As a general principle of caution Rameshwar Dayal avoided making new friends older than himself. He was willing to make the acquaintance of young people. The young looked on him as a sort of curiosity. At worst they treated him with surly condescension or decided to have endless ideological differences with him. But at best they became props to lean on—they booked his gas, paid his telephone bill, rushed to the power station when there was a power failure and called the doctor when he was taken ill. But persons of his own age or older could always commit the irresponsibility of predeceasing him, an act of inconsideration that Rameshwar Dayal was not equal to coping with. At seventy-five he avoided every occasion when opportunities for making the acquaintance of the old came his way.

Still, situations arose from time to time to introduce new persons into his simple existence. Nothing surprised him more than the unexpected association with old Saghir Ahmed Siddiqui, the last—and in some ways the best—friendship of his life.

Theirs was a morning walk association. Saghir Ahmed's sudden appearance in the park had a touch of the incredible about it. Rameshwar Dayal entered the Company Garden at his usual hour, one late February morning. It was the hour when an ashen sky, already plastered with Kanpur murk, began thinning with a slow-filling dust of light.

Between a quarter to six and seven in the morning Rameshwar Dayal laboriously covered two circuits of the park. Then, face to the east, twenty-five inhalations and exhalations. Six waist turns, conquering the obdurate old spine; six iron-willed advances towards. Followed by half an hour's tranquil meditation on an old stone bench. Sometime between six and six-fifteen the dense sky stretched to its ultimate resistance and gave way. Above the massive outline of the LIC tower the skin of the sky cracked under some internal tension and a cold shower of light fell through. A sharp little breeze came along and shuffled the sheaves of lit-up leaves above the Bata building. The park, the greenhouses, the oblong blocks of faded concrete in the distance lifted themselves out of the morning steam, emerging motionless with an opaque shine on all their sunward surfaces and furred over with mist in their unlit hollows. A polished note of rare birdsong sounded like a plucked string twanging in a vast, empty room, and miraculous little parrots and squirrels appeared in groups, taking their walks. By the time Rameshwar Dayal returned to the stone bench and his shawl, a glassy light had already pitched itself like a smoking tent astride the park.

Looking back after a space of months, it was the shawl which had started everything. Returning one morning he found it flung upon the grass and an unfamiliar gentleman on the bench. He stood, looking upon both with undisguised displeasure.

The stranger, when the pause grew strained, turned slightly and indicated the shawl upon the grass with enquiry in his eye.

'Yours?' he asked. He had strange, lighted eyes. Rameshwar Dayal nodded.

'Am I encroaching upon your space?' asked the stranger politely. 'This, I understand, is your place in the sun, which I have inadvertently occupied. But this . . .'—he poked the limp shawl with the ferrule of his stick—'this mantle of yours . . .' His words trailed off. He shifted to one side of the bench. 'Do I suppose that it is regularly laid upon this bench to guarantee occupancy?

As they lay books and papers upon railway berths or cinema hall seats? And you leave it here for any interested party to purloin? Bespeaks a very high opinion of human integrity, if I may say so, sir.'

His words followed a chiselled, old-fashioned formality of diction, blending syrup with acid with no loss of friendliness.

Rameshwar Dayal pulled his mouth into an apologetic grimace. 'The ragged old shawl was not likely to arouse acquisitive feelings in any but the most abject mendicant,' he murmured. On its worn weave the dyers had done their work and the darners as well. And over and above the activity of human agents, several decades had wrought their relentless service of decline.

'And yet,' added Rameshwar Dayal, reaching out to retrieve it from the grass, 'you may find it hard to believe it but it is a genuine old pashmina. An antique piece, you might say. It has seen better days.' He was tempted to add, 'As I have', but he stopped himself in time. The unfinished implication was sufficient for instant transference.

'I can well believe it,' responded the stranger. 'One can see how proud you are of it. Did you receive it with a citation, may one ask? Ah, the vanity of Antisthenes shows through the holes in his cloak—eh, what?' He laughed. 'But,' he went on, 'is it any special subtlety of yours or any slowness of mine that I fail to grasp the function of this relic?' He turned a quizzical glance upon the object under discussion. 'I used it as a duster—my apologies—but what do you use it for? Evidently it is not employed to armour your person against the chill, or why would it have been left behind? Even if, meaning no disrespect to its sacred antiquity, it had the capacity to cover or the power to protect . . .'

This touched upon a painful matter and one most private to Rameshwar Dayal. It embarrassed him a great deal but he was constrained to come clean.

'I use it to sit on—you know—this hard stone bench—I suffer from a troublesome and tragic ailment . . .' And in a hushed and shamefaced whisper he mentioned its dreadful name.

The stranger took no such deferential view of the malady. He flouted its sanctity with an outburst of hooting merriment.

'I see it all!' he said, laughing. 'But why blush to utter the sacred syllables of its name, sir? Fistula is a most respectable and melodious name. By the way, Dr Johnson wrote some pretty observations about fistulas, did you know?'

Rameshwar Dayal shifted uncomfortably on his perch upon the bench. He wished he had not bared his heart. Bared his arse would be more exact! He cursed himself. He flung his reproaches upon himself in angry self-loathing. But the stranger prattled on in an unstoppable flood of amusement.

'Have you ever reflected, sir, how diseases have names as dainty and tuneful as the names of delicate maidens—Primula, Ursula, Petula, Fistula, I could name dozens more. It must be the Latin roots, I guess. So, I perceive, this shawl interposes its tender mediation betwixt bench and backside. Interesting, eh, what? You don't share my humour, no? My humour is banal-anal too, ha, ha! You keep a straight face—I see that you are a gentleman, sir. And the gentleman, I maintain, must now be declared a protected species and threatened with extinction. There must be special national parks for him to wander about at large in sweet civilization, unmenaced by all barbarity—like the Maharaja of Rewa's choice white tigers. But what, you may ask, constitutes a gentleman?' The explosion of eloquence ceased and the strange lighted eyes came to focus sharply on Rameshwar Dayal's tremulous countenance, so insistent, so piercing, that Rameshwar Dayal was indeed compelled to obey their command and mutely signal the question: What constitutes a gentleman?

'If you know the answer, sir, I am happy to withdraw the question. But if you don't . . .' the eyebrows bristled, black-quilled, rubbed the wrong way by an imperious brush of the hand, '. . . if you don't, let me bring to your attention, Mr—'

'Dayal,' prompted Rameshwar Dayal.

'Dayal,' declared the other. 'Let me bring to your attention, Mr Dayal, that the matter has been one of pre-eminent interest in my life. I have subjected the question to the analysis it deserved and in the course of a long career lecturing in the university . . .'

'You are a teacher, then?' ventured Rameshwar Dayal.

'That's right. I was. In Allahabad. Retired. Well, university makes strange bedfellow, as I was fond of saying. And exposure to the rank and file of humanity gave me a great many insights into the subject. A gentleman, in short, is a man of our times who, living in this Kanpur of ours, still happens to remember or suspect that a Titan could be something other than a brand of watch and Milton something more than a brand of insulated tableware.'

The next morning saw Rameshwar Dayal become the embarrassed recipient of an uncommon gift. An inflatable foam cushion, doughnut-shaped.

'You fill it with air—and comfort the rear, ha, ha! Sorry, I have an unhappy proclivity for poesy,' laughed the boisterous stranger. 'It's time to relieve the patrician pashmina, you know, from the ignoble functions you compel it to perform. All you do is produce this little pneumatic marvel from your overcoat pocket—' (And although it was late February the stranger still wore an oversized overcoat and a thick woollen cap and muffler)—'you puff a few lungfuls of God's air into its flexible interiors—and put a stopper, thus, and presto! A cushion to please the most fastidious of fistulas—what?'

Rameshwar Dayal flushed in discomfort.

'I'm afraid I haven't the stamina,' he stuttered.

'The stamina for what?' queried the other. 'Puffing air? Not to worry. For me it's just what the doctor ordered. Just right for my asthma. A few deep puffs and you have your cushion and I have my deep breathing exercises. What do you say to that? What did you say your name was, sir?'

Rameshwar Dayal told him again.

'Saghir Ahmed Siddiqui is mine,' returned his companion.

The stranger, his narrow cheeks ballooning wide, put the cushion to his lips, wheezed laboriously into it, plugged the stopper to the valve and flicked his fingers with playful satisfaction.

So the cushion it was that necessitated a collaborative constitutional every morning after that. The mornings unfolded around them as they walked, the trees of the park awoke in thick swoops of bouncy green fleece, muffled in tatters of smog. Some days a strong wind blew down from the river, bringing its curious pungent stench of tannery decay. The bunches of whipped green tumbled and tossed about, churned stiff by the wind, the green ladled on in rich, foaming dollops. Then the breeze died away and a shred of light dribbled across the park. Presently the entire path was trapped in a fine net of light. And as they walked, matching stride with stride, and stride with the rhythm of the blood, Rameshwar Dayal found himself talking more and more.

'Funny.'

'What?'

'I mean to say—when the pressure of strength grows thin the pressure of the blood goes up. Hardening of the arteries along with softening of the brain.'

'These are life's little antitheses.'

'But all the same,' pondered Rameshwar Dayal, 'it seems to me that far from blunting the powers of perception, age has served to sharpen the keenness of those senses still left. So that, you know, with the slowness of the blood, there awakes a corresponding accuracy of attention to all this.' He meant a lot of things. He could not always verbalize his meanings. He waved his hands about. His hands hinted at many suggestions—the detail and display of life, tracing the polished curve of things, the grain of the world's surface, 'with leisure and detachment,' he finished helplessly.

But Siddiqui knew exactly what he meant.

'What did I do for a living? Let me tell you, Siddiqui sahib, that I had one major occupation and two minor ones. Ministering to the wife's caprices was my major life work. Working in the Directorate

of Education and gardening were my two minor ones. My major
occupation ended forever six years back when she passed away,
God rest her soul. My two minor ones ended when I retired and
I realized that gardening tires me out and the water supply grew
erratic in my area . . .'

Siddiqui cupped a hand behind his ear.

'Erotic,' he asked, astonished.

'Erratic,' repeated Rameshwar Dayal loudly.

'Oh,' beamed the other.

Rameshwar Dayal's voice was sombre. His stride was measured.
'The water supply seems to correspond to the flow of my personal
enthusiasms, if you get what I mean.'

'An ex-educationist?'

'That's right.'

'Come to think of it, isn't it strange that most of us, retired men,
are still introducing ourselves by our former positions? I am, for
example, an ex-professor. That tall gent there with the mutton-chop
whiskers, who waves his stick as he walks is an ex-colonel. It's sinister.
Sometimes I feel we're ghosts in this world. I wonder if the dead meet
and converse thus, you know.' "I used to be so-and-so. And you?"
Ex-Siddiqui meeting ex-Dayal. But we wouldn't be Siddiqui and
Dayal then.' He took a few more paces, musing. 'Do you think that
each of us has one constant name, quite distinct from our present
name—a name we've mislaid in memory—when we die we may
recover it—and our deceased buddies may be calling us that even
now?' He thought in silence and Rameshwar Dayal walked along,
expectant. 'It must be a name as elemental as light, as impersonal as
mathematics, something non-syllabic, a sort of symbol.' A sudden
smile appeared on his face. 'And talking of names, just listen to this
one. I read somewhere that in 1933 Mustafa Kemal Pasha decided
that the Turkish must choose surnames for themselves. So, given
the option, the Turkish set about exercising their wits to choose
ideal names. Some chose names like Fisek, which means cartridge,
or Zararsiz, which would translate as Mr Harmless; or Nalbantoglo

which means son-of-the-blacksmith; and some were Nazik or Mr Polite, and there were more ambitious attempts—Mr Mad Smoke, Mr Monster and adventurous ones like Pure-Nut, Swollen-Leg, Mouldy, Head-Of-Stone and Dwarf-Man-Of-Iron. But what impressed me most was an original number like Mr Son-Of-The-One-Who-Does-Not-Lie-Down-and-Sleep-Under-Poplar-Trees. Names, I felt after reading that piece, must be personally and imaginatively chosen. Maybe I could run a name-selecting consultancy.'

And so it was day after day. February gave way to March. To Rameshwar Dayal his new friend combined the contrary virtues of alienness and insight. And he spoke to him as he hadn't spoken for years, finding new words, hitting upon unarticulated realizations, sharing confidences as one shares them with a stranger in a train, who receives them in the fullness of their reckless indiscretion to vanish into oblivion for all time.

They sat upon the bench for an hour after their walk and the branches of the drumstick tree threw up its delicate paisley upon the sky. They questioned one another and spoke of what they knew.

'For my part, RD, I have decided to hold all theories about life in abeyance—sort of suspend philosophy and just drift along.'

'But drift towards something?'

'Well, yes. Maybe the currents of time and situation shall blow me to some final truths of existence. But I'm not going to work too hard at it now. I maintain no steady insistence upon theories about what you call the "human condition".'

'Have you noticed,' asked Rameshwar Dayal after a brief moment, 'how there are periods of intensified eventfulness in one's life? Suddenly people begin falling ill, dying out . . . then there comes a long fallow expanse when time seems to fade out. No child is born in one's immediate circle and no new deaths occur either. But you sit in a home left vacant and you're surprised at its emptiness. It's that neutral phase between middle age and old age.' He brooded, his eyes fixed upon the grass. 'It seems to me that it's these eventless spells that give life its consistency, when our understandings are digested, as it were, when our meanings are worked out and happiness is defined. It gives you time to catch your breath. I often think, Siddiqui sahib, that our real enemies are our own emotions.'

And Siddiqui answered, 'All said and done, my dear fellow, the real thing is the way you put yourself together again after each big fall. But, then there comes a fall you can't recover from—right at the end.'

'I believe that someone does come along to lend you a hand at that instant.'

'This may just be a case of bogus mysticism.' There was soundless laughter in Siddiqui's voice.

'What do you believe then?'

'Well, I've kept my spiritual options open.'

'Anyway, it's all behind me now. And I'm grateful too, in a way. I mean a life without any major misfortunes is a good life to have, isn't it?'

Sitting on the bench together, at the far end of life, some things sorted out and a great many left unsorted by private disinclination, they tasted a wondrous, simple peace.

Their talks sometimes ended in disagreements. Some days Rameshwar Dayal resented Siddiqui's debunking. It wasn't right or wrong that was important—it was argument for its own obstinate sake. An old man's ball game.

'What do I still want to do with my life? I don't know. In the time still left to me I'd like to be able to chalk up a few final truths of life for my own reference. It'd be such a great pity going off without having understood a great many things . . .'

But Siddiqui interrupted, his sallow face turning smug. 'A logical fallacy there. Even if you were to understand a handful of things, what use would they be to you in the meagre time left? You'd soon move on, beyond your own understanding, so?'

But Rameshwar Dayal persisted, wrestling with indescribable uncertainties and conquering them with his stubborn, comforting convictions.

'I don't really know. I mean, surely something would carry over to the next page, some . . . some grand total reduced to an . . . an ultimate figure, a sort of a general impression . . .'

'What a naïve optimist! It's like taking an insurance policy for the afterlife, if there is such a thing.'

'Is there such a thing, d'you think?'

But Siddiqui just wouldn't notice that question and went his own rambling way.

'. . . or like making a fixed deposit of wisdom—to be encashed upon death. But then, death may be, you know, how shall I put it?—a sort of an absolute insolvency of self.'

Rameshwar Dayal dreaded such dark doubts. He set his face against their threat. 'I can't say anything—no one can—but I feel it's not that way.'

But Siddiqui was apparently enjoying himself. 'What vanity, RD. In my reckless moments I feel that living things are just chance expressions of some wayward force, neither good nor bad. We fulfil no purpose. We only act as temporary stations of that energy. A river flows through us but it doesn't know or care for us. Then it moves away and we're so much dead dust upon an abandoned bank.'

'And what does your religion say?' That was Rameshwar Dayal's trump card. Siddiqui's face softened. 'Ah, that. That occupies another compartment of my mind and I take it very seriously.'

Rameshwar Dayal never could understand how this could be.

'Actually,' continued Siddiqui, 'as the old argument goes, since I am part of the problem I seek to solve, I can't ever hope to be right.'

'Exactly.' Rameshwar Dayal sat up. 'Since I am part of the problem I'm considering, I share in its general pattern, so . . . so I can claim to have access to some of its laws.'

They were back to square one. Both fell silent and sulked on the stone bench. In that stalemate the drumstick tree stole its furtive shadow a few inches along the chequered grass.

And one morning in May, the sky flooded hot blue, Rameshwar Dayal brought Siddiqui along to share a bite of breakfast at his shabby apartment overlooking a bazaar. It was an occasion, an unknown and shadowy one that he wished to seal with a small celebration.

Siddiqui, it appeared, did not care for coffee or for tea.

'No, Mian, not for me. A man with your high blood pressure would do well to keep off that morning cup of coffee. For my part, I have no wish to drain this bitter cup. Ugh! It fills my mouth with bitter taste. It fills my mind with bitter thoughts!'

Rameshwar Dayal was surprised. 'Do you never drink tea or coffee, then?'

'Just once. At four-thirty in the afternoon. Ah, that's the hour of agony. The question one asks at one-thirty is: Is there a life after lunch? For me, no, there isn't. Not since I retired—a good fourteen years back. But there's a price to pay for that sleep. I haul myself out of the jaws of slumber as a babe drags itself out of a restful womb. A shudder overcomes me. I could fret and shed tears of sheer despair. It's absolute misery. Such a lethal reluctance of the limbs. I know what Keats meant by the drowsy numbness paining the sense and the hemlock. Then and only then do I seek strength from tea or coffee. But in the mornings, no. No hemlock for me. It's buttermilk for me. Buttermilk makes you live to be a hundred and I hope to do so. Those chaps in the Caucasus live on barley bread and buttermilk.'

Rameshwar Dayal scoffed at this patent lie. 'Buttermilk, eh? And what of the eight-thirty whisky, Siddiqui sahib?'

'Oh, that.' His friend leaned back upon the deckchair. A smile melted the muscles of his thin face. 'That, Mian, is a man's tiny bit of jannat in this sinful world. It's the twenty-fifth hour of the day and no earthly clock can measure it. I dare not presume to claim responsibility for that holy hour.'

'I couldn't disagree with you more,' protested Rameshwar Dayal, pouring buttermilk into two steel glasses. 'For me clarity has always held greater joys than oblivion. It's a pity losing the shape of real things, think what you're missing—there's oblivion enough ahead, without losing touch with actual things, you know.'

'I look on it differently,' said Siddiqui, sipping from his glass. 'Let me tell you of the time I was operated on for cataract.' He produced a muslin handkerchief from his kurta pocket and wiped away the fine white whisker of curd from his upper lip. Ever since he had lost a front tooth, Siddiqui was overly conscious of his mouth, afraid of spraying spittle or breaking into an uncontrollable lisp.

'Before the operation, how milk-white the world seemed. Fuzzy. Ordinary women looked like houris. Ordinary things appeared lovely. Miracles of light and shade. Shapes shrouded in soft suspense. Ah, once I saw not one moon but six! And after the operation how disappointing everything looked—unmysterious, drab, every colour turned hard. Bland—like the salt-free food you're given for your high BP.'

'Oh, I'm not on salt-free stuff now,' said Rameshwar Dayal. 'It's sugar I crave. And have you heard that one about the doctor and the diabetic?'

'No.'

'"Well," the diabetic told the doctor, "My urine report's fine. So can I now eat a gulab jamun, doctor sahib?" The doctor said, "Well, not a whole gulab jamun, sir. Maybe half." So the diabetic rushed to a sweetmeat seller and ordered a gulab jamun, a single kilogram-heavy one . . .'

'—and proceeded to chop it in half and—'

'Exactly,' laughed Rameshwar Dayal.

'Ha, ha,' laughed Siddiqui. 'That's how man may read the will of God if he's smart enough.'

'Ha ha ha!' echoed Rameshwar Dayal. 'Just what I pine to do myself.'

'And that's just the spirit in which I sneak up to the whisky bottle, Mian. I love it. I sip its sweet splendour and it brings out the best in me, the ideal man, the noble being, fresh from Allah's hands, unsmirched by the mire of this evil world. Ah, it makes me recognize all the hidden resources of my brain and find words for them. I rise in self-esteem. I'm amazing, I assure you. My begum used to be quite exasperated by my fluency. "No use, Mian," she said, "In offering namaz five times a day, no use your charities and your pieties." "Begum," I would tell her, "Allah shall grant me a period of grace, be sure, and I shall do adequate penance, but that shall come when it shall come, so please God, but meanwhile . . ."'

They finished the buttermilk and Rameshwar Dayal's servant brought in the tray of savouries.

'Wah!' said Siddiqui with relish. 'Did I tell you that I have conducted a linguistic survey of menu cards? Sweeping changes must now be made in our English dictionaries, I feel.'

Rameshwar Dayal brought mint chutney. 'The first of this season, Siddiqui sahib,' he said.

'Do you know, sandwiches have been "witches" for more than a decade now. And cutlets are often "cutlettes." What would you call it? Indo-Gallic transmutation, ha! I even once ate "Damn Aloos" in a vegetarian restaurant.' He put his plate down upon Rameshwar Dayal's cluttered table, pushing aside the piled-up books and papers. 'Hullo!' he exclaimed. 'What's this, now?'

Rameshwar Dayal's pale, lined face coloured slightly and his mouth went tight. He kept his eyes fixed upon his chutney.

'A pocket calendar,' he said, tonelessly.

'Hummm.' Siddiqui did not put it down but continued to study it with uncalled-for attention. 'A lot of dates encircled in red. What's this? A private holiday list?'

'Something of the sort,' answered Rameshwar Dayal.

'I see that the sixth of May is circled in red? Today. What's all this, RD?'

'The sixth of May is my late wife's birthday,' said Rameshwar Dayal slowly. He pushed his plate aside and went and stood at the only window overlooking the busy bazaar.

The Greeks had called it nepenthe. A drug to induce forgetfulness of grief. He thought of her. A vivid image, exact and entire, every detail in place, ambushed his mind and left it staggered. Another sixth of May and she had stood, forty-seven years old, on the brink of age, her skin papery and bravely withstanding, with the fine lines enforcing the strength of the struggle, her dyed hair upholding its determined twin waves, last bastions of resistance, and large ruby drops in her earlobes, supporting the strong red of her bindi in the desert of her forehead and the staunch oasis of her crimsoned lips. Suddenly he had noticed that she could still look good and in a voice unaccustomed to ardour had clumsily muttered approval. And she darted her old accusing look at him and said 'Oh, you!' in that typical blend of pleasure and disgust. And when he had protested she looked away and busied herself with the table, saying in a voice of complaint which ever guarded her privacies, 'Well, it's getting harder and harder to manage. Don't look at me too closely after today.' That was already more than twenty years ago. And Rameshwar Dayal remembered how much she had suffered before she died, and how disfigured the disease had left her. It came to him in a shock of pain that she knew nothing of the new things that had happened to him in the last six years—the coat he had bought, the shrubs he had planted, the weight he had put on, she, who while she lived, knew everything about their life by natural inquisitiveness or uncanny conjecture.

Somebody joined him at the window. They stood a long while in silence. In their separate solitudes they gazed down upon the city of their childhood and retirement, its dense sky with its charcoal rivers of soot, its burnt smells and strong suns, its spice and sewage and smoke, its carved balconies and chattering alleys, its buffoonery and bluster and, surmounting all, its tall chimneys sending smoke signals up into the sky, tall quills writing an endless, rolling smoke script that boiled away into the ragged clouds.

'And the thirty-first of May?' urged Siddiqui.

'The anniversary of my retirement,' answered Rameshwar Dayal.

'Indeed. And the twenty-first of July?'

'My birthday.'

The low voice prodded him repeatedly and he disclosed his secret almanac of associations with relief, with embarrassment and with some annoyance too.

'The second of September?'

'The birthday of my only son.'

'Where is he now?'

'In Bangalore. We fell out over his marriage,' came Rameshwar Dayal's brusque reply.

'And the tenth of October?'

'My marriage anniversary.'

'And this one here, the tenth of March?'

Rameshwar Dayal took a deep breath. 'That,' he said, 'is the birthday of my special God, Lord Shiva.'

Siddiqui stroked his beard.

'Strange,' he mused. 'Each man carries his own calendar. I do too. But I'm one of those lucky ones who have the skill of forgetting. But you, ah, poor chap, must you embalm it all in red circles upon paper?'

Rameshwar Dayal uttered a stiff laugh. 'Just a tiny private habit. A New Year's Day rite. I buy a pocket calendar and circle up my special days.'

'And stranger still,' mused Siddiqui, 'that in all our personal calendars there's one date hidden from us all—the anniversary of our own death. There it lurks, somewhere between the first of January and the thirty-first of December and we live through it year after year, unsuspecting . . .'

This was such a new and unnerving thought that Rameshwar Dayal turned to stare abruptly at his companion. The idea inflated slowly in his brain.

'You're right,' he murmured. 'It's there all this while. It's been there all these years. Sown in like a weed.' His best, most natural metaphors always came from gardening.

'Like a bomb.' And Siddiqui's metaphors came from war.

'Or like the bulb of a lily, underground but alive, waiting to sprout in season,' said Rameshwar Dayal, the gardener.

'Or explode in my face and fragment me.'

'And isn't it strange? That everybody else shall recognize it as the day of our death, but we ourselves may be beyond that recognition.' There was a long, numb pause. Then, on an impulse, Rameshwar Dayal declared his faith. 'On the whole, I prefer to think of it as a lily bulb—a future flowering, a . . . a further growth. Not a . . . a killer bomb.' Some urgency filled him with words and more words. He seemed to be pleading his case against a deadly sentence. 'Do you know, Siddiqui sahib, you may feel that one bomb does it all and then you lie waiting for God's judgement, but we Hindus believe we continue to flower, season after season, wearing different stems and petals, the seeds of our being ever reverting to that original buried bulb beneath the surface . . .'

'For us it's a flowering too,' mused Siddiqui. 'We lie waiting beneath the earth and our season shall come when all earthly seasons are over . . . and that is when the bulb shall sprout . . .'

A piercing siren from the mill tore its way through these meditations, and both old men grew self-conscious with the unease of unwitting self-disclosure.

'What a giant mailbox,' remarked Siddiqui, standing on the last step behind the collapsible gate. 'You must be receiving a lot of letters.'

'Scarcely,' answered Rameshwar Dayal. 'None, in fact. That mailbox remains, from other times.'

Siddiqui stopped for a moment. Then his ironical old man's grin creased his face. 'Well, RD, someone said that in this world nothing is unavoidable except death and taxes. On the whole I prefer the former.'

They laughed, and salaamed one another.

When Rameshwar Dayal returned to his apartment on the third floor he discovered, to his perplexity, that his pocket calendar was missing. He fretted over it all day, gave it up as lost without trace. All the same a nebulous suspicion continued to aggravate him.

He had always had a deep dislike for these special days. They nagged his memory into unwanted recollections. There was no refuting their claim. The hours hung around the mind like silent drapes and, palpable behind their thin opacity, lay complete tableaux of the past, indestructible and demanding. The day had to be lived through, a grim country of the mind to be crossed. And it was much worse when evening came. Between five and seven-thirty were the hours of special desolation. He did not know what made them so. And inevitably sleep cheated on him too. It was only when midnight struck, remote and metallic in some dusty clock tower, in some distant, drowsing pocket of the night, that he felt himself released from the dreadful spell of the memorable day. Then, let loose once more in the steady current of uncalculated time, he breathed again, absolved.

So he lay. Ten-thirty and the old cooler turned the steamy air in the room into a clammy sponge. He recognized the oppression. He switched on the TV and switched it off. It was the heat, he thought. It was the stale air. He drank a glass of water, went to the loo, dripping slow and long, an old man's nightly test of patience. He returned to his bedroom, stood at the window. And looked out upon a smudged night sky, a half-erased moon. At the back of his mind he knew who troubled his peace. It was the sixth of May. It was she. And the endless unease of a human being having once been intensely present and now so intensely missing in every pore of the air and every place of his soul.

He stood at the window. And saw a telegraph boy propping his bicycle against a wall. He saw him rattle the collapsible gate and heard the loud jangle and the clink of keys in the doorman's loop. The mutter of voices. Footsteps were rushing up the staircase towards his apartment. And his heart began hammering out its dread. A telegram at eleven in the night! He thought of his son, that reckless, heartless boy with his violent, headlong choices, his proud defiance, his intractable, unmerciful, wilful, wondrous face. And his knees began to tremble with fear at some dreadful event, unknown and away at Bangalore, on that other extreme outpost of his weak, hopeless heart. The doorbell rang and a voice called out his name.

His hands trembled. He shot back the twin bolts, lowered the bar. The door grated open and a rhombus of light fell upon the musty corridor, enclosing the short, khaki-clad form that stood outside, telegram in hand.

'R. Dayal?' He nodded.

'Sign here.' For an instant he didn't remember the letter R and which way to steer the distracted pen.

'Where?' he asked. The man looked up, confused.

'Where is it from? Bangalore?' His tongue was dry and layered with sand.

'No. Local. Urgent.'

The door shut once again on the retreating night caller, the curtains drawn, Rameshwar Dayal read the long message over and over again, spelling over it, revising its many errors and replacing them with likely words, taking up a pen to write out the garbled message correctly upon a sheet for better perusal.

MY DEAR RD STOP ALLOW ME TO EXTEND HEARTFELT THANKS FOR THE COMPLIMENT YOU PAID ME THIS MORNING IN INVITING ME TO SHARE AN OCCASION AS PRIVATE TO YOU AS A LATE WIFE'S POSTHUMOUS BIRTHDAY STOP I OFFER THE ONLY GIFT THAT CAME TO MIND STOP MAY IT REACH YOU ON THE SIXTH ITSELF STOP THIS IS JOHN DRYDEN'S EPITAPH FOR HIS WIFE—HERE LIES MY WIFE—HERE LET HER LIE STOP NOW SHE'S AT REST AND SO AM I STOP WHEN YOU GO TO SLEEP TONIGHT MY FRIEND MAY YOU BE AT REST AS WELL STOP WITH WARM REGARDS STOP SAGHIR

Rameshwar Dayal peered at the sheet. He raised his eyes to consult the watch. It was a quarter past eleven. He must have paid through his nose for this, he thought. Suddenly, noticing the quaint twisted spellings, he smiled, remembering the voice saying 'Damn Aloos'. He hunted around for his spectacles, wondering why a mist obscured the sheet. He found his spectacles, put them on and studied the sheet again, but the mist did not go. He cleared his throat which was unaccountably full. And it was just then that the faraway metallic chime struck its twelve faded hammer clangs upon the air. And Rameshwar Dayal noticed the peace, the knot loosed in his mind, the tiny clot of pain dissolved in grace, the strain laxed. He lay down at last. Sleep lapped its slow waves against his stilled brain. He slipped, unawares, into its cool interior depths and lodged there, inert.

If Rameshwar Dayal had planned to thank Siddiqui he did not get a chance. Riots broke out between their communities. From his window overlooking the scorched bazaar Rameshwar Dayal looked down upon the sun-bleached street, all its shutters down, a city temporarily muffled and blindfolded, all pavements empty of vendors, no carts or voices anywhere as though the torrid season of killings had prompted a wholesale human migration. And, shrill with sirens, roaring through the empty tunnels of the streets, sped grim police vans, their engines grinding like savage rock drills burrowing fiercely through the solid wall of heat. Helmeted squads patrolled the lanes in the bone-white sun. And sometimes of an evening the dun Kanpur sky admitted new streaks of mongrel smoke, unparented by the familiar old chimney towers. No newspapers came and the newsreaders on TV used cautious, guarded phrases of assurance. Living in Kanpur was like building a home in the crater of a dormant volcano. From year to year the mighty tremors came, the blinding explosions, and the hot lava poured in endless burning streams over the lip of the flaming crater. But Rameshwar Dayal was used to his quixotic city of fumes and furnaces, its activities as combustible as its people.

On the empty streets the tar melted. Away at the other end of hearsay, shops were burning. And homes. Flaming objects landed in the abandoned courtyards like tinder. And from his window

Rameshwar Dayal saw the flag-march, the long columns of the army, their stern instruments of threat nosing up like the snouts of prehuman predators, leashed but ever poised to spring. And what was strange was that, year after year, the hot ash from the crater settled in yet another layer of faded human sediment upon the ruins of the old. The human furnaces dimmed to charred dust and the smoke from the mills silently replaced the smoke from the bazaars. The sky patched up its shreds. The murmur of traffic knitted itself together again. The seams of commerce closed gently over the scars in the crust, until it was hard to believe that, embedded in the body of the earth, the old excitable veins pulsed still. But the mills began clacking and the bazaars humming and the great grist of the city went pouring into its giant turning wheels. And thus did the great maw of history consume one generation of human raw material to generate a new generation of finished goods, waiting, in turn to be carried on that overwhelming flood of event back into the churning mess of time, and pulped into grist for a future mill. But in the middle of it all, his bicycle wobbling, under its load of clinking cans, came the milkman, through the back lanes, and knocked gently upon the door, exemplar of peace and evidence of the comforting truth that in the debris and ruts and grooves, life wormed along with all its secret chores, crunching and inching forward under cover of obscurity, and knew that it would always overcome.

Rameshwar Dayal wondered distractedly about Siddiqui. Harboured in the Muslim pocket of Becongunj, Siddiqui perhaps waited, as he did, watching his city from behind the chick of a balustrated window wondering when the curfew would lift. Three weeks went by. Rameshwar Dayal sat down to write a long, breathless letter:

My dear Siddiqui sahib,

I have anxiously waited for these present troubles to end. I wanted to call on you but apart from the fact that you live somewhere in

Becongunj, I do not have your address. I learnt of the big fire and the terrible bomb blasts in Becongunj and was extremely alarmed and worried about you. Can I be of any help? Why don't you move in here with me? If I could only locate where you live.'

He stopped writing. Becongunj was a small area. Surely an enquiry or two would lead him straight to Siddiqui's house. What he wrote did not ring true. He did not go in search of Siddiqui because he was afraid. No Hindu could ever dare to step into a Muslim pocket in riot-torn Kanpur. He wished he could frankly confess it but could not bring himself to. The letter was never completed. It came to lie in tiny shreds in Rameshwar Dayal's basket. Rameshwar Dayal never managed to communicate his sleepless nights to Siddiqui.

And one afternoon when the postal service had begun working again, Rameshwar Dayal found a white packet stuck inside his big mailbox.

'Salutations,' it read, 'on the auspicious anniversary of your retirement, RD. Disraeli once said that when a man falls into his anecdotage it is a sure sign for him to retire. And say I, my friend, that having both retired from service, and due to retire soon from life, may we now enjoy our mutual anecdotes once more. All said and done, we are, as they said in calmer times, *par nobile fratrum*, a noble pair of brothers; *omnes eodem cogimur*, all driven into the same fold when our time comes.

'May I cherish the hope that the opportunity may soon come to resume our walks and share our anecdotage upon the bench, Insha-Allah, so God willing, Saghir.'

Then Rameshwar Dayal suddenly realized that it was the thirty-first of May. Climbing slowly up the stairs to his rooms, he understood now where his pocket calendar was.

The second week of June had arrived by the time things had quietened down, the curfew lifted, the shops reopened and the police vans departed. Approaching the gates of the park, Rameshwar Dayal spotted Siddiqui casually perusing a morning edition of the local paper, standing between a gram seller and a tea stall. And, greeting one another with a salaam and a nod, the two resumed their walks as though nothing much had happened.

Rameshwar Dayal had inwardly experienced some instants of awkwardness. How was he to allude to the recent disturbances between the Hindus and the Muslims which should normally have been the likeliest subject for conversation? To speak of it all would have been treading sensitive ground. Not to speak of it would have been an unnatural evasion. And there were belated thanks to be expressed too.

But Siddiqui seemed full of his latest purchase—a pair of specially designed shoes in finest patent leather, picked up from the back alleys of Ram Narain Bazaar. He took small mincing steps, sat down upon a bench to take them off and display the soles to Rameshwar Dayal, bent to wipe away the dust and eventually complained of footsore fatigue.

'Hardly the shoes to wear to a morning walk, Siddiqui sahib,' observed Rameshwar Dayal mildly.

'I know, I know, my dear RD. But how else was I to show them to you? I bought them just before these confounded killings and lootings and waited all this while to show them to you. Why, I was all for risking breaking the curfew had my neighbours not dissuaded me.'

Rameshwar Dayal bit his lip. 'That would have been unwise, Siddiqui sahib,' he said. But Siddiqui answered, 'To a retired man a pair of shoes is a major investment, you know, I've achieved in twelve months.'

'A very good bargain,' murmured Rameshwar Dayal.

'But,' said his friend, 'may I suggest a rest? I seem to go all breathless these days. And I confess that the state of my soles is of some concern to me.'

Rameshwar Dayal forced a laugh. 'My feet ache too. We're out of practice,' said Siddiqui in English, sitting down with a sigh.

'What d'you think is the circumference of this park?' he asked, after a brief pause.

'Three kilometres, I imagine.'

'Strange. We must have covered a great distance together, RD.'

'Yes,' mused Rameshwar Dayal. 'But always going round and round together, passing the same trees and wicket gates and gravel walks, the same things happening to us at regular intervals.' He laughed. 'We need a pair of tough soles, Siddiqui sahib, to cover so much distance together. As it is, it isn't the best of parks but we've got to make the most of it. We didn't design it, did we?'

'And talking of shoes and soles, let me tell you a Sheikh Sadi parable.' And Siddiqui recounted the tale of the man who had no shoes and who envied all those who had shoes, until one day he saw a man with no feet! And he fell to praising Allah for His mercy. And Rameshwar Dayal remembered a Ramakrishna Paramhansa parable about the man who found the ground too hot and thought of covering the whole earth with leather, and who was advised by his bull to make for himself, instead, a pair of shoes! And then they fell silent and watched the June sun singe white-hot blades of steel through the foliage overhead.

'I've hit upon an astonishing thought, RD,' said Siddiqui, at length. 'That consciousness might be an electronic phenomenon. Life too, who knows.'

And when he returned that morning, Rameshwar Dayal was a little dissatisfied with himself for not having managed to overcome the senseless reticence he was sometimes afflicted with, and not having uttered his thanks.

As it happened, after the riots came the rains and they could not meet too frequently. Some mornings they arrived with umbrellas and squelched laboriously through the puddles which glittered among the stones. But Rameshwar Dayal soon began experiencing the old threatening twinges in his rusted knee and ankle joints, and had to plead for respite.

Then on the second of September, by a miracle of accurate timing, came an inland letter, pale as a flake of submarine memory, surfaced upon the waters of the mind. Rameshwar Dayal lighted upon it one wet afternoon, lodged in his mailbox, like something that the rain had washed up, much spattered and soaked, its letters afloat upon beads of random spray.

'Your son's birthday, RD!' was the forthright preamble. 'I wish you and him the best. And leave Bacon to say the rest. The joys of parents, he wrote, are secret, and so are their griefs and fears. But then, children sweeten labours but they make misfortunes more bitter. For "he that hath wife and children hath given hostages to fortune for they are impediments to great enterprises, either of virtue or of mischief". So, RD, rejoice in your solitude and in the achievement of a life over and completed, with or without satisfaction. Regards. Saghir.'

Reading it over, Rameshwar Dayal had an impulse to write back once again. He began:

'My dear Saghir,

Are you practising your scholarship on me, my friend, now that you have no classroom to hold forth in? Am I your last student, I, a confused old man, past seventy?'

He didn't quite like that bit of self-abasement on his part and decided not to continue with the letter. It found its way into the waste paper basket.

'But, Siddiqui sahib,' he laughed when next they met. 'Why did you forget my own birthday. Remember, the second of July? I waited for a word or a line, you know.'

'Hish! man, you are like a woman!' rebuked Siddiqui. 'And do not understand tact or finesse. An old man doesn't like his birthday remembered.'

'I do,' said Rameshwar Dayal lightly. 'It's a luxury I had forgotten after she went. But you've made me expect it, you know. Well . . .' he became confused. 'It's good to know someone remembers. One isn't exactly a piece of lumber in the backyard then.'

'Shall I risk another scholarly allusion, RD?'

'Go ahead, sir.'

'This time it's going to be Frost. "A diplomat," he said, "is a man who remembers a woman's birthday but never her age."'

'Ha, ha,' laughed Rameshwar Dayal.

'I,' said Siddiqui, 'I am no diplomat. I'd hate to remind you—'

'What?'

'Well, you were seventy-six this year. Or am I wrong?'

'No,' said Rameshwar Dayal slowly. 'You aren't.'

'I imagine,' Siddiqui went on, 'that having walked so many miles together, we may hope to complete a century.'

'In years?'

'No, in kilometres, Mian.'

'But, of course we shall!' exclaimed Rameshwar Dayal, strengthened in some mysterious way. Suddenly assigning himself an undismissible project to prove himself, he added, 'We have got to complete a hundred kilometres, Siddiqui sahib. Even if I creak and limp every step of the way.'

Autumn came, the air in a glistening web. Mornings threaded with beads of early dew. And a gentle, sifted sunlight against the pastel skyline of the city. They walked and talked. They paused at the stall and bought leaves filled with sprouted gram, though neither had teeth strong enough to chew hard. They took to drinking a morning tumblerful of buttermilk together. They frequently returned to the park and sat, speechless, and tired, upon the bench an extra half-hour. And the first little bite had come into the breeze when Siddiqui announced:

'Well, my dear RD, it's time for my annual visit to my second son in Delhi. I spend a couple of months with him every year. But I always return to Kanpur in February.'

'I hope,' responded Rameshwar Dayal, 'that you will keep walking your hour and a half each morning. We have a century to complete.'

'Oh, be sure I shall,' answered Siddiqui. 'Not a day shall go without my assiduous efforts, RD. And the same holds good for you. No shirking, eh?'

'Absolutely not,' laughed Rameshwar Dayal. They were silent for a while. Then, on an afterthought Rameshwar Dayal spoke. 'Doesn't your son ever insist on your staying on in Delhi?'

Siddiqui shook his head. 'I wouldn't stay on even if I could. I can't stay away from this mongrel city of ours. It's fashionable to say—Oh, this filthy city! I hate it! But most of us have been returning to it year after year. I always come back to it.'

After he left, Rameshwar Dayal kept up with his walks, panting along on the coldest of days, appearing at the crack of dawn when all the trees were shawled in mist. And a fortnight later he received a letter with a Delhi postmark.

My dear RD

What have you to remark about a time of life when a man cannot even cross a street? He waits, patiently marshalling his rusted reflexes, steadying his unsure shanks, for a lull in the traffic when a life-or-death urgency pumps an autumnal rush into his limbs. (Sometimes, RD, I feel we're all on one side of a torrent of traffic, just waiting for our crossing to be made, all of us nervous, all of us trusting to luck.) I always congratulate myself when I've crossed a road without mishap. This gives me food for reflection. Is our first emotion after our big crossing one of relief and self-congratulation?

I detest this city. Everybody seems to be putting on an act. Everything measured in money. I feel a poor man. But then I belong not only to a different place but also to a different time. Nineteen fifty, roughly, is my temporal habitat. I am still living off the glow of that decade.

You find me depressed. I am not too well. This morning in the market I had a curious experience. I still haven't sorted it out. Emerging from a shop, I caught sight of a person I used to know. He was short, a little stooped, heavily muffled, and he wore a furred Kashmiri cap and kept his eyes fixed on the ground. I recognized him as Dr Shahabuddin, our Persian professor in the old days. I hadn't seen him for ages and it surprised me that he should still be around—and here in Delhi, buying groceries. All these confused thoughts flashed through my mind in a brief second and also concurrent thoughts that it could not be—he would long have been dead. Then, as I stepped closer, the illusion vanished and I perceived him to be a stranger. I let it go. But a few paces ahead the same thing happened. Getting out of an auto was a young lady in a coffee-coloured saree with beads in her chignon and a knitting bag on her arm. And my heart leapt and I inwardly cried: "What's Rehana doing here? I thought she was in Karachi". And suddenly the lady lifted her head and I saw that it was not my beauteous cousin but an unknown young woman. When the thing happened a third time I became uncertain of my wits. At a fruit juice stall, standing with his back to me, wearing Aligarh pyjamas with Lucknow kurta and a thick Jawahar vest, was the unmistakable form of Shariq, my Aligarh University friend. And I knew now that here was another deception of the senses. The youth shifted his position and, predictably, it turned out to be an unknown young man. And I was suddenly confounded and afraid. Was I seeing things? All those persons I believed I saw were no more in this world. They weren't the ones I mistook for them but they had somehow supplanted the living world with their remote forms. And it occurred to me that at this point of time I am perhaps trapped in two different currents of traffic, moving in different directions, this world and another one. I am their point of intersection and who knows, maybe I am about to abandon one for another. Maybe a part of me is already a denizen of another zone of self. Enough! This gets altogether too dismal. I hope to snap out of my present melancholia and join you in February as planned, God willing. With warm regards, Saghir.

Flipping over the sheet, Rameshwar Dayal could find no address to write back to. And February came and went, and March and April too and he continued to plod along alone, morning after morning, measuring the sum of his acquisition against the slow circuits his old feet covered, quantified as kilometres of conquest. And the great heat came in May. The sky, as the day broke turned the colour of chalk, the mornings windless with only a few small strings of breeze floating idly by. Then, as the hours advanced, the heavy multi-storeyed hulks pulsed with heat. The hot air rose from the bazaars, spicy from the stalls, fermenting from the gutters, and faint with the concentrated sun which sank of its own weight and curdled about the feet as one walked.

Rameshwar Dayal came down the staircase and stepped into the heavy gold gravy of the air. A tinfoil midday sun threw down its light in sharp metallic wires that bore into the eyeballs and made them smart. The drone of coolers sounded on the pavements and hot jets of air swept out of the air-conditioned showrooms on the Mall. And a wind as dense as sawdust, as rough as sandpaper, came dehydrating the throat, and the long highways turned steel grey with heat and lied about water.

June came and went and Rameshwar Dayal wondered what had become of Siddiqui. And the light grew clouded, the sky coated and streaked, the air stained with the scum of approaching storms, and suddenly the grim sky blurted out rain. And Rameshwar Dayal picked his way down the small back lanes, between slimy, mildewed old walls, humid and suppurating with weeds, grasses pouncing wild out of pustules in the cracked stone, the gutters thick with a darkly rolling wash. And as the lane opened into the main road, the city swung about in front of his eyes behind a shifting veil of rain.

Then one day, quite out of the blue, on a day without association of guilt or loss or any advance hint of foredoomed pain, tucked neatly into his mailbox, Rameshwar Dayal spotted a little stamped note, black on white paper. And even before he extracted it he knew what its formal Urdu words carried.

786
17/B, Gulbagh Complex,
Muhammad Shah Marg,
New Delhi

Venerable Sir,

With profound grief I inform you that on 11 July 1993, at 1.20 a.m. the soul of my revered father, Saghir Ahmed Siddiqui, flew,

released from the mortal cage of its corporeal form. We are left bereft
of the hand on the head and dare hope that you shall extend your
benediction upon us and pray that God may grant unto our revered
Walid sahib the highest plane in His sacred heaven,

Obedient tabedar,

Israr Ahmed Siddiqui.

He read it slowly, read it again. He went up the stairs, holding
on to the banister rail very tight, dropping his keys, fumbling for
the electric switch, feeling a sinister shrilling miles within his head.
He sat awake in his chair till midnight. Then he fell asleep, so deeply
that he might have absented himself from humankind for a night.
And when he awoke to find the calendar fluttering upon the wall, he
had one large, limpid moment of innocence before the knowledge
of Siddiqui's death leapt out at him from a crevice of memory and
nauseated every sense.

Rameshwar Dayal was a man with a trained heart, obedient and
discreet in most of its responses, and practised in negotiating grief
with proper skill. And in the long years he had progressively perfected
the old age strategy of doing without. To shrink one's ownership of
things down to the barest minimum of one's own surviving self, to
reduce one's wants from the avidly desired to the merely feasible,
was the training of a decade.

The first thing to do was to write a properly worded condolence
note. He directed it to 17/B Gulbagh Complex, Muhammad Shah
Marg, New Delhi.

My dear son,

How did it happen? Was there an illness? I received your note and
my one regret is that I was not informed earlier. I trust that you shall
write to me giving me all the details. They shall serve no purpose but
they are important to me.

Against the scale of the years, your father and I knew each other for a relatively short time but in that brief period I like to think that we shared a pleasurable and meaningful chapter of our lives. We two, your father and I, belonged to a generation in which idle and sustained friendships were still possible. Perhaps your generation is not so fortunate. Do I sound patronizing? Forgive an old man's illusions if such you find them.

Words cannot express the grief I feel. I shall pray, in my own way, for the peace of his soul.

He signed it, sealed it and dropped it into a mailbox.

It was observed by other walkers in the park that for a day or two Rameshwar Dayal did not walk, but sat, withdrawn, upon the stone bench, all trace of expression buried irretrievably behind the intricate map of lines that traversed his face in many sunken hollows and lapse of tissue and of time.

Whether it was the rain that kept him from his walks on subsequent days or whether it was indisposition or disinclination, Rameshwar Dayal took care not to sort out. He sat in his armchair beside his open window, as he sat upon the stone bench in the park beneath the drumstick tree and let his thoughts drift. He watched the early monsoon slick down the street until it shone like a dark glass stirring with an inverted life of its own. He gazed blankly down upon the red-hooded rickshaws, the spools of smoke from the coal braziers uncurling in the grey wind, the soaked little dogs, the flowered parasols and mobile tents of polythene sheets held over the heads of scurrying schoolchildren, the crystal bells of bicycles, ringing liquid with an extra sweet trill in the washed air, the polished gold skin of opulent mangoes stacked in big pyramids upon vendors' carts. And several afternoons stole past with no name or date to them. Until one evening a neighbour rapped upon the door, greeted him and held out a sealed envelope, murmuring that it had been mistakenly dropped in his mailbox.

Rameshwar Dayal took it with relief, believing it to be the awaited response to his letter, anxious for detailed circumstances about Siddiqui's death. Then he caught sight of the handwriting on the envelope and felt his breath stop halfway down his throat and a lone, loud thump in the intense stillness of his chest. Tearing it open, fumbling over the single white sheet, he stared, dumbfounded, at the words slanting across in a fine, filigreed script.

My dear RD,

I wish you as many returns of the day as are good for you.
—Saghir

Lifting his eyes to the wall, Rameshwar Dayal noted the date in the calendar and had to concede its significance.

There was no address. And no, there was no evidence of postal delay. A clear date, just four days gone, shone, stamped within the Delhi postmark!

For an instant an absolute stillness waylaid his senses. Then, as he sat holding the letter in his hand, a pleasant warmth, a flush of comfort rose in his limbs and in his numb heart. It was as though a faint voice had sounded far ahead and addressed his soul, accented with strangeness and immeasurable space. Something had spoken to his mind, accosting him in the vacancy of his spirit, to assure him of unutterable things. As a child Rameshwar Dayal frequently had a curious dream of travelling in a jeep towards the western border of his city, speeding past the last level-crossing into the empty fields beyond and discovering with an outburst of surprise that the city had not ended, but hamlets and gardens continued to appear, cottages as existed in picture books of the mind, toy pastures, fields of mauve and pale blue flowers, orchards of shadowy boughs, scent filled and still. He experienced a similar sensation now as though he sensed, if not continuity, then at least contiguity, as though a neighbouring reality stood just outside the circumference of his own. And most of all the final fear was put to rest that Siddiqui was no more. For a brief instant Rameshwar Dayal felt a bridge open before him and felt confident that no man ever ended, that though in death personality may grow rarefied until it grew insensible of itself, some last claim over oneself persisted, some last syllable of self left unsubmerged.

Then workaday sense returned and Rameshwar Dayal gave himself a little shake and reasoned that the explanation for posthumous letters was more likely to be ordinary than occult. It was an actual letter he held—paper and ink and stamp. There had to be a perfectly banal explanation for it. Turning it over, he studied the Delhi postmark again and the four-day-old date. And half an inkling of understanding started in his mind and gathered speed. And climaxed in a burst of rage. For the third time in their association, Rameshwar Dayal sat down to write to his friend:

My dear Siddiqui sahib,

Several times I have tried to write to you but somehow the communication was never made. You will ask why. To tell you the truth, I find it difficult. I have neither your style nor your wit. Too many things prevented me—let us leave it at that. Today I must overcome my inhibitions and tell you how strongly I disapprove of the recent liberty you have taken with my feelings. There is a limit to what a man may risk at another's expense. You may not be aware that your latest practical joke has cost me my sleep and made my blood pressure soar. I have not been able to walk or eat or work. Can I do justice to the state you have put me in? You always had the better of me. I was the witless one, the timid, the coarse-grained, the gullible, and you the suave sermonizer. You were the learned professor, preaching Bacon and Ghalib and Frost. I told you everything about myself, but you? You kept yourself enclosed. You would not reveal yourself, you guarded your life from me. I did not even know where you lived. There was a part of your life that you would not share. You kept yourself apart, aloof, exclusive, even when you shared my life, learnt my past and overcame my present. You stood apart from me, always apart, different, too different, preserving something you would not disclose. It was not fair—

So Rameshwar Dayal wrote and wrote—four garbled sheets which he did not read over and which he posted hastily lest some untimely afterthought made him withdraw his charges.

It was seen that Rameshwar Dayal commenced his walks again, hobbling with effort, striving to complete his century alone. Some days he muttered to himself as he walked. Sometimes he opened his eyes wide and looked about him in astonishment at the world around him. It did not matter to the trees or the paths that Siddiqui did not complete his century. They kept no count of such things. It would not matter to them that he, Rameshwar Dayal, perhaps would not. The only entity for whom it mattered was himself. The only person for whom he now assumed responsibility was his own self. And completing the century was somehow bound up with his resolution to savour the essence of this current chapter of his self. Siddiqui's note, whatever the circumstances of its arrival, had made him believe that this was by no means the last chapter, that everything, park, trees, walk, would accompany him in a fine impress wherever the laws of life chose to take him.

The doctor put him on a salt-free diet once again. His head spun when he awoke in the mornings. Nights he kept awake, stumbling to the loo a dozen times. Two rounds of the park were no longer possible. And one unidentified day there arrived a telegram.

MAY HEAVENS RAIN CHOICEST BLESSINGS ON THE YOUNG COUPLE.

It reminded Rameshwar Dayal that it was indeed his wedding anniversary, a day lost and without meaning.

By the New Year Rameshwar Dayal had to have his chest X-rayed and his heart declared expanded. Late that afternoon there came a gift by post—a small pocket calendar with a Shiva on it and the year blacked out and every single day encircled in red. And a little note:

My dear RD,

Greetings on this first day of the year. Let this year be a special one and let each day be full and special, a gift from God, to be cherished and put away. Regards, Saghir.

By mid-January it was just not possible to go to the park at all. Sitting in his window-side chair Rameshwar Dayal reluctantly applied his mind to the question he had suppressed. Why had Siddiqui sent a fake message of death? Why had he continued to write to him his brief, natty little notes, failing to return but unfailingly punctual in his messages? Rameshwar Dayal was sorry they could not complete the century together now. Siddiqui would just have to complete the century on his behalf.

'Or someone else might,' he muttered aloud. 'In our place, on our behalf. Someone we don't know and who doesn't know us and maybe doesn't even know why he is compelled to cover a hundred circuits of the park. Bless him, I say,' muttered Rameshwar Dayal distractedly. 'Bless him whoever he is, for picking up where we left off. And maybe there won't be one but two of them. And maybe one shall be a Hindu like me and his partner a Muslim and despite all that's happened recently, through the thick of riot and rage, they shall achieve this century, walking calmly together each morning.'

Then one day in March there arrived a thickish packet by post.

'It's that old fool again,' muttered Rameshwar Dayal. 'Up to his senseless tricks. Pretending to be dead!'

But instead of one note he found six, all neatly tied together. And a seventh, in a different hand and paper, attached to the rest with a pin. He unfolded it with slow, unsure hands and read:

92/C Vijayanagarpuram

Most revered Chacha sahib,

I must take the liberty of addressing you thus although I have not seen you nor had the honour of making your acquaintance and perhaps now never shall. But I feel that you are known to me, so frequently did my revered Walid sahib speak of you during his last illness here. He did more than speak, as you may have realized. He wrote out for me a bundle of notes to be sent to you and left me a pocket calendar with certain dates encircled and many instructions as to the proper time of dispatch for each note. He had trouble holding a pen but if you knew my Walid sahib, you would remember how zestful was his spirit and how enduring. This is what he said to me: "My friend, RD, is alone, Israr mian, and has no one to remember or write to him. I propose to remember him, even if Allah in His wisdom should send me immediate intimation of promotion and transfer." I have carefully followed my father's directions. Alas, it is not possible for me to carry them out any longer. I leave for the Gulf at the end of the month and therefore take the liberty of sending across to you the entire bunch, along with the pocket calendar, with my deepest respect and best wishes.

Israr Ahmed Siddiqui

Slowly Rameshwar Dayal noted the changed address and understood. Slowly he untied the packet. Half a dozen cards fell into his lap. He picked them up, one by one, and studied them. He counted them carefully and counted them again. There were six of them left to the future. He felt breathless. He arose and opened the window, striving to let his emotions out. There were six little notes left in all, he told himself repeatedly. Siddiqui had allowed him just a year, no more.

And after countless repetitions he felt calm at last and released from the imperative to complete the century he had set himself. In some curious way he felt he already had. He felt there was nothing he was now defying or pitting his strength against. There was nothing left to prove, no vanity to confirm, no cherished fortress to defend. He felt so light, weightless, exempt at last from many unmerciful demands.

When he went down very slowly to buy a match next morning, he stood a long while, waiting to cross the street. Suddenly, on the opposite pavement he spotted a tall, muscular young man, intently studying a shop window, and his mind exulted, 'Ghanshyam! That's him!' Then the man turned and Rameshwar Dayal saw his mistake. Soon afterwards, walking down to where the street narrowed and the crossing would be easier, he came face to face with a plump woman with a wide face, a large red bindi and two big waves of hair, and his heart almost stopped for he was so sure! Then he realized it wasn't the one he thought. Suddenly the words of Siddiqui's letter came back to him and he stood still, just as he was, astonished at his two recent illusions. He began to understand what was happening to him.

The street had reached its narrowest point. He waited alone, ready to cross it when the moment came.

Through the Looking Glass

I haven't told Bulbul, my wife, yet. I'm nursing the pleasure of this revelation, waiting for the opportune instant, a moment of stalemate in a quarrel or the hesitation of an unequal rejoinder in an argument. Then with a casual shrug, I shall break it to her. I can see the fury collapse in her voice and the reflexes of her face stagger.

'Bulbul,' I shall say, 'I do believe I'm going blind. Kapoor told me so.'

I can just see the overflow of self-reproach, the wrongs, real or fancied, that she believes she has done me, take charge of her expression.

Need I state that I enjoy our quarrels immensely. Even the last one.

'There's nothing I have to say to you and nothing I have to ask!' she fumed. 'God, why do I continue to live with these people!'

I could answer that one well enough. I continue to live with things and people because what they have done for me is greater than what they have failed to do.

But I didn't say a word. My wife is a strong, wilful, vital woman, hungry for places she has never visited and people she has never known. For my part, it's good to be alone for a space.

I love being alone temporarily. It helps me regain ownership of myself. The house accommodates itself to my states. The rooms free themselves of the reverberations of people. I savour the taste of books and ideas in the fullness of their flavour. If ideas are furnishings of one's inner life, the clothes the mind wears, I love being alone to experiment with this internal costumery of the mind.

So, three months all to myself with my books, my groves and grounds, my dog and parrot and laboratory. I spend the first day taking a tour of my orchards, Voltaire at Fermeé.

I suppose you could call me a very rich man. These groves alone amount to a good deal, to say nothing of the old mansion, the library, the mills which my brothers manage in the city. As for me, I like to call myself a gentleman of leisure, a sort of an aristocratic hermit.

I look down the slope along the canal. Those mango groves are my pride. I have a name for each tree and a relationship with it. I do not know what hope and meaning I get from them. We coexist in beautiful dependence, sharing the same home, maybe the same laws. And after a thousand storms have passed over your head, is it not wonderful and strange that a single tree or stone or poem can still make you happy?

I mean to spend much of my sabbatical this summer in my groves. The mornings anyway.

In my mango groves the low trees cluster close together. I step into this moist dark cavern of the mango grove; light translates itself to green; the shaded air is so porous you can sponge your face with it, squeeze its cool wetness right on to your skin. There is in the grove a shanty and a cot. Armed with a book, I mean to dip into this well of satiny green darkness and cool my heart of human longings. Reclining upon my string cot, I look up into the dense rich heights. And remember Turgenev writing about trees—how gazing up into the heights of a forest is a lot like gazing into the depths of the sea. This is one reason why I never taste real aloneness. My ideas crowd round me in cool, concentric circles of allusion and echo. Other voices speak up in my head, snatches from books that have become preceptors, companions, the utterance of men from other times, whose signature my senses recognize.

Appropriately, the book that accompanies me the very first morning of my sylvan retreat is the *Brihadopnishad*. Appropriately the passage I decide to read is the one which draws a correspondence between a man and a tree. I put on my reading glasses and peer into the page:

> As is a mighty tree, so, indeed, is a man;
> His hairs are leaves and his skin is the outer bark,
> From his skin blood flows forth as sap from the skin of the
>   tree . . .
> His flesh is its inner bark, his nerves are tough like inner
>   fibres.
> His bones are the wood within and the marrow is made
>   resembling the pith.
> A tree when it is felled springs up from its root in a new
>   form;
> From what root doth man spring forth when he is cut off
>   by death?
> If a tree is pulled up with the root, it will not spring again.
> From what root doth a mortal spring forth when he is cut
>   off by death?

It was a struggle reading the passage to the end. There was decidedly something the matter with my eyes. Sometimes, quite without warning, flares of light erupted. Flies lay strewn upon a blank white wall, little blots of darkness upon a white page—as though I carried in my head a negative of the starlit sky. And I had this array of glasses—reading, distance, bifocals, photochromatics, pale goggles, dark ones.

Reading has grown increasingly difficult lately. It seems to me that my understanding cannot now travel down a page. It jerks to a stop on certain phrases and I stumble back and read everything again until I'm moving more backwards than forwards. It was different when I was younger, when there were books that seemed to blow through my mind like tempests, leaving only a sedimentary dust of unidentifiable tones and unclaimed thoughts.

I must not complain, I told myself. It will pass. Maybe my eyes are just tired with forty-six years of strain. I put away the book and looked up into the heights of my mango grove again. And thought of the many courtly and poetic names our ancestors gave to their mangoes—husn-ara, embellisher of beauty, nazuk-pasand, liked by connoisseurs, samarbehisht, fruit of paradise, ashraf-us-samar, greatest of fruits, nazuk-badan, of delicate form, suvarnarekha, line of gold! Even our blunt old langra that is in places known as har-dil-aziz, dear to all hearts, and David Ford and Ruh-e-afza. The langra that grew off a tree from a village called Langra near Benaras, a tree that looked bent and crippled. My favourites are always my special dusehris, first grown in the garden of the Nawab of Lucknow and presented to Alamgir Khan of Malihabad, who planted the first saplings in his groves. And thinking of mangoes, my mind passes to Amir Khusrau and his fourteenth-century quatrain on the mango. And thence to Ghalib's and thence to Zafar's. Well, maybe this is the decadence of spirit of an affluent scholar but just turning over those classical names of men and mangoes is enough to send such a sharp pang of perfection through my mind that I can believe in absoluteness and order with the full force of my faith. I fail then to notice this faint hairline crack running across the world.

And not only the poetry of Ghalib on mangoes but that of Kalidas on trees and flowers fills my heart with fullness. Eyes shut, I recall Kalidas's verses on the ashok tree, which with its drooping leaves makes the maidens sorrowful. And his verses on the palash which is like a nuptial furnace in the wind. I turn over the names of Kalidas's flowers in my head, touching their fragile syllables with care—the kadamba, kesara, kakubha and ketaki.

I grew drowsier, languorously indulging my extravaganza of echoes. I remembered that in my childhood saplings were treated like human babies, bathed in herbs and scents, adorned with flowers, wrapped in fine cloth. Their 'ears' were pierced with a needle of gold, their 'eyes' treated with collyrium applied with a golden rod. And that thought brought me back with a jolt to the subject of my own eyes. It was becoming increasingly clear to me that my reading days were going to end. Nothing for me spelt greater horror. I would be a man dispossessed, banished from the precious estates of his wanderings. There was this appointment I had again with Kapoor, my ophthalmologist, on Friday. He'd said once that an operation might not really be the answer but it would be prudent to try. But I had caught the false note in his voice and it now troubled my days and nights. The sight of my library, lined with books from floor to ceiling, stretched a small nerve in pain. I had picked up those books over an expanse of forty years and more. I had been infatuated by the promise in their names, and the colours of their jackets. There were books I had inherited from my father and books I had received as gifts. And books I had argued with and defied and books I had challenged and conquered. And still so many of them lay half read, unread, awaiting me. Why, Solomon in his seraglio was not richer than I. And now, with such a stab of deprivation, I confronted the likelihood of never being able to read again. Three months, six, eight, maybe a little more, and what then? Already I was having such trouble. And Kapoor only evaded my insistent queries.

Maybe if some vision remained, I could turn to painting. A semi-blind view of the world might have interesting mindspectives to offer. Form and colour in retreat. I used to love painting my forests and groves—endless splurges of green in the complete gamut of its shades. I'm a pretty bad painter, because I never managed to create the forest I wanted to. I wanted a picture that would engulf me, that would hurl its colours across and make them flare about, sweep, drench, submerge my brain. A vast wall-length picture that reached the tentacles of its shades and arrested me in the marsh of its moods, that dwarfed and reduced me to a speck in the cyclone of its passion and left me dizzy, cast exhausted upon its shore. A large, lonely green universe in canvas. I then committed an unforgivable blunder. I introduced a single human form. That ruined it. My painting had been like the world before God created Adam or like a vast echoing hall before the grandeur of its emptiness is ruined by the introduction of the first article of furniture. Now, all of a sudden, a limited, local meaning separated itself from the soaring solitude of the whole. I tried to erase my error, but only increased the mess. The world after man has left will never be the same as the world before man arrived. I put it away, resolving to paint my fantasy again at a future date when my experience was ready for it. That too, I realized, could now never be. How much I needed my eyes, now more than ever before to complete the undertakings of many decades. Yes, there were things I had planned to write as well. I wrote poetry once. 'Wrote' is the wrong word. It seemed to me that there were poems in my head lying already written and I was only discovering them. Reading over those pale poems, I found them useless and threw them away. Some day I would write something worthwhile, but when would that be? Another undertaking left unfinished.

But suppose, I brooded, I tried something really short. There was still time for that. I could condense all my intuitions into one compact expression, or I could sift through them all, eliminating whatever seemed no longer convincing to me, and come at last upon the central fiction of my life.

There was a theme I had constructed and I planned to get down to it on the second day of my sabbatical. There was no time to waste now.

I'm a better writer than a painter. I had even once designed a monogram for myself—a toy monkey sitting upon an antique typewriter, clutching a Rubik's cube. It said everything about me and my writing. They say, in theories of probability, that were a monkey to sit at a typewriter, in a million years he'd come to produce the works of Shakespeare. The Rubik's cube stood for all those multiple possibilities which that monkey might blunder through, all their degrees of inchoateness and clarity on the road to perfection. I sat down, on the second day, to work at my story, a story that was breathed down into my mind like the exhalation of some alien force. I called it *Alice in the Library*. The idea fascinated me. Alice steps into a new wonderland, my own library, in fact. She goes from book to book and hey presto!—she comes upon a book called *Alice in the Library*. And in that book there's another Alice wandering in another library, going from book to book, coming upon yet another book called *Alice in the Library*. Philosophers might call it an example not of infinite regress but of infinite ingress, the inward sinking of a mind endlessly in the maze of its own constructions.

It was afternoon. The curtains burned faintly. The white light rolled down and emptied its force upon the floor. Another beam branded a white patch upon the wall. I wrote and wrote until I was exhausted. Alice had just reached the fifth Alice wandering in the fifth library in a fifth recess of self, when I put down my pen and stretched myself out for a brief nap on the foam couch on the floor of my library.

I suppose it was a psychic experience of sorts. Above my head I heard someone speak:

'I've chopped the firewood.'

'Put it in the grate.'

'Shall I light the fire for you?'

'No, Stepan, thank you. I don't need one.'

'Your chamber will be cold.'

'Where is it written that chambers must be warm?'

And from the far end of the wall came another whisper:

'It is right before your eyes.'

'Why do I not see for myself?'

'Because you are thinking of yourself.'

Then two voices spoke up in altercation and one overcame the other: 'No, listen awhile. There is something I must say, only my brain is befuddled. Draw that chair hither. Can you comprehend things that are told you?'

'Indeed, I do. I am good at comprehending.'

And a gusty voice broke in impetuously: 'This is intolerable! What are we to do, my lord Eurypylus? I am on my way to Achilles, my wise master, with a message from Gerenian Nestor, the Warden of Achaea. All the same, I am not going to leave you in the lurch, exhausted as you are.'

A strong, solemn voice interposed: 'The majesty of God is in no way reduced by the limits of bodily experience. But mankind is raised to understand nobler things.'

In my drowse I lay, attentive, trying to catch more. But the next words escaped my grasp. There was a small lull and then I heard a slow, meandering voice close beside me: 'Surely,' said I, 'surely that is something at my window lattice. Let me see, then what thereat is, and this mystery explore—Let my heart be still a moment and this mystery explore—'Tis the wind and nothing more.'

And a prompt rejoinder came from some place near the ceiling:

'Therefore in this ordering we find a wonderfully symmetrical world and a sure bond of harmony for the movements and magnitude of the orbital cirles such as cannot be found in any other way . . .'

At some point of a dream continuum we nudge our supine brains alert and grow mindful of a sudden resumption of sense. And as I did so, a fantastic thought flashed upon me—these were my books speaking. Who else could they be? There was no one present in the library except for me. I woke up with a start and lay staring at the silent shelves. A large, diffuse sentience seemed to inhabit them. I had always known my books for the comrades that they were, but that they could reach out to me in ways I had ever suspected struck me for the very first time. I felt one with them a great fellowship, disembodied presences pouring their intuitions into a reservoir of understanding spread over the centuries. There were central truths of life still to be harvested, but as far as I was concerned, time was running out. I felt like the man in Pushkin's story who had a book beside him and who never got down to reading it, little suspecting that that book contained the key to his own life. Somewhere in this room, folded up on a shelf, there existed the quintessential formula of my own life and I would have to read and read and read, I would have to traverse miles of print and expanses of mind to come across it. There had been smaller fragments of truth I had recognized. Sometimes I had said: I love this paragraph. I had closed the book, promising to return to it surely once more in this lifetime. I never did. And then, lying there half-awake, I had a brainwave. Suppose, now that time and vision were both limited, suppose I went through my entire library, rather as my Alice did, reading just a single random paragraph out of each? Maybe all their separate meanings would link up and a surprising grand meaning take shape, the single central sense I had been waiting for. I decided to apply myself to this exciting exercise on the third day of my holiday.

But before I could do so, a small ripple of agitation upset the even tenor of my life. My old parrot flew away. I haven't said anything so far about my dog and my parrot. We three lived amiably together. I spoke to them and they responded in their own ways. I began trying to teach the parrot to speak. Whimsically, I decided to teach him to repeat Einstein's formula for relativity. I even named him Albert. But, alas, my parrot did not take kindly to physics. He went mute. And then one day he looked significantly at my dog and imitated a bark! Poor fellow, I thought, I was going too fast for him. Man too can't learn what is too advanced for him and not all the libraries in the world can teach him. And then another day my dog tried to bite my parrot. I rebuked the dog, comforted the parrot. Then I comforted the dog in his shame. This, I mused, must be one of God's routine functions. When I'm alone, I spin little parables for myself. Everything that happens to me seems significant. I return to my parrot, the dog's attack left it depressed. So one day I switched on my old phonograph and turned its trumpet towards Albert's lovely brass cage.

Slowly, to an antique lilt, my parrot began to dance, lifting one foot, then another, dipping his round head to left and to right, rotating upon his brass perch. The tempo increased. He closed his beady eyes, his round lids slid down, he went on circling the space in the cage.

'Sahib, stop!' cried my old servant. 'Notice that drowsy rhythm. It's going into a trance, sahib. Who knows what spirit lodges in that parrot form. Stop. Don't meddle with such things.'

I switched off the music. The parrot awoke slowly.

For a long time he sat staring mournfully at the big world. Then he applied himself to sawing with his beak at the brass bars of his cage.

Once earlier he had managed to get away. Someone caught him in a towel and put him back. He sat in his cage, dejected. Now, after a long, patient year of sawing away, he had managed to unlatch the door of the cage. I hadn't the heart to catch him again. I sat, motionless, watching from my chair. He found himself in a plant-filled balcony with a grille. He thought he was in a larger cage and tried now to saw at the grille. I watched, fascinated, as he turned his small head and gazed for a long time at the sky. Then he hopped around, found a small gap in the grille and slowly, very awkwardly, gave a flap of the wings. The air replied and, with a sort of upward bound, he swayed in a wide arc up into a mango tree. I stepped out, craning my neck to spot him on his low branch. Apparently he was tired. His belly heaved, adjusting his breathing to the flutter of his heart. The he took the plunge—a long, lone competent flight up into the sky and away into the tall eucalyptus. I watched his maiden solo flight, sad and thrilled as a parent. There, I said, there goes $E=mc^2$. I had tried to teach him the formula for relativity and named him Albert. Icarus would've been a better name. There he goes, I said, learning the formula of flight with his whole, small, concentrated being. He was not content with the relative—he wanted to measure the irrelative sky with his small wings.

That night we had one of our terrible pre-monsoon storms and I worried about him. I got out my telescope to scan the branches of the trees. There was no sight of him. The sky snapped and shuddered with lightning. God must be like that, I thought—an energy field crackling with positive and negative charges. My telescope could spot nothing in the sky, as all my glasses could teach me nothing beyond the fuzzy shape of written words on a page, as my eyes too could teach me little. I thought tomorrow the weather shall change. Albert would be thirsty. So I made a bird bath in my garden where he could, if he wanted, alight for a drink. I made it with stones and shells, ferns and floating flowers. The little pool trapped the entire sky, the floating clouds and branches in its circular lens and integrated them all with its stones and flowers in a compound image. I even put the little mirror he used to play with.

My parrot loved looking at his face in a mirror. So do I. I've always loved mirrors and microscopes. Have you ever concentrated upon your face in a mirror, looked really hard at it and really close? The face you know slowly alters. All its lights go out. Its outlines dim and flow, slow down and set again. Strong bones reorganize their slopes, crags and crannies appear. It's an ancient and terrifying self, neither man nor woman.

And microscopes. Sometimes I would put a leaf beneath the glass. The veins suddenly seemed like streets in a busy city, involved in its all-important commerce—so many lanes, by lanes, high streets, thoroughfares. Each leaf a complete world. And what if our universe is a leaf hanging on the branch of a larger universe and so on and so forth till the brain tires of its convoluted fancies. And what are these crazy ideas the brain generates? I just don't know why I should expect my ideas to have a corresponding equivalent in reality. Why should anything make sense? In the leaf I spot an answer—because the leaf has its own internal sense. Maybe the world is a conglomeration of many relative self-enclosed truths. But if conflicting truths were to clash, would one truth annul another? Then how can any truth, even a larger one, survive if a smaller truth perished?

I do believe I'm going distracted.

Only the empty hours brought home to me how much I missed my parrot. I locked myself up in my library. Now or never. One paragraph out of each book I would read, no more. There wasn't time enough. One paragraph would have to suffice.

That was the most wonderful day in my recent life. I know what I am talking about. I do believe I was blessed with a personal miracle.

There I was, worrying for my eyes, for my bird, for my books. It was evening and the light was dim. I didn't feel like switching the electric lights on. I went up to my shelves, reached out for the first book. I put on my glasses and discovered an old favourite—Chekhov's *Seagull*. I read a paragraph, put it back. I reached out again, pulled out another book from another shelf and looked at it. Ibsen's *Wild Duck*. I read another paragraph, I put it back. I walked round to the far end, extracted a third book—an old volume of Shelley's poems. Of course the page fell open at the 'To A Skylark'. I took out something from the bottom shelf—*Jonathan Livingston Seagull!* That was when a mind-boggling revelation staggered me, every book I seemed to be picking up was a bird book! I grew baffled, breathless. I seized a sixth book. Short stories by Nadine Gordimer—and the first story was The Bird. There was a faint tremble in my hands. I quickly went to my Indian shelf and took out my *Ramayana* and let its worn pages cascade under my thumb—it opened precisely at the Jatayukand! I put it back and randomly pulled out a *Purana*. And it was the *Garuda-Purana*. Every book was echoing every other book, weaving contexts artfully, making no human sense, yet assailing me in such persistent unison! I groped about my Sanskrit classics shelf and my hands fell on the *Sukasaptati*—the parrot tales! I wasn't imagining this. To Ghalib I turned and the page smoothly fell open to the poet's toil, the laying down of webs of mind and ear, evenings turned to morning, rivers of milk brought forth. 'Meaning was the bird that alighted not,' Ghalib told me.

There was no question of withdrawing from this experience. Feverishly I went through book after book and came across peacocks, papihas, chetaks, bulbuls, albatrosses, nightingales, kingfishers, phoenixes! I read late into the night, realizing that I was in their hands, those books, or rather that all of us were in the irresistible control of an intelligence that was returning my lost bird to me, that was making me know that all those books were at some further point of sense one single book which did not end with personal vision or with words. If I couldn't reach understanding, understanding might still come in search of me and what did it matter then if I no longer read or wrote or painted or saw?

The last book I picked up, late that night, was, of all things, Gibbon's *Decline and Fall of the Roman Empire*, putting my experience to a last playful test. And read, weak with excitement:

'. . . the clamours of his army compelled Attila to relinquish the enterprise and reluctantly to issue his orders that the troops should strike their tents the next morning and begin their retreat. But, as he rode round the walls, pensive, angry and disappointed, he observed a stork, preparing to leave her nest in one of the towers and to fly with her infant family towards the country. He seized with the ready penetration of a statesman this trifling incident which chance had offered to superstition; and exclaimed in a loud and cheerful tone, that such a domestic bird, so constantly attached to human society, would never have abandoned her ancient seats unless those towers had been devoted to impending ruin and solitude. The favourable omen inspired an assurance of victory, the siege was renewed and prosecuted with fresh vigour, a large breach was made in the part of the wall from whence the stork had taken her flight; the Huns mounted to the assault with irresistible fury and the succeeding generation could scarcely discover the ruins of Aquileia.'

I laid the book down. It was long past midnight and my eyes had begun playing tricks with me. Flares of light exploded in my head. The page swarmed with dancing dots. I curled up on the couch, the book still beside me, and slept in perfect peace for the first time in weeks. And when I awoke, quietened and refreshed, I went down the stairs, opening doors, letting in air and light. I shot back the bolts of the outer door and stood on the doorstep. There on the topmost marble step at my feet, lay a single green feather.

My parrot had come for a drink after all.

Pretty Woman

Nishant Sharma had always had a scientific interest in women. Over the years he'd compiled an extensive list of women who never quite forgave him for his neglect. They had thrown themselves at him beseeching, 'Be mine! Be mine!'—And he, fastidious, had found them quite below par. The rest was history—hell hath no fury, etcetera.

In the old days he had playfully toyed with the idea of amusing his friends with an enlightened and insightful work—The Theory and Practice of Seduction. The epigraph was to be a sombre and scholarly quote: *Casta est quam nemo rogavit*—The nymph may be chaste that has never been tried. He never got round to committing his researches to paper but he was given to discoursing at length on the subject, twiddling a glass of scotch, absently admiring the impeccable crease of his trouser leg and the luminous leather of his shapely boot.

His primary talent was an ability to spot the likely woman. It needed finesse to begin a conversation, dexterity to detect the vulnerable spot. The field was complex, the technique sophisticated. It was a fine art demanding an uncommonly sensitive operation. No one could ever say that he didn't esteem women, but there was this thing—you had to sink your own ego, come down to their level to succeed in this sort of thing. He often fantasized about the very last woman he would sleep with. Someone vulnerable, sweetly-shrinking, young? Or maybe a seasoned thirty-five. In these visions he never clearly stated his own age. He thought back in moments of languishing sentimentality to his first woman. He shook his head often, saying sadly, 'No. Can't remember them all, you know. But the name rings a bell.'

He never knew how it was that she got him started on this theme. In a speeding train of all places.

'You could say I'm an obsessive traveller. A student of culture,' he had informed her. 'Now, to know a country you have to know its history and its art, its markets and its music, its seasons and its scenery. You've got to taste its wine and its confectionery. You've got to sample its women.'

She had a way of putting her head to one side and studying him with laughter in her eyes. There was in her pretty face a teasing disbelief of every word he uttered, and a dainty mockery. And when she spoke it was in little coaxing queries and tender taunts, stroking each syllable with honeyed tongue.

'You're rather intensive in your approach to culture, no?' she asked, so satirically sweet, so sharp that he laughed outright with pleasure.

'Oh yes,' he agreed. 'I'm extremely thorough.'

He had watched her surreptitiously all morning. She was the fourth person in the compartment, and by Kanpur station, the only one left. And it was she who had opened the conversation.

'Fat,' she twinkled, shrugging at the last man who left. 'And not at all nice.'

'I beg your pardon?'

'Now, you aren't fat.' She smiled a brilliant smile. 'Therefore you must be nice.' She had a baby voice full of little cadences.

He marvelled at the quaint illogic of it. And seized the opportunity.

'The same, madam, may be said of you,' he murmured.

'You bet,' she replied. He studied her closely, noting the little porcelain fingers, the tiny gold ear-bobs, the shimmer of raven hair. He observed with approval the ivory feet, the small oval face, gazelle eyes, the lovely, elegant form. It was a very transparent face through which a swarm of expressions plunged their way. You could, he fancied, actually separate the thoughts as they dropped, one by one, into her black eyes, sending little shocks across them. Dry leaves dropped one by one upon the black surface of a shivering pool, he remarked to himself. Behind that still face lay a very noisy mind.

She turned away from the window and frowned at him. He cleared his throat.

'I hope you don't object to my smoking.'

Her face unfroze. Suddenly her eyes danced in a soundless giggle.

'Smoking, yes. Smokers, no.' She had an elfish smile, a little pout, a quick, disarming grin, pearly-white, reaching, yet not quite achieving, that promise of a dimple.

What a buxom, fuxom woman, he exclaimed inwardly. On her lips everything seemed to turn ambiguous, rich in many shades of complex insinuation.

'What are you, madam?' he asked gravely.

'Me?' she trilled. 'I'm a philosopher. You don't believe me? I think for my living. I live to think. I think to live. Remember the Mad Hatter's Tea Party?'

He rose equal to the craziness of the exchange and remembered, 'Why is a raven like a writing desk?' he roared with laughter.

'No, why is a writing desk like a raven, uh huh?'

'Because . . .' He did some swift thinking. 'Because it makes your mind take wing and soar.'

To his amazement, her coquetry turned to instant outrage. She shrugged, full of loathing, mercurial. 'It's all lost on you, of course!' He sat rebuffed. 'How many pearls can one cast, after all!' She looked at him with hate. Then, slowly, her face unclenched in a ravishing smile that seemed to leap out in ambush and cry: Peek-a-boo! Did you think I was serious? He relaxed and decided to try again.

'You're married, of course,' he hazarded.

'Why?' she demanded, baleful. 'What's "of course" about it?'

He turned on the old, unerring charm. 'I mean, how can a pretty woman like you stay single? The stronger sex would never be fool enough to let you remain that way.'

'I have a husband, yes,' she conceded.

'Lucky man. And is he nice?'

'Now this is official. He's a husband. He's always nice. Except when he isn't.' There was a delicate stratagem in every sentence and then, out of the blue, came a wicked observation, a piercing insight so heartlessly honest that it disturbed his poise completely. He covered up his discomfiture with a quip.

'And what does this so-nice man do?'

'He owns a couple of newspapers.'

He whistled. 'You can afford to think for a living,' he exclaimed.

'Well, fortunately or unfortunately, I'm very wealthy.'

'I can see that,' he answered.

'It wasn't always that way, though,' she went on. 'When we first met he was a poor correspondent and I was an art student. We met in Munich.'

'Munich?'

'Yes. In a Youth Hostel. You know those cosy little places. Well, this one had a self-catering kitchen with litte signs posted up on the walls. "Please wash your dishes"—*Bitte waschen Sie ihr Geschirr ab. Danke.* And things like *Wenn Sie den herd benutzen wollen, mussen Sie auch dit Zeit scaltuhr*—"When using the stove, you must also turn on the timer." Those Youth Hostels on the Continent are great places for making new friends. The kitchen used to be full of people meeting and chatting. You cooked, you shared, you compared notes—Australians and Brazilians, Japanese, Koreans, Americans, Malays. Well he was staying there too. I'd slunk into the kitchen when it was deserted. That's where I was caught red-handed . . .' She giggled wickedly.

'Red-handed?'

'Yes. I was caught undoing his . . .'

He stared, held his breath. She laughed a long roguish laugh, stretching it out, tuning it to silver, allowing it to take wing and tumble off the scale.

'His?'

'His packet of noodles, I mean.' She uttered a tiny shriek of mirth. He sank back and laughed a little nervously. A master of the unfinished utterance, saying but not quite, the unexpected naughty thing, checking herself in time with a bat of a fluttering lash and a mischievous moue. He thought he had summed her up—a delicious, refreshing creature and altogether amoral. He liked her.

'And what did he have to say?'

She jiggled her shoulders in a theatrical shrug. 'He tapped me on the head and pointed at a sign on the fridge—"This is a community kitchen but the food is not. Please do not consider the whole fridge your private one."'

'And then?'

'Well, I said sorry in six languages and offered to cook it for him ... one thing led to another ...' She stopped, suggestive, every word elliptical. He watched, fascinated. 'You ever been to Munich?'

'No.'

'Ah.'

'And the wedding bells rang soon afterwards?' He chose to pursue.

'They almost didn't. I mean we almost didn't—what am I saying?—oh yes. They did. They jolly well did. That's what got me trapped in this great family experience.'

He noticed the sudden tension in her hands, clasped tightly together. There was a peculiar pinched look about her nose; her face had grown stern and there came from her such emanations of tension that he felt oppressed.

'Ugh!' she shuddered. 'Haven't you known the great family experience? "What d'you want for your birthday, dear?" she mimicked. "Please, let me not see your faces for one whole blissful day!" That's what I want to shout. Oh God!' She buried her face in her hands, then shot bolt upright and glared at him, menacing, malevolent. Her eyes simmered, gripped him with such overpowering magnetism, that he could neither look her in the face nor look away. Abruptly the hold slackened and he was released. He breathed again. A voice, remarkably composed, addressed him, 'I could do with some tea.'

'Oh, but of course.' He went out, found the attendant, placed an order.

Her hand shook as it held the teacup. That flower-like hand seemed unequal to the weight of the heavy railway pottery. She spilt a bit. He sprang to help, cleaned up, getting close to her, risked putting a steadying arm reassuringly round her.

She sighed gratefully, smiled a shaky smile. 'Oh, you're nice,' she breathed. This was what he liked most about her, this directness. She wasn't oblique like most women. He poured her a second cup and asked, solicitous: 'Is anything wrong?'

'Why?'

'Your hand.'

'Oh, this? It's all these medicines I have to take. They make my hands shake. Can't be helped.' She evaded his eye.

'On the whole it's better to be a mannequin in a shop window than a human being in a house,' she declared decisively, flung him a pretty smile, steadied her hands. 'No, don't laugh. I'm speaking from experience. I love the shop windows of Paris or Milan. And I adore the mannequins most of all. They seem to twirl in a magic light, an . . . an ideal world. So slender, so perfect. And their shining wigs—auburn and blonde, peroxide, copper, corn gold. And their skins—of cream, or ebony or silver or gold! And those arctic eyes—so fixed, so opaque, looking beyond everything . . . like ghosts . . . or saints . . . into abstract space. Think of it—the real people stand outside the glass, looking longingly in. They never achieve that . . . that ideal beauty. It's the mannequins that are . . . beyond good and evil . . .'

He stared at her, incredulous. Her hand as she drained the cup shook violently. Her face was deeply thoughtful; and yet, as she spoke on, her pupils dilated and the reeling discourse turned into a soft surf of sound, an incredible whispering to herself. Weird expressions blew across her face and in that twitter and glitter, every feature seethed. There was some witchery here. All the women he had counted as conquests had good skins and noses and curves. But this one had something different—this one had enchantment. He wondered at the secret of that sinister charm and hit upon a sudden definition of beauty. Beauty wasn't the perfection of ideal lines, no, it was the fruit of a chance accident of composition, erratic and unexpected.

As he produced his wallet to pay the attendant she interrupted him. 'No, no. I absolutely insist. This is on me.'

He protested, was overruled. She fished out a delicate snakeskin bag and searched its interiors. It took him a whole minute to grasp that something was wrong. Her smile had crumpled up, her eyes were muddy, she hung her head, thrust out an underlip. He reached out and took the bag from her nerveless hands—and found it empty save for a powder compact and a lipstick. 'Sorry,' she whispered, such a shamed ache in that baby voice. 'It's all with Bhushan Singh.'

'Bhushan Singh?'

She clamped her lips tight and would not answer. He was embarrassed in the presence of the attendant and quickly paid him off, placing the wallet with a sigh of relief on the mica ledge.

'Who is Bhushan Singh?' he asked cautiously.

She beamed, took out her lipstick, winked at her image in the powder compact, twiddled an eyebrow, wrinkled her nose.

'One of the reasons why I detest tea or coffee is that it washes away my lipstick. I feel quite . . . quite nude without my lipstick. Not at my best at all.'

He decided to try the old formula of flirtation, the naughty innuendo to resolve the unease.

'Oh, I'm sure you're quite at your best then.'

'What?'

'Nude, I mean.'

She pouted. 'I lost a lovely French lipstick the other day,' she lamented. 'Amit said it's suiting you a helluva lot. And guess what? I came back from a party and found it gone. The dog ate it. It was all over his snout.'

'And was it suiting the dog too?' he teased.

She shrieked with laughter, wagged a finger at him and with a swift movement, flung the 'lipstick' out of the window.

'This is my Nurjehan act,' she giggled. 'Sometimes I'm so sorry I can't be her all the time. I'm her only part of the time. But I'd love to hold a pair of pigeons in my hand, send off one, then send off the other as well . . .' She lunged forward. The compact went flying out of the window too. She swung round and grabbed his wallet and it dawned on him in a flash that it would follow the fate of the lipstick and the compact. He jumped to his feet, sought to get between her and the window. She ducked to the left, giggling, found herself impeded, twisted and swung her arm to the space on the right. In a crazy scuffle he managed to grab hold of both her wrists, trying to force her down, arguing frantically, managed to snatch the wallet from the dainty clasp of her hand, only to find his own wrist twisted. He felt himself pulled close, brush against her. Her hands were strong as a wrestler's and gripped him like a vice. Alarm and pain shot through him. This was not how things usually proceeded between him and the women he conferred his appreciation on. In the middle of the general confusion there sounded a gentle scrape and a knock. The door of the first class compartment slid open and there stood the ticket-checker with the attendant close behind him.

'Here!' exclaimed the ticket-checker as the scuffle subsided and the combatants sank, confused, into their respective seats. An expression of swift deduction, of suggestive unction, came into his swarthy face. He smiled a knowing smile, coughed in apology. Nishant Sharma felt a hot flush race over him at the man's familiarity.

'Sorry to disturb,' smiled the offensive fellow with a great show of contrition. 'Tickets, please.'

Nishant Sharma fumbled with his retrieved wallet, produced his ticket. The man turned to her. Her fixed smile had crumpled up in an instant, all that delightful mummery and mimicry evaporated. Melancholy swept down her face. Her eyes filmed over and she hung her head. So vulnerable did she look that the odious man swelled, empowered.

'Madam,' he repeated. 'Your ticket, please.'

She turned, suddenly smouldering, to confront him. Her rage swooped down upon him like a crackling electric charge, her molten face belying the composure of her voice.

'I am not accustomed,' she said, 'to having underlings of the railway hector me. May I suggest that you check with the attendant.'

The man, baffled at the sudden transformation, stammered, took a step back.

'Madam's tickets are with one Mr Bhushan Singh, travelling second class,' whispered the attendant.

The man turned slavish, oozed sweaty apeasement. 'Very sorry, madam.' And turning with exaggerated apology which Nishant Sharma found maddening in its suggestiveness, he addressed him. 'And very sorry, sahib.' Retreating, he closed the door behind him with the same conspiring caution. His air plainly conveyed that he left resigned, leaving the rich to their incorrigible promiscuities.

Nishant Sharma looked at his travelling companion with misgiving. A small foot tapped playfully on the floor. Long pink nails rested languidly on a magazine. His mind raced. That flower-like delicacy that could scarcely hold a heavy teacup and that brutal strength didn't go together. He nursed his twisted wrist, wrung like the neck of a helpless fowl. He turned it gingerly and winced. He looked up to see a pair of large moist eyes fixed sorrowfully upon him.

'Sorry,' she whispered. There was such pain in her little voice, such pathetic embarrassment.

'Don't mention it. It was a pleasure,' he answered drily, with elaborate mock courtesy. She threw him a wide, bland smile.

'Do you know,' she said, 'I rather like you.'

'I am delighted,' he replied, caustic, putting his wallet carefully into his trouser pocket.

'You're very careful about your money,' she remarked.

'Also my tickets,' he corrected. 'I can't risk any further Nurjehan acts. Might as well put it away safely.'

'Is it safe there, are you sure?' she asked, all concern.

'I imagine so. A trouser pocket's better than most places.'

'And do you always have your trousers on, sir?' she twinkled, her voice perilously soft and mocking.

He took one look at her face and burst out laughing.

'Now this is unofficial,' he quipped. 'I frequently don't.'

'Thank God for that,' she beamed. And it was at this point that Nishant Sharma realized how gratifying it was to be the object of seduction by a delicious woman.

'But who's Bhushan Singh?' he suddenly remembered.

'Oh him?' she lilted. 'That's my accomplice.'

'What?'

'Yes, he carries my tickets and my trinkets and my money and my vanity box and my firearms and little things like that.'

'What on earth?'

She went into a long tinkling laugh. 'Honest,' she teased. 'I run a terrorist gang. I love kidnapping handsome men. Some day I'm going to be a human bomb.'

He started. Her eyes waited, snapping with a derisive glint in them, ready to ridicule his response, whatever it happened to be. There was such poisonous patience in every muscle of her face, drawing him out carefully in order to make him slip, encouraging him to speak in order to sting him to silence. He chose to say nothing.

'You aren't surprised?' she coaxed.

'Madam,' he said gravely. 'Nothing about you will surprise me now.'

'It shouldn't,' she smiled. 'I'm really bright, believe me. You just don't know how clever I am. When I speak to others I'm so disappointed—I find everyone else so dull. And as for my looks—

d'you know I won the Miss Lahore in 1965 when I was twenty. I've been cover girl for *Vogue*. I read the national news on TV in the '40s.'

'Just a minute,' he interrupted. 'Lahore in '65! I doubt if beauty contests were popular there in '65, my dear young lady. They were all too busy fighting. And if you were twenty then, you should be about fifty now—which you're plainly still many years from. And TV in the '40s! You must be joking. Come on, who is this mysterious man travelling with you?'

'Oh, him?' she said, looking deliberately vague. 'I think I'll tell you after all. Bhushan Singh is my husband's orderly. He's supposed to look after me—keep me out of mischief.'

'What?'

'Pays my bills, gives me my tablets.'

He found the suspense of it unbearable. Why on earth should an orderly carry her money and her medicines unless? . . . A penniless woman travelling alone, the picture of affluence.

'Exactly where are you coming from?' he asked.

'Me? Mussoorie.'

'Mussoorie?'

'I was sent there for a rest. Everybody needs a rest, you know,' she discoursed very sensibly. 'One longs for a place where . . . where one may recover fom life, from relationships and responsibilities, shed this . . . this taste of self. I'm filled with such disgust and bitterness. Such absolute, intense loneliness. You know, I get into real black states. My brain is tired of ideas, my heart is tired of feelings, my tongue is tired of speech, my body is tired of work. Sometimes, I think I'm living at the bottom of a well and I'm scared I'll live forever.' He looked at her transformed face, her brimming eyes.

'Easy,' he said. 'Easy.'

'To see that look on my husband's face . . .' she went on. 'To surprise him in that look. He dislikes me. Maybe he too surprises the same look on my face.' She was pale and subdued, all the vivacity gone.

'I think you need to sleep,' he said gently.

'Sleep? Oh yes, I sleep lots. But the trouble is, no matter how far one wanders away one always wakes up in the same bed. The same boring self. I . . . I seem to have used up all the resources of sleep. What I'm interested in is not waking up in the same bed.' She stopped and considered him gravely.

Then she said very softly: 'But maybe in yours . . .'

And he whispered back, just as softly, 'And why not?'

There was a pregnant silence. But she waved a hand and went on speaking. 'Maybe there are things I haven't tried. Drugs? Hell? Maybe even death. My sleep is troubled by such noisy dreams and I wake up tired and angry. It's like moving from one noisy family living room to another. Even in sleep there are so many routes to choose from. I speak as though it's got an actual geography. Believe me, it has. You stand, playing truant, wondering where to go. Then you choose your lane. But even then it's thus far and no further. The alarm rings. You rush back.'

He marvelled at the intelligence in her broken mutter. Then a strange lisp crept in, a sibilance that turned into a slur. 'Well, this time I've settled my account. I've counted all my omissions and commissions. I've got myself . . . sorted out now. I know . . . exactly who I am.' Her words loosened, slid down the scale, tripped and fell about. A glassy stare fixed itself on him. 'I . . . know what I amount to . . . the . . . measurements of my mind, you'd say the . . . the vital . . .'

'What?' he asked. She smiled, suddenly gleeful.

'The vital statistics of my soul!' she announced. 'We're wearing too many things on us. It's not right so I'm trying hard to drop 'em all, one by one, whenever I can. It's possible to drop time and situation too. I often drop them. Now if I were to drop off all my clothes, first this kurta, unknot and . . . drop this salwar, then my time, my soul, my bra, and all my dreams, wouldn't it be heavenly to . . . to stand free and . . . empty and . . .'

Her eyes gushed all over him, snapped, stood still, raked his face. Oh, hell, he thought, if there ever was a confusion of the sublime and the suggestive, this was it. But for some reason beads appeared on his forehead. He shrank into his corner. It was getting uncanny. The dreadful suspicion that had been shaping itself in his mind now turned into a horrified certainty. He knew now what that terrible beauty was, the unnameable enchantment.

She lifted a lovely arm, pulled a jewelled hairpin out of her hair. The raven locks tumbled loose in a glossy, velvet mass down one shapely shoulder. She held out the pin with an exalted flourish. 'Those're diamonds, see? Four of 'em. See this pin? I thrust it into my baby's face.' Her eyes shot a flash of steel right through him.

'You what?' he cried, appalled.

'I pushed my baby into my bath tub and held him down till he choked. D'you know that nursery rhyme—"I had a little duck. His name was Sunny Kim. I put him in the bath-tub to teach him how to swim."' She sang the rhyme in a childlike lisp that made his blood turn to ice. '"He drank up all the water, he ate up all the soap. Next day he choked with a bubble in his throat."' She stopped singing and turned heavy, sulphurous eyes upon him. 'Just like that . . .' Her fists unfolded in a fluttering, fluent gesture. Her eyes simmered, a jaw worked, a gulp. 'Floating in the water . . . like a small pink ball. All squeezed up . . . like a man's . . .' Her radiant smile flowed sideways down her face, her wanton eyes laughed, oblique and full of innuendo, her cheek dimpled askew, her voice floated up in a reckless crescendo, tuneless and tipsy. She rose slowly to her feet, staggering slightly on her high heels, a look of intense venom on her face, and advanced towards him.

In the years that followed Nishant Sharma never could remember how he got to the door and opened it, how he hurtled out and ran headlong down the corridor of the thundering train, past the locked doors of four first class compartments and straight into the welcome society of the attendant, snoring in his little bunk beside the door. He was perspiring all over, he shook like a leaf and his words were garbled in helpless panic.

'Eh?' exclaimed the attendant, rousing himself.

'Please,' gasped Nishant Sharma. 'I'd like to move into a different coach.'

'Ha!' exclaimed the attendant, grinning slowly. 'Not possible.'

'In that case, I'll spend the night here,' spluttered Nishant Sharma. 'You've got to help me retrieve my suitcase.'

As one in imminent hazard of molestation and possible ravishment, Nishant Sharma's distress on that shameful occasion was not one that he cared to dwell upon in later years.

The man consulted a sheet of paper and clucked. 'Sorry. No vacancy,' he pronounced maliciously.

'In that case I'll have to make do with the corridor,' said Nishant Sharma, deeply upset. 'If . . . if you could get Mr Bhushan Singh, whoever he is, to fetch my suitcase for me. Perhaps I could exchange berths with him . . .'

'Next station,' said the man, and went to sleep.

Nishant Sharma spent half the night squatting on the cold floor of the corridor outside the lavatory, causing some damage to his impeccable trousers and considerable damage to his self-esteem; and the other half of the night bunched up on a wooden bunk among a gaggle of smelly citizens.

In subsequent tales of conquest the ignominy of that winter night remained for his select circle a suppressed chapter.

A Lane in Lucknow

Thank you all very much indeed. Words have always been my trade but they often fail me now. I can't tell you how moved I am to be in this old lane again. I remember it so well. It was, of course, very different then.

There were several old havelis with ornate studded doors, carved stone pillars. There were basements with arched gates where the last phaetons and buggies were housed, and also the horses and grooms. Doors opened to allow glimpses of cool paved courtyards and shady, chik-hung verandas.

I found, as I came today, a beauty parlour, a coaching centre, shops, a stockbroker's, an STD/PCO booth. But, looking down, I found that the flagstones which paved the ground were unchanged. I knew them instantly. As a child I had measured my expanding stride against their changeless chart, first stepping into one at a time, then taking in two, then three, then forgetting all about them. But seeing them again . . . it's as though these faded stones have always been with me, paving the floor of my mind.

In fact I used an idea somewhat like this in a lyric I wrote for an old film of the forties. It was called *Saba Aur Bahar* and it had stars like E. Bilimoria and Gohar and Sabita Devi acting in it. That was the first song I wrote that became a popular hit. And my introduction to the Bombay film industry as Veeran Lucknavi, not Mohan Chand Khare, which happens to be my real name. I wonder if any of you remember that film or that song. No? I thought not. Well, your fathers might remember it. Ask them if they heard that song, *'Tere kuche mein aahat mere kadmo ki hai'*.[1] And did you know that it was in this very lane that I became Veeran Lucknavi? Why else did I feel compelled to drop all my engagements and rush down to inaugurate this mushaira? I felt I had to. There's an old debt I have to repay. To this lane and to a man long dead.

Does anyone remember a poet named Siraj Hasnain? No? I thought you wouldn't, but again your fathers might, though even that is unlikely, considering Siraj sahib's self-chosen obscurity. Well, he used to live in a tiny stone-balconied chamber in a house where now your STD booth stands. And it was to him that I owe my penname. And so much more. I think of him often.

Siraj sahib used to sit on his string cot, pulling at his hookah. The young men sat around him, some on mats, some on low wooden divans, reading out their verses, earnestly seeking his advice. Poetry was so much in the air then. And Siraj sahib was our sage and consultant. He edited a local poetry paper called *Siraj-e-Mehfil,* which, as you know, means 'lamp of the gathering'. That's just what he was.

'Siraj sahib,' a young scribe would ask 'what is the function of *tarannum,* and is music really essential to poetry?'

And Siraj sahib would reply, 'Sikandar mian, know you the answer that Amir Khusrau made unto a musician. "Poetry may be likened to a bride and music to her ornaments. For doth the beauty of the bride depend on her ornaments? Nay, ornaments do but enhance a woman's charm, as doth music enhance the sweetness of a lyric." For poetry is a knowledge that is complete in itself, as Khusrau well said.' And he would recite Khusrau's Persian verse for our benefit.

Then another young man would venture, 'Siraj sahib, wherein does the poet reside—in the world that gives him food for verse or in his thought which turns that world into verse?'

[1] In thy lane the sound of my footsteps remains.

Siraj sahib would reflect and then answer, 'Zebunnissa, Aurangzeb's daughter, once said: "Like the perfume of the rose I dwell, hid in my verse, he that wishes to see me can see me therein." Now, Zebunnissa's poetical name was "Makhfi", which also means in Persian "the concealed one". Hark you now and mark how she plays on the word "makhfi" to mean both herself and "the hidden one".' And he would spell out the Persian pun slowly for the young men to take down.

Not all his tales had to do with poetry. Endless were the stories of conquerors and princes, sallies of wit betwixt masters and slaves, when a witty answer could alter a sentence of death and a courtly message could disarm a threatening army; tales there were of caliphs, qazis and courtiers, of the honeyed repartee between kings and their consorts.

'Said Jehangir to Nurjehan, "Not like the bulbul am I, that with his loud complaints doth annoy the ears of others. Nay, rather like the moth am I that for love of thee doth burn in silence without complaint."

'And Nurjehan made prompt reply, "No, not like the moth am I that loses his life in a single flash. Like the candle am I, burning all night without complaint."

'Then said Jehangir to Nurjehan, "'Tis not the colour of saffron that hath come to rest upon thy collar—'tis the colour of my face, pale with love of thee, that hath caught thee by the collar in reproach."

'And answered Nurjehan, "You wear a ruby button on your silk tunic, my lord. Say rather it is a drop of my blood that hath settled on your shirt, demanding retribution."

'And uttered Jehangir to Nurjehan, "Thou art intoxicated with the wine of thy beauty. Command those narcissus eyes of thine to waken and watch over this durbar."

'Thereat did Nurjehan make reply, "O cupbearer, waken not these eyes from their voluptuous slumber lest, full of witchery, they baffle the entire assembly."'

When Siraj sahib ended his recitals, the young men took turns to read out their countless verses on wine or beauty or love, agonies of estrangement woven into deep ambiguities.

One said, 'Were it not that fire comes constantly from my heart, the whole world would have been turned into an ocean from the water flowing from mine eyes.'

And another said, 'This world and the next are, thou sayest, thy price. Raise thy price still higher, for even yet thou art cheap.'

And a third said, 'Every stone that I hit on my breast received thine image on itself, until the stone itself became an idol worth my worship.'

A fourth recited, It is jealousy that keeps me from speaking of you. I do not utter your name lest my heart should hear it.'

And while the sighs and raptures of the assembly filled the chamber, a fifth contributed, 'On her delicate cheek the ringlets stir with the breath of my sighs, as the shadow of the hyacinth trembles in the water of the pool. Her eyes with their stolen glances capture my heart like the birdcatcher who scatters the grain little by little. And when she walks forth, 'tis like the agitation of the rose on the gentle rose branch.'

To hear us then was to marvel how no cares of pocket or of purse, of life or livelihood could trespass in our midst, our sole joy in life being the chiselling of conceits and the inlaying of artful images.

And it would be Siraj sahib himself who always intoned the final winning verse of the evening.

'In thy casket of pearls, the cornelian of thy lips hath hidden such charm as is worth purchasing with my very life. The lips form a ruby lock over the casket and thy lovely mole an amber seal thereon.'

When the applause died down, Siraj sahib explained, 'Do you know, sirs, this qasida was written in the style of Zahiruddin Farabi, at the request of Sultan Oweis and his mother Dilshad Khatoon. For it the poet received a grant of two villages as a reward.'

In the middle of the exclamations of wonder, a young voice sang out yet another verse. And so did the evenings pass unnoticed until all the lamps stood lit in the niches.

Then one day, I, Mohan Chand Khare, dared to present before Siraj sahib a verse of my own.

He read it with a sceptical face, asked my name, flicked the paper over once, twice, and condescension and pity appeared in his polished voice.

'I shall tell you a Persian story, Mohan Chand,' he said in his silken voice. 'A poet once went to a critic with his verses. The poem was full of lines taken from other poets. The critic, having read the poem, said, "You have brought me a caravan of camels tied together, let anyone untie the cord and each shall escape to its original master."'

My face burned. But Siraj sahib was in an unpleasant mood and had more to say. 'And once the young poet Saadat Yar Khan Rangi approached the great Mir for advice on the composition of ghazals. Mir sahib told the young man, "Sir, you are rich, the son of a rich father. Learn to throw the javelin, practise archery or horsemanship. Poetry must lacerate the heart and burn out the liver. Take care and do not knock thoughtlessly upon her door."'

He returned the sheet of paper to me. I hung my head. He was in a mood for further malice. Some entrenched dislike, some bitter prejudice was having its sport.

'Do you like wine, Mohan Chand?' he asked suavely.

'No,' I answered.

'It is forbidden in your pious home, eh?'

I said nothing.

'Especially for beardless young striplings,' he went on. 'And do you like women?'

I blushed and remained silent.

'And have you thirsted for God and chosen death above breath? No, how could you at your age? And do you know what it is to smite and let blood by the strength of your arm? Of course not. Go then, my boy. It is not by dining on lentils and greens that a man learns to write real poetry. No, one needs the mists of wine and of love, the aromas of saffron and of musk, the passion and pain of a dancing girl's bells, the pungent strength of garlic and onions in one's meat to train the liver for Urdu verse.'

And he turned away towards another young poet, leaving me humiliated and trembling with rage.

I remember how I could not sleep that night. It would never be nightingales and candle flames and moths for me any more, I swore. I rose in the small hours of the morning and wrote a long poem called 'Bakr-Eid'. It was not about wine or beauty or love or 'inquilab' or 'tasawwuf'. It had new words inadmissible in the prevalent vocabulary of poetry. It uttered my mortification in a wild current of rage repressed into a rhythm of reflection. I decided to risk it again. Let him scoff at it. Let him tell his endless Persian stories and make mock of it. I was determined to make my voice heard, if only to be rebuffed. I took it to him and handed it across, sullen and speechless.

He read it out slowly. It had a curious rhyme scheme:

My father read me a story from a book,
How Abraham hoisted the logs up the hill,
His son by his side and his heart in pain.
And when Abraham cried in a voice that shook:
'God of my fathers! I consecrate to Thy will
This, my son !'—there sounded again
A cry in the heavens—'Stop!'
And the son was spared, something tested and proved,
And a ram appeared, trapped in the bushes,
Sitting prepared, waiting unmoved
For the axe to drop.

'Ah!' said Siraj sahib, pausing to smile into his beard. 'Let me tell you a Persian story, Mohan Chand.'

I expected it, of course.

'One Bakr-Eid day a desert Arab sacrificed a camel to Allah. Then he went boasting of his sacrifice everywhere. A mulla admonished him for displaying such unseemly pride. Thereupon the Arab said: "Subhan Allah! Allah did sacrifice but a single goat which he put in Ishmael's place when Abraham took him to be offered up. And yet this sacrifice has been referred to repeatedly in the Koran! So should not I, who have sacrificed a camel, so much grander than a goat, mention my sacrifice as many times?" But a camel sacrificed by a desert Arab isn't the same as a ritual goat, you know, Mohan Chand.' Everyone laughed. 'So let's get on to the second verse of Mohan Chand's poem,' said Siraj sahib playfully. He resumed his reading:

'I wonder,' says my father, always mild,
'Did the ram have no pang in its dense head?
Did numberless ages of beasthood inherited
Exclude from its skull
The formula of grief?
Did its butt head, dull
In its curdles of hair,
Poor fool, prove
Too small for prayer,
Holding just a bleat, senseless
And brief?'

Here Siraj sahib stopped and turned his eyes thoughtfully upon me. Then he cleared his throat. 'Reverence for other forms of life isn't alien to the spirit of Urdu poetry, Mohan Chand,' he said a little gently. 'Why, the poet Zauq, when he offered namaz, prayed even for a sick bull that belonged to a local scavenger, so tender was his heart. And it was Iqbal who addressed a verse to a roasted partridge which goes thus:

Ai murgh ke bechara, zara yeh to bata tu
Tera woh gunah kya tha yeh hai jiska mukafaat?

Takdeer ke qazi ka yeh fatwa hai azal se,
Hai jurm-e-zaeefi ki saza marge-mufajat.[2]

'However,' said Siraj sahib, 'Let us read on and see what this junior Iqbal has to say.'

My father, vegetarian, munches lentils and greens
Day after day, and when somebody leans
Forward to say, 'This meat in strong onion
Tastes good,' he snaps, 'Pray,
Did anyone ask the ram's opinion?'
I do not know what conspiracies advance
These confluences of chance.
But it was on another Bakr-Eid day,
My father tottered shakily to his feet, put away
His cup, swore at the hot loo[3]
When the axe fell hard and struck him down too.
Two days he choked before he died.
It was a lengthy sacrifice. Those whose whim
Loads the dice, took time over him.
I knew then that the oracles lied.
It was all long ago, I can now sit and spell
The probable programmes of the universe well,
Its hypothetical hierarchies, compute
Its coherences, recruit
Its syllables of sense, in my old strife
To learn the likely lineaments of life,
The things that persist and what our words denote,
But it's this matter of mercy that still gets my goat.

[2] O innocent bird, do but explain
What was the crime that hath this punishment deserved?
This sentence from times ancient (is pronounced by) Fate's judge:
The offence of frailty is punished by death untimely.
[3] loo: hot, dusty winds that sweep across north India in summer, often
causing fever and death from exposure.

Siraj sahib stopped reading and fell silent. Then, very softly he intoned, '*Kya khoob!*' Slowly he turned to face me. 'Mohan Chand,' he said, with equal slowness, 'that was well said indeed.'

He seemed to be pondering a point. 'Indeed,' he murmured on, very low, as though he now spoke only to himself. 'And where would Urdu verse be without the kafir[4] and the but-khana[5] to allude to? And what would Ghalib have done without Hargopal supporting him with money and Maheshdas arranging for his liquor? And Raja Sahab Ram arranging for Zauq's education? And Mir seeking refuge with Dewan Mahanarain and Raja Jugal Kishore?' Suddenly he seemed to remember me. And spoke with great feeling.

'Your father is no more?'

'No, sir,' I said.

'Whom do you have at home?'

'My mother, two younger sisters.'

'And how old are you?'

'Seventeen, sir,' I said.

'Have you written much?'

I nodded.

'Then, bring it all along next time,' he said decisively. 'And Mohan Chand . . . in case you should ever require a father's advice . . .' He did not finish his sentence. As I left his chamber I realized how silent all the others were.

From that day Siraj sahib gave me special attention, going over my work, meticulously correcting my juvenile efforts, lending me books, tutoring me in Persian. I read the poems of Hafiz, Sadi, Jami and Nizami, the *masnavis* of Rumi, the anecdotes of Lukman. I was instructed in the poetry of Ghalib, Majaz, Zauq, Mir, Iqbal, Dagh. I was made to memorize the *Gulistan* and the *Bostan*. I was even allowed to offer my opinion on choice verses handpicked for *Siraj-e-Mehfil*.

[4] kafir: idolator.
[5] but-khana: temple where idols are worshipped.

Now *Siraj-e-Mehfil* was owned by Nawab Muzaffar Beg and edited by Siraj sahib. Nawab sahib seldom came in person to Siraj sahib's house but chose to send his messages by word or letter. But one evening Nawab Muzaffar Beg's shining new Alfa Romeo came hooting down the lanes, putting to flight the swarms of squawking hens and squealing urchins. It created a rare flutter in the little lane. Chiks were hastily lifted to catch a glimpse of the motorcar. Women ran to balustrades and balconies and peeped shyly through the trelliswork. The car stopped where the lane grew too narrow for admittance. A retainer in turban and cummerbund opened the rear door and bowed. Nawab Muzaffar Beg alighted, gracious in sleek black shervani and snowy pyjamas and bearskin cap aslant upon his head. His patent leather shoes stepped cautiously between the drains and doorsteps and picked their way towards Siraj sahib's home.

Nawab sahib bowed slightly, ever graceful and soft-spoken.

'Salutations, Siraj sahib,' he greeted the poet.

Siraj sahib rose from his divan and received his fine visitor with equal urbanity. 'That you should grace my humble dwelling,' he murmured.

'Ah, no, that I should impose on you the affliction of my presence.'

'That you should deem my threshold worthy of your lustre,' murmured Siraj sahib.

'That I should presume to intrude into your noble pursuits,' murmured Nawab sahib.

It was a contest in civility.

'I do regret that you had to walk.'

'A mere ten paces,' Nawab sahib reassured him.

'These lanes were built for the unshod feet of litter-bearers, not of nawabs,' said Siraj sahib. 'But pray be seated.'

'Thanks be to you.'

Nawab Muzaffar Beg beseated himself and looked intently at the crease of his snowy pyjamas and at his gleaming shoes. Then he spoke softly.

'Report has it that you are unwell, Siraj sahib.'

'The temper hath turned enemy, Nawab sahib. It is the rebuke of age, no more.'

'And does poetry stand rebuked as well?'

'Poetry is that magic filly that grows youthful with time. The more she is exercised, the more supple she gets,' answered Siraj sahib. 'And how may I serve your pleasure?'

'Do not trouble yourself,' begged Nawab sahib. 'The hakeems have seen to it that I partake neither of meat nor wine, neither of sugar nor of salt.'

'As man on earth may partake neither of *jannat* nor of *jahannum* but a bit of both,' remarked Siraj sahib.

'Well said, well said,' smiled Nawab sahib. 'But I, unfortunate man, am now a stranger to both.'

'You are not of humankind, then, sir, but share the lot of the angels,' said Siraj sahib. 'Then may I tempt you with some wine at least—a drink made for the angels but drunk, alas, by immoderate man.'

'No angel am I,' declined Nawab Muzaffar Beg 'but an ordinary erring son of father Adam. Place not this bait before me, Siraj sahib, lest I, weak mortal, fall from grace.'

So Siraj sahib passed the ornate silver spittoon and betel box, which Nawab sahib graciously accepted.

There was a moment's silence. Then Nawab sahib spoke.

'I come on a matter of some delicacy.'

'So I divined,' responded Siraj sahib.

'Yesterday I received a letter from Maxwell, the editor of the English newspaper *The Empire*. Apparently some offensive verses have been published in Urdu, lampooning certain public personalities. The District Collector has taken umbrage. I have been sent a page out of *Siraj-e-Mehfil* for my comments.'

Siraj sahib remained silent.

Nawab sahib bent forward and, casting courtly converse to the winds, spoke with great earnestness. 'Siraj sahib, why don't you stick to your Sufi songs and your love laments? Why must you mess around with politics too?'

Siraj sahib answered very steadily with a couplet from Ghalib:

Bakhadre-shauk nahin zurf tang naye ghazal,
Kuch aur chahiye vus-at mere bayan ke liye.[6]

'At my age, Nawab sahib, I can't go on writing on the mole on a maiden's damask cheek. Inquilab gives fresh air to the lungs.'

But Nawab sahib looked troubled. 'There is an allegation that *Siraj-e-Mehfil* is only a cover for a secret resistance group. The poetry is but a pretext for young men to meet. That anti-government pamphlets are being printed at our press and being circulated, concealed in the leaves of Urdu verse books.'

Siraj sahib's voice was constrained but steady. 'I discourage no one from raiding my premises, no, neither dogs nor Englishmen,' he said.

Nawab sahib laid a placating hand on Siraj sahib's sleeve. 'Please do not be heated, Siraj sahib. You and I, we understand one another. Have we not shared a special bond these twenty-five years and more? Recollect, it was my brother, our Bade Nawab, God rest his soul, who first noticed your verses and besought your gracious employment with our house. We still remember the *sehra* you wrote for my wedding. And *Siraj-e-Mehfil* was like a precious offspring to both of us, need I stress? Do not compel me, Siraj sahib, I do beseech you.'

'Let not your excellence embarrass my humble compass,' said Siraj sahib testily. 'It is not for high-born patrons to crave the indulgence of lowly poets.' His voice had assumed its silken note of satire.

'You do not deny composing those verses, then, nor publishing them without my consent in *Siraj-e-Mehfil*?' insisted Nawab sahib.

---

[6] The ghazal's narrow lane constricts my joy in verse.
   A wider compass doth (now) my narrative demand.

'I am not bound to admit or to deny,' said Siraj sahib stubbornly.

Nawab sahib sighed and rose to his feet. 'I bid you farewell then, Siraj sahib. This unpleasantness is not of my seeking.'

'Nor mine, Nawab sahib, I do assure you,' rejoined Siraj sahib, bowing stiffly. 'Khuda Hafiz.'

All through this exchange I had sat behind a screen of sacking in the courtyard within, poring over a faded Persian text.

It was when the Alfa Romeo had purred away that all hell broke loose. The only way in which Siraj sahib could give vent to his fury was by unleashing a torrent of tales on me.

'Patrons!' he seethed. 'Buying poetry for a pittance! Let them all know, let word go round—I, Siraj Hasnain shall sell neither my poetry nor my pride. Know, Mohan Chand, money must be wrested from their fists, these lackadaisical, languorous ones. One's got to bow and scrape, anoint appease, frolic, flatter, dance, *en deshabille* if one must! There's no honour in it, boy, none. A man's a bawd, grooming his lines and rhymes for a nobleman's couch. All for a handful of silver.' He paused for breath. 'But,' he added, 'there have been some, men of pride and worth, that would not be underlings. It is said that Mir sahib and Nawab Asaf-ud-Daula once sat a-talking. Great was Nawab Asaf-ud-Daula's lustre, many the favours he had done unto Mir sahib. Well, said Nawab Asaf-ud-Daula, "Mir sahib, will it please you to pass me that book?" Mir sahib would not lift a finger. Turning to the Nawab's lance-bearer, he said, "Attend to your master, sir. What sayeth he?" Nawab Asaf-ud-Daula, abashed, himself did reach out and pick up the book. And, Mohan Chand, my memory does instantly grant me another Persian story which, I am sure, your fresh and enquiring interest shall not disdain. Once the Sheikh-ul-Islam of Tabreez presented to the poet Mulla Mohammad Assar an old and worn-out cloak. The poet, dismayed at the shabbiness of the gift, did send it back with the message, "Your holiness has sent me a blest garment of rare antiquity. In the first days of Creation its warp was made by Eve for Adam; Mary wove it on the loom for Jesus. Later the torn places were patched by Fatmah with thread made from the wool taken from the camel of the Prophet. Who am I, base mortal, that I be honoured with the cloak that has been blest with the light of so many prophets?" That, Mohan Chand, is the way to handle these patrons! Impress that upon your young mind.'

Siraj sahib had turned suddenly cheerful, much uplifted by his own anecdotes. 'Go, Mohan Chand,' he said, 'it is late. Take the book along if you wish. See me tomorrow.'

The next day Siraj sahib drew on his shervani, put on his cap, picked up his stick, and left for Nawab sahib's villa. He was away for a long time but when he returned, it was evident from his expression that some final breach had occurred. He hung his shervani and cap on the peg, strangely silent. He put away the stick in its corner, still silent. And it was in silence that he sank into his divan and leaned back upon the old bolster. No accusations, no bitter jibes, no Persian tales. It was alarming. After a long while he spoke.

'I have washed my hands of *Siraj-e-Mehfil.*'

'The mehfil shall then be dark, sir,' remarked I.

He shrugged. 'I care not,' he said in great bitterness. 'Sarfaraz Khan, the upstart from Aligarh, is the new editor. I was to be kept on in the editorial board, but I would have none of it. Ah, Mohan Chand, verily hath it been said, this evil old world is like the great ocean in which the weeds are always at the top and the pearls at the bottom.'

He heaved a world-weary sigh. He looked a broken man. It was time, I realized, to show him a verse I had long kept waiting.

'Sir,' I ventured, 'there's something I've composed. Would it please you to examine it?'

'Give it here,' he said in a tired voice. I produced it. He read it through with a listless face.

'Addressed to a young lady?'

'No, sir.'

'To Allah, then?'

'No, sir.'

'Then, who is the fortunate object of this devotion, Mohan Chand?'

'It is dedicated to you, sir,' I stammered.

Siraj sahib turned to stare. On his face flamed a look of confusion and pain, a shock of alarm and shame that turned swiftly to a flush of pride and bashful eagerness. He conquered the mutiny of emotions with a grim expression of stern censure which still retained a tell-tale afterglow of embarrassed radiance. He plunged headlong into literary criticism.

'*Beet gaye zamane safar-e-alfaz mein.*' He pondered over the opening line. 'Ages have passed in this journey of words. *Safar-e-alfaz?* The journey of the word. Hmmm. Ghalib wrote, "*Safar-e-ishq mein ki zauf ne raahat talabi*".[7] And Iqbal wrote, "*Khulta nahin meere safar-e-zindagi ka raaz*".[8] But *safar-e-alfaz?* It sounds well, though.'

He went on to read the next line, *See diya nakamiyon ko apne libas mein.* (I stitched my failures into my garment.)

'A sewing metaphor!' he exclaimed. 'Quite authentic really. Do you know that Mir has written somewhere "*Majrooh apne chhati ko bakhiya kiya bahut*".[9] And Zauq wrote, "*Samajh ye daro rasan taro sozan ai Mansoor, ki chake parda haqeeqat ka hain rafu karte*"'.[10]

He went on to the third line. *Ab tasawwur zarooratmand nahin.*[11] He reflected. '*Zarooratmand?*' He questioned the sound of the word. 'Why not use "*haajatmand*" instead, Mohan Chand, as Ghalib does?'

'I need three syllables there, not two, sir,' I said.

---

[7] In love's journey the frail one did crave rest.

[8] The secret of my life's journey doth not reveal itself.

[9] Much did the wounded one his torn bosom hem.

[10] O Victor, consider the hangman's rope and noose the needle and thread that darn the vent in the torn curtain of Truth.

[11] Now imagination in no longer in want.

He spelt over the line. 'Very true,' he said. He came to the second half of the line. *Khayaalath na hain veeran.*[12] "Why *veeran*? Why not *bayan*? It'll rhyme just as well?'

'I like the sound of "*veeran*" better,' I insisted.

He came to the last line: *Aapki awaaz ne de di hai jo meri khamoshiyon ko zaban.*[13]

And he had nothing to say. He sat motionless. Then he spoke in an unsteady voice.

'*Veeran*, hmmm? Look at me, Mohan Chand. From this time forth you are not Mohan Chand Khare. Your name shall be Veeran. Veeran Lucknavi.'

Slowly, not knowing why I did so, I rose to my feet, dazed like a knight newly initiated and named. It was one of those rare and luminous moments of life, never to be forgotten. So it came to pass that every stanza I wrote came to carry my signature—Veeran, the desolate, the estranged.

Nawab Muzaffar Beg kept sending pleading messages and propitiatory gifts, but Siraj sahib sent them all back.

'Go and tell your master,' he addressed the servant, 'Siraj sahib sends his greetings and begs leave to decline his generous invitation. Say, Siraj sahib is busy at something he is composing and solicits Nawab Muzaffar Beg's kind concession.'

Word went round that Siraj sahib was working at a definitive collection of verse and much curiosity was generated. Poets came to call and asked guarded questions. But Siraj sahib put them all off with mysterious replies. For my part, I believed he worked all night, writing as never before, and I had great hopes from this volume of verse whenever it chanced to surface.

Then, some months later, there came a written invitation from the Nawab sahib's villa that Siraj sahib did accept.

[12] My thoughts are no longer desolate.

[13] Now that your voice has conferred speech on my silences.

Nawab Muzaffar Beg offers his warm salutations and craves the august presence of Janab Siraj Hasnain at a Mushaira this evening at his villa.

Dare we hope that Siraj sahib shall graciously vouchsafe us a reading from the new diwan he is busy writing, which, we do not exaggerate in saying, is sending ripples of speculation in the world of Urdu letters.

We look forward to being fervent auditors of the same, and remain

Ever in admiration,
Your faithful friend . . .

'Tell your master that I accept,' Siraj sahib told the bearer. 'Tell him also that he shall hear my composition tonight if he so desires.'

'Come, Mohan Chand,' Siraj sahib bade me. 'You shall accompany me to this mushaira. A friend of Nawab Muzaffar Beg's is here from Bombay. He is a well-known film producer and his name is Salman Alvi. He is bound to be present this evening.'

I was filled with consternation. 'I, Siraj sahib? I read with you? No. Don't embarrass me.'

'Rubbish!' dismissed Siraj sahib. 'They're not going to eat you, you morsel of lentil and spinach!'

So to the mushaira we went that evening. All the way, seated in the tonga, Siraj sahib gave me last-minute tips, his voice supported by the trotting tattoo of the horse's hoofs on the wet stone cobbles. I was numb with stage fright which my mentor did his best to dispel.

'Be wary of Sarfaraz,' he cautioned. 'He is all vinegar and vitriol. At a mushaira it isn't just the verses one carries along that matter, or the way one renders them. It's the verse one may be called upon to improvise in an instant, to say nothing of the skill of turning a jibe or a sally to one's own advantage and spinning out an immediate couplet or quatrain. It's a contest in subtlety, it's the artistry of poised and polished repartee . . .'

'Sarfaraz may be jealous,' he said after a moment's thought. 'Let it not disturb you. Jealousies are common among writers. There have been classic rivalries between Ghalib and Zauq, Mir and Sauda, between Insha and Masahfi. There is an interesting Persian story I must tell you before we arrive. At the court of Sultan Sanjar there were two rival poets, Rasheedi and Ama'ak Bokhari. Once Rasheedi said of Bokhari, 'He is a good poet but his verses have no salt in them.' To which Bokhari, incensed, retorted, 'Thou art right. My poetry is like honey and sugar. It is your poetry which tastes like boiled turnips and beans and requires salt to make it palatable!'

He followed it up with a handful of other anecdotes till such time as the great cast-iron gates opened and the durwan admitted our clopping, gluttering tonga into the imposing tree-lined drive through the vast lawns of Nawab Muzaffar Beg's villa.

I remember that evening vividly. On a rich Kashmiri carpet, in a circle round a large brass lamp, sat the guests with Nawab Muzaffar Beg presiding. At his side, a delicately built man who, Siraj sahib whispered, was Salman Alvi, the producer from Bombay. Wine was bubbled out of silver carafes into cut-glass goblets. There was melody in the air and the fragrance of jasmine joss sticks and rose water and Kanauj attar. A dozen voices rhapsodized and repeated lines, sighed in appreciation and sang out in ecstasy. Nawab sahib beamed with pleasure, making room for Siraj sahib and me on his left. By the filigreed light of the brass lamp, I distinguished the faces of some of the poets I knew. There were Janab Ejaz Hussain Rizvi, Janab Faiyaz Ahmed Farooqui Bismil, Hazrat Zahid Ali Kanpuri, Hazrat Anwar Allahabadi and a tense young man who would surely be Sarfaraz Khan. There were dozens more whom I did not know. To my unpractised eye and ear, there never had been such a galaxy of celebrities. Such wonders of versification, such marvels of melody.

Siraj sahib's turn came late by his own preference. Much was hinted about his new collection. There came searching queries and whispered requests for a recital. Finally, Siraj sahib, primed by wine and sweet praise, decided to satisfy the popular demand.

'Gentlemen of the gathering,' he began. 'Presented in your service sundry modest verses I composed . . .' He looked enigmatically at his host, 'in deference to the advice that I henceforth dedicate my humble poetry only to Sufi songs and love laments . . .'

Nawab Muzaffar Beg flushed while Siraj sahib cleared his throat and the assembly murmured in expectation. The word for commencement was given.

> Her face is beautiful like the day of Eid
> And her brows like unto the arch of a mosque. Her nose
> is the pulpit and the mole on her cheek
> Verily is the black-robed preacher delivering his sermon.
> Ah, do not ask why her dark tresses, scented like the musk
> Seem too short on her beauteous face.
> She is the season of spring and her curls are spun of night.
> Everyone knows that in springtime nights are short.

He stopped. 'That's all,' he announced. 'The rest shall see print shortly.'

There was a weak rustle of applause, uncertain, disappointed. Then Nawab Muzaffar Beg took the lead and, with a brave show of pleasure, cried—'Subhan Allah! What a lively conceit! What felicity of fancy!' And, the tension relaxed, everyone began repeating the ultimate line as befits the reception of an excellent poem. 'Wah! Everyone knows that in springtime nights are short!'

I don't know why I felt personally let down. Why had Siraj sahib recited this tawdry poem? Was this a sample of what he was writing now, the great work everyone hinted at? Why, it was in the same school of poetry that connected the unloosening of a woman's long dark hair from head to heel with the burning of the poet's heart and the candle flaming from top to bottom!

'Go on, Siraj sahib,' urged Nawab sahib gently.

'That is all,' repeated Siraj sahib stubbornly. 'But allow me to present to your distinguished judgement now a young poet, Veeran Lucknavi.'

It is at this point in my story that my memories grow blurred. Everything is bathed in an unreal light. As I slowly intoned the opening lines of my ghazal, *Ik saya meri kalam mein leen ho jata hai,*[14] I was attended by a tolerant but alert silence which the minutest discord could crack.

I was treading on thin ice, walking, word by word, on a taut heart-string stretched tight to snapping between my own nervous breath and the intent stillness in the room. It was as I uttered the last two lines of the stanza, *Gosh-e-murmur aur ye gardish ki lakeerein, khauf lagta hai gumnaam bekhudi se,*[15] that a palpable stir went through the audience, an audible intake of breath, and a low hum of men's voices took up the refrain for instant repetition. And from that point forth, each line was taken up and repeated again and again until the ghazal ended in a hubbub of excitement. I recovered from the spell, my cheeks hot and beads of perspiration on my brow, to find Salman Alvi's eyes resting reflectively on me. I saw him reach forward to Siraj sahib across the width of the carpet and whisper in his ear. In Siraj sahib's eyes there was a strange fluid shine.

The banquet, the compliments, everything is misty. But as we left, Salman Alvi turned to me and said, 'Well, Janab Veeran Lucknavi, that was truly splendid for one so young. Shall we meet again tomorrow? There is an offer I have to make which may possibly interest you.'

So that, to cut a long story short, is how I came to leave Lucknow and move to Bombay. I joined Salman Alvi sahib's production unit as apprentice lyricist and went on to write songs and screenplays too numerous to recount. I was associated with well-known films like *Vatan Ki Awaaz, Bansri Bala, Gulam Daku* and *Nazar Ka Shikar.* I wrote songs which were picturised on actors and actresses you may remember—Sohrab Modi, Leela Chitnis, Moti Lal, Feroz Dastur, Pahari Sanyal, Kanan Bala, Bibbo, Baburao Pendharkar. On the side, I turned out several volumes of Urdu verse which were appreciated by

[14] A shadow dissolves into my pen.
[15] White isolation and these revolving lines,
   Nameless oblivion of self frightens me.

connoisseurs and did no damage to my reputation. Money I earned in plenty, as well as acclaim and friends.

My attempts to persuade Siraj sahib to move to Bombay proved unavailing. He had dropped out of the first circle of writers, looked upon by some as a spent force, forgotten by others. His long-awaited diwan was not published and I felt ashamed and conscience-stricken sending him my own steady output of books.

And then, one day at a library, examining an old volume of medieval Persian poetry, I lit upon a verse that set all the chords jangling in my head:

Her face is beautiful like the day of Eid.
And her brows like unto the arch of a mosque.
Her nose is the pulpit and the mole on her cheek . . .

I could not believe my eyes. Wasn't this the poem Siraj sahib had recited at the historic mushaira, ingeniously translated to Urdu? Why did he need to pass off another's poem as his own, he who was so fine a poet? Or had I been wrong about him? At seventeen one is easily impressed by persons one dethrones at thirty-seven.

So disturbed was I that I wrote a well-thought-out letter to Siraj sahib, seeking an explanation.

Most esteemed Siraj sahib,
Tasleem.

I do hope you received the books I sent. Among them were two of my recent efforts. I await your reactions, ever more valuable to me than all the reviews put together.

Recently I came upon a verse in a Persian book that unlocked in me a great many confusions. I enclose it for you to look at. If you happen to detect a question, I shall gratefully await an answer. If you do not discern a question, I shall erase it from my own mind. And if you should discern it, yet deem me unworthy of an answer, that too is acceptable to me.

I have long looked forward to the appearance of your long-promised diwan but have waited in vain. I've always felt that your immense gifts are wasted in Lucknow and that a city like Bombay might well prove the worthier arena for your powers. Might I not, as an old disciple, make the arrangements for you to come?

Your presence shall be an inspiration and a reminder of old and more gracious days.

Your devoted shagird

Veeran

The letter I received in answer to the one I wrote still brings the blush of shame to my face. I have it still as a testimonial of my own worthlessness, as Subuktigin, the father of Mahmud Ghaznavi, kept his old, torn quilt as a testimonial of his former poverty.

Most cherished Veeran,

In your letter I discern not one question but three. I shall seek to satisfy your queries as best I can.

The poem you sent me, yes, the poem I read out in Urdu at Nawab Muzaffar Beg's mushaira, as you have discovered, was not my own. I had a substantial reputation to live down and no wish to shine that evening, but only to act as a poor foil against which a better light might shine. And do not credit me with either nobility or modesty. A Persian couplet—you know my weakness for those—aptly says that as the rose branch gives the rose a place at the top and as the sandal tree knows that the oil from its wood is sweeter far than its entire self, so it is proper for a father to grant a place to his son higher than his own.

Your second question, implied in the last paragraph of your letter—why I continue to choose Lucknow and my present humble state above all the affluence and recognition of Bombay, and why I therefore have taken the liberty of once again declining your kind invitation—I shall answer with a story.

When Timur conquered Persia, he called the poet Hafiz and rebuked him thus: 'O poet, much effort and trouble have I expended conquering Samarkand and Bokhara. How is it that you, ragged poet, in your futile verses, dare to claim that for the mole on a damsel's face you are ready to give away both Samarkand and Bokhara?'

Answered Hafiz: 'O Sultan, now you may see why I am ragged. It is by making gifts of entire cities in my verses that my condition is thus reduced.'

I am like that poet, Veeran, who still prefers the power to gift away cities in his raggedness than to make a gift of himself to cities though they dress him in gold.

Lucknow is dear to me, though now an altered city. Partition has emptied my chamber of poets but I stay on in an unaltered space.

Finally, you asked—when my diwan is to see the light of day. I attributed to you greater understanding, my friend. My diwan saw the light of day years ago. It has earned laurels everywhere and shall go on earning them. And it is, I beg to submit, an achievement exceeding all your own excellent ones.

You created the poems, exquisite and accomplished, but I, my dear Veeran, created the poet.

That, you shall grant, is no small feat. And I am grateful to Allah for my good fortune which the poet Zauq enumerated better than I can:

All that is required is His name, O pen,
The beauty of the page, alluring, well renowned,
The sky that ensamples all nature;
The ink-well wrought with a thousand arts.
To the countenance of the paper gave He clarity.
To the ink gave He luminosity.
Gave to the white bird the heart's refrain of verse
To the tall verse gave stature statelier than the tree . . .

All this have I known in my life and more, desiring nothing further than to remain what I am,
Your sincere well-wisher,
Siraj Hasnain

That is the man, long dead, to whom I dedicate this mushaira.

ACKNOWLEDGEMENTS

I must mention my debt to the 12 April 1865 issue of the *Pioneer* for certain references in 'Coming of Age' and the journal *Al-Risala* for the quotations from the Koran in 'Goddess of Clay'. In 'Through the Looking Glass' the whispering books utter sentences taken from *The Iliad*, a Zen kōan, *The Battle for the Soul of Man* by the classical Roman poet Aurelius Prudentius Clemens, Edgar Allan Poe's *The Raven* and the writings of Copernicus. The Tagore poem in 'Play' is taken from *Geetanjali* and the Persian anecdotes in 'A Lane in Lucknow' are taken from an antique collection compiled by M.N. Kuka, published in 1894. The poems by the character Veeran Lucknavi, in Hindustani and in English, are, however, my own.

I thank my family in whose enabling proximity these stories could be conceived and realized, my friends for believing in me and my publishers Penguin India for standing by me these many years.